TO THE WILD HORIZON

IMOGEN MARTIN

Storm

To request permissions, contact the publisher at rights@stormpublishing.co

Ebook ISBN: 978-1-80508-174-6
Paperback ISBN: 978-1-80508-176-0

Cover design: Emma Rogers
Cover images: Shutterstock

Published by Storm Publishing.
For further information, visit:
www.stormpublishing.co

ALSO BY IMOGEN MARTIN

Under a Gilded Sky
To the Wild Horizon

For my daughter Naomi—the kindest, most talented, and resilient person I know.

PART ONE

ONE

Grace knelt over the man she had shot. The pistol slipped from her trembling hand, and clattered to the floor of the mudbrick house.

Pushing her hair out of the way, Grace forced herself to put her ear close to the man's mouth. She flinched at the foul stench of tobacco, cheap bourbon, and rotting teeth. But he was breathing, thank God. That was something.

She heard footsteps on the wooden stair and turned to see her younger brother, standing there in his nightclothes. Tom gripped a candlestick, his eyes fixed on the body on the ground. How much of the fight had he heard?

"Is he... is he dead?"

"Nope."

Not yet anyway.

She looked back at her landlord. The dark stain grew on the thigh of his pants as blood seeped through the cloth.

Grace's heart was pounding as she scanned the dimly lit room.

"My sewing box." She nodded to Tom, who put down the candle and fetched the wooden case.

"What happened?" he said as he handed it to her. "I knew something was going on. Why didn't you holler?"

Grace ignored the question. It was her job to protect her ten-year-old brother, not the other way round. She grabbed her scissors from the box and her hand shook as she cut the coarse material where the bullet had grazed the man's leg.

A warning shot, that's what Pa had taught her.

"I don't understand." Grace shook her head, desperation rising inside her. "It's not deep. He shouldn't be out cold." She shifted round to raise his head, and gingerly pushed her hand underneath. Feeling warm blood on her fingers, she recoiled and wiped her hand on her apron, an icy terror creeping over her.

"He must've hit his head on the hearthstone." She glanced up at Tom and swallowed hard. "Fetch something. Anything. If I can stop the bleeding—"

Tom stared back, his mouth gaping.

"Now!"

He scrambled up the narrow stairs, and his steps creaked on the boards above. In a moment, he returned with bed linen.

"'S'all I could find."

Grace snatched the bundle, then hesitated. Good linen she couldn't afford to waste. But then she shook her head; she wasn't thinking straight. What was worse: no linen or a dead man?

Her thumb felt too large for her scissors as she snipped the threadbare cotton of the pillowcase and ripped it in two. She flashed a look at the man's face, both dreading and hoping the noise stirred him. Nothing. He looked halfway to the pearly gates already.

Her fingers were clumsy as she folded one half into a pad and tore the rest into strips, then tied the pad over the wound and pulled as tightly as she could.

"What now?" Tom whispered.

Grace sat back on her heels and took a deep breath. "He'll be mad as hell when he comes round. Mightn't be for hours, given the bellyful he's drunk. *If* he comes round." Her words faltered.

"Are we in trouble?"

Grace struggled to her feet. "Could be. My word against Mr. Boyd's. And he's the one with the bullet wound." Next step would be jail, or worse—the noose. She raked both hands through her thick brown hair and groaned.

Tom's face crumpled. "Don't leave me. Not you as well. We're gonna make a new life with Zachary. That's what you said." His eyes were wide.

Grace stepped toward Tom and hugged him, stroking his sandy hair. All those fine promises. In a couple of weeks, once the weather was better, they'd join a wagon train west, that was the plan. She'd persuade one of the many parties of ill-matched emigrant wagons to let the two of them tag along. Maybe pay a mountain man to accompany them. By the fall, they'd be with their older brother, Zachary, in Oregon: what was left of their family finally together and safe. She would fulfil the promise made to her father on his deathbed.

"We've managed over the past few months, haven't we? And we're gonna keep on dealing with things together." She held him at arm's length and looked him straight in the eye. "You've been the bravest boy. Pa and Ma would've been so proud of you."

Tom wiped the back of his hand over his nose. "What we gonna do?"

Grace let her arms drop. What *were* they going to do?

She picked up the pistol, feeling the familiar weight of it in her hand, the barrel still warm. It was a damn fool thing to do, shooting him like that. But she'd pull the trigger again, if she had to.

"We've no choice but to set off for Zachary's now. There's a wagon train leaving town in the morning." Grace's stomach clenched as she saw Tom's doubtful face. "We'll be on it somehow. Go get dressed and pack everything in the trunk. We'll spend the rest of the night in the wagon."

Tom ran back upstairs. Grace's hands shook as she wiped away the blood on the floor. She paused a moment; the man was still breathing, but his eyes remained shut. She needed to act quickly in case he woke.

Grace gathered their few belongings into a canvas bag: the sewing box and woolen stockings she had been mending, a book with an iridescent feather marking her page, a small leather purse with savings. It did not take long; they had been traveling from town to town, and most of their possessions were in the wagon, ready for the long journey westwards once they secured a place on a train.

She stood over the open gun-case on the table and carefully placed the richly decorated pistol next to its twin. She hated those guns and how they had caused her family to fall apart. But who could blame her for keeping them loaded when traveling alone—and not just alone, but with a brother who'd already lost so much and relied on her?

Closing the lid, she slipped the wooden case into the canvas bag.

Tom hauled the trunk down the stairs and across to the door.

"Wait." Grace glanced down at her apron, and stared at the bloodstains in horror. She untied it and rolled it tight in a ball, shoving it in the stove, where it smoldered for a minute and then broke into a blaze.

The golden light flickered over the man's body. Grace looked at where his belly pushed at the buttons of his greasy waistcoat, but she wasn't sure if she could see the chest rise and fall. She was too afraid to go close again and check.

Tom slipped his hand into Grace's. "What were you arguing about? Money again?"

Grace closed her eyes to shut out the memory. She'd paid him all the rent for this dump up front, and was justified in locking the door against him. It was darn stupid of her to think he didn't have another key. He'd forced his way in, steaming drunk, ranting about how a pretty girl shouldn't be alone, about him not getting his dues, insisting on more payment. *Other* payment. The kind that didn't involve coins.

She put both hands to her mouth, as if praying. "I'm so sorry, Tom. I tried to talk to him. He just..." Grace's hands became fists as she battled to stop tears from falling.

"What if he don't wake up?"

"I don't know." She took a deep breath and picked up one side of the trunk, waiting for Tom to take the other. She might be slender, but there were strong muscles under her demure dress. "Come on. The Oregon Territory isn't part of the United States. There's no way they can bring me back. We get to Oregon and we're safe."

Grace wasn't sure if this was true but tried to sound confident. She blew out the candle, opened the door, and stepped into the muddy alley.

The streets of Independence were never completely quiet. Even in the early hours, the noise from saloons disturbed the corrals of horses, mules, and oxen, making them stamp and groan.

Grace lay staring at the patch of indigo sky where the canvas flap on her wagon bonnet had come loose, Tom asleep beside her under a blanket. She shivered, and knew it wasn't the cold, but fear, still running through her veins. Knowing their dog, Kane, was tied underneath the wagon bed was a comfort.

There were only a few hours before dawn, but slumber was

a long way away. She listened for her brother's breathing; the gentle rhythm showed he was asleep.

They must leave town immediately, there'd be no waiting now for a later train when the weather improved.

Grace hoped there'd be a few places left with the group leaving that morning. People were reluctant to gamble every-thing on the first train of the season: the trail would need to be broken in places, the weather could be stormy this early in April.

Grace and Tom had made their way from Pennsylvania to the Midwest, eking out their savings. They had reached Inde-pendence, and prepared for the long haul west. Their mother had died of cholera just three months before, striking swift and heartless. Four days later, their father had succumbed, heart-broken at the death of his wife. Grace had promised on his deathbed to get those pistols to Zachary, to tell him their pa was sorry for everything that had come between them.

Zachary had been one of the earliest settlers in Oregon, as far west as it was possible to go. He'd written, urging the rest of the family to follow him for a new start. Now, even with the dangers of the journey, it seemed like the best bet to keep her younger brother safe.

Grace's mind circled back on the night's events, and she shuddered. She forced herself to itemize the remaining tasks. As soon as day broke, she would buy extra mules. It would be a poor deal, but needs must. And food. All the dried goods were packed. She would send Tom to get as many perishables as possible. Then, when sign-up opened for the last places, she would be waiting.

TWO

The painted words on the wooden sign above the door read INDEPENDENCE COURT HOUSE. The aptness of the name of this town was not lost on Captain Randolph, who sat at the table on the porch. It was what the people who came through here were looking for. Independence. Freedom. A new life.

The Court House was the only fine building in this frontier town. The rest were hastily thrown-up clapboard stores and dwellings, petering out to tents down by the Missouri. In the square out front, creaking carts and braying animals filled the air with noise, kicking up dusty red clay. Smithies and wagon shops rang with iron over the babel of tongues: Shawnees and Kansa wrapped in blankets, Mexicans smoking shuck-rolled cigarettes, Black stevedores carrying crates up from the steamships, bullwhackers and mountain men hollering their services.

A line of hopeful overlanders stood before him, and Randolph saw among them carpenters, millers, lawyers, cabinetmakers, tailors, coopers, preachers. But most were farmers with their wives and children, looking for a better life. He wondered how many understood what was ahead. Were they courageous, just ignorant, or downright stupid?

Randolph flipped up the collar of his military overcoat, even though the April air had the first shimmer of spring. He frowned at the ramshackle line, and sighed.

A pioneer stepped up to the table.

"Name?" Randolph asked.

"George Hollingswood, sir."

The corporal sitting at Randolph's side wrote down the details.

"How many traveling?"

"Wife and six kids."

Randolph raised an eyebrow. "That's a lot of children to take on this trip."

"Can hardly leave some behind. Wife won't let me," Mr. Hollingswood said with a grin.

The captain's mouth remained a firm line. "Any of them going to be of use on the trail?"

"My eldest boy is sixteen, next boy is thirteen. They're good and strong. The others are girls."

Randolph eyed Hollingswood, weighing whether to let him join. He looked strong as a buffalo, but *all* those children.

"What are you driving?"

"Standard prairie schooner with eight oxen, and a cart with two more."

"Reserves?"

"Already bought the provisions and I've still got fifteen hundred dollars for the trip and to set up in Oregon."

Perhaps the man wasn't entirely foolish then. "Good. That should see you through if you're careful."

"Does that mean we're in?" Mr. Hollingswood stepped nearer.

Randolph tapped his fingertips on the table. He could think of no good reason to refuse. He signed his name on Corporal

Moore's paperwork with elegant lettering. "Take this to the quartermaster, and report your provisions. We leave at ten."

Mr. Hollingswood beamed as he shook the captain's hand, before rushing off to find his wife.

Next was an older woman with the ruddy complexion of someone who had worked many years in the sun. Homespun cotton strained across her bodice.

"Mrs. Lila Pengra," she said in a strong Texan accent.

"And your husband?" asked Randolph, looking beyond her.

"Not with us, sir."

"Then, where is he?"

"Passed on, three year back. Just me now."

Randolph ran his fingers along a short scar on his chin. "So... why are you here?"

"Same as all the others, sir. Wanna see if the air in Oregon is as sweet as they say."

"Ma'am, it may be sweet as honey, but you will not be coming on my wagon train."

The woman folded her arms below her generous bosom. "Captain, I been running a farm by myself since my man died. Done pretty darn good. Got plenty of savings."

Randolph's jaw twitched. "Can you drive a wagon for twelve hours a day? Cross rivers, haul your cart up hills? You would not make it as far as the Little Blue, before turning back."

"But, sir..."

The captain stood to make sure his words were heard by other people waiting. "I've traveled there and back twice now and I can promise everyone here, it will be the worst six months of your life. Two thousand miles of mountains so high, water turns to ice in your bucket at night, even in high summer. Deserts so hot and dry, you go crazy. Mosquitoes so thick, you can't breathe. Rattlesnakes. Bears. And God help us if we don't make it before the snows come in."

He looked straight at the woman. "Now, madam, you can

ignore my advice, and try your luck with one of the parties leaving later. But hell will freeze over before I take you with this company."

The woman dropped her eyes, and turned away in disappointment.

As Randolph sat back down on the rickety wooden chair, he felt a brief pang as he wondered what the widow would do next. Still, it couldn't be helped and she wasn't his problem.

Corporal Moore struck a line through the half-written permission, and shuffled it to the bottom of his pile of paper. "That's why women need a man to take them in hand."

Randolph grunted, and watched the widow disappear into the crowd, brushing past the next person in line as she went: a young woman, waiting with a boy. The woman's dress was buttoned to the neck but suggested a trim figure. He thought her perhaps in her early twenties.

He watched as she hesitated a moment, pushing back wisps of chestnut hair escaping from her calico bonnet, and she seemed about to follow the widow, but then turned back and walked toward the table, with the boy following.

"Mr. Thomas Sinclair, and my name is Grace Sinclair, sir."

Randolph glanced up. Her eyes were deep brown and framed by dark lashes. His breath caught for a moment, and then he frowned and asked, "Why isn't Mr. Sinclair signing you up?"

She paused and darted a quick look at the boy. "We only just arrived at Independence. We're sorting out our wagon and the last few things."

Randolph breathed out and nodded to the corporal to take the details. The captain's strictness on overlanders had led to a smaller wagon train than usual. But his superiors had made it very clear that he needed a few more, to make it worthwhile for the army to accompany the civilians.

"Any idea of life out West?"

"We have family in The Dalles, Oregon. Just above the Cascades. Went out in '43. Here is a letter from them." She put a folded paper on the table.

Randolph perused the letter. The outside showed signs of being passed from hand to hand, with copperplate lettering in different colored ink, and various stamps.

"And we have savings."

"How much?"

"Sir?"

"The savings."

"Oh. One thousand, one hundred, and forty-three dollars."

"Just your husband, you, and the boy?" he asked.

She hesitated before murmuring, "Yes."

The corporal wrote down the figure as Randolph looked up at her. "That's still sort of tight for setting up fresh. What are you driving?"

She cleared her throat. "A small wagon: oak-made. A double sailcloth for cover."

"What's pulling it?"

"Six mules."

Randolph shook his head. "You'd be better with oxen."

She folded her hands and stood a little taller. "We have a good mare. She'll take some of the weight when needed."

The captain tapped his steel pen against the table, drumming out a beat. Something unnerved him about this woman, but nothing she had said so far would justify a refusal. "Tell me —" Randolph looked down at the corporal's notes to check her name. "Mrs. Sinclair, have you supplies?"

"My relatives wrote me what's needed, there in that letter. I've got things covered."

"And are you fully equipped?"

"Oh, yes. Er... A good cooking pot, a stand—"

The boy began to count things on his fingers. "Grease bucket, shovel—"

Randolph waved his hand. "I don't need a darn inventory."

He sat back in his chair, and stretched out his legs. He looked at her as she took the boy's hand and gave him a quick smile, then turned and held his gaze. He was struck by the darkness of her eyes, the fullness of her lips. The prettier the woman, the worse the trouble. But it was her husband's job to keep her safe, not his.

He scanned the corporal's list of overlanders already accepted. Regrettably, still a few short. He looked up at her and raised his eyebrows as he said, "I'm determined to deliver the same number of wagons to Oregon as leave this godforsaken town. Understand?"

"And we're determined to get there." Although her voice was soft, there seemed to be iron behind it.

He made a decision. "Check your list with the quartermaster. We leave at ten. Sharp." He handed back the letter, and their fingers brushed as she took it from him. She flashed him a look of something like alarm, muttered, "Thank you," and pushed her way past the line, the boy following in her wake.

As Randolph watched her go, he felt something like regret, and hoped he hadn't made a terrible mistake.

THREE

Grace sat bolt upright on the sprung bench at the front of the wagon, reins in hand. At ten o'clock, around thirty wagons carried over a hundred pioneers out of Independence and in the direction of the Kansas River.

"We made it, Grace, we made it." Tom sat close beside her, their dog lazing behind in the shade of the canvas bonnet.

"Sure did!" Grace bit her lip to stop herself smiling. Then she lowered her voice and said, "But you need to be careful to call me 'Ma' from here on. It will make people more likely to think there's a Pa here too."

Grace felt a pang of guilt about the untruths she had told. At least the letter was true, they *did* have family in Oregon: brother Zachary had urged them to join him. Grace had merely failed to say that Mr. Thomas Sinclair was ten years old, and her brother; not her husband as, she admitted to herself, she had perhaps implied. She cringed at the memory of the one outright lie she'd told the captain, but then she blew out a breath and told herself she'd done what she had to; keeping Tom safe was more important. If something happened to her now, Tom would be left alone, a child at the mercies of a pitiless world.

Grace felt sick at the memory of the previous night. She squinted back at the frontier town, glad to be gone. First to disappear was the weathercock perched at the top of the tower above the courthouse, then the redbrick building faded into the haze. Grace prayed they would be far away from Independence before anyone noticed the absence of her supposed husband. A woman driving a wagon was not an unusual sight—the men frequently rode on horseback or walked beside the wagons. She already had her next web of stories worked out for when the moment came: Tom was her son and they were traveling to meet up with her husband.

She needed to find her mother's ring and keep it on her finger. Maybe, just maybe, if she pretended to be married and trying to reunite the family, this stern army captain would give her a chance.

She thought back to their encounter. His voice had been low and gruff, suggesting exasperation with these latecomers. When he had stared at her with those steel-blue eyes, she had feared he could see right into her, recognizing the lies.

Grace shook the reins and tried to focus on the road ahead.

By the evening, they had covered ten miles—not bad for the first day with a late setting-off time. The going had been easy enough: gentle inclines, plenty of grass. Drivers drew up the covered wagons near the river's edge. From her place near the back, Grace watched the captain effortlessly take control from his tall black stallion, giving orders for the smaller carts to be drawn into a circle to corral the livestock. Unlike most of the travelers who were worn out, he seemed unaffected by the day's journey. To her relief, the army tents were erected in rows away from the overlanders. She and Tom needed to keep out of the captain's way.

Small fires crackled and the smell of salted bacon spread

through the air. Children ran about laughing and playing leapfrog. Many of the travelers eyed their companions, trying to get the measure of folk who would share the next six months of hard work and danger.

An older lady in the next wagon was struggling to put a hen back into its cage hanging over the wagon bed. "Where you from?" she asked Grace.

"Pennsylvania, just a small town."

"I'm Mrs. Perriman. We used to have a farm in Kentucky. I like to see my chickens scratching the ground of an evening."

"Mrs. Grace Sinclair." She offered her hand. "Pleased to meet you."

Grace turned back to tighten the ropes fixing the canvas bonnet to the wagon. She needed to keep her head low and get as much land as possible between her and Independence.

"I know what you're thinking," Mrs. Perriman continued. Grace's eyes snapped back to her. "I'm a bit old to be making the journey."

She shook her head. "No, I didn't—"

"I have two sons out West already, staking their claim. My husband thought it best to join them and stop running the farm. And I used to teach a little group of kids in my home. I'm gonna miss them."

Grace yanked a knot tight as she gave a polite smile. "I guess it'll be worth it."

"He's a great reader and thinker, my husband. Believes we need to spread our civilized way of life wherever we can. So we sold up, and here we are."

Grace opened her mouth to discuss the Perriman view of civilization but thought better of it. "Would you excuse me? I need to get our horse settled."

The less conversation at this stage, the better.

. . .

When they'd finished tending to the animals, Tom and Grace sat on boxes by their small wagon, eating beans and rice. Grace wondered if Tom's thoughts were running on what had happened in Independence, as hers were. Kane barked at the cattle who were moaning in protest at their captivity.

As the sun set below the horizon, someone took out a guitar and another found a squeeze-box. A crowd gathered, and a few voices raised a song. Grace watched the musicians at a distance. They all wanted a better life; perhaps others, like her, were trying to leave bad experiences behind them. There must be many reasons for embarking on this life-changing journey. But now was not the time to join her fellow travelers and find out.

Grace climbed into her wagon, and arranged some boxes between their wooden furniture to make two platforms. She threw a couple of quilts over them for comfort, and prepared for an early night.

When the army bugle blew at four the next morning, a few of the overlanders were already up and about—Grace among them. Tiredness had helped her fall asleep, but she had suffered disturbed dreams of men laughing and shouting, one of them the drunken figure of her landlord. She had woken in a sweat before the sun rose, and had been unable to settle again. Her head swam with anxieties and what-ifs.

She had crept around Tom to get dressed and climbed down from the back of the wagon to start the fire and make sure everything was prepared for the day's journey.

Watching the camp come to life, Grace saw Captain Randolph striding out to talk to the guard. The air was crisp and the grass still damp; his polished boots made footprints in the dew. He was another early riser—already immaculate in a dark blue uniform, tapping his hat against his thigh, his belt buckle catching the morning sun. His dark hair was thick and had an unruly wave, which caused it to fall across his brow.

When he reached the soldier, he ran his hand through his locks to push them back, before putting on his hat. Captain Randolph's height made him incline his head toward the straight-backed guard. The dawn air was cold enough for Grace to see his breath.

As the captain turned, Grace looked down to hide her face in the wings of her bonnet, and her heart beat faster. She needed to avoid his attention for as long as possible, and chided herself for allowing her gaze to settle on his movements.

As soon as the army company had eaten, Randolph called them to inspection, forty men in two lines. It had come to his notice that some soldiers had broken open a keg of beer during the night and he knew he had to address it head-on.

"We have many months ahead of us; months of hard work and danger. Our government says it's our destiny to spread from East to West across this great continent. Whether you believe that or not, time was, we could travel without much trouble. We all know there has been more unrest recently, particularly in the disputed Indian territories. Even the Shoshone have demanded payment for crossing their lands. In my experience, it is better to negotiate with the chiefs. But we must be prepared to defend these civilians if necessary."

There were a couple of grunts in response.

"So, let us get things straight right now. Some of you have made this journey with me before and know what to expect. For those who are new to my command—I insist we arrive in Oregon Territory as smart and disciplined as our first day."

He paused in front of a soldier who was swaying on his feet. Half the company would relieve Fort Laramie, and Randolph was already marking those he'd want to leave behind for a different commander to straighten out.

"I will not tolerate drunkenness in my men. If we get attacked, and you're only half-sober, you won't be of use to anyone."

Randolph moved on to the next man. His voice was low, but the soldiers heard every word.

"Nor will I tolerate debauchery. I expect my men to behave with dignity, not as the drunken animals some of you became yesterday."

A few men shuffled, while others stood straighter than before.

Randolph walked along the line, casting a critical eye over their uniforms. Some of these privates were so young, and it was perhaps their first time away from hearth and home. "Let me give you some advice about your personal conduct." He straightened the belt of a private who looked too young to need to shave. "Don't get too close to the civilians. Your job is to escort them to the West safely. But keep a distance. Otherwise, you will be... compromised. Some of these pioneer girls are looking for a good catch. I've seen many a promising military career ruined by a moment of weakness."

The captain paused, and looked hard at the company of men.

"Privates Willard and Lewis: my quarters now. The rest, dismissed."

The two soldiers exchanged a glance. The captain had an unerring ability to pick out the ringleaders when there was trouble. Nobody quite knew how he did it. The pair would be severely reprimanded and could expect the worst duties for many days.

·   ·   ·

A bugler signaled departure at seven o'clock sharp, and the wagons rolled out. No stragglers, no last-minute panics. Everyone was trying to make their best impression on the captain, who rode at the front of the line.

The sun rose and warmed the air. The countryside was lush and verdant, rolling hills covered in long grass. Captain Randolph possessed a fine pocket watch, of which he was very proud. There would be a break at ten for the animals to rest and then a meal at noon. They would move on at one o'clock and the traveling would end around five. He planned to stay to this regular pattern through the trip—as far as the landscape and weather would allow.

This part of the journey was familiar to him and his right-hand man Lieutenant Turner. Not only had they crossed the Continental Divide together, they had been posted at Fort Laramie for two winters.

The golden rule of traveling West was to follow the rivers. Randolph knew the best overnight camps and would push hard to reach them. The second evening's camp was at Elm Grove. Maybe once, there had been plenty of trees, but not anymore. Nevertheless, it had a tranquility that restored his spirit. He was uneasy about the number of untested soldiers for the months of hardship ahead. But he put that out of his mind so he could savor the peacefulness. He had to grasp these moments when he could; there was no telling what dangers tomorrow would bring.

FOUR

On the second evening, Lieutenant Alfred Turner wandered the campsite, making sure the cattle were secure, watching men play cards, checking the soldiers on picket duty. When invited to sit by a campfire with a group of women, he readily accepted, dropping heavily onto a camp stool that threatened to collapse. The smoke from the fire kept insects at bay, and the evening air was cold. As he smiled genially at the group, Turner's kind eyes suggested a gentle preacher, rather than an experienced soldier. He was a large man, with a uniform belt that sat under his ample gut. His graying hair belied his forty years, although his impressive mustache and beard were still thick and dark.

Turner was a confident and composed career army officer. He traveled with his wife whenever possible, and this journey was no exception. He liked the comfort a wife was able to give: coffee in the morning, holes darned in socks in the evening. His wife, Eunice, was generously proportioned, like her husband. They had no children, something Eunice had grieved for a long time. Nevertheless, they were a well-matched partnership, her sharp insight balancing her husband's tendency to think the best of people.

Lieutenant Turner had first served with James Randolph in the Texas Revolution in 1836. He had known him as a cadet at West Point, wild and young, taking risks that gained him a reputation for bravery with some, and recklessness with others. Over the past decade, Turner had watched Randolph develop into a fine officer. Visceral experience of the reality of combat made him put the lives of his men above all else. If there was a way out of conflict, he would take it. If there was no alternative, he was swift and ruthless. Turner and Randolph became brothers-in-arms, trusted friends, despite the decade between them. Turner knew most of his friend's history, knew what had shaped him into the man he was now—the good and the bad, the triumphs and the times of trouble.

Convivial by nature, Turner was glad of the opportunity to get to know the people with whom he was traveling, be they soldiers or civilians. He looked around the campfire; few of the women had idle hands. Mrs. Hollingswood mended a hole in a child's breeches. A redheaded young woman twisted rags into her sister's golden curls. At the edge of the circle, sitting in the shadows, Turner could make out Mrs. Sinclair, struggling to read a book by the firelight. Mrs. Perriman sat center and conducted most of the conversation. As always, it turned to discussing other people.

"So, Lieutenant, what sort of a man is the quartermaster? I don't trust him myself," she said, stating her own opinion before Turner could speak. "Looks shifty. But maybe that's because he's got that squint. I hope he's honest about distributing supplies."

The lieutenant tried to give an accurate and positive assessment of the quartermaster, and then of each of his fellow officers, in response to Mrs. Perriman's questions.

"And what about the captain?" she asked, a question many people had been waiting for her to get round to. "Seems like a mighty proud man to me."

"I should not want to cross him about anything," added Mrs. Hollingswood. "One look from those grave eyes would have me quaking in my corsets."

Chuckling rippled around the campfire.

"Yes, he can put the fear of God into you if he so chooses." Turner pulled at his whiskers. "But you will find him a fair man and true to his word."

"And what is *Mrs.* Randolph like?" Mrs. Perriman asked. A good many of the ladies present had waited even longer for this question.

"There is no Mrs. Randolph," Turner replied.

"Why ever not?" Mrs. Perriman raised her eyebrows, scandalized that a good man should go to waste. "He's a mighty handsome man, if one dares to look at him. And he must have a good annual income to support a family. The army pension is generous, should the worst happen."

There was more laughter at Mrs. Perriman's summation of the captain's prospects, both alive and dead.

Turner paused to choose his words carefully. "I think his dedication to the army leaves him little time for the fair sex," he replied. "Although that doesn't stop many trying to capture his attention."

Turner deftly turned the conversation to other subjects, and the merriment continued until it was time to prepare for bed.

The slope of the glade forced different families to huddle close together, with a tent for two young women pitched close to Grace's wagon. She watched the girl with the long red braid crouch down to crawl into the tent, and heard the complaints of her older sister already settled inside.

"Ow. Jane, I do declare you sharpen those elbows with a whetstone. Why can't you be more careful?"

"Why can't you keep to your side of the tent?"

"And some of these rags have come slack. You need to fix them for me."

"Oh, Sarah, I'm beat. Your curls will be fine."

"No, they won't. If you'd done a better job, you wouldn't need to fix them again now."

The side of the tent bulged as the girls moved round.

"You're a sly one, little sis. Trying to ask questions about young Corporal Moore. I can tell when you're sweet on someone. Your freckly face goes all red to match your hair. Ow! That hurt."

Grace wondered if she should cough, to hint that every word could be heard, but didn't want to wake Tom.

"You should sit still. Anyway, I saw you trying to make eyes with the captain all day."

"It's a free country. And somebody's got to make such a handsome man into a husband. I'm gonna make sure he notices *me* before the journey is over."

"Sarah, you heard what that big lieutenant said. Girls have tried and failed in the past."

"Other girls didn't take the time and effort to make sure their hair was in pretty ringlets, even in a tent in the middle of nowhere. Now, have you finished? I need my beauty sleep."

Grace put a hand to her mouth to stop laughing out loud. She had no doubt Sarah would do all she could to be noticed. She had the coquettish confidence of someone who knew herself prettier than those around her. She agreed with Sarah's assessment of Captain Randolph: he was indeed one of the most striking men she had ever encountered, tall and authoritative, with eyes as blue as his uniform. Her breath hitched, remembering him this morning, pushing his dark hair from his face.

Then she recalled what she had overheard when he gave his soldiers a dressing-down that morning. His every gesture showed a man discontented with the world and all its weaknesses. Reading between the lines of what the lieutenant had said at the campfire, women were obviously among the weakest things, and thus worthy of little attention.

Grace shook her head ruefully, pretty sure all Sarah's attempts would meet with disappointment.

Then she thought about what she had seen in line at Independence, how harshly he had treated the brave Texan widow. There had been a moment when Grace had almost turned around. But Tom deserved a chance and it was essential they got on this train, even at the price of bare-faced lying.

But oh my, that speech he'd given about hell freezing over... She had no doubt he would throw both of them off the train if he knew the truth.

FIVE

The thirty covered wagons heaved out each morning, oxen plodding and lowing with pain from cracked hooves. Grace smiled to herself that a couple of larger families with many children were always rushing at the last minute to get everything loaded. One pioneer, Mr. Davies, journeyed alone and was often at the rear of the train. He was a late riser and slow to make breakfast. Grace worried about his underfed oxen which Davies would hook up to the wagon in haste.

Overlanders walked beside wagons, or chased after cattle wandering off in search of better fodder. With the flat prairie, there was space for the wagons to fan out and avoid traveling in the wake of the dust kicked up by the next wagon. Grace and Tom tried to take a place toward the edge, as unobtrusive as possible. From there, she could watch the Perrimans urging their oxen onwards, a little ahead of the others, Mr. Perriman trying to engage the officers in talk about the route, progress so far, the best choice for the next day's journey.

One morning, the front wagons had begun to snake up the bluff that surrounded the previous night's campsite like a bowl. Tom was taking his turn on the driver's seat and Grace walked with the pair of mules at the front of her team. As she urged them up the slope, Captain Randolph rode past, his face dark with fury. He reached Mr. Davies, who was straggling at the back as usual.

"You'd better sharpen up or you won't be going all the way out West." The captain sat on his black horse, looking down on Mr. Davies. He didn't raise his voice, but the deep timbre echoed up to the line of wagons.

"How's that?" Davies chewed on some tobacco.

"When we reach Fort Laramie, I will leave you there."

"You can't do that. I paid the government. You *have* to take me."

"I *can* do it. And I will, if necessary. Nobody risks the lives of those under my protection. If you're straggling at the back, you endanger others. Either you buck up your ideas, or you'll be off this train, first chance I have."

Grace's mule tugged its head away from her, as if it could sense her heart beating faster. She muttered some soothing words and patted the velvety muzzle. "Not gonna happen to us, Moppy," she whispered, "not to us."

They had been traveling for almost a week, and had stopped for the midday break by the river. The sun warmed Grace's shoulders as she unhitched her mules and pulled the headstall to lead the most docile to the bank, knowing the others would follow. She took off her bonnet and gathered her skirts to step into the shallows, then scooped up a handful of water to splash on her face and neck. She washed away the dust with her hand.

Mrs. Hollingswood was watering her team of oxen. A tall, wiry woman, she wore a man's wide-brimmed hat which made her seem even taller. Under it, there was something fox-like in the alertness of her eyes, the sharp chin and cheekbones. Even with six children, she made time for anyone else who needed help.

"My. Isn't it a beautiful spot?" Mrs. Hollingswood said.

"Very peaceful. I thought you would get one of your boys to do this chore."

"And miss quiet time to myself? Not a chance. The oxen don't go whining, 'Mama, where's my hat?' 'Mama, he's taken my stick.'" Grace laughed and Mrs. Hollingswood put her palms in the small of her back to stretch out the aches. "But, y'know, if *you* want a hand, I could get one of my boys to help you out. You must find it difficult."

Grace glanced across at her. "Find what difficult?"

"Being alone like this. Just you and your son."

Grace stiffened. If Mrs. Hollingswood had noticed, then surely others must have; yet nothing had been said by the over-landers.

"Though, I must declare," Mrs. Hollingswood continued with a shake of the head, "I don't know how you persuaded Captain Randolph to let you come."

Grace's mind froze and she kicked her way back out of the shallow water. But she liked what she had seen of Mrs. Hollingswood, and, already feeling the loneliness of having to keep herself to herself to avoid attracting attention, she realized she longed for a friend, someone to chat to at the end of the day. She turned and took a deep breath. "He doesn't know. I didn't tell him I was alone and, so far, no one seems to have noticed."

Mrs. Hollingswood turned to look straight at Grace. "Oh my! But he'll never let you carry on once he knows. And then you'll be stuck at some ramshackle fort in the middle of nowhere. Whatever made you do it?"

Grace struggled to keep her lower lip from wobbling. "I just *had* to join this wagon train, had to travel West. We have family waiting for us out there."

"So why didn't your husband come back to accompany you?"

"I... I couldn't wait that long."

The two women fell silent, watching the water flow past.

"I'm guessing there's more to this than meets the eye. And it's none of my business. But you can't go on like this for long. The captain's bound to notice soon."

"I know." Grace closed her eyes. "But I hope by then I'll be so far across the country, he won't be able to send me back."

Mrs. Hollingswood nodded and glanced at her, curiously. "Perhaps you're running away from something, not traveling to it."

Grace looked into her face, and saw kindness and understanding. She wanted to tell her, wanted to share her fear of returning to Independence and finding that her assailant was searching for her. Or, far worse, that he had died and she was now a murderer. These were the thoughts running through her mind every day as she sat, reins in hand, and every night as she tossed in her sleep. But these things she had to keep to herself.

Her eyes filled with tears and Mrs. Hollingswood put her hand on Grace's arm. "Honey, things seldom turn out as bad as we fear. And until then, we must live each day as an adventure."

The animals had finished drinking and were nibbling at the grass.

"I'll keep your secret safe."

"Thank you. I am forever grateful, Mrs. Hollingswood."

"Call me Lillian."

Grace gave a slight smile. "Please call me Grace."

"And if there is anything I can do to help, just holler."

Grace pulled on her cotton bonnet and tied it at her neck.

The two women led their teams back to the wagons, pulling at the ropes and using a switch to keep them moving.

"You know, there is one thing. That would help, I mean. Some of the men were talking of shooting small game tonight."

"That's right," Lillian said. "So we can have fresh meat for the sabbath tomorrow."

"I would like to go with them. I'm trying to keep back the cured bacon for later in the journey, but Tom could do with some proper meat."

"Don't you go bothering yourself. I'll get my husband to bring some back."

"Oh no, I couldn't take food meant for your family," Grace said. "I can shoot my own game. I would just be less... conspicuous... if I were not alone."

"Very well, I'll speak to my husband, George, and make sure he accompanies you."

They returned to their wagons and within the hour were traveling again.

That evening, the wagons reached their destination in good time. Soon, a small group of pioneers gathered as a hunting party. The men each carried a shotgun and boys ran alongside, holding sacks and setting the dogs barking. A few women joined the group as they strode out across the river plain, but Grace was the only woman to carry a gun. Her skirts pushed against gray sagebrush, filling the air with a savory tang, while flies danced above the grass. Tom scurried along with their flat-coat retriever, Kane, the dog's long black nose twitching at a scent.

The prairie had lots of small game—long-legged and lean jackrabbits, fire grouse, pigeons. The party found a low mound to start hunting.

A few of the men joked as Grace raised a rifle to her shoulder and took aim.

"Want a hand lifting that thing? Make sure you know which end to point."

Tom scowled up at them, but his face changed to a grin when Grace took down a jackrabbit with her first shot, followed a minute later by a wildfowl. Tom whistled to send Kane out to retrieve the limp bodies.

"See?" Tom said, jutting his chin. "I'll bet she's the best shot on the whole wagon train."

"Good to see a boy so proud of his mother," said George, trying to counter the laughter of some of the men.

Grace flashed Tom a look to remind him not to respond to the comment. It was good that people were accepting him as her son.

"I just want to get on with catching our supper," Grace said, reloading the rifle and adjusting the pad of cloth strapped over her right shoulder.

After the next two shots also met with success, she was ready to halt; the catch would easily take them through the coming week. She didn't want her shooting skills to draw even more attention.

Half an hour later, the sun was touching the horizon; the party strolled back to the camp, laden with rabbits still soft and warm, birds' legs tied to belts, wings spread out as if mid-flight, rangy hares held by their hindquarters. Tom ran on ahead with Kane, throwing a stick he had found.

Grace was grateful as George fell into step with her.

"My wife told me you're traveling out to your husband," he said. "I thought you were crazy. But looks like you'll be able to protect yourself. I never seen a woman shoot like that. Where d'you learn?"

"I've been shooting for as long as I can remember." She spoke quietly. "You could say it's the family business."

George coughed. "Gunslingers?"

Grace laughed. "Goodness, no! Father and grandfather

were both gunsmiths. They saw it like a calling. Pa would spend night and day in his workshop, trying to create the perfect rifle. I was a good shot, even as a girl; it amused Pa, so he kept encouraging me. I would try out each new modification for him, particularly when his eyesight began to fail—for things in the distance anyway."

"Were there no brothers to follow in the family trade?"

Grace glanced up at George, as this question came uncomfortably close to the mark, but realized he could know nothing about her family connections. "Yes, I have an older brother, but he and Pa had a falling out and he took up and went West to start out fresh. Both my folks are dead now, so we're going to join him."

"I'm sorry to hear that. Your parents, I mean."

A red-tailed hawk screeched and circled above them. "It was cholera. Took lots of fine people."

They walked in silence for a while.

"Can I take a look at the rifle?"

"For sure." Grace stopped walking and gave it to him. "Pa built up the stock so I can rest my cheek and get a better sight. It's got a beautiful balance. Truth is, anyone would be a better shot with that rifle."

"How d'you mean?"

Grace took the rifle back and showed him the barrel. "Now, I promise you this is empty. But look closely. See? It's not round. It's actually hexagonal inside the barrel. And see these bullets?" Grace took a handful from a leather pouch at her waist. "My pa made them specially for this gun, with six sides. It means the bullet flies straight. So long as you're lined up right, and judge the wind right, you shouldn't miss."

George squinted into the chamber and drew in a breath through his teeth. "Why aren't all guns like this?"

Grace shrugged. "Each gun takes a long time to make." She put the rifle back over her shoulder and they walked faster to join the group. "Pa said he was going to get a patent. But he never got round to it. I have two of my father's prototypes for a new pistol. Pa still hoped my brother would follow him in the business, even on his deathbed. One day, you never know…"

They reached the edge of the encampment. Fires crackled in the half-light and the smell of a dozen meals wafted toward them.

"Thank you for letting me come with you tonight," Grace said. "Here, take the jackrabbit."

George put up his hand, but Grace insisted.

"Tom and I could never eat all this."

"Thank you. What I'd really like is a chance to try out that rifle."

She smiled. "I hear we'll be in buffalo country soon, so next time we go hunting, I'll let you borrow the gun. Goodnight."

George took the rabbit and disappeared into the gloom to find Lillian and his many children.

Sunday broke with warm sunlight. Tom had responded to Kane's insistent barking and got up to take him for a walk. Grace stayed wrapped in her blanket a little longer and listened to children, up as early as ever and freely playing around the camp.

At nine o'clock, she joined others at the short service, standing near the back, a straw bonnet casting her face in shade. Tom had not yet returned, no doubt avoiding the dose of religion. Captain Randolph led the prayers, his voice strong, but with little feeling in the set words. Mrs. Perriman sang a hymn with gusto, encouraging others, and frowning at the accordion player for taking the tempo too fast. Grace made a silent prayer for forgiveness for what she had done in Independence.

Everyone ate well that day. There was a trail tradition that the overlanders cooked for the officers each sabbath. The women took turns to provide the food and made it a point of honor to cook a large and elaborate feast. Mrs. Perriman and Mrs. Harriet Long eagerly took up the challenge of providing the meal on this the first Sunday of their trip.

Most men and soldiers spent the afternoon at leisure. Some chatted in small groups, a few read, many slept. Some women took the chance to launder clothing in the Kansas river, drying chemises and shirts on bushes, and grumbling that it was no day of rest for them.

Grace made sure all the tackle was in good shape, and then crept off for a walk up the river with Kane. Away from people, she watched the spring sunshine glittering on the river. After almost a week, her presence was still unremarked by the captain. She had hidden herself among the hustle and bustle of thirty wagons, and thankfully a company of forty soldiers took a lot of his attention. Lillian and George had asked no further questions, and resisted the temptation to gossip. But it couldn't last forever, a storm was going to break over her head sooner or later, and she'd have to face the consequences of her actions.

SIX

Captain Randolph was pleased to have reached Sunday without incident. He hoped for an evening's rest for himself and his men. Turner, however, had suggested that a dance celebrating one week on the trail would be a morale-boosting treat for everyone. Randolph recognized Turner's ability to judge peoples' mood and reluctantly agreed. In no time at all, there was a buzz around the camp, as the younger travelers pulled cleaner clothes from the bottom of trunks, and many of the soldiers made an extra effort to polish buckles and boots.

Randolph suggested a flattish area for the gathering and told a couple of privates to stand torches around the edge. Overlanders unloaded tables and chairs from wagons, and the fiddle and accordion players tuned up. The first dancers to take their places in the middle were the married couples, happy to get the evening started, while younger folk flashed looks and tentative smiles at each other. After the first couple of songs, the soldiers edged forward to join the groups and some gallantly asked the ladies to dance.

Randolph stood by one of the torches and watched. Corporal Moore approached a slight, redheaded young woman.

He pulled at the cuffs of his sleeves as he turned toward her. Randolph caught Moore's look of disappointment as the girl's eyes stayed determinedly fixed on the dancers. Moore moved away, but then turned on his heel and extended his hand toward her. The girl took it and, although trying to keep her eyes demurely on the ground, could not disguise her wide smile.

Randolph shook his head, an inkling of regret at allowing this dance. While Lieutenant Turner had taken Eunice to make up a set for the Virginia Reel at the first opportunity, he was not at ease in such situations. It brought back painful memories of earlier years at military social events. Yet it was his duty as a leader to be here, so he walked over to a couple of his officers and tried to make light conversation. Turner joined him, and Eunice took Randolph's arm.

"I think everyone will be more comfortable if they see you dance," she whispered to him. "People are intimidated by your disapproval."

Randolph snorted but did as he was told, respecting Eunice's ability to perceive the truth about people. It was a slow waltz, and Randolph was happy to take a turn with the wife of his oldest friend. This had the effect Mrs. Turner had predicted, and soon many more couples were dancing. At the end of the waltz, they rejoined Turner, and the fiddle player changed to country dances.

"Captain Randolph?" A sweet voice called his name.

He turned to find a pretty face, surrounded by blonde ringlets.

"I seem to be without a partner for this dance," she said, dipping her head and looking up through her lashes, her hands clasped and her shoulders swaying.

Randolph scratched his ear. "And you are...?"

Eunice Turner stepped forward. "James, this is Sarah Eliot."

He nodded and considered suggesting one of the other officers, but no one was close. He then thought of the hurt and embarrassment a refusal would cause the girl. "Perhaps I could help?" and he gave her his arm.

Sarah sashayed as she took her place among the dancers, taking in the looks and whispered comments. He put his hand on the small of her back, and she reached up to lay her hand on his shoulder.

Sarah attempted to engage Randolph in conversation. She commented on what a pretty night it was, what fun everyone was having. Randolph nodded but said nothing.

"The army must be such an exciting life," she fluttered.

"Occasionally."

"Have you met with any Indians on your duties?"

"Occasionally."

"You must have been very brave. I hear they are mighty dangerous."

Randolph looked down at her, regretting his decision to dance with this girl. "The Native threat is much exaggerated. Treat them with respect and you generally don't get any trouble. We are traveling through land they've lived on for generations, after all."

Sarah fell silent and Randolph frowned at his poor manners. He cast around for a neutral subject for conversation.

"Are you from a large family?"

"No. Just one sister, a year younger than me. Jane. Over there."

The redheaded girl was laughing as Corporal Moore spun her round. Randolph guessed how his own fair dance partner would lord it over her younger sister in the days to come, how she would crow that the captain had invited her to dance. His mind filled with memories. He had seen it before, experienced it before; the woman who would never be satisfied with what she had while there was more elsewhere; who would not be happy with a corporal while there was a chance to dance with a captain.

A whelp from Sarah told him he had tightened his hand into a fist. He muttered an apology.

The dance came to an end, but the fiddler promptly struck up a well-loved circle dance in which each lady progressed around the gentlemen partners. Before Randolph could lead Sarah off the dance area, Eunice was by his side.

"I hope you are not thinking of bowing out, James," said Eunice, a hand laid on his arm. "You dance so well, and we need some good partners for this circle dance."

A muscle twitched in Randolph's jaw, but he turned to Sarah. "Are you happy to continue, miss?"

The smile didn't quite reach the girl's eyes, and he suspected she was less interested in a dance where she had to change her partner.

Nevertheless, the high spirits were infectious, as partners marched forward and back, swung each other around, and laughed as someone inevitably tried to move round the circle the wrong way.

Randolph's irritation subsided as he danced with a succession of matronly women who simply wanted to enjoy themselves.

He reached out his hand to the next partner and was aware of a gentleness of touch. He looked down: the woman was younger than most and her gaze was fixed somewhere beyond his shoulder. It was the fine-looking woman from the final morning of sign-ups.

"Mrs. Sinclair?"

She nodded. "Sir."

"You were the family who joined at the last minute. On the day we left Independence."

Finally she looked up at him, and then away, biting her lip. "That's right."

Standing opposite each other, both hands clasped, he could feel a tension in her, something suggesting she didn't want to be here. They galloped eight steps to the right and then back again. She was not wearing a bonnet, and her hair, which reminded him of hickory wood, fell in wisps from where she had twisted it behind her head. While other couples used the paired spin to twirl wildly, he placed his arm carefully around her trim waist. He felt her begin to relax, to mirror his moves. When she laughed as a couple in front moved the wrong way, he looked at his partner for a moment. She glanced up, and his breath caught as he took in the dark eyes and bright smile. Maybe Mrs. Sinclair was another careless flirt.

Randolph frowned slightly as a memory from years before flashed through his mind. Then it was time for her to move on round the circle. She curtseyed in response to his bow, and greeted her next partner with the same smile: a large man over fifty years, with unruly whiskers and two left feet. Not a flirt then. Just a young woman enjoying herself.

When the dance ended, Randolph was quick to leave the floor. He had done his duty.

He found Turner in an unusually pensive mood. "Come now, you are normally the life of a party."

"I've been watching you dance."

Randolph raised an eyebrow.

"You and Mrs. Sinclair seemed well matched," Turner continued. "And then something troubled me. Or someone. Someone who does not appear to be here."

"What d'you mean?"

"I will tell you as soon as I am sure, James. I don't want to go setting any hares running unnecessarily." Turner moved away from the dancers.

The musicians took a rest and everyone made the most of the chance to fetch a drink, or sit down to get their breath back. Randolph scratched his scar, wondering what Turner was up to.

.   .   .

Grace slipped free the top button of her dress and pulled the fabric to waft cool evening air onto her neck. Why had she remained at the dance so long? Earlier, she had told Tom that to stay away would draw attention. They needed to stay hidden *amongst* the travelers. And, oh, how she loved to dance, becoming one with the rhythm of the music. But to have ended up dancing with the man she most wanted to avoid!

She couldn't help but think about those few minutes, as she sat down on a log to tighten the laces that had come loose on her boot. She fancied she could still feel the heat from the captain's hand on her waist. They had danced so close, she could smell his musky aroma. She might not like his manner, but she had to admit, being near him was nothing less than exhilarating.

Exhilarating and foolish. She needed to make herself scarce, retreat to the shadows.

She hurried back to where she had left Tom, near one of the fires closer to the wagons. She could see him stroking Kane's black coat. An officer stood with his back to her, talking to her brother. Tom nodded and looked serious, as he fondled Kane's ears. Then Tom's eyes drew wide and his mouth fixed, slightly open. He pulled Kane closer, and dropped his gaze to the officer's boots. Something was very much amiss.

Grace quickened her pace. "Can I help?" Her tone was sharp.

Lieutenant Turner stepped to one side. "Yes, ma'am, indeed, I think you can. I was asking young Tom about his father. Mr. Sinclair. His whereabouts."

Grace's mouth went dry. *Please, not here, not now.*

Captain Randolph was walking towards them; it seemed he had followed Turner through the crowd. "Is there a problem, Lieutenant?"

Oh God. Things had just got much worse.

"I think there may be, sir. I was struck that I couldn't place Mr. Sinclair in my mind, couldn't picture him." Turner addressed Grace directly. "He's not here, is he, Mrs. Sinclair?"

The moment had come, she must face it.

Grace swallowed hard. "No. I am alone. Just me and Tom."

Her head throbbed. Should she tell the whole truth now? *I'm not married, Tom is my brother.* But there was still a chance... Captain Randolph might allow a wife and husband to be reunited out West. A single, unmarried woman would not have a chance of traveling onwards. She had to keep up her story somehow, if she could possibly do so.

The captain narrowed his eyes. "I don't understand. Where is he?"

"Waiting for us in Oregon. I gave... the impression... he was here, in order to join the expedition."

Randolph's face went dark. "You *lied* to get on this train? It's just *you* and this *boy*?"

Grace's cheeks burned. The music had stopped; all eyes were upon her, people sidling closer to overhear what was being said.

"Yes." She stared back at him, holding his gaze. She had to make this journey. She was not going to let Captain Randolph leave them behind.

Randolph glanced at the men and women gathering. "In my tent, both of you. Now!" he growled. "Turner. Come."

He marched toward his command tent.

Grace took Tom's hand and he looked up at her, his face pale. She gave his hand a squeeze and followed Randolph, along with Turner and a few more soldiers eager to hear more.

Turner ordered the soldiers and overlanders to stay put. "This is a private matter," he said. "Fiddler, play some more."

SEVEN

Captain Randolph paced back and forth in the large canvas tent from which he ran operations. Deep under his anger was humiliation at being made a fool of—how could they not have noticed, for *seven* days!

By the time Grace Sinclair reached the tent, he had lit the oil lamps and was waiting for her.

"I would prefer Tom to stay outside," she said as soon as she entered. "This is my fault, I should take the blame; it has nothing to do with him."

"Very well," said Randolph. "Tell him to return to your wagon."

She did so as Turner arrived.

The tent was big enough to stand in and had a table and several chairs. Grace stood stock-still, just inside the canvas door. She looked infuriatingly calm. The button at her collar was undone, showing white skin that had not been exposed to the sun. Her hair was even more untidy than when they had danced together.

"I don't understand how this came about. Who registered as Mr. Sinclair?" he asked.

"As you remember, sir—" Grace coughed to clear her throat, and he wondered if she was more nervous than she appeared. "I joined the train on the morning of its departure. I registered myself and Mr. Thomas Sinclair. I admit I was not clear about Tom's age."

Randolph stared down at her, a pulse throbbing in his temple. She was blithely admitting her deceit. "You knew the bar against women traveling alone?"

"Yes, sir, I did."

"But you damn well chose to ignore it."

"I just *had* to join this train."

Randolph loosened the collar of his uniform. How could it be so hot, this late in the evening? "Might I ask *why* you should abandon all sense to make this journey alone?"

Grace hesitated. The blood had run from her cheeks, leaving them paler than the tent canvas.

"My family is in the Oregon Territory. We miss them. Tom and I wanted to join them as soon as possible."

So, truth was, she was emotional and impatient under that cool exterior. Typical.

"Could you not have waited for your husband to come East and fetch you?"

Grace shook her head slightly. "That would have taken so long—and the new farm could not be abandoned for so many months. I believe the Preemption Act means land can go back to the government if it's left idle."

"But the government doesn't own Oregon Territory."

"Not yet. But they're going to. Everyone knows that. I mean, otherwise, well, what's the point?"

He looked at her; she was better informed than expected. God knows who she got this from. The husband? "Then why did you not go West with him in the first place?"

Grace glanced up at him, but her eyes slid off to a space

somewhere over his shoulder. "He wanted to prepare things. And some wagon train leaders *do* allow wives to travel out later."

"But *I* don't." Randolph started to pace again. "And you *knew* that. For darn good reasons. It's dangerous enough doing this journey, without having to carry dead weight."

A line appeared between her brows. "Women aren't dead weight! Look how hard we work."

Dear Lord, she was answering back.

"You get sick, become childish, petulant. Obstinate. Women just aren't built strong enough to do this trip without a man. And don't get me started on the effect on the men's moral fiber, having lone women around. In no time at all, a whole platoon is chasing round, just to get one wagon to keep up."

Grace bowed her head, and he saw her hands were balled tight.

"Why didn't you wait for the next train?" Turner's tone was gentler but suggested bewilderment. "You said yourself, some leaders take wives out to join their husbands."

Grace shook her head. "I... I don't know." She sniffed and stood up straighter. "What happens now?" Her voice was unsteady.

"Well, that is obvious." Randolph shrugged. "When we reach Fort Laramie, you remain there. Or wait for a guide foolish enough to take you onwards—which may be a long wait."

"But, sir, we don't have enough money or supplies to wait at Fort Laramie for months."

"Then you join the next group of turnbackers. Plenty of them."

"But that's not possible."

"Everything is possible." He spat out the words and sank into a chair by the table.

Grace bit her lower lip and blinked several times, looking like she was fighting back tears. "But, please, sir, you are not being fair."

"Life's not fair," he snarled.

"Sir, consider for a moment." Grace moved to the table and leaned on it. He was surprised by her boldness but tried not to show it. Her hands were close enough for him to see a slight tremble. "You say a lone woman can't do this, but I went for a week without being a bother to anyone. I agree there are some who are not fit for the rigors that lie ahead— and they should not be allowed to put everyone else's chances of a new life at risk." She clasped her hands together as if she were praying. "But, sir, surely those left behind at Fort Laramie should be the ones who have *shown* they can't adapt."

Randolph raised his brow and stared at the woman. None of his officers would dare to speak like this.

Grace stood meeting his gaze. "If I do indeed behave as you describe, then leave me at Fort Laramie with all justification. One day's sickness, one complaint, and I will stay there. But I *beg* of you, sir, if between now and Fort Laramie, Tom and I have proved we can be pioneers, then take us further."

Randolph snorted. "Fort Laramie is at least four weeks away."

"I know, sir, but please, give us a chance. I promise we won't call on your men for help."

She had spirit, he gave her that much. "Why in God's name should I give a chance to someone who has already disobeyed me?"

Grace tapped her forefinger on the wooden table, her eyes blazing. "This country is built on justice for all, on each being counted for their own worth, not on... on birth, or inheritance, or... or having a father with fancy connections. Please, let me prove my worth. Give me a chance."

As he saw her chest rise and fall as she fought for breath, his jaw tightened so hard it hurt.

Randolph knew a thing or two about having to prove one's worth. He had fought his way to his position of authority through his own determination but had watched in disgust as men with lesser abilities were promoted beyond their worth because of family influence. He dreamed of a land of freedom and opportunity. This woman showed the fighting grit he most admired. He felt everything shift for a moment, as if he'd stepped on ice and was fighting to stay upright.

He pulled a hand across his face and breathed out through his fingers. "Very well, it's a deal. If you do as you say, you can travel on; if not, you stay at Fort Laramie."

He heard Turner let out a low whistle.

"Th-thank you. Thank you, sir," Grace stuttered. She shot out her hand to shake. "A deal?"

He looked at her hand, but what else could he do? He took her warm hand in his and shook on the bargain. The back of his forearm prickled and he pulled his hand back to gesture toward the doorflap.

"You may leave, Mrs. Sinclair."

Grace ducked through the canvas opening and stepped outside.

Lieutenant Turner dropped down on a wooden chair, which protested at his bulk. He stared at the captain, waiting for him to speak first.

Randolph shook his head. "How on earth did we fail to notice?"

Turner shrugged. "I suppose we weren't expecting it, weren't looking for it. They say when Columbus first came to this land, the Natives couldn't see his ships because they didn't know what to look for."

Randolph poured two short glasses of whiskey and put one down in front of Turner.

"Many of the women take their turn at driving the wagon, while the men walk by the team. Or ride on the spare horses," said Turner. "It was not *unusual* to see her driving." He swallowed down the whiskey. "What on earth made you agree to Mrs. Sinclair's proposal? You could have knocked me down with a feather."

Randolph gave a short laugh. He felt far too uncomfortable to reveal how deeply Grace's words had touched him, even to his closest friend. "I wanted her out of here. What do I have to lose? She hasn't a hope. Four weeks—and the terrain gets harder from here. Rivers to cross. She will break. Mark my words, by the time we get to Fort Laramie, she'll be begging to stay there."

Grace took a deep breath, threw a few words up to heaven to ask forgiveness for all her lies, and dashed back to the wagon to tell Tom about the deal that had been struck.

The dance was still in full flow, but neither felt like facing the crowd, so they huddled under the arched sailcloth. There was a knock on the wooden tailboard of the wagon.

"It's me: Lillian."

Grace untied the bonnet and leaned out into the cold night air.

"I wanted to check you were all right."

"Yes, thank you, Lillian. That's kind."

"Was he terrifying?"

"To begin with. I thought my legs would buckle, they were shaking so." Grace remembered the strange exchange. "But by the end, he had... changed."

"Is he sending you back?"

"Not if I can help it." Grace's slight hand movement drew Lillian closer. "The captain agreed that if we can prove to be no trouble between here and Fort Laramie, he'll take us on further."

Lillian's eyes rounded. "My goodness! That *is* unexpected."

Grace nodded. "So all I have to do now is keep my head down, work hard and hope no one notices me."

Lillian laughed. "That will be easier said than done. You are now the center of gossip for the whole camp. Half of them saying how scandalized they are that you're by yourself, and the other half pretending they knew all along."

"I feel pretty bad about it all."

"Never mind, my dear." Lillian tapped Grace's arm. "You get a good night's sleep. Tomorrow things may look different."

Lillian returned to her wagon and Grace tried in vain to take her advice. She tossed and turned; not for one minute did she regret sinking deeper into the lie about being married. She would do *anything* to keep Tom safe and avoid being sent back to Independence.

But she knew she'd struck a crazy bargain, and things were about to get even harder.

The next morning, Grace rose before dawn to make sure her wagon was in order. The air turned colder and gray clouds made the sky feel oppressively low. When the train was due to pull out, many were still worse for wear after their late night of dancing and merriment. Captain Randolph rode on his charcoal-black horse, barking orders, his back ramrod straight and hat lower over his eyes than usual.

Grace cringed as she felt people's eyes upon her.

Mrs. Perriman swung past with Mrs. Eliot, speaking loud enough to be overheard. "We can all guess why the captain's in a fierce mood this morning." She nodded toward Grace. "An' there's a wagon won't be going much further."

Grace took her customary place in the middle of the train, Tom by her side. She tried to hold her head up high, and was grateful for the long wings of her bonnet, but what she really wanted to do was crawl back under the canvas and hide.

Randolph trotted past but didn't so much as glance in her direction.

EIGHT

Tom had no idea there would be so many rivers to cross. the Kaw, the Big Blue, the Black Vermillion. But then, he had little idea of what to expect from the journey. The two letters that had managed to reach them since Zachary had left in '43 had told of a peaceful paradise, a beautiful land beyond huge mountains. But Zachary had written little of the journey to get there. Maybe his big brother didn't want to put the rest of the family off. Not that there was much of the family left now; just him and Grace. He didn't like to admit how often he missed his father, how he still ached for a hug from his mother before settling down to sleep.

Over the next week, the overlanders got better at crossing the rivers. Most times, the Perrimans were the first of the wagons to follow army carts. Tom couldn't help but be amused by Mrs. Perriman, clutching the seat, her face white as her knuckles. Most of the travelers waded across, cold water reaching their thighs, as they pulled at yokes and bridles, hollered to urge the cattle to follow. He found each river had a different bed: small stones which hurt his feet, or sand which shifted with every step. One time, Mr. Gingham lost his footing and ducked under but bobbed back up, sad to see his hat float away downstream.

Walking alongside the team gave Tom plenty of time to think about things. He felt bad for not coming up with a clever response to Lieutenant Turner's questions that night of the dance. He went over the evening in his mind's eye, each time imagining himself as the hero who kept their secret hidden. But Grace had made it all come out right—just like she always did. Now he had to do everything he could to make sure the deal with Captain Randolph held. He knew months of hard work were ahead of him, but he'd show everyone he wasn't the boy they thought he was; he'd show them he was a man.

Prairie land undulated, almost like the sea when a storm was brewing. The skies were so vast, they seemed to mock the men and women scuttling across the earth and towards the distant horizon.

Randolph knew there would be arduous trail-breaking as the first company to set off West this season, but it started even earlier than expected. Time and again, a wagon got stuck, unable to pull out of a rut, or a boulder would make the path too narrow. Each time, the soldiers and overlanders got down from their horses and physically maneuvered the wagon on its way. They laid down planks, or smashed rocks with picks and hammers. Always at the center, Randolph assessed the situation, gave orders, and took his turn with the physical graft.

Whenever the cry went up that a wagon had got into difficulty, Randolph looked back, expecting and half hoping it to be the Sinclairs'. Then he'd have good reason to leave the troublesome woman at Fort Laramie and no one could say he had broken his word. But, frustratingly, it never was the Sinclair wagon. Theirs was small with few belongings, so it more easily followed the path. Their mules were strong and well-kept, so had no difficulty hauling the wagon onwards. He had to admit they had done well over the past week. But there was a very long way to go.

Halfway through the following week, around the middle of the morning, with the sun already beating down, the wagons at the front of the train crawled like ants along a narrow trail, up the ridge of hills beside the river. To one side, a landslip made the earth fall to a deep creek, so Randolph told everyone to take it carefully, holding the yokes, guiding the animals to a firm footing.

A loud crack of splintering wood cut through the air. A louder crash followed, with a woman's scream, then the clatter of pots and pans rolling away.

Randolph hollered at wagon drivers to pull on reins, and soldiers jumped down to see what had happened. The back axle of the Perrimans' wagon was split, and one wheel nowhere to be seen. Randolph saw Mrs. Perriman sitting on the ground and Mr. Perriman running round, gathering belongings which had spilled from the sloping wagon. Mrs. Perriman was in tears but unhurt and the wagon was in no immediate danger.

The wheel had rolled down the ravine and caught in a scrubby tree clinging to the cliffside. Beyond this, the land fell straight down to the river below. The Perrimans were lucky; if the wheel had rolled over the edge, it surely would have been smashed on the rocks.

Randolph stood at the trailside, looking down, discussing the options with Turner. "Fetch the ropes," he ordered.

When Turner returned with two heavy cables, Corporal Moore stepped forward, eager to prove himself, but Randolph shook his head.

"No, son. You'll have your time." Randolph tied a rope

round his waist, tugging to make sure it held. "But be sure your end is good and secure."

Looping the end of a second rope to his belt, Randolph stepped his way backwards down the steep slope toward the ravine, his legs stiff against the earth and rock, his pulse running faster with the strange sensation of leaning into the void. Moore and Turner stood above, easing out both the ropes, hand by hand, as overlanders' faces peered down at him. The tumble of water over rocks echoed up the ravine.

He reached the tree which clung to an outcrop with exposed roots, the wheel precariously caught by the trunk. Randolph fed the spare rope through the rim, yanking a secure knot.

"Start pulling," he yelled.

The wheel came free from the tree, loosening pebbles which scattered into the emptiness. With each tug from the soldiers, it inched its way back up the hillside. At one point, the hub became wedged in some rocks and Randolph climbed up to release it. A rock fell away, releasing an earthy smell and scattering bugs startled by the sudden light. His mouth went dry, as his eyes followed the rock bouncing downwards until it splintered on the rocks below. He let out a long slow breath.

Once the wheel was pulled to safety, Randolph was relieved to start scaling back up, looking for secure footholds and digging his hands into the dirt, trusting his men and the rope should he slip. He pulled himself back over the top, breathless and muscles aching. The onlookers broke into a ripple of applause, and now he was no longer in danger, Randolph flashed a rare grin, brushing the dirt from his uniform.

"Everyone might as well settle down and take their midday meal here," he said. "It's not ideal, but fixing this axle will take some time."

Lillian invited Mrs. Perriman and her husband to join her family for lunch. While they ate, soldiers unloaded the whole

Perriman wagon, turned it on its side, and worked together to repair the axle.

When it was done, the captain spoke to the Perrimans. "You must decide what belongings can be left behind."

Mrs. Perriman grasped a candlestick and clutched it to her breast. "But these are all family heirlooms. We can't leave anything."

"Ma'am, your load is too heavy. You can replace that axle at Fort Laramie. Until then, you must not put a strain on the repair."

Mr. Perriman pulled at his gray whiskers. "Maybe folk could take a piece each?"

Randolph frowned and looked at the other wagons. Most of them were full to bursting too. When people left to make a new life in the West, familiar objects were a defense against the unknown. "I'm sorry, that would put an unfair burden on other travelers and risk more wagons ending up broken."

Mrs. Perriman's chin began to wobble.

Randolph pulled on his gloves and sighed. He really didn't want the crying to start again. "You may ask people if they have space for small items. Linen, or clothing, I mean. Nothing heavy, mind."

Mrs. Perriman dissolved into floods of tears once more.

Randolph winced and wondered if a softer touch was needed. "Lieutenant Turner, please supervise the reloading of this wagon. Perhaps your good wife could help."

Mrs. Turner spoke in a gentle voice to draw from the Perrimans which belongings were most precious to them. They were a little wealthier than most of the overlanders and agonized over each item. Mrs. Perriman couldn't leave this dress because she had worn it at a gala evening, or that ornament because it had been a gift from the town mayor. Some folk made room for kit—but the Perrimans were not particularly popular, and most were reluctant or unable to help. Turner persuaded the Perrimans about the usefulness of each item, and gradually the wagon was reloaded with the basics.

After an hour or so, a forlorn gathering of treasured pieces was left beside the trail: an oak washstand, a bronze mirror, a much-used rocking chair, half a dozen dresses, a delicately carved crib. These would not be part of the Perrimans' new life.

With the delays, overnight camp was made in an exposed spot where the wind whipped up dirt and grit. Randolph visited each wagon to check for repairs and, if necessary, persuade the pioneers to leave some of their own belongings, as the Perrimans had done.

He strode up to the Sinclair wagon on the edge of the camp, wondering if he would find anything amiss. He expected his inspection would not take long with the Sinclairs: either they had few possessions from life in the East, or they had packed with haste.

Randolph looked at the animals first and then walked round the wagon. He uncomfortably acknowledged his disappointment that their mules were fed and groomed, the wagon in good shape with the wheels greased, and water butts filled.

As he wondered where Mrs. Sinclair was, Randolph knocked on the backboard before pulling the canvas to one side. He found her inside, packing away the Perriman crib between her own meagre belongings. She paused, and they exchanged a look, those dark-brown eyes seeming to hold a challenge.

"It was breaking her heart to leave it," Grace said quietly.

It was true, Mrs. Perriman had cried more over this crib than anything else. She had told anyone who would listen that it had been in their family for generations, and she had hoped to rock her own grandchildren in it.

He shook his head. Another example of how darn foolish and pig-headed the Sinclair woman was, taking on unnecessary weight. Randolph grunted and moved on. Reaching the next wagon, he glanced back at the small wagon. An unfamiliar warmth spread inside his chest, as if something had melted inside, something softened by her act of kindness. He shook himself to dislodge the feeling, and returned to his inspection.

NINE

Captain Randolph clenched his fists. A simple challenge from nature and the settlers had failed miserably. There had been an overnight downpour, so in the morning the travelers found themselves surrounded by mud. Randolph marched around camp, giving orders, pointing out tasks which should have been done the night before. A few women managed to light fires for breakfast, but most thought it not worth the effort with the wet wood, despite their menfolk grumbling about not getting hot food.

Turner handed the captain a tin mug of coffee. "They'll get more disciplined in time, James. But they're civilians. Think how long it takes to lick new recruits into shape."

Randolph nodded and sighed. He gave orders to his men to push and haul the wagons out of the mire as soon as each was ready.

Mr. Davies was Randolph's biggest problem; he had started coughing the night before and had not yet risen. He ordered two young soldiers to put everything in order. They dressed Mr. Davies in his coat and pants and sat him in the front of the wagon, reins in hand. The coughing soon started again.

.   .   .

After so many smaller rivers and creeks, Grace was surprised by the wide Platte with its slow-moving, muddy water. Short cottonwood trees clung to its low banks. Parallel rivulets meandered away from the watercourse, only to bend back to the main river, leaving low islands and sandbanks between the dark water. Hundreds of migrating sandhill cranes chattered and chirped at each other as they delicately picked their way through the grit and dipped their long heads into the water.

The trail followed the twisting banks of the river, slowing the progress of the wagons. The wind changed direction and turned fresher, making Grace's damp clothes cold and heavy. She pulled on her gloves and made sure Tom stayed warm inside under the sailcloth.

By lunchtime, squalls brought smatterings of needle-sharp rain. They stopped, and as Grace stepped down into the mud, Lillian appeared, slipping her arm through Grace's.

"Haven't you heard? The captain wants to talk to us. Sounds like we're all in trouble and need to be chastised. Every man, woman, and child." She shook her head. "You too, Tom," she called over to where Tom was unbuckling a harness.

The pioneers huddled together to get some shelter, Grace and Tom near the back, close to George and Lillian. Captain Randolph's voice rumbled over the heads in front as he lectured them about their failings that morning, how they had endangered the whole trip, that they must be more disciplined, that they could not expect the army to bail them out every time things got tough.

His eyes ranged over the gathered people and stopped on her for a moment. Grace shivered and pulled her pa's coat closer round her. She had struggled as much as everyone else this morning. This warning felt like it was targeted right at her.

She heard a fair bit of grumbling as folk returned to their

wagons: Who did he think he was? Couldn't he see it was raining? Grace kept her counsel.

"Things will only get tougher, though," George said, loud enough for those around to hear. "Might as well get ourselves sorted now."

His eldest lad, Simon, ran up. "Molly's no better. Just been sick again. Went everywhere. Disgusting."

George and Lillian exchanged a look. Their youngest child, Molly, had vomited the day before, and now had a high fever. Lillian quickened her step, eager to make Molly comfortable in the back of the wagon.

"I could take your other boy," Grace offered. "It's too wet for him to walk in this weather." Their attempts to keep their heads down at the beginning of the journey meant Tom had not made any friends yet. She worried that he was getting lonely.

"You sure? Benjamin can be a handful."

She turned to Tom who was kicking stones, a few steps behind them. "You okay with Benjamin traveling with us?"

He shrugged. "Yeah. S'pose so."

She sensed he didn't want to seem too eager but was pleased that Tom went on ahead to the wagons with something like a spring in his step.

As the day continued, a fever spread through the travelers and soldiers. It began with a cough and aching in the bones, then a high temperature and the sweats. Molly Hollingswood continued with her fever, then her brother Simon went down.

Captain Randolph sent his army surgeon, Dr. Trinkhoff, round the camp. This was the doctor's first trip West with a wagon train, having emigrated from a small German principality five years previously. He was used to dealing with soldiers, and boasted that on the European battlefield he had amputated seventeen limbs in one day. Nevertheless, that poorly prepared him for this new posting. He was nervous and uncertain with civilians, especially women.

Dr. Trinkhoff returned to the command tent to make his report. "A light fever is going round, sir."

"Not serious then?" asked Randolph, giving the doctor his full attention. He knew how quickly disease could spread among groups of tired people camping so close together.

"No, I think not." Trinkhoff removed his wire rimmed spectacles and polished them with his kerchief. "Many of the weaker sex, and children, have taken to their bunks. But, in my educated opinion, a robust male would be best working on through. The fresh air, it will blow it away!"

"Should we not rest here?" Randolph was eager to push on but wanted to be sure that was wise.

"Oh no, *mein Herr*, that is not necessary."

"And you're *sure* it's not cholera?" Randolph asked. "I've seen it strike without warning, taking men as strong as oxen as easily as a young child."

"*Nein*. The symptoms are very different." Trinkhoff held up a thick forefinger. "For one, cholera victims rarely run a temperature."

Randolph nodded. At least that was something. "Is there any medicine you can give?"

"I suppose I have a few tinctures which *might* ease the fever," said the doctor, puffing his cheeks, "but I advise against using them now. We have many months' journey ahead. Who knows what we might need."

Having given the travelers a firm lecture about discipline, just hours earlier, it would be a disaster to ease up the very next day. "Very well. We leave tomorrow at seven as usual." Randolph returned to his logbook. "However, Dr. Trinkhoff, before we leave, I need a further report, plus a list of all who've gotten the fever."

.   .   .

A disheveled group of wagons pulled out at seven in the morning. Many had missed breakfast and stowed bedding and tents anywhere they could. When Davies' wagon did not move, Randolph sent Corporal Moore to investigate. Davies lay in the back, coughing and delirious. The corporal hitched up the oxen, tied his own horse to the back, and led the animals out.

The bad weather stayed with them with torrential downpours. In the rush, some of the wagons were not battened down properly and the canvases flapped and banged in the wind.

Randolph was frustrated that Dr. Trinkhoff did not appear with a list until midway through the morning. The paper showed almost every wagon had at least one sick person.

At the noon break, Randolph questioned the doctor closely about whether to proceed, or wait until people were better. Lieutenant Turner shared the discussion.

"Might be better to slow up a little so we do not exhaust folk," Turner suggested. "We left on time this morning, but at a cost. People were not prepared."

Randolph scanned the list. "Seems mostly women and children affected so far. Few men, so there is no reason why we cannot push on."

"Indeed, few of the soldiers also." Trinkhoff hooked his glasses over his ears and stood close to jab a podgy finger at the list in Randolph's hand. The captain curled his lip at the unmistakable whiff of spirits.

"But, James, on a trip like this, the women are very important in keeping the wagons going," Turner protested.

Randolph frowned at him. Turner wouldn't normally use his first name in front of other soldiers.

Trinkhoff let out a high laugh. "I think you will find, with the women out of the way, the wagons may leave earlier!"

Turner sighed. "And what happens where the man is sick?"

"We will allocate one soldier to each wagon where that

happens," the captain replied. "As long as the doctor confirms they are indeed sick. I will not have any malingering."

"D'you not think a day's rest might be of help?" Turner persisted.

Randolph took a few strides as he thought through the problem. "What worries me most is that when we reach the south fork ferry crossing, it will be too dangerous to cross." He looked out at the land, the dark clouds low and heavy with rain. "With all the rain added to the spring melt, the Platte will get faster by the day. The sooner we get there, the better. No, Turner, we keep pushing onwards." It was a fine judgement, with arguments on both sides, but he didn't want them stranded on this side of the river. His instinct was always to move westwards and he just hoped it would prove to be the right decision.

TEN

The wind dropped as the wagons were wedged still, and tents erected for the night. More people had gone down with the fever through the day, so camp was quiet, except for the dogs barking and the sick coughing. Folk who remained healthy divided into those who kept a distance for fear of catching the illness, and those who worked twice as hard to look after the sick and their animals.

Grace was determined to keep her side of the bargain with the captain and show she could be valuable to the train. She quickly started a fire using the kindling she had dried out in last night's embers and had kept dry under canvas. She cooked a large pot of stew and took food to the weakest travelers, but it soon ran out.

She was sure fresh meat would build up the strength of the sick. She went to ask George Hollingswood to accompany her on a short shooting trip, and was dismayed to find he had also succumbed to the fever. Lillian was nursing most of her family.

"Ask Mr. Gingham to go with you," Lillian said. "He's a good man. George says Gingham was impressed with your shooting that first time you went out."

Gideon and Hanna Gingham were a young couple who had left a farm in Tennessee in the hope of a better life. Mr. Gingham had a thick brown beard that reached his chest. His nose was peeling because it was not quite protected by his battered straw hat, his proper hat having been lost in the river. He was happy to help out, and hoped to bring his wife something to cook over the coming days.

Gingham and Grace hurried away from the camp to shoot some game before the evening drew in. They pushed their way through the long grass to a hillock with a view over the featureless prairie beyond. Kane flushed out what wildlife he could find, and Grace's rifle shots rang through the evening air.

At the sound of hooves, Grace lowered her gun and turned to see Captain Randolph cantering toward them, Sergeant Knox a length behind him. Randolph's jaw was dark with evening stubble, and as he came close, she could see in the shadow of his hat a streak of mud on his cheek. This was not the well-turned-out captain she was used to.

"What in God's name d'you think you're doing?" the captain roared.

Grace bit her lip in utter frustration. It would have to be the captain that found them.

Gingham removed his hat. "Evening, sir. Mrs. Sinclair suggested fresh stew would do the sick people a power of good, so we're catching us some jackrabbits."

"Why did you not inform one of my men?"

"Everyone seemed so busy, sir," Grace said. She glanced up at Randolph, as his horse stamped and circled.

"More like you thought no one would notice the two of you slipping off together."

Her cheeks burned and she dropped her gaze to the ground, embarrassed at what he was implying.

"No, sir," Gingham protested. "Was nothing like that."

"You decide to go shoot rabbits but bring a woman with you?" the captain snarled, narrowing his eyes at Gingham.

"It was my suggestion," said Grace. The look of contempt from the captain made her realize she had made things worse. She could have kicked herself.

Gingham rolled the brim of his hat. "Mrs. Sinclair is a good shot. She wanted to hunt food an' I said I would accompany her." Gingham gestured to the two jackrabbits and three prairie chickens piled near their feet. "She's already caught most of this."

The grass rustled as Kane lolloped to his mistress, tail wagging and a bird drooping from his mouth.

The captain snorted. "You expect me to believe that?"

Grace's stomach lurched. This suggestion of indecorum was exactly the behavior the buttoned-up captain would most deplore.

"If you need extra food, Mr. Gingham, you ask one of my soldiers to help, not some girl. But then, I guess Sergeant Knox here does not have the attractions of Mrs. Sinclair."

"Sir, I must protest." Gingham raised his chin. "Your suggestion is insulting to both Mrs. Sinclair and myself. I have told you the truth of the matter."

Grace felt a surge of gratitude that Gingham was prepared to challenge the captain and defend her honor.

At that moment, a trio of rabbits broke cover on the grassy turf nearby.

"Sergeant." The captain nodded toward the bobbing tails.

Knox drew up his gun, took aim, and fired. The rabbits scattered, none of them hit.

"Not easy in this light, sir," Knox said in a low voice.

The captain rolled his eyes and turned his impatient horse. "Evening is drawing in fast. Return to camp. And I mean now!"

At that moment, Kane startled a covey of quail into the air, squawking and beating their wings to gain height. Grace raised her rifle to her shoulder, laid her cheek along the stock, and fired: once, twice.

Captain Randolph turned in his saddle as two birds spiraled out of the evening sky.

He looked back at her in surprise and she stared straight at him.

"If the Pawnee attack, remind me not to stand behind Knox."

The captain's blue eyes burned into her. His lip curled. He dug his heel into the side of his horse and cantered back to the camp, the sergeant following in his wake.

Grace let out a long groan. What a stupid, peevish thing to say, no matter how angry and insulted she felt! She shook her head. There was so much at stake, she really needed to learn to hold her tongue.

Randolph stretched out his legs and leaned back in his canvas chair, looking up at the sloping tent roof of his private quarters. As usual, he shared his nightcap with Turner while they checked all was settled at the end of the day. He swilled the whiskey round his glass and studied the amber liquid, frowning.

"Mr. Gingham. What's your assessment of him?"

"Seems a good man to me," Turner replied carefully. "Works hard. Has two young ones with him. Wife's no trouble."

There was a silence.

Randolph swallowed a mouthful. "Alfred, you ever seen a woman aim a gun good as a man?"

Turner smoothed out his mustaches. "There's Gertrude Gill. I saw her once at a fairground display."

"Gertrude Gill?"

"A novelty turn in one of them traveling fairs. Dressed up like a fur-trapper but a head of blond curls, going all the way down her back. She shot bottles way off."

"And it wasn't trickery?" asked Randolph.

"Maybe. Looked real enough to me." Turner leaned back. "What you getting at, James?"

He swallowed more whiskey. "Mrs. Sinclair..."

"Ah." Turner nodded knowledgeably.

"What d'you mean, *ah*?"

"Well, I heard Mrs. Sinclair is a remarkably good shot."

Randolph frowned. "When d'you hear that?"

"While back. When the overlanders went hunting to stock up supplies, she went with them. And I'm told, had a truer eye than any."

Randolph closed his eyes and passed a hand over his face. "How come *you* know this and I don't?"

"Because, James, as well you know, I make it my business to find out about folk so you don't have to. Seems to work well that way. Would you like to share whatever's been eating you all evening?"

Randolph drained his glass and got to his feet. "No, it's nothing. A passing incident."

He remembered Grace's final words about Knox. By God, that woman had an infuriating lack of respect. If she'd been one of his soldiers, she'd be on report by now.

And yet, her mischievous wit, the quickness of her retort; she really was something else.

ELEVEN

Rain during the night meant the travelers yet again woke to find muddy puddles and rivulets around their wagons and tents. At five o'clock, the camp was quiet, with few people willing to go about their chores. Grace went to the Hollingswoods' wagon, where Lillian was tending her husband and two of the children. Lillian herself now looked ill: her eyes were red and her cheeks were flushed.

"We had a difficult night," said Lillian. "Molly seems more settled, but George's coughing has gotten worse, Simon's too. I betcha it's measles. Molly's got a red rash on her tummy which is spreading."

"I've brought you some breakfast, so you get something warm inside you."

Grace sat and drank coffee with them for a few minutes.

"Lillian, I'll go see if a soldier can be allocated to drive your wagon. I heard the army is willing to help, particularly when the husband has gone down with the fever. Now, don't you worry."

Grace pulled on her overcoat to keep out the drizzle. The mud caked her boots and made each step heavy. There was more activity around the camp now, with men rounding up cattle who had wandered off during the night, but mostly it was soldiers sorting everything for the day's journey.

A private led a bay horse to be tied up behind a wagon.

"Excuse me. Would it be possible for you to help—"

"You'll have to ask the sergeant," he interrupted. "I've already got my detail for the day."

"Where can I find the sergeant?"

The soldier jerked his head. "Striking the mess tent."

Grace picked her way through the boggy earth. The sergeant stood with his back to her.

"Excuse me, sir," she started again.

He turned and her stomach fell: Sergeant Knox. He grimaced at the sight of her.

"I... I was wondering"—she hesitated—"would it be possible for one of the soldiers to help me..."

He looked her up and down, the disheveled hair, the muddy boots. "You don't look sick to me."

"No, I'm not."

Knox returned to looping a guy rope. "I have priorities, you know."

"Yes, you see... it's not me—"

"Look around, woman." Knox threw down the rope. "Do you see any men spare? Doin' nothin'?"

"No." Grace's mouth was dry.

"Everyone's been allocated. Got no one left."

"But please, sir, it's for—"

The sergeant stepped so close, Grace could smell his stale breath. He was tall and broad, a shaggy mustache shaped down the sides of his mouth to his chin. A lower tooth was missing, suggesting a man who preferred to sort things with his fists. "I heard you don't git no special treatment. If you're stupid enough to come on this journey alone, then that's how you'll do it—alone. No favors. That's what the captain said."

The sergeant snatched up the rope and marched away.

Grace trudged back to the pioneer wagons and thought what she could do. None of the privates would help without permission; there was no point speaking to Knox again. And she didn't want to cause a fuss.

She reached her wagon, where Tom was hitching up their mules.

"Tom, how near are we to being ready to leave?"

"Pretty much there now."

"Good, well done. Look, d'you think you could handle the wagon by yourself for some of the day?"

Tom looked up anxiously from the harness. "Where will you be?"

Grace waved toward the big wagon. "The Hollingswoods need a hand."

"If you think I'm ready for it."

Grace patted one of the mules. "I'll send Benjamin over. Did you get on with him?"

"Sure, he's all right." He gave a little shrug, but Grace thought he looked pleased.

"And you think you can manage, between the two of you?"

Tom stood up and planted his legs wide, tucking his thumbs into his belt as he'd seen men do. "Yeah, we'll be fine."

"Right, let's get this tidied up then."

Grace quickly made sure everything was stowed in her wagon, then hurried back to Lillian.

"I'm going to stay here and help you today. Could Benjamin travel with my Tom?"

Lillian's shoulders dropped. "Won't the army help?"

"They seem very busy, I'm afraid." Grace chewed her lip. "But don't worry, everything will be fine." She gave Lillian a quick hug.

Grace remembered when she and the whole of her family had caught measles; Tom had been very young and they were afraid he wouldn't pull through. Lillian would need all the help she could get.

It was almost seven o'clock and wagons were preparing to move off. Grace dashed round trying to gather everything. The Hollingswoods were a large family, and spread their belongings wide. Their wagon was pulled by a team of eight oxen and took a long time to yoke up without any children to help.

The train pulled out at seven, filling the air with shouted orders and lowing animals. Grace whispered a prayer of thanks when she spotted her own small covered wagon taking its place in the middle. *Please, Lord, help Tom today.*

Grace was still struggling with the oxen when Captain Randolph rode up. The canvas bonnet was pulled tight against the rain, the Hollingwoods safe inside and out of sight.

"Mrs. Sinclair, you are holding us up."

She looked up at him—his chin now smooth, his blue eyes fixed on her. "Almost there, sir, just a moment." She fumbled with the unfamiliar tackle.

"This is the last wagon to leave. Why are you so unprepared today?"

She noticed that his uniform was back to being as smart as ever, as if the mud and rain had been repelled by his stern aura. She glanced down at her mud-splattered coat. "Sir, I am very sorry, we had some difficulties." She briefly motioned towards the wagon and returned to securing the yoke.

"This is *exactly* what I warned you about." He leaned forward on the pommel of his saddle.

"But, sir, please—"

His nostrils flared. "I said you would be a burden on the rest of the travelers."

She paused in her work to stand up straight and address him. "But this isn't even—"

He threw a look heavenwards. "Woman, do you never stop answering back? I don't want to hear another word." His black horse shook its head as if sensing the rider's anger. Captain Randolph reached forward to pat its neck and calm the animal. "You have proved you're unable to manage alone. I can't wait here with you while you catch up. I'll send some of my men to accompany you."

The captain rode away before Grace could explain that this was not even her wagon. She angrily pulled the last buckle in place and went to the front of the team, using her stick to encourage the front pair to move off. She forced back the tears of fury and frustration.

Turner angled his hat to let the water drain as Randolph reached him. The army-issue coat was cumbersome but thankfully kept the worst of the rain out.

"I need you to get the rear wagon moving. Mrs. Sinclair hasn't left yet. Just as I predicted, it didn't take long for her to crack."

Turner couldn't miss the irritation in Randolph's voice. He frowned. "The Sinclair wagon has already passed, James."

"On the contrary, I have just spoken to Mrs. Sinclair. Now, let's not waste any more time."

Randolph dug his heel into the horse's flank to canter away.

Turner was mystified and rode to the back of the train, where he recognized the Hollingswoods' prairie schooner. As he drew closer, he saw the woman trudging beside the oxen team was Mrs. Sinclair, wrapped in an overcoat, a man's hat with a wide brim pulled well down over her bonnet.

"Ma'am, would you like me to get the team moving faster?" he asked.

"That won't be necessary," she said, tapping the hide closest to her with the stick. They were a good distance behind the rest of the wagons. "I'll catch up, soon enough."

Turner touched his hat and turned to the main group which

had fanned out across the prairie. It seemed the bad weather on top of all the sickness was making everyone short-tempered. But that didn't stop him wanting to find out what the confusion was this morning.

After an hour or more, the wind dropped and a few shards of sunlight broke through the gray clouds. The sky turned pale blue as the morning progressed, dollops of cloud forming lines into the distance across the rolling land.

The wagons slowed as they trundled up a low incline; those at the rear came to a halt, waiting in line. Turner rode back to Grace Sinclair and thought her face looked a little puffy. Was that the sign of tears? He dismounted and tied his horse to the back of the wagon and then walked next to Grace.

"Why don't you have a rest on the driving seat? I can keep an eye on the team."

"I should think not." Grace looked straight ahead and gripped the stick more firmly. "You were there when I struck my deal with the captain. You're not allowed to help me."

"I've helped lots of other travelers over the past couple of weeks," he said gently. "I don't see why you should be treated differently."

Grace bit her lip and tears gathered on the edges of her eyes. "Anyway. What will people think? Captain Randolph caught me out hunting with Mr. Gingham last night and regards me as some kind of scarlet woman, not to be left alone with a man."

Turner laughed. "I'm sure my wife trusts me."

Grace left the oxen and went back to the wagon, where she pulled a canteen from below the bench. She drank deeply, her head dropped back. Turner followed her and she offered the water. He took a mouthful.

"Would you like to tell me what happened this morning?" he asked.

Grace looked at him sharply and raised an eyebrow. "What d'you mean?"

"What led to the mix-up with the captain? He must know this isn't your wagon. Why didn't he realize?"

"Because he's blind, as well as arrogant." Grace screwed the top firmly on the canteen.

Turner thought about these words and moved closer. "I think he *is* blind when it comes to you. He's smarting because you tricked him in order to knowingly go against his rules."

Grace told Turner what had happened that morning, about how ill the Hollingswoods were, how Sergeant Knox had refused to help.

"None of you seem to *listen*," she cried. "You're in the army and civilians don't count."

"Now, ma'am, that's just not true."

"Twice this morning I could have explained things. *Twice*. But, oh no, the sergeant and then Captain Randolph wouldn't let me. And now *I'm* going to have to pay. I've tried so hard to keep my side of the bargain with the captain." Tears came to Grace's eyes once more. "And now... now he's not going to let me carry on beyond Fort Laramie."

"Maybe it won't come to that."

Grace passed her forefinger below each eye to make sure any tears were swept away. "He was looking for an excuse and now he's found one. It's just not fair!"

"I'll talk to him at midday break and explain things to him."

"That will just earn you a reprimand." Grace sniffed hard. "He'll think I've *lured* you into making up excuses for me. He'd *never* admit he was wrong over whose wagon this is." She ran her hand over the wooden wagon bed.

Turner untied his horse from the backboard and mounted,

pausing beside her before riding on. "To be honest, Mrs. Sinclair, you don't know the first thing about the captain."

As he threaded his way through the wagons, he thought about the man he had known for a decade. Randolph exuded confidence at all times, but there was a great deal of responsibility on his shoulders. Was he above admitting his mistake?

TWELVE

With the sun drying the trail, the wagons stopped for their midday break at a pleasant spot by the Platte among short shrubby trees. As soon as the wagon halted, Lillian jumped down from the back. She had been half asleep against the canvas just behind the driver's bench and had heard the whole exchange between Grace and Turner. Lillian was determined to put things right for her friend, even if it meant challenging the captain.

She approached the officers' area, where Captain Randolph was seated, a bowl of cold bean stew in his hand.

Lillian gathered her courage. "Sir, I wonder if I could have a few words?"

He nodded, still fixed on his food. "Yes, but they'll have to be here while I'm eating."

"Of course. I wouldn't want to interrupt. I don't know if you are aware... you probably are not... I mean, why would you? But my husband, George, has gotten this fever. I don't feel too well myself."

"I'm sorry to hear it." Randolph tore a hunk of bread and

used it to soak up the gravy. He looked up at Lillian for the first time and frowned. "Your color is up. You should take care."

Easy for him to say. It was hard to take care when your whole family was sick and you felt weary yourself. That was why Grace had been such a godsend. Lillian was determined that Grace shouldn't suffer for her sake.

"So would it be possible for one of your men to be assigned to us until we are more able to, well, paddle our own canoe? Mrs. Sinclair has been divine, but I can't expect her to help *all* the time."

"Mrs. Sinclair?" The captain put down the bread.

Lillian spoke rapidly so the captain might not interrupt. "Yes, she made sure we were all fed, she's done most of our clearing up. And today even drove our oxen team for us. An absolute angel. But, of course, she has her own things to look to. Young Tom to look after."

The captain tilted his head and narrowed his eyes. "I'll send Dr. Trinkhoff to see how ill your husband is."

"Thank you, sir, that is very kind." Lillian made a quick bob and returned to the camp, her head aching even more than before but glad she had done what she could.

Randolph didn't feel like finishing his meal; a wave of nausea came over him as he thought of Mrs. Hollingswood's words. He made his way down the slight hill to the wagons but had not gone far before Turner approached him.

"James, do you have a moment?"

Randolph stifled a sigh, guessing this would be to do with Mrs. Sinclair. "Not really. I'm on my way somewhere."

Turner fell in next to Randolph's brisk stride. "It's about the wagons this morning," he started.

"Yes, I know."

"You know?"

They stopped at the Sinclairs' wagon, where Grace was seated, dishing out lunch from a skillet. Dear God, he *knew* that this neat and tidy wagon was hers. How the devil could he not have noticed that she had been hooking up oxen, not mules? That she was leading a large schooner?

Grace looked at the captain as he approached, her head to one side. Was it defiance? He could never be sure what was going on in her mind and wished he knew.

Randolph cleared his throat. "I want you to know, one of the soldiers will drive the Hollingswood team this afternoon. You will be able to concentrate on your own wagon. Boys as young as Tom shouldn't be put in such a responsible position." It was hardly the first time a boy had driven a wagon, but he just couldn't stop himself from finding something to chastise.

"Very well, sir." She put down the skillet and spoon. Her voice was steady, and gave no hint of what she might be feeling. She glanced over at Turner, who stood at some distance. What did that look mean?

Randolph shifted his weight. "Next time, speak to the appropriate person when one of your fellow overlanders has a problem. Don't take things upon yourself."

She folded her arms. "I did try, sir." Her voice was clear.

Ah, yes, defiance. That's what she was feeling.

"Try *harder*."

His jaw stiffened and there was a moment's pause. He looked down at her mahogany-brown eyes, and felt slightly ashamed as Grace blinked and turned her face away, as if trying to hide the tears that threatened.

Randolph removed his hat and ran his fingers through his hair to push back the lock from his brow. What was it about this woman? "I spoke harshly to you this morning. For that I apologize."

A movement of her head put him in mind of a prairie antelope, always primed to bolt in an unexpected direction.

"Does this mean…" She took a small step closer. "Does this mean we can continue beyond Fort Laramie?"

He balled his fists. Why did she always have to push so damned hard? "Our arrangement stays in place. Nevertheless, it would be foolish for you to build your hopes. I was in error on this occasion, but it is only a matter of time before *you* make the mistake."

Randolph walked away briskly, his heart beating hard, banging his hat against his leg. He heard Turner's steps behind him.

"Alfred, I don't want to hear it."

"Hear what, James?"

"Whatever pious homily you're going to give me. You think I'm being unreasonable. But I have to think of the welfare of *every* person on this expedition."

"Of course. I think you are right to have this… arrangement with Mrs. Sinclair." Turner puffed to keep up. "If she's not strong enough, she shouldn't carry on."

Randolph stopped and raised an eyebrow at Turner. "But?" He knew Turner well enough to be sure something more was coming.

"But I think you have to be completely fair about it," Turner said.

"Fair—"

"Treat the Sinclairs *exactly* like everyone else."

He hardly needed a lecture about fairness. "That is what I am doing."

"With respect, my friend, you're treating her more harshly than everyone else. You're *trying* to catch her out. This morning, for example. That can be the only explanation for mistaking that wagon. And then you didn't give her a chance to explain. You assumed the worst. Perhaps you could look at this from the other end."

Randolph narrowed his eyes. "The other end?"

"A few more people like Mrs. Sinclair and we'd have fewer problems. People who are prepared to help out other folk."

Randolph put his hat back on and pulled the brim down. "Alfred, you have always been kindhearted. Be careful the charms of this young woman are not drawing you in."

With that, he returned to the mess tent, wondering why his blood was pumping so hard when the incline of the hill had been so slight.

That evening's camp was quiet. Randolph consulted Dr. Trinkhoff at the infirmary—which was, in truth, nothing more than a tent with two benches and three boxes of medical supplies. A few more people had fallen sick, a few seemed on the mend. Some soldiers were now ill. Although less certain in his diagnosis, Trinkhoff nevertheless felt they should be able to move on.

Randolph returned to the mess tent to speak to his lieutenant. He dropped his hat onto the table. "I've decided we push on tomorrow."

"Even though it's Sunday?" Turner raised an eyebrow.

He shook his head. "Can't be helped. Survival is more important than the sabbath. We need to push on for a few more days until we reach the ferry to cross the Platte."

"Do you think people are well enough?"

Randolph shrugged. He wasn't sure how far he could trust Trinkhoff's advice, but he had to hope the travelers were strong enough. "Once we're the other side, then we can rest."

THIRTEEN

During the first weeks of the journey, Randolph had been amused by the pioneers' excitement at the new territory they were crossing, each day making progress toward the promised land. Now they were easily dispirited. Progress beside the Platte River was monotonous, mile after mile of flat earth, of gritty gray-brown dust that worked its way into shoes and clothing. Fresh water was scarce: the Platte carried so much sediment, a bucket needed to stand for an hour before the water at the top became clear. A few buffalo grazed in the distance, but not the huge dark herds they had hoped for. Hawks made circles in the sky, balancing on the air thermals, and sometimes swooping down with a flash of red wings to stab at a ground squirrel.

Most distressing of all were the occasional mounds of earth, marked with a cross made of whatever came to hand: the graves of previous overlanders whose dreams had come to a bitter end. Seeing them made even Randolph's hardened heart feel a little sore.

Yet still they pushed on, day after day.

. . .

Thursday morning, they reached the fork of the North and South Platte rivers. Until here, the Platte had been too wide and deep to ford, and too shallow for a ferry to cross. The South Platte was deeper, and in recent years an enterprising frontiersman had set up ferry crossings for the growing number of people heading West. He'd built a wooden platform large enough to take two wagons, made buoyant by oak barrels. The ferryman pulled on ropes, and used poles to push his way across the river, charging a high payment for his service.

The wagons reached a clearing between cottonwood trees on the riverbank where Randolph expected to see the ferry tied up, but there was nothing. He sent Corporal Flanagan upstream with a couple of privates to see if the ferryman had set up elsewhere.

Flanagan returned after half an hour to where the wagon train waited.

"Sir, I think I found the remains of the ferry. There were some cut logs and a few barrels washed up on rocks a couple of miles upstream."

"Any sign of the ferryman?" Randolph asked.

"No, sir."

This was troubling news. "Could we build our own raft from what you found?"

Flanagan pulled at his lower lip. "There might be a dozen logs, but not enough for a whole platform. All of the barrels looked smashed up and we couldn't see any rope."

Randolph wondered what had made the ferryman change his crossing place. Had a bad winter or ill luck forced him to abandon his lucrative trade? Or had something more serious befallen him?

A crowd had gathered around Randolph, looking to him to decide what to do next. He mounted his horse to speak, so they could all hear.

"This has been the location of the ferry for the past two

years. My corporal has found remains upstream. It's too deep to cross here without help. We will continue up the South Platte until we reach a place where we can ford the river, where it's shallower and has a firm riverbed."

There were mutters of discontent. But the rivers they had forded before now had not been so wide and fast as this one. Anyone could see they had no alternative to moving on.

"Let's get this train moving," said Randolph, encouraging them back to their wagons. "Think of the money you have saved from not paying the ferryman."

All day they pressed on, until in the evening they reached the crossing place where the riverbed made the water run wide, but not deep.

Early the following morning, Randolph sat tall on his horse to survey the river. The beige surface looked flat and calm but belied dangers beneath. It was running faster than usual, swollen not just with the spring snowmelt from the mountains to the west, but from the unseasonably wet weather of recent weeks. They could gamble and wait a few days for the river to subside. But there could be another deluge and the river get worse. Randolph was not a gambling man. He called his officers to him.

"Get everyone prepared. When we are ready to go, each wagon must move fast."

They got to work setting up guide ropes across the river. Moore fixed a long rope to a boulder, and Randolph tied the rest of the rope to his saddle to feed out as he crossed. He pressed his horse into the river, feeling for the current. The water soon reached the horse's shank, cold and sharp, but thankfully not getting much deeper. He glanced back at the settlers huddled at the water's edge. By mid-river, the flow was near Randolph's boots and the horse needed more urging as it resisted the numbing water. Nearly there. But the unseen riverbed dipped, the horse bucked and lost its footing. A few sharp digs of the captain's boot forced the horse on, and it struggled up out of the river, eyes wide with fear but safely on the other side.

Randolph tied the end of the rope round a mature cotton-wood tree near the riverbank. He signaled to Moore to start crossing with the second rope, which they then tied to a tree, a wagon-width further down. The two men pulled each cable taut so they spanned the river, about three feet above the roiling water. The ropes would guide the wagons on the most direct route, forming a path. If necessary, a rider could grab one for safety.

Randolph knew this was going to be a difficult crossing for everyone, but they were out of choices. The best he could do was make it as safe as possible for the overlanders. When the first few soldiers had crossed the river, he detailed a pair to go downstream and be ready to rescue any belongings, or worse: folk who might get swept away. He sent Corporal Moore forward to a site, half a mile hence, to prepare fires so people could dry themselves as soon as they arrived.

Grace stood by the riverside watching Randolph span the river, with her hands pushed into her armpits, hugging herself to stop the fear that he might not make it. So much of the overlanders' futures seemed to rest on this one man.

When his horse emerged on the other bank, she felt her shoulders loosen, unaware that she had been so tense.

Now the first few soldiers were over, it was the pioneers' turn.

Grace went back to her wagon, telling herself if others could do it, so could she. She moved firewood and food as high as possible; clothing and bedding would dry eventually, but grain would be ruined if it got wet.

Grace guided her team to her place in the line and waited with Tom. Kane settled behind the bench, and everything was wedged or tied.

Lieutenant Turner was at the bank, checking every possible thing was battened down, giving advice and encouragement.

"I'll lead the way," said Mr. Perriman, his wagon at the river edge.

"Where's your wife?" asked Turner.

"Decided to stay inside," Perriman replied, nodding to the canvas behind him.

A soldier on horseback went to the front of the team of mules to guide them into the water. Perriman snapped his whip, and they lumbered onwards.

Grace shielded the sun from her eyes as she watched, holding her breath as the Perriman wagon progressed. As it neared the far bank, Captain Randolph went into the river to reach it and pull the mules clear.

The Eliots were next. Sarah protested; she might fall in and couldn't swim.

"Stop your fussing. I can't swim neither," said Jane.

Turner took a couple of half-empty barrels from the quartermaster's cart. "If something happens, hold on tight to one of these," he said.

About half the wagons had crossed and it was nearing their turn. To Grace's surprise, Corporal Moore climbed up to the driving seat.

"Whatever are you doing?" asked Grace, edging toward Tom.

"Lieutenant Turner sent me. Said I was to drive your wagon over."

"You most certainly shall not. I will drive it myself."

"Got my orders, missus."

Grace's hands formed fists where they held the reins. She squared her shoulders. "I thought the order was for you to assist people who are sick. There is no one sick in this wagon."

"There ain't no man in this wagon neither," persisted Moore.

Grace fixed him with a glare. "Please return to Lieutenant Turner. Give him this message: *The captain shall have no excuse*. He'll know what I mean."

Moore shook his head and climbed down again as Grace proceeded to the river's edge. When she was given the signal to start her crossing, she took a deep breath, slapped the leather straps on the backs of her mules and urged them onwards.

The dark water eddied around the mules' legs and they hesitated. Grace shouted and they strained forward, the wagon's wheels slowly turning. Grace gripped the reins so tightly, the leather of her gloves was stretched smooth. The lightness of the wagon might work against her, the slightest stumble from a mule might overturn it and send them all hurtling down the river. She briefly lifted her eyes from the backs of her animals to assure herself of their destination and saw the captain in the water, his eyes fixed on her wagon. For all her posturing a moment ago, she was relieved he was there.

Tom shivered beside her, his face pale.

"You can hold round my waist if you want," she suggested. Would he be more scared if he could feel how fast Grace was breathing?

The spray splashed the hem of Grace's skirt, making it damp and heavy, the water seeping through her boots, sharp like a knife.

Time slowed and she felt an hour had passed, but they were only halfway. The worst part was yet to come. She silently cursed herself as she struggled to control the mules; she should have been less damn proud, and taken Corporal Moore's offer.

She urged the mules on as the wagon plunged downwards, and for a moment the water came right over the sideboard, making her gasp in fright. The soldier in front pulled the mules onwards and the wagon emerged from the water. She had never been so relieved as when the captain grabbed the halter and guided them to dry land, although he kept his eyes on the animals and still refused to look at her and Tom.

Grace stopped at the top of the bank and jumped down to calm her team. Water dripped from her wagon like a wet dog, and she and Tom were soaked through. Kit had moved around in the back, but everything was still there—even Kane, looking doleful.

Turning back, she was pleased to see the Hollingswoods crossing, so she waited for them, sitting with her back against a tree and gazing across the river. The captain was again at the water's edge. How on earth could he bear the cold? He'd been in and out for more than an hour now.

George Hollingswood had insisted on driving their wagon, even though he was weak from his fever. As they reached the deepest part, Grace was alarmed to see a huge log sweep past, startling one of the oxen. It panicked, trying to pull away. The upstream side of the wagon lurched into the air but was pulled back down by the weight of the remaining animals. But dear little Molly was tossed into the river. George seemed to forget about his team, his instincts no doubt turning to the child.

Grace jumped to her feet in alarm.

"Pull the wagon to the bank!" Captain Randolph shouted at the soldier heading the Hollingswood team.

Molly screamed as the current dragged her away.

Grace ran after her, but the captain was far quicker. He dug a spur into his horse's flank to force it downriver, and when he reached a little beyond the girl, he dived into the water. With a few firm strokes, the captain grabbed Molly's outstretched arm. He pulled her close and held her head above the water. Swimming toward the bank, the captain was reached by the soldier who had been posted downstream earlier.

The three struggled from the river, soaked to the skin, Molly clinging to the captain's neck and sobbing. Lillian and George joined Grace at the bank to meet them, breathless and exhausted. Molly's hands were clenched so tight, George could barely undo her little fists and pass her to her mother. Lillian covered the girl in kisses, while George tried to thank the captain and apologize for causing the accident.

"A piece of bad luck," Randolph said with a shrug. "Might've happened to anyone." He strode back to the crossing point. "Come on," he shouted to his men. "Let's get these last wagons over."

Thankfully, the remaining wagons crossed without incident. Grace waited at the crossing place to watch all the cattle and spare horses being steered across in one large herd, each following the other, the Sinclairs' precious horse among them. She marveled at how long the captain had stood in the water. He was a different sort of leader from any she had seen before. Yes, he was rigid, authoritarian, even dictatorial. But all other men she had known had used their power to force subordinates to do the dangerous and difficult tasks. She remembered the day the Perrimans' wagon wheel had fallen down the ravine. The captain had climbed down to rescue it rather than ask another soldier to hang on a rope over the perilous drop. And today, there was not a moment's hesitation before he dived into the roiling water to save Molly. Perhaps there was more to this man than she had originally thought.

At the camp, Grace was grateful for the fires lit by Corporal Moore, ready for the travelers. She dropped down next to one, shivering.

Captain Randolph announced they would spend Saturday here to rest, and ordered the soldiers to distribute hot drinks to raise everyone's spirits.

Grace fetched buffalo chips from her wagon and stoked the fire. Steam rose from damp clothing as she held it close. The Platte was so full of alluvial mud, the fabric stiffened as it dried.

"You look ill," Tom said, pushing a piece of cottonwood where it would catch light.

"I'll be fine."

"You were sniffing all morning. The cold water has made it worse."

The coat Grace was drying slipped through her fingers and the edge singed in the fire.

"I'll do this," said Tom, snatching the coat. "*Please* rest."

"Well, maybe I will—just for a little while."

Grace stumbled on her way to the wagon.

Tom set out her bed for her: the blankets were dry, but damp seemed to seep through everything. Grace was so tired, she barely noticed.

Instead of soothing sleep, she experienced a hallucinatory nightmare. Her hands grew huge, as if rolls of hard fat insulated her fingers from her body. She floated; not a restful floating, more the sensation of being at sea, with her body moving up and down, her head spinning and throbbing.

She was surrounded by darkness so thick, she could push through it. A man stepped out of the shadows, smelling of tobacco and spirits. She lifted her gun... fired. A dark patch of blood spread over his thigh, but he didn't stop: he kept walking toward her. She fired at his chest; blood oozed onto his waist-coat. Still he moved toward her. She screamed and hid her face from him.

The cries drew Tom. He tried to rouse her and wiped away the sweat, cooling her arms with a damp cloth. With the cool-ness, the bad dreams subsided and Grace fell back to sleep.

. . .

Tom went to the Hollingswoods for help but found them still in uproar over the incident with Molly.

Mustn't make a fuss, Tom said to himself. *Grace says we mustn't show any weakness. Be strong, be a man, not a boy.*

He returned to the fire and systematically dried their belongings. Everyone else was so preoccupied, they didn't notice Grace's absence.

He heated up soup and when he took it to Grace, she had woken up. He was sure she had the fever. She shivered as if frozen, yet sweat beaded on her face like grains of sand. She tried to eat the soup but felt too sick.

Tom sat on his wooden box looking at the graying embers of the fire and thinking how he would manage the wagon all by himself, how he would play his part in making sure the deal with the captain was won. Making sure they were not sent back to Independence to face the consequences of that awful night.

FOURTEEN

Fortunately for the Sinclairs, the captain ordered Sunday as a rest day as well. Now they were across the river, they could take a pause. Tom foraged firewood from the gnarled cottonwood trees and continued the chore of drying their belongings. Lord be praised, the May downpours had finally passed.

Lillian asked Tom about Grace, but he hedged. She was cooking, or in the wagon, or fetching water. All the time, *mustn't make a fuss* ran in his head. He knew what was at stake. He remembered their landlord's body on the stone floor the night they left Independence, the gleam of blood in the flicker of candlelight. That smell like wet iron. He wrinkled his nose and a shiver went down his spine. Most likely the man was dead, and a whole posse of sheriffs galloping West to track them down.

He might only be ten years of age, but he'd learned well from his sister. Everything was down to him, and he was going to show her. He packed their belongings on Sunday evening, knowing there was never enough time in the morning. Monday, he rose with the sun barely up, grabbed breakfast, and prepared the horse and mules.

He looked up and saw Grace struggling down from the back of the wagon. Her skin was pale and shiny, with dark rings under her eyes.

"What you doing?" Tom asked, hooking the grease bucket under the wagon bed.

"Helping you."

"It's all done. Everything's ready."

Grace looked around, unsteady on her feet. "So I see."

"You should carry on resting today. I can handle the wagon."

"I feel a little better, Tom." She put her hand on his shoulder. "You know the captain has forbidden you to drive the mules. He'll be furious if I let you sit out front alone again."

Tom's shoulders dropped, but he climbed up to the driver's bench, followed by Grace. She was dressed in her father's coat, buttoned up against the elements. Despite saying she felt better, she did not look it.

They pulled out, one of the first wagons to be ready for the prompt departure at seven o'clock. The wagon dipped and rocked as the mules pulled it over ruts in the earth.

"I'm not sure I can do this," Grace whispered to Tom.

"You lean on me while I hold the reins." It was typical of his sister to try to take on too much, but at least he could help.

Grace let him take the leather straps.

"I'll keep a lookout for the captain and if he comes, I'll nudge you and quickly give the reins over," said Tom.

Grace nodded and made no protest. The captain usually rode at the front of the train but would occasionally trot through to the back to check everything was well. This was what made Tom afraid, but luckily, this morning it was the lieutenant who rode back.

.   .   .

Turner had noticed Grace had not been around the previous day, and now, as the Sinclair wagon passed, one look at her face told him why.

At the noon break, Turner found Tom sitting on a box, wolfing some bread, but no sign of Grace.

"Mrs. Sinclair in the wagon?" Turner asked the boy.

"Yep, she's tidying up in there." He nodded toward the wagon and returned his attention to his plate. "Doesn't want to be disturbed."

"Happen like she could do with a breather."

Tom silently stared at him through his overgrown hair but kept on chewing.

"You're doing a grand job here," Turner tried again. It would be so much easier if the boy opened up. "I mean, with your mother ill."

"She's not *really* ill," Tom said quickly. "Just a little... under the weather. We'll be fine."

"Look, Tom, you don't need to pretend to me. I'd like to help."

"We don't need help," he said with a scowl.

He reminded Turner of a new army cadet, all bravado and bluster, covering up the fears beneath. He crouched down next to the boy, his knees complaining. "The captain has allowed soldiers to help other wagons when someone's gotten sick."

Tom gave him a sideways glance. "Not the same with us, though, sir, is it? The captain doesn't want us here."

"The captain doesn't have to know." Turner winked at the boy. "If I send one of the privates to drive the wagon, the captain probably wouldn't notice. And if he did, it would be on my orders."

"My sis—I mean, Ma won't hear of it. There's no way she'll risk it, no matter how bad she's feeling."

Turner let out a long sigh. "Maybe you two *would* be better off waiting at Fort Laramie. You could join a later wagon train. Or a message could be got to your father, and he could travel back East to meet you."

Tom shook his head vigorously. "No, sir. That wouldn't work. We've *gotta* keep moving West, we've just gotta."

Turner stood up and stretched his legs. This boy was scared of something. There was more to the Sinclairs' story than they were letting on, he was sure of it.

The afternoon felt endless to Grace as she sat on the driver's bench, leaning against Tom. Her head throbbed and the reins weighed heavy in her hands. Her muscles burned as she struggled to control the mules. She longed for the day's traveling to be over so she could sleep.

The Great Plain was a monotone sea of beige grass all around them, devoid of trees, the horizon unchanging except for some strange rock formations in the far distance. The sky was blue with wispy clouds like white feathers, and the heat rose.

At last they reached their destination for that day. As soon as the wagon drew to a stop, Grace climbed back under the canvas bonnet, laid out her bed, and flopped down. She no longer cared if they went beyond Fort Laramie. She longed for rest, for the aches to be over.

The next few days followed the same pattern, with Grace huddled against Tom. The rock formations drew closer. First the lump of Courthouse Rock, like a castle rising abruptly from the plain. Then the strange Chimney Rock standing tall above the flat land, a central finger of rock which seemed to have spewed flour into the sky to fall as a gray-white cone all around the base.

Grace fretted that Tom was taking on too much, but he smiled as he went about his chores, proud of his toughness. He was at the age when people still treated him as a boy, even though he thought of himself a man. Grace felt for him, with his slight build for his age, but he was proving he had inherited the Sinclair grit and bloody-mindedness.

Each evening, Tom watered the animals and fetched stinking buffalo chips to burn on the fire for supper. A few people might ask after Grace, but he gave his usual bland replies.

By Saturday night, people gathered for their customary singsong and dance. There were fewer than usual and the merriment ended early. The strains of the journey were wearing folk down, but thankfully, the next day they would rest.

On Sunday morning, Grace woke and sat up, but her head reeled so bad, she snuggled down again. It was the sabbath. She could relax in peace. No one would notice she was absent; after all, many travelers had been patchy in their attendance at Sunday morning prayers.

"I thought I might attend morning service," Tom said.

"Really?"

"Kinda got stuff to be grateful for."

"What like?"

"We got this far. And you're better than you were."

Grace rearranged the bag of linen she used as a pillow. "You go spend some time with the Hollingswood boys afterwards. You need a break from everything."

The day of rest did Grace a power of good. She woke on Monday morning and, dear Lord, her muscles didn't ache. A good cooked breakfast and she would take on the world. She remained careful, though, taking things easy, Tom still holding the reins.

That evening she visited the Hollingwoods who were all on

the mend. Lillian handed her a tin mug of coffee and they sat on a log for a gossip, watching the children play chase around them, the sounds of laughter traveling through the evening air.

Maybe Tom was right, maybe they did have a lot to be thankful for.

FIFTEEN

Randolph unbuttoned his military jacket, shrugged it off and placed it over the chair by his campaign desk, brushing away some dust with the back of his hand. He sat on his camp bed and pulled off his leather boots, then leaned back, stretching his legs. Heck, he was worn out. He closed his eyes and rolled his shoulders.

"Sir?"

A small voice made him sit up sharply. There was Molly Hollingswood standing tentatively just inside the canvas door of his tent.

"What is it, Molly?"

She stepped forward, holding her hands behind her back.

Randolph lifted an eyebrow. "Is something wrong?"

"I... I wanted to give you these." She held out a large bunch of wildflowers: butter-gold mules' ears, white-and-yellow daisies, and a few purple mountain irises. Some of the stems were broken and the heads hung down over her small hand. "I've been gathering them all day, along the trail."

Randolph stood up, towering over the girl. "That's mighty kind of you."

"I wanted to say thank you. For saving me, I mean. I was very frightened and I bet you were frightened of that river too."

Randolph smiled and dropped down on his haunches so he was level with her. "Sometimes we do things even if we are frightened."

"Ma says you saved my life." Her blue eyes gazed straight into his face and she straightened her arm, still holding the flowers. Randolph was abashed by this little girl's directness.

"Well, don't know about that." He took the bunch carefully. "Why don't you sit here at my desk while I find something for these?"

She climbed onto the chair, her feet dangling.

Randolph looked around, uncertain of what to put the flowers into. He glanced at his whiskey glass and felt a twinge of unease: too small of course, but more than that, it did not feel right for such an innocent gift.

He laid the flowers on the camp bed and pulled on his boots. "Stay here a moment."

He slipped out, reappearing a minute later with a small metal water jug.

"Hopefully the quartermaster won't notice it's gone." He winked at Molly and she broke into a wide smile.

He shoved the flowers in, doing his best to keep the stems upright. Molly seemed unperturbed by his clumsy efforts. He placed the jug on the table by his camp bed.

"What are you writing?" she asked, looking at the book on his desk.

"That's my log."

A line appeared on her forehead. "It's not made of wood."

"It's like a diary of things that happen each day. Look, a week ago"—he leaned over and turned the pages—"I made a note of what happened to you."

Molly eagerly leaned forward and traced her name. Then a

shadow crossed her face. "Are there any more rivers to cross before we get to Oregon?"

"I'm afraid there's lots," he said. "But not many as wide as that one."

Molly curled her lips inwards, seeming to ponder his words, and swung her feet.

"You need to learn to swim," Randolph said, sitting on the bed. "That will keep you safe."

She hooted. "Don't be a silly goose! Girls can't swim."

"I don't see why not."

Molly's eyes opened wide. "Will you teach me?"

Randolph grinned. "I'm not sure I'll get the chance. I have all my soldiers to look after. But why don't you ask your father? Or one of your brothers. Do they swim?"

Molly pursed her lips. "They do, but I don't think they'll want to teach me."

"Look, why don't I take you back to your wagon now, and I'll ask them to do it myself." Randolph stood up and slapped his thighs.

"Would you?" She seemed excited by the idea.

"My pleasure."

Randolph held open the canvas door of his tent and Molly jumped down from the chair. As they started down the slope to the wagons, she slipped her hand in his. He looked down and smiled.

"You're nothing like as scary as everyone says."

Randolph laughed. "They say I'm scary?"

"Ma says you're very angry. And another word that I think is the same. Agnorant."

"Agnorant?" Randolph chuckled as he tried out the word. "Do you mean *arrogant*?"

"That was it!"

Randolph shook his head.

They came to some brambles across their path, so he

scooped Molly up and perched her on his right hip. She put her arm round his neck and giggled.

Randolph saw Lillian and Grace sitting on a log and strode toward them, aware that he was more disheveled than he would like to be when out in public, his dark hair unbrushed, with his wayward fringe falling across his brow, his white shirt unbuttoned at the neck. He hadn't expected Grace Sinclair to be there.

Lillian's mouth fell open when she spotted him and she shushed the children.

Randolph swung Molly down as the Hollingswoods gathered.

"Molly and I have been discussing things, and we both think one of you should teach her to swim this summer."

The family stared mutely at him and Molly swayed his arm back and forth, grinning from ear to ear.

Lillian stepped forward and took Molly's hand. "You *know* you should not be bothering the captain. He's an extremely busy man." She frowned at Molly.

Randolph folded his arms. "So, Mr. Hollingswood, d'you think you might do that?"

George looked like a startled hare. "Yes. Yes of course. I will make a point of it."

"Good." Randolph turned on his heel, took a couple of steps, before turning back to Lillian. "You have a very well brought-up little lady there, Mrs. Hollingswood. You can be proud of her." Then he set off back to the soldiers' camp, leaving the family speechless.

Lilian turned to the little girl. "Molly, what were you *thinking*?"

"I wanted to say thank you," she replied, looking up with big innocent eyes. "I took him some flowers. He's not scary at all."

The tension broke and everyone laughed. Lillian gave her a

big hug. "Off to bed with you, honey. That's enough excitement for one night."

Lillian looked at Grace and their eyes met, sparkling with amusement. She nodded to where the captain had been standing, a heart-stopping mixture of virility and tenderness.

"By the color in your cheeks, that's enough excitement for you too."

Grace gave her a friendly shove. "Wonders will never cease. According to your six-year-old daughter, he's not scary at all."

They both started to laugh, stifling their giggles in case Randolph was still in earshot.

The trail became easier and Grace's strength returned. A few days later, as she walked beside her mules between the mammoth bulks of Scotts Bluff and Sentinel Rock, Molly's giggles rang out behind her.

Grace watched open-mouthed as the captain's horse trotted past, Molly tucked onto the saddle in front of Randolph, his arms keeping her safe as she bounced along, hooting with glee. The captain's face was mostly shadowed by his hat, but she thought she could see the slightest smile on his lips. She shook her head at this unexpected bond between the stern captain and the little girl.

She looked around and took in the landscape, which was changing with each mile. Ridges rose on each side, the rock exposed and layered, strange shapes at the summit. There was no doubt: they were nearing Fort Laramie. Only a week's drive. Maybe a bit less. Then they would get their first sight of the Rockies.

Dear Lord, they might do it, might reach Fort Laramie without giving Captain Randolph a single excuse to leave them behind. As long as he kept his word, they would be on their way to the far West, to the safety of brother Zachary, where surely no one would drag her back.

SIXTEEN

The weather turned bad again. As rain fell, it had nowhere to run off, so the earth became sodden and muddy. Progress slowed as the mules and oxen plodded and pulled their way onwards. Flash floods gathered where the land undulated. Small streams running down to the river boiled into noisy torrents.

Each day they covered less ground; Grace looked back one evening and was able to see where they had spent the previous night. Tempers flared if a wagon held up progress. An argument broke out between Mr. Eliot and Mr. Davies when the path narrowed and their animals clashed. Captain Randolph calmed heightened feelings: "Patience now, gentlemen. A good push today and we will reach Fort Laramie by tomorrow evening."

Late that afternoon, the trail was forced to leave the side of the river and go over some soft sandstone. Grace was walking by her front pair of mules when she felt the wagon judder.

Tom jumped down, Kane following him with a wagging tail. "It's the back wheel. It's jammed in a rut."

She supposed something like this was bound to happen

sometime, but why so close to Laramie? She urged the mules to strain forward, but the wagon stayed put.

Grace ran to the back. She needed to sort this quickly, before anyone could criticize her. She crouched down to try to unwedge the large rock which blocked the wheel. It shifted a little, but she didn't have enough leverage.

Private O'Hara saw the problem and got down from his horse to help. Between the two of them, it came loose and rolled away.

Unfortunately, Randolph trotted up to see what was causing the delay. Grace stood up and caught his disapproving eye as he turned his horse away. How did he manage to *never* let things escape his notice?

She went to the mules' harness and encouraged them onwards, while Tom slapped the reins on their backs. They hauled forward, but a creaking sound came from under the wagon and then a crack.

Grace ducked under the wagon bed, her heart in her mouth. An axle had split under the strain, but not yet broken.

"Do we stop to repair it?" Tom asked anxiously.

Grace bit her lip. "I'm not sure what's for the best. If we stop now, it could take an hour to mend, and that might prevent the whole train reaching Laramie tomorrow. That would be a black mark against us."

"But Grace, if it completely breaks, then we won't be able to move on at all."

She could tell from Tom's tight voice that he understood how serious this was. Grace covered her mouth with her hand and shook her head. "I know. I know. Surely we can't be going much further today."

She shaded her eyes to look ahead, but it was useless. That told her nothing. She paced, trying to make a decision. "We'll risk it. Carry on to tonight's camp, and hope and pray it doesn't break before we get there."

· · ·

Grace's throat was dry as they drove for an hour, every moment listening out for the sound of cracking wood. She breathed a long sigh as they reached the camp without further damage.

It was a windy, inhospitable place with no trees, just low shrubs. The ground was saturated and soon churned to sludge as people walked between wagons.

Grace went under the wagon to inspect the damage close up while Tom started supper. The front wheel axle had begun to split along a weakness in the wood. Probably the damp weather had stopped it breaking completely. It would have to be replaced, but that was a job for a professional wheelwright. There should be no problem fixing it at the Fort, but they needed to reach there first. If Grace could splint the axle with another piece of wood, then, with luck, it should hold for one more day's traveling.

She had brought pieces of planking for repairs. Most pioneers did this and patch-ups were common enough on the long journey. Wheels were replaced, wagon beds strengthened, ripped bonnets repaired. Hers was not the first axle to have had problems, and wouldn't be the last.

Grace and Tom ate their food and tended the animals. They didn't want to start work too soon, as that would draw attention. By making the repairs later, people would be settling down and there would be less of a fuss. Grace prayed Randolph wouldn't notice there was a problem with their wagon.

Darkness fell early; the clouds were gray and low, threatening more rain. Grace lit a storm lamp and ducked down to work out how to make the repair: the new joist could slide under the axle and be secured in the hound braces at right angles. But she would have to lift the rear bolster by about six inches, to slide the joist in.

She and Tom unloaded the heavier luggage, and then

created a pivot to lever up the bolster and axle. It was slow work. The sky was black and the drizzle started again.

"What's going on here?" A soldier on his rounds was drawn by the lamplight under the wagon.

"Nothing serious, sir. Just a minor repair." Grace crawled out and stood up hastily. "Ah. Corporal Flanagan."

The corporal's eyebrows raised as he took in her mud-splattered dress and the wrench gripped in her hand.

"I'll take a look," he said.

"Thank you, sir, but it's all in hand."

Undeterred, Corporal Flanagan crouched down and looked at the undercarriage by the light of the lantern. He was a thickset man and when he took off his hat, his red-gold hair stuck up like a brush.

"You've got a split axle there, ma'am."

"Yes, I know." She exchanged a look with Tom, and he rolled his eyes heavenwards.

"That can be fixed at Fort Laramie."

"That's what I'm hoping, sir."

"That joist ought to hold it, if you can get it secure."

Grace tapped her fingers on the wrench. "Like I say, that's what I'm hoping."

"Look, if I can give you a hand with—"

"That won't be necessary, thank you." Grace took a calming breath. "We can manage."

Corporal Flanagan stood up, his bushy eyebrows set in a frown. "But, ma'am, all I have to do is lift the—"

"I am sure you are trying to help, but it is not required."

"But this is foolish—"

"Thank you, but I'll decide what is and is not foolish in respect of my own wagon." Grace set her shoulders and looked straight at him. "And as I'm a civilian, I believe you have no authority over me in this matter." She picked up his hat and handed it to him. "Good evening to you, sir."

The corporal's ruddy face turned redder and Grace waited for the dam to burst. Instead he marched off.

Grace's shoulders dropped and she and Tom continued their labors under the wagon.

Turner's card game with some of the men in the mess tent was not going well. One more hand and he'd turn in with Eunice. The tent doorflap banged and Corporal Flanagan entered, his mouth a grim line.

"You can take my place in a moment, Corporal. I'm almost through."

Flanagan shook his head and poured himself some water.

"You've got a face as dark as this weather," Sergeant Knox said. "Maybe you need a glass of the strong stuff after all." He winked at his companions.

"Can you believe it?" Flanagan banged the glass back on the table. "You offer help and it's flung back in your face!"

"Playing the Good Samaritan again?" Knox picked up another card. "Who were you trying to help this time?"

"One of the overlanders. Mrs. Sinclair—she's got some serious repairs to fix, and she *insists* on doing them alone."

Turner put his cards face down on the table and pushed them to the dealer. Mrs. Sinclair. Was her luck about to run out?

"What exactly has happened, Corporal?" he asked.

Flanagan told him of the exchange with Grace.

Turner stood and got his hat. "Let's go see if we can sort this out, Flanagan."

They went out into the light rain. Reaching the wagon at the bottom of the slope, Turner could hear tapping. Grace was underneath, hammering at something, with Tom moving a storm lamp so she could see.

"Mrs. Sinclair," Turner called.

The hammering stopped and Grace edged out and struggled to her feet. Her dress was gray-brown from where she had lain on the earth, and her hair had loosened, falling in tresses around her shoulders. There was a smudge across her cheek. Turner suppressed a smile that threatened.

"Lieutenant Turner." Grace gave a slight nod.

"The corporal here says you got a problem."

"As I told him," she said stiffly, "it is all under control."

"May I take a look?"

Grace stood her ground for a moment, but then stepped aside.

Turner crouched down, inspected the damage, and stood up again.

"Mrs. Sinclair, it could take you and Tom all night to get that joist in. With the corporal and myself to help, it will be done in ten minutes."

"I'm sure you understand why I cannot allow that," Grace replied firmly.

Yes, Turner well understood what she meant. "But the captain isn't around at the moment."

"He often does a tour of the camp in the evening. I just can't risk it. To be so close to Fort Laramie... To come this far..." Grace pushed away a strand of hair that had stuck to the mud on her face. "I won't give him a reason not to take us onwards."

There must be a way to persuade her. "The army has helped many other wagons with repairs," Turner remarked.

"It would be different with me, sir. You know that." She looked up at him, her eyes shining.

Turner shook his head, wishing others truly knew Randolph as well as he did. "The captain is by no means as unreasonable as you believe."

"You may be right. But I cannot take the chance. There's too much at stake." Grace bent down to pick up her hammer. "Now, if you would excuse me, sir, we have work to do."

They left her, the most stubborn woman he'd ever met. But Turner could not abandon the situation. He sent Flanagan back to the mess and went to the captain's tent to see if he could move things on through stealth.

"May I disturb you?" said Turner.

Randolph was drinking a small whiskey and reading a book by the light of a single lamp. "Come in. Would you like a nightcap?"

"A whiskey would warm me through." Turner sat in the spare canvas chair and shook the drips from his hat.

"There seems no end to this rain," Randolph said, passing the glass. "We've sure been unlucky this trip."

"Ain't that the truth. The weather's taken its toll." Turner nodded. "I declare, there's one wagon out there making repairs as we speak."

"Late to be doing that, isn't it?"

"Indeed it is, James. But some of these pioneers, they're so proud. Won't accept help from no one. Stubborn headed, they are."

Randolph took out his pocket watch. "Look, why don't you take a few men and finish the repairs so everyone can get some sleep."

"Tried that, James. I was told by the pioneer that we have no jurisdiction over the wagons. Is that true?"

Randolph considered the question. "The wagons are their property. But I believe it's our duty to make sure everyone gets to Oregon safely."

"So we could *order* them to allow the soldiers to make repairs?" Turner hoped a challenge to army authority was just the thing to lure Randolph to get involved.

"I would say we could," Randolph replied.

"Perhaps *you* could have a word with the family. It would come better from the captain."

"I don't see why."

"Y'know, less of a challenge to the pioneer pride."

Randolph shrugged and swallowed the last of his drink. "If you truly think that would help. Let's get down there."

Randolph took his hat and, for the second time, Turner made his way to the stricken wagon.

The drizzle was easing off as they crossed the camp. When they neared the Sinclair wagon, Randolph gave a tired sigh of recognition and glanced at Turner.

A lamp under the wagon gave a warm glow and spread lines of shadows through the spokes of the wheels. The earth had been trampled into dark mud. Tom squatted next to a second oil lamp placed on the ground, surrounded by an assortment of hammers and tools and lumps of wood of varying sizes.

Randolph paused and folded his arms, looking straight at Turner. "Is this a test?"

"James?"

"Of my principles."

Turner thought for a moment about the question. "Maybe. You like to play the misanthrope. But I know you're a just man."

Randolph gave an exasperated shake of his head, and walked on to confront Mrs. Sinclair.

SEVENTEEN

"Tom, pass me the large wooden mallet, would you?"

Lying on her back on a tarpaulin, Grace had managed to wedge a piece of wood between the axle and the iron flange. If she could only hammer it inwards, she could start maneuvering the broken shaft.

"Tom? Are you there?"

There was no response.

Grace turned her head to look along the ground to the wagon side, expecting to see Tom offering the mallet. Instead, there were two pairs of military boots, one set with distinctive burgundy leather around the top: the captain's.

Dear Lord, no. She felt like a cattle rustler caught by a rancher.

"Mrs. Sinclair?" The captain's voice was low and controlled.

She ought to slide out and start making explanations, but was too defeated to move. "Yes?"

"I understand you're having a few problems down there."

"All under control, thank you, sir," she called, trying to sound confident but feeling on the edge of tears. All their hard work to come to nothing. Just one day's journey from Laramie! "It might take a while, but I promise you, Tom and me, we'll fix it in the end."

"You say you need the mallet?"

"Um..."

Captain Randolph crouched down on his haunches. In the shadows, Grace found it hard to read his face. He unbuttoned his blue jacket and pulled at the cuffs.

"If I'm going to get covered in mud, I'd prefer it to be this shirt. Easier to launder than my uniform."

He picked up the large mallet at Tom's feet and crawled under the wagon.

Grace dropped her head back onto the tarp and closed her eyes for a moment, knowing further protests would be useless.

Captain Randolph settled down on his back next to Grace, and by the light of the oil lamp examined the broken axle. "I see, this is beginning to split," he said, running his hand along the wood. "And you're trying to put in this strut to support it."

"I thought I could get it replaced in Fort Laramie."

"Yes, well, this seems the most sensible thing to do. How were you going to lift the bolster so you could put in the strut?"

"I'm using these wedges and then was going to use levers."

Randolph frowned. "That could take you hours."

Grace swallowed; her mouth was dry. "Time is not a problem."

"Turner and I could repair this in minutes." He folded back his shirtsleeves, uncovering his muscular forearms. "Right. Let's get this wedge in first." He used the hammer to knock it in place with a few sharp blows.

"Another one at the other end?" he asked.

Grace had the wedge to hand and he took it from her.

"Turner?" he called out. "Pass me the long strut. Let's check it fits where we need it."

"Sir, I've already measured..." Her throat was so tight, the words would not come.

He hefted the large piece of oak into place under the wagon. "Could you hold that end there, Mrs. Sinclair?" He studied the length. "Yes, that will be fine."

For the first time, Randolph looked directly at Grace. Her stomach tightened.

"But I expect you already knew that, didn't you?" Crinkles softened the edge of his eyes.

"Yes, I *had* measured it."

"Of course you had. Would expect nothing less." A slight smile played around his mouth. "Now, let's get this in place." He hollered: "Turner, could you lift the wheel when I say?"

"Will do, sir."

"Mrs. Sinclair, when I lift here, I want you to slot in the strut. Ready?"

She nodded.

"Now!" he called to Turner.

He flexed his arms to take the weight and raised the bolster enough for Grace to push in the supporting strut.

"Good." He glanced at Grace, a look of satisfaction on his face. "I'm afraid you need to be the other side of me to slide it in at the other end."

Grace's mouth opened slightly and she feared Randolph could see her color rising, despite the mud on her face.

"It would be quickest if I lift up while you roll," he said.

Turning, he leaned over her and lifted his body up with his arms. Grace rolled to the other side. Their bodies were in contact briefly. Her heart beat so hard, she could feel the palpitations in her neck.

"That wasn't too bad now, was it?" he teased.

She slid her eyes toward him, and he bit his lip as if trying to stop himself smiling. He seemed to take pleasure from embarrassing her.

"Turner! We're ready to go again down here."

They repeated the process, Randolph lifting and Grace pushing the other end of the wooden strut in place. Randolph tested it and nodded.

"Now, could you hold the lamp while I secure things?"

While the captain hammered home nails and wedges, Grace closely observed him without fear of being caught. His full attention was on the task, making sure each nail was perfectly placed, and using as few blows as possible. The sternness had melted from his face; instead the skin around his steel-blue eyes creased in concentration on the job in hand. His teeth bit slightly on his lips as he thought where to put the next wedge.

She had never been close to a man in this way before, never experienced this mixture of apprehension and excitement. She studied the bristles of the dark stubble on his jaw, noticed a line of scar tissue and was surprised by how hard she had to resist the temptation to use her fingertips to find out what it felt like.

Grace thought ahead to which nail or hammer would be needed next. She felt a flutter of pride when he flashed her a smile as she handed him the right tool before he asked. She watched the dark hairs on his forearms, the ropes of muscle flexing as he grasped the hammer. She breathed in his musky masculine smell. As they worked together, aware of nothing beyond the pool of golden lamplight under the wagon, it dawned on her that far from resenting him for helping her, she wanted this to last for hours. Even in the cold and mud, she felt warm and secure beside him—and, oh, she wanted more of this feeling. All too soon the repair would be done, and the time for confrontation would begin again. He would still be the austere captain, they the troublesome Sinclairs.

"That's the last bit." Randolph turned to face her. "Should get you as far as Fort Laramie."

"But what about beyond?"

He frowned. "Let's talk about that standing up, shall we?"

He crawled out from under the wagon.

Grace followed and Randolph leaned down to offer a hand to help her up. The misty rain had stopped. Her hair had completely escaped its pins and tumbled over her shoulders. Her dress was damp from the mud and she tried to beat some clods off the skirt. She decided to get on the front foot and put her case forward first.

"Sir, Tom and me, we were working slowly, but we would have gotten there, in the end."

He began rolling his sleeves down. "I know you would."

"And we didn't *ask* for military help."

"I know that too. The lieutenant fetched me."

Turner handed Randolph his jacket, but he chose not to wear it. Instead, he ran his fingers through his damp hair, pushing it back from his brow.

"As I see it, I agreed to take you all the way to Oregon if you proved you could take care of yourselves and be no trouble. Frankly, it was an easy deal to make, because I never thought you would do it."

Grace opened her mouth to interrupt, but Randolph raised a hand.

"Until tonight, we've spent less time on this wagon than most." He stepped past her and placed a hand on the wooden sideboard. "And it's true you would have repaired the axle eventually. Turner would be the first to point out the army have helped other overlanders with practical difficulties."

He turned back to face Grace whose heart was thumping, waiting for his decision.

"It's clear you kept your side of the bargain—and I will keep mine. You may continue journeying West with me—as long as you maintain the behavior you have shown so far, of course."

Grace gasped. She reached out and clutched the captain's

hand and, before she knew what she was doing, brought it to her lips. Randolph frowned in surprise.

"Thank you. Thank you," she breathed. She grabbed Tom and squeezed him with joy. Laughter bubbled out of her, mingled with tears of relief which she swept from her eyes. She wouldn't be going back to Independence, leaving young Tom to fend for himself.

"You've made the mud on your face even worse," Tom said.

She laughed again.

Turner clapped Tom on the back and gave Randolph a triumphant smile.

Randolph rubbed his hand where Grace had kissed it, as if it had been burned and needed soothing.

This young woman was doing everything in her power to reach her husband once more, undergoing hardships and great toil. He had never experienced such devotion from a woman; feared he never would.

His jaw tensed. Was this unfamiliar sensation a creeping jealousy of a man living on a homestead somewhere out West? What was so damn special about this Mr. Sinclair that he inspired such loyalty?

PART TWO

EIGHTEEN

Fort John had been built to service the overland fur trade, perhaps ten years earlier. Now it was a garrison fort, taken over by the US Army and renamed Laramie after the river that protected one side. Captain Randolph knew the approaching overlanders were always impressed by the wooden walls, although many ramshackle huts sheltered in the shadows, along with lodges and tipis. Soldiers would be stationed here for months at a time, and men with an enterprising nature catered to their needs. Over recent years, Laramie was the first place for overlanders to stock up on supplies. But it was also the end of the trail for turnbackers who no longer had the energy or inclination to go all the way West. Randolph thought the fort and surrounding area had the air of a transit camp and a place of failed dreams.

The entrepreneurs who had settled in and around the fort studied the wagon train with interest. This was the first of the season and unscrupulous traders hoped for rich pickings. Randolph advised the pioneers—and soldiers—to keep all valuables secure, and never buy the first thing offered, no matter how good a bargain it seemed. *Caveat emptor*. They had been warned.

His advice was not universally followed. The overlanders' relief at having covered a quarter of their journey made them inclined to celebrate. The soldiers felt the burden of responsibility lift from their shoulders, and some indulged in heavy drinking and playing hazard or three-card monte late into the night.

Over the next few days, useless equipment was bought, jewelry stolen, and good horses exchanged for lame. Randolph tried to adjudicate as many problems as he could, but some travelers were left disappointed.

The Sinclairs, as always, kept their heads well down. They had left Independence in such a panic, there were things Grace had failed to buy. Now she knew they could travel onwards, she risked her precious savings. Many wagons had a cow or goat tethered behind for fresh milk on the journey. Grace bought a quizzical-looking black-and-white goat and a butter churn. The movement of the wagon would produce butter by hooking the churn to the axle. She chose three hens from an ancient gray-haired trader who said he'd been a mountain man once, and was reduced to selling poultry rather than pelts. The chickens would travel in a wooden crate fixed over the back of the wagon bed. If she could keep the animals alive, they would set her up in Oregon.

Grace asked around for recommendations for the best wheelwright to repair the wagon, but the choice was limited and none was cheap. The morning of the second day in camp, word must have reached Captain Randolph, because he brought a Lakota to Grace's wagon.

"This is Gray Eagle. He is very skilled at repairs."

She stood rooted to the spot. She had never been so close to a Native before. The man was unusually tall, with a wide face and a firm jaw. His black hair was parted in the middle and braided at each side. He was dressed in a mixture of clothes: a long American coat and buckskin pants. Threads of beads made of bone lay over the neck of his cotton shirt.

"For the axle," said Randolph when she failed to reply. "You haven't had it repaired yet?"

Grace swallowed and found her voice. "No. Not yet."

"I recommend him. You won't find better."

She looked at the man in front of her. From a distance, she had watched Native families traveling across the Great Plain, and some Kansa had approached the wagons as they had passed, hoping to trade—but she had not had to have a conversation.

Grace turned back to the captain. "You think it's for the best?"

Randolph nodded.

Grace took a breath. She had come to trust the captain and knew he had her best interests at heart. "Very well."

"Good. I'll leave you to agree the price," he said, and walked away.

All those stories whispered between the overlander women flooded into her mind, tales of kidnaps, mutilations, and murders, which some of the gnarlier pioneers seemed to take a perverse joy in retelling.

Grace lifted her skirts to hurry after him. "Sir, are you sure?"

"Gray Eagle has good English," he said over his shoulder. "His mother was Lakota but his father was a fur-trapper."

Grace plucked at the sleeve of his uniform. "No. I didn't mean how we agree the price. I mean... Are you sure you should leave me? Alone?"

Randolph turned, and Grace felt herself get smaller under the intensity of his gaze. She had a sense of disappointing him.

He pulled the cuffs of his uniform sleeves. "You'll be perfectly safe. Gray Eagle often visits the fort. He's scouted for me before." His voice was more clipped than usual. "Try to pay him a good price, though. It's his land we're traveling through after all."

Grace frowned. "He owns all this land?"

"His people, I mean. Don't know if they own it as such. But they've lived here for as long as they can remember. So I guess that counts for something." He adjusted his hat and swiftly left.

Grace looked after him and was unsure why her heart felt so heavy at losing his regard. She turned back to her wagon, and saw that the man was already busy gathering tools.

It was a bright Wednesday morning in the middle of June, when the wagon train trundled out West once more. Grace noted a number of changes. A few wagons were left behind, the drunken and inadequate Mr. Davies among them. One new wagon joined them. Its occupants had been struck down with cholera the year before, and even though they had buried all four children, they had decided to continue on to Oregon. A few of the soldiers also changed. Some had been detailed to remain at Fort Laramie, replaced on the wagon train by garrison soldiers.

Grace's breath caught when she saw the man riding next to the captain. The tall figure of Gray Eagle was unmistakable, even though he was in a blue army coat. He rode without a saddle, instead using a brightly woven blanket. His riding seat was relaxed and he seemed at one with the movement of this fine white-and-brown Paint horse. As the captain had predicted, Gray Eagle had done an excellent repair of the axle and charged a fair price. Grace had felt embarrassed by her fears, and tried to make amends by offering refreshments. None were accepted by the man and he had maintained a distance. She wondered how long he would be traveling with them.

The next part of their journey began the long, slow, upwards pull toward the foothills of the Rockies. Early in the day, Grace walked beside her mule team as birds sang, floating high on the air currents. By midmorning, the unforgiving heat made the birds fall silent. Instead, the constant clicking and chirping of grasshoppers and cicadas had a hallucinatory effect. Cracks emerged in the soil, narrow to begin with, but with each day, the crevices grew wider and Grace looked out for the mules' hooves. There was little visible wildlife in the yellowing grass—the occasional antelope scampered away; prairie dogs sat up on their hind legs to sniff the air, before bolting back down a hole in the dry earth.

They had been back on the trail for a week and a half when the turgid, muddy Platte veered south. On Saturday evening, they reached the Sweetwater River, a meandering river which would take them to the South Pass and over the Continental Divide.

The river lived up to its name: first thing Sunday morning, Grace washed her belongings in its clear, cool water, scrubbing the grit embedded in every garment, the dust that worked its way into crockery boxes and food stores and blanket boxes.

The sabbath duty to prepare the officers' meal had fallen to Grace and Mrs. Betty Eliot. Mrs. Perriman still organized the rota, making sure each wagon took its turn, like a rooster showing who was in charge.

Mrs. Perriman had spoken to Grace and Mrs. Eliot the day before. "You know this is your chance to say thank you. Betty, it's such a blessing to have grown daughters—maybe they should help."

Mrs. Perriman's clucking made Mrs. Eliot anxious. She was

a mouselike woman, always scuttling from place to place, her head down to make herself smaller. Her daughter Sarah's beauty was evident in her small features, but the only signs of Jane's luxuriant red hair were the wiry wisps that escaped the cotton bonnet.

"The ladies of this train have succeeded in producing a magnificent spread nearly every week and I trust you two will not be among the few to let us down," Mrs. Perriman had continued, straightening her shawl. "A woman's touch is always appreciated by the menfolk." She had looked sharply at Grace. "And I know how independent you like to be, Mrs. Sinclair. Look on this as a more feminine way of showing how self-sufficient you are."

The problem was that there were few wild animals to be found in this sparse countryside. Mr. Eliot was not a good shot, and Grace had gone out with her dog Saturday evening but only got two buckrabbits. These hung in Mrs. Eliot's wagon, but she was worried this was not enough to feed seven officers.

"We will just have to kill one of our chickens each," said Mrs. Eliot, looking doubtfully at the rabbits.

"Mrs. Eliot, you must agree that is not a very sensible solution," said Grace, trying to be calm but firm. "We will need our layers for when we reach Oregon."

"What else can we do?" Mrs. Eliot's thumb rubbed at the palm of her other hand. "I won't let my family gain a reputation for being miserly. Everyone else has provided proper meat—and the officers won't have anything less."

Grace found this hard to believe. "Surely there have been other Sundays on this journey when meat was short."

"Yes, indeed there have. So the women have wrung the necks of a couple of chickens instead. Mrs. Long has, and Mrs. Morris."

"Well, more fool them!" said Grace, her color rising. She

folded her arms. "If the rest of us do without, then the officers will have to also."

Mrs. Eliot smoothed an imaginary crease from her apron. "There'll be ructions, Mrs. Sinclair."

"There'll be even more ructions if I'm forced to sacrifice my chickens to such foolishness," said Grace. She'd only just bought them and now was expected to feed one to the officers. She needed to persuade Mrs. Eliot to cook something different, so she unfolded her arms and laid a gentle hand on her shoulder. "Come, now, Mrs. Eliot, you're a clever woman. I'm sure you can make *any* dish taste good."

"My husband does say I'm a fine cook," said Mrs. Eliot, flattered by the suggestion.

"I bet you've passed on lots of secrets to your daughters."

"Jane, now, she's a good girl. Already able to skin a rabbit in double-quick time. But Sarah?" Mrs. Eliot sucked at her teeth. "Maybe less so. I guess she's relying on her looks to snare her a husband. Doesn't like getting her hands dirty."

Grace remembered Sarah's flirtation with the captain in the first week, and doubted she'd made much headway.

They decided to make a thick stew with the little of the rabbits worth eating, bulked out with plenty of vegetables, grains, and pulses. This sort of dish needed to mature, so they started immediately, to let the flavors infuse. Grace added dried herbs, crushed pepper seeds, and a bulb like an onion.

By Sunday evening, the stew was ready to be transferred to the three large pots Grace borrowed from Lillian and Mrs. Gingham. They neatly laid out the officers' mess and Grace waited with a touch of nervousness to see what sort of reception their meal would receive.

NINETEEN

The officers gathered; Mrs. Eliot again patted at her apron and even Grace's mouth was dry as she wondered if she had done the right thing. The air in the tent felt close and stuffy.

Turner walked in with Gray Eagle. "Captain Randolph has been held up by a dispute between some overlanders. He won't be long, but he said we should not wait for him."

The six officers stood behind their places, muttering agreement.

Corporal Flanagan had trained for the clergy in his early years, so the blessing fell to him. He removed his hat and ran a hand through his bristly auburn hair to tidy himself up.

The men sat, Gray Eagle taking a place on the end of the bench, ignoring the hostile body language of the men. Grace lifted the lid off the first pot and ladled out the stew. A silence fell. Mrs. Eliot poured ale into glasses, the bottle clinking as her hand shook. Dr. Trinkhoff grasped his and downed it, tapping the glass on the table to indicate it should be refilled.

Quartermaster Hooper was very particular about his food, as testified by his wide girth. He poked his portion with a knife. "Darn it. What is this?"

"An old French dish passed down for many generations," bluffed Grace, unable to meet anyone's eye.

"That may be so," replied Hooper, his voice rasping, "but it's hardly Sunday roast, is it?"

"I hope, once you have tasted it, you'll find it satisfying." She placed a dish in front of the doctor.

"Woman—the meat! It is where?" Dr. Trinkhoff joined in, slamming his glass to the table.

Some of the other officers shuffled uneasily, knowing the doctor had begun drinking long before the evening meal.

Grace stood her ground and continued to serve the food, giving a plate to Gray Eagle. He put his head to one side and used his fork to stir the vegetables, then swallowed a mouthful.

"There's a little rabbit in it, doctor," said Grace. "It's a shame we were unable to provide you a proper roast dish this Sunday. But please, do taste it." She glanced at Gray Eagle, but nothing in his face revealed if he approved.

"I'm not eating *that*." Hooper pushed his plate into the middle of the table and leaned back, his arms behind his head. "And I'm sure as eggs is eggs, the captain won't want to eat this muck neither. He looks forward to a proper meal once a week. We all do. For pity's sake, it's not much to ask."

"I'm afraid that's all there is," Grace said, plonking a ladleful on the last plate with less care than the first.

Mrs. Eliot took a few steps back until she met the canvas of the tent. At that moment, Captain Randolph strode in, removing his hat. He frowned as he noticed the men's faces and saw that only Gray Eagle was eating.

"Problems?" he asked, and took his place at the head of the table.

"Mrs. Sinclair and Mrs. Eliot have seen fit to ignore our traditions," said Hooper. "All this journey, the overlanders have provided us with a proper dinner on Sunday evening. And tonight these women have insulted us with farmhands' food."

Randolph looked at the stew, and then at Grace.

"There may be some explanation," said Turner, trying to keep the peace.

The captain raised an eyebrow. "Well, what is it this time, Mrs. Sinclair?"

Grace's skin prickled under Randolph's steady gaze. She tried to speak, but no words came. She coughed and tried again. "No insult was intended. I am sorry, but with the dry land we've been traveling through, we've not been able to hunt wild game to cook for you... except for the small amount of rabbit in the stew."

Randolph scratched the evening stubble on his chin. "I can understand that, Mrs. Sinclair. However, the ladies before have always provided a proper roast. This spartan meal does seem to show you have not really tried."

Mrs. Eliot was close to tears and couldn't contain herself any longer. "I told her we should kill some of our chickens, but would she listen? No! I *told* her."

"That is true, sir," Grace said, returning her face to the captain. "Mrs. Eliot did think we should kill some chickens. And it's my fault we didn't. But I can't kill one of my layers for this meal. I shall need them to start a flock when I reach the end of our journey. I daresay Mrs. Eliot needs every one of hers as well."

Corporal Moore tutted audibly. "You have let your fellow overlanders down."

Moore was treating her like a child. Did no one understand the situation?

"The women before were *fools* to kill their own livestock rather than, as you say, let the side down," replied Grace, the sarcastic words out of her mouth before she could catch them.

"Mrs. Sinclair, that is an uncharitable accusation," said Corporal Flanagan.

"'Tis the truth," said Grace, her eyes blazing.

Randolph's gaze was still on her. "I need to get to the bottom of this." He turned to Corporal Moore. "Mrs. Perriman organizes this duty, does she not? Bring her here as fast as you can."

Moore left.

"In the meantime, this food is getting cold and it appears to be all we have." He looked over at Gray Eagle who had already finished his plate, and Grace thought something passed between the two men, something like an eye-roll.

"It's good," said Gray Eagle with a shrug, loud enough for everyone to hear.

Captain Randolph leaned forward and took a large spoonful of the stew and put it on his plate. The aromatic smells filled the air. He swallowed a mouthful. "Well, men, Gray Eagle is right. I can heartily recommend this. It tastes delicious. Come now, eat up."

None of the men were going to disobey the captain. Once they started, most eagerly continued their meal. Turner pushed his plate forward for a second helping.

Mrs. Perriman entered the mess with her bonnet strings untied and a sheen of sweat on her brow. "I cannot apologize enough, sir," she started.

Randolph put up his hand for silence. "What I want to know is whether some of the women have been killing their stock in order to provide us with our Sunday meal."

"Well... er, now, sir." Mrs. Perriman rolled her lips and looked at Grace for a prompt but received nothing. She turned to the red-faced Mrs. Eliot, seeking a cue as to how to respond, whether the captain would be pleased or angry. "I believe it may have happened once or twice, sir."

Randolph slowly nodded as he thought about this, but his face gave nothing else away. "They have killed their laying chickens?"

"Indeed, sir, and the occasional breeding stock." Mrs. Perriman seemed to have decided to use the issue to demonstrate the pioneers' dedication. "We were proud to do it so you could be properly fed—unlike this evening's offering." She waved a hand toward the table. "Had I known—"

Randolph interrupted. "I want to make this very clear. I am a man of tradition. As a general rule, there should be a good Sunday meal for my officers, using the wildlife hunted on the journey. However, when this is not possible, I want there to be no circumstances where breeding stock and layers are killed. Does everyone understand?"

He looked at his men and then the women.

"Mrs. Perriman"—he gave her his most charming smile— "thank you for the excellent way you and the ladies have provided for us so far. However, I want you to ensure that no stock needed to set up in the West is slaughtered. Can I rely on you?"

"Indeed, sir. You can *always* rely on me. And my husband."

"Good. I'm sure you'll be wanting to return to his company."

Mrs. Perriman bobbed a curtsy and left the tent.

The men returned to their meal, including the quartermaster.

"Thank you, Mrs. Eliot and Mrs. Sinclair," said Randolph. "You may leave now. And perhaps you could give Hooper the recipe for this stew."

The tension had been broken and the men laughed.

Grace's eyes met Randolph's; he gave a slight nod and there was an unexpected connection. She smiled, unable to help herself. This meal duty seemed a silly thing to Grace, and yet Mrs. Perriman had invested it with such importance. But now no more women would feel obliged to kill their own stock in order to keep face.

She was surprised the captain had seen things with such clarity and speed. Here, at last, was something they could agree on. She only realized how flushed her face must be when she stepped out into the cool air as she left the tent.

TWENTY

Most evenings, Grace walked Kane around the edge of the camp. She enjoyed the solitude, the chance to breathe in the evening air and watch the clouds drift across the huge skies. Because of the officers' meal, she set out later than usual that night. It was the last moment of dusk, the sun had set and the shadows were darkening.

Grace made her way upstream, Kane splashing in and out of the water. At first, Grace could not tell what the whimpering sound was. Had Kane hurt himself? She climbed over the rocks to a shape in the shadows.

A figure sat scrunched in a ball, arms covering the head.

"Hello?" Grace called tentatively into the gloom.

The sound of anguish cut through the air. Kane barked and bounded closer. The figure lifted a head of tangled red hair, and Grace saw that it was Jane Eliot.

"Whatever are you doing here?" Grace asked.

There was no reply.

She stepped closer and touched Jane's arm. The girl flinched and moaned.

"It's me, Grace Sinclair. Tell me what's happened! Are you hurt?"

Each question was answered with silence.

"I'll go fetch your mother."

Jane whipped up her head. "No! No, you mustn't... mustn't do that! My ma... Please don't do that." Jane's cheeks were streaked with tears. "Promise me you'll not... not fetch my family."

"But, Jane—"

"*Promise* me... please!"

"Very well. I promise. But you must tell me what's happened. You must allow me to help."

Grace sat on the earth close to the girl, and Jane's slight body convulsed in sobs. She put her arms around her and found Jane's clothing dislodged and torn. Dear God, what had happened? She waited as the convulsions slowed; the evening grew darker and the sound of the water louder.

"Can you tell me, honey?" Grace whispered, stroking Jane's hair. It was not in its usual neat braids; instead tendrils sprung loose around her head.

Jane spoke so quietly, Grace could barely hear. "A man, he attacked me. He grabbed me... and... hurt me."

In Grace's mind's eye, she immediately pictured her landlord looming over her, remembered the terror of knowing the man in front was bigger and stronger than you, the look in his eyes of hatred and contempt. She shivered as she remembered how her hands shook as she had pointed her gun at him, and how he had laughed at her, confident she would not pull the trigger. Violence had ended that evening in Independence: violence which meant she feared persecution, even now.

"Who? Who was it, Jane?"

Jane shook her head. "He was behind... grabbed me from behind. My neck... He had a knife. Held it to my neck, just here." Jane's hand trembled. "Said he would kill me if I moved. I stayed still... like he said... hoping he'd go away. Then he punched me. Here. In the stomach." She shook her head. "Said I was a whore. And then he... then he kicked me."

"You poor sweet thing," Grace whispered.

Jane looked up. "I tried to wriggle away, I really did. But he just pulled... just dragged me back. The knife... And then... on top... crushing... no air. Pushing. Pushing at my legs. He ripped them, my pantalets..." Jane fell silent and the tears fell.

Grace pulled her tight and rocked her like a child. "We will find out who did this and we'll make him pay. I'll ask who was on guard. Find out if they saw anything."

Jane shook her head frantically. "No, you mustn't. I mean... what if he *was* the guard?"

"But if you couldn't see him—"

"It was a soldier. I know that much. Wore a uniform."

Grace was startled. The army—well, they were their honorable protectors, prepared to die if need be, to get them safely to their journey's end. How dare a soldier betray them. As God was her witness, he was not going to get away with it, not if she could help it, treating this poor girl like that!

"What else do you know of the man?" she asked.

"Nothing. Nothing at all. He wore a hat and his... his..." Jane searched for the word. "His neckerchief was pulled up."

"Was he big, small... fair or dark?"

"He seemed big. Real big. And smelled disgusting. I think he drank."

"What about his voice?"

"I'm sorry, I can't... He kept whispering at me. Saying horrid things. Up close. My ear. It was almost like a... like a snarl." Jane shuddered.

"I must get you back to your family," Grace said.

"No, no, I don't want them to see me."

"Why ever not? Your ma will take care of you."

"But they'll blame me," Jane said, sniffing back her tears. "It was my fault, you see. I wasn't supposed to be out here. It's my just reward."

Grace was bewildered by Jane's fear of her family and how she could think she was being punished. "Why *were* you out here?"

"You mustn't tell." Jane scrunched up torn fabric from her skirt in her fists. "I was meeting Daniel. You see... we... But he won't want me anymore. Not now." Jane started crying again. "An' I'm being punished for being wanton. For wanting Daniel like that."

Grace took Jane's chin and looked straight into the girl's tear-filled eyes. "What happened is not your fault. Now, tell me: Daniel—that's Corporal Moore, isn't it? You arranged to meet here?"

Jane nodded.

"But he never turned up?"

"No. Never. When that man grabbed me, you know, from behind, I thought for a moment, I thought it was Daniel. Playing a prank. I even called out his name. The man just laughed. And started hurting me."

Grace's mind ran through an unsettling possibility that the corporal had shown a different side, once he was alone with the girl. But she dismissed the thought. Corporal Moore was slightly built, with the same delicacy about him that Jane had. It could not have been him.

It was dark except for the pale light of the half-moon. Grace tried to think what to do, her brain racing with thoughts. What was for the best? "We must get back, honey. It's getting cold. Why don't you share my wagon tonight? I'll think of some excuse to tell your parents."

"You promised, remember," Jane said. "You promised not to tell them."

Grace sighed. This was unreasonable, given the circumstances of her promise, but Jane had faith in her, and at this moment desperately needed someone to trust.

She called Kane, who lolloped after the women as they slowly made their way back to camp, Jane leaning heavily on Grace's arm, hunched over, pulling her torn clothing together, each step causing the girl pain.

Grace always set her wagon on the edge of the camp, and darkness hid them from anyone who was still up. Inside, Tom was already fast asleep, the sleep of the just; he never woke once his head hit the pillow.

Grace gently helped Jane with her clothes and brought water to wash the blood and stains from her body. She gave Jane her softest linen nightdress and a draft with a couple of drops of laudanum to bring sleep.

Although she felt reluctant to speak to Betty Eliot so soon after the meal debacle, Grace then went to make excuses to the Eliot family. Jane had not been missed. Mrs. Eliot thought she was in the small tent with Sarah, while Sarah assumed Jane was doing chores for their mother. Grace told a story about Jane helping with some embroidery, how she had fallen asleep and would it not be best to leave it that way until the morning? The Eliots seemed unconcerned.

Grace went back to her wagon and to bed, but sleep would not come for many hours. She kept going over in her mind the best way to find the man who had so cruelly violated this young woman. Each time she neared sleep, a vision of her own attacker loomed out of the darkness. She had never shot a man before, and her heart pounded at the memory. Was he dead? Or was he still alive and coming after her, the full force of the law behind him?

Grace was up as soon as the first stripes of gray appeared on the horizon. As she dressed, she decided the first step of what she had to do. Grace had promised not to tell Jane's family but made no further promises. It was her duty to inform Captain Randolph of the incident.

Grace walked over the wet grass to the soldiers' neat row of tents. One of the officers nodded good morning to her. It was Corporal Moore, and she took a sharp breath, then said a quiet good morning as she reached the captain's tent. She stood, uncertain for a moment, and asked the corporal to find out if the captain would see her urgently. He ducked into the tent.

TWENTY-ONE

Randolph stood in front of a bowl of water, a mirror clipped to the wooden tent pole.

"Ask her to wait until after breakfast—I can hardly see her now." Bare to the waist, his braces hanging around his hips, he was about to start shaving, and he hated to be interrupted.

"She was quite insistent, sir. It seems urgent," said Moore.

"Well, tell her that if she insists on seeing me now, she will have to take me as she finds me." He wasn't going to be made late, no matter what the problem.

It would have to be Mrs. Sinclair, of all women. There was something about her. But he damn well wasn't going to change his routine, just to suit her.

Grace entered the tent. "Thank you for seeing me so early," she said quietly.

He turned and he saw darkness around her eyes, tension at the edge of her mouth. "Sit down there, Mrs. Sinclair." He nodded to a wooden chair next to the table where he wrote his log. Having bullishly agreed to this interview, he felt a fluttering sensation in his chest and was intensely aware of her presence, and that he was standing shirtless. Her eyes had passed over his torso before moving to the ground, and a slight color had risen in her cheeks.

He turned his back as he lathered soap in a small tin with a brush. Maybe this was a mistake, but she was here now.

"You will have to excuse me. I can't be late for the morning inspection."

"'No, of course not." Her voice was soft. "But this is important."

"Well, ma'am?"

Grace cleared her throat. "I was walking my dog last night, sir, up by the river. I walk him most nights, you see. And I heard... I came across one of the young women. And she was not very well, sir."

Randolph picked up his razor and lined himself up with the mirror. "Not well? Has she seen the doctor?"

"No sir. It's not like that... You see, she was in a dreadful state, crying. She had gone there to meet a young man she's sweet on. One of your men."

Randolph raised an eyebrow. "And what? You think I need to stop this dalliance with one of the soldiers?" he asked, watching Grace through the mirror. "Easier said than done."

"No, sir, that's not it..." Grace dropped her chin and fidgeted with a thread that had come loose on her sleeve. "Sir, this is very difficult to say..."

She seemed to have come to a complete halt. He really did not want her there any longer than necessary. "For the love of God, spit it out."

She lifted her chin slightly. "Very well. The girl has been attacked and raped."

Randolph stopped his razor in mid-stroke.

"It was one of your soldiers. That is what I came here to tell you."

His stomach lurched. He turned to Grace and looked down

at her. "And how much of this do you *know*? Is the girl telling the truth?"

Grace looked up, her eyes bright. She swallowed hard. "Oh, yes, sir. I am sure of that. She was in great distress. Her clothes were torn. I had to... clean the blood from her. I assure you, she was telling the truth."

He felt cold, right inside his chest.

He slowly turned back to the mirror, and made a few more razor strokes around his scar to finish his shave and gain some thinking time. "I will deal with this immediately. I have authority to take any person into custody. In all likelihood, the man will be charged and tried at Fort Boise."

Grace bowed her head. "She doesn't know who it was, though. It was dark and he covered his face."

Randolph narrowed his eyes. "Then how can she be sure it was a soldier?" Was the girl sullying the honor of one of his men?

"He was in uniform." Grace raised her head to him, a frown line forming on her brow. "I have seen the bruises the military boot made."

Randolph sucked in some air. Grace had forcefully made her point. The attack was brutal.

He wiped the remaining soap from his face, and splashed it with cold water from the metal bowl, wishing the water might clear his head. He needed more information. "Who was she meeting? Could he have been her attacker?"

"No, she's sure of that. She was supposed to meet Corporal Moore."

Randolph picked up his linen shirt from the back of a chair and pulled it over his head. "Then... it was the redheaded Eliot girl. Am I right?"

Grace nodded.

"She must be only, what, seventeen?" Turner's words about

being above the comings and goings of the civilians had hit home: he'd started to observe the overlanders more closely.

"Seventeen next month."

Randolph let out a long breath. "And how's the family taken this? What has Mr. Eliot done?"

"They don't know. She hasn't told them."

"Not told them! Dear God, why ever not?"

Grace gave a slight shrug. "She feels overwhelmed. And embarrassed. She blames herself and thinks they will disown her."

"So have you—"

"I promised her I wouldn't tell the family. She trusts me. She needs some time. And perhaps... perhaps it will be better they don't know for the moment."

"What do you mean?" A bugle sounded. "Damn! That's the first reveille. I'm sorry, Mrs. Sinclair, but I must finish dressing." He buttoned up his shirt and hooked over his braces.

Grace stood and spoke quickly. "Sir, I have barely slept, thinking about this. The most important thing is to find the man and stop it from happening again. Because I assure you, sir, a man who can do this once will do it again, given the chance."

"Agreed." Randolph jerked on his blue military jacket and tugged the sleeves.

"But if we... if you go out there and announce what has happened, it will have a dreadful effect on the whole expedition. Accusations will start flying and the girl will be humiliated."

"But it would put everyone on their guard." Randolph saw anguish in Grace's eyes.

"But from whom?" Grace paced the small tent. "The overlanders will not trust the soldiers because it was one of them. They will demand to use their own guns to protect their families."

Randolph nodded slightly as he thought about her words.

"Discipline may break down." He pulled his belt tight and fastened the brass buckle. "I could grill the soldiers one by one. Given enough stern warnings, it may stay within the platoon long enough for me to gather evidence." Randolph pulled his fingers through his hair, knowing it was a long shot. "The man may confess—or his friends may have noticed something."

Grace sighed and sat back down on the chair, looking weary. "He would never confess. Not a man like this. And he will just become more devious next time. The man will know you're on the lookout, so we might not catch him. And at the end of the trail, he will be free to go and attack some other poor girl. And that *must* not be allowed to happen."

The second bugle blew. Time was running out.

"Could you pass me those boots?" Randolph indicated the leather boots near the table, and he sat on the camp bed to pull them on. "So, Mrs. Sinclair, what do you suggest?"

Grace shook her head. "I don't know. It's still not clear in my mind. All I know is that we must tread carefully and not make the situation worse."

Randolph stood and unhooked his hat from a nail. "As soon as inspection and breakfast are over, I'll come to your wagon. I'll think of some excuse. I must see where the incident happened, before we move out."

He looked at her and she held his gaze for a moment. Her brown eyes were still beautiful even though the dark smudges beneath showed she had not slept. It was clear that she had struggled with their awful predicament all night.

Thank goodness she had had the courage and sense to come to him. And she was right: marching out there and making an announcement wouldn't solve anything.

"And, thank you, Mrs. Sinclair."

She nodded and perhaps understood that he meant more than those simple words conveyed.

Randolph strode out of the tent and pulled on his hat.

Grace followed and made her way back to her wagon unre-marked. He breathed in the cool air, stunned by the god-awful news.

Grace gave Jane breakfast and told the same story to Tom as she had given to the Eliots the night before. She then went over to the Eliot wagon.

"I'm sorry, Mrs. Eliot," she whispered. "Jane has been brought real low by her monthly course. It might be kinder to leave her where she is for the day. She can rest in the back of my wagon."

Mrs. Eliot readily agreed. One fewer person to worry about was fine by her.

The captain and Gray Eagle walked over to the wagon as Grace was clearing the plates.

"I want you to tell me about overlander food supplies, after that interesting meal you served up last night," he said loudly as he approached.

Grace glanced at Gray Eagle, puzzled as to why Captain Randolph had brought him. She had thought they were trying to keep the issue private. But she needed to behave as normal. "Yes, sir. I'd be happy to."

Once he was near, he dropped his voice. "Gray Eagle is the finest tracker I know. He's the best person to search for signs left on the ground."

Grace felt foolish for a moment. Of course Randolph would trust Gray Eagle with this task. She nodded to him and received a slight bow back, as way of acknowledgment.

"Can you describe the place where the attack happened?" asked Gray Eagle.

"I'll fetch my shawl and show you."

Randolph reached out to stop her. "It would be better if

Gray Eagle and I went alone. People would be sure to notice if you came with us."

Grace nodded. "Up the river, to where the banks begin to get steep. There's a sharp bend to the right by some shrubby trees. You will find a sandy area just beyond the turn, out of sight from the camp."

"Good. Now, I need you to get any information you can from the girl about the attacker. Even the smallest detail might help to identify him."

"I will do what I can through the day."

Randolph carried the heavy cast-iron cooking pot back to the wagon so they could stay close. "I have been thinking. This knowledge is a burden for you to carry alone."

"But—"

"I know, you don't feel able to tell the family. Is there someone else you trust? Someone wise who might help judge the best way forward."

Grace thought for a moment. "Mrs. Hollingswood... I'll tell her."

"Good. Now, where's your grease bucket?"

"Sir?"

"I need to look like I'm doing something here."

Grace unhooked the bucket from the axle. Randolph applied a small amount of lubricant to the wheel hub.

"Mrs. Hollingswood is a good choice," he said quietly. "I'll inform Lieutenant Turner. He's experienced, and can be trusted not to take action until I have decided what's best. You and Mrs. Hollingswood will meet us as soon as camp is set up this evening. I want to know any details about the attacker. And how the poor girl is faring."

"But won't meeting you get people asking questions?"

"At noon break, I'll let it be known that, in view of last night's difficulties with the officers' meal, I have decided to find out if there are any more problems that should be addressed.

You and Mrs. Hollingswood will meet me under the guise of a... well, consultation. The four of us can think what to do next. Until this evening then?"

Grace nodded, and handed him a cloth to wipe a smear of grease from his hand.

"That new axle is looking fine, Mrs. Sinclair," he said loudly in case any overlander were nearby, and then she watched him as he marched away in the direction of the river, the Lakota just ahead.

TWENTY-TWO

Grace invited Lillian to travel in her wagon during the day. She related what had happened and, after Lillian had got over the shock, they turned the problem over and over, looking for the best solution to make sure the man was caught.

As soon as supper was finished, the women approached the army camp. When they entered the mess tent, the captain was seated on one side of a pair of trestle tables, Turner at his right hand. Yellow oil lamps threw shadows on the creamy canvas.

Captain Randolph indicated for Grace to sit directly opposite him with Lillian beside her. "May I offer you some coffee?"

"Thank you, sir," said Lillian, and Grace nodded.

Randolph rose and poured coffee from the pot on a burner behind him. He placed a tin mug in front of each woman.

Grace felt confusion; this man, who usually intimidated her, engaged in the simple act of making coffee. Memories of this morning came unbidden to her mind: the shoulder muscles on his naked back moving as he shaved, the dark hair on his chest as he buttoned his white shirt. She fixed her eyes on the cup of coffee, cursing herself for her thoughts, given the purpose of this meeting.

"Thank you for coming this evening," Randolph began. "I wish it were not such a serious problem we have to address. Mrs. Hollingswood, may I assume Mrs. Sinclair has told you everything?"

"Yes indeed, sir. We have talked of little else since this morning. Dreadful."

"And I have briefed Lieutenant Turner." He nodded to Turner and then faced Grace. "Mrs. Sinclair, first tell us, how is Miss Eliot?"

"Um, yes, sir." Grace's heart thumped and she coughed to clear a frog in her throat. She took a sip of coffee but felt foolish because it was too hot.

Turner pushed a glass of water toward her.

"She's rested in the back of my wagon all day. I gave her laudanum to help her sleep last night, and she seemed drowsy through the morning. A couple of times I looked in on her and she'd been crying again."

"The poor poppet," Lillian said, shaking her head.

"Have you found out anything else about her attacker?" Randolph asked.

"It's been difficult to get two words from her, but I did try, sir. You said any detail would help. There seems to be so little that would distinguish the man. Jane says he was in uniform— blue shirt and pants, the dark boots—but was unable to think of anything that would give his rank. He might be dark-haired, but she could not be sure because he wore a hat. He *may* have a beard. She remembers a roughness on her skin. But he wore his neckerchief around his face, so she cannot be sure."

"What about his build?" Turner asked.

"She could only say he was not a slight man. He was big and powerful."

"For a young girl being attacked, any man would seem big," Lillian observed.

Grace took a sip of water before continuing. "There was a

smell. She thinks it was tobacco. It may have been drink. Jane has not been in mixed company much. She said the smell was, well, unpleasant."

"Most of our men smoke or drink spirits," Randolph said. "Was there anything else?"

"No. I'm sorry to be of such little help."

"Not at all. Even these details help us to discount a few of the men."

Randolph touched her hand, his fingers resting on hers a moment. She looked up; there was a softness around his eyes she had not seen before.

"We can forget Corporal Flanagan, for one," said Turner with a shrug. "He never touches drink, nor tobacco."

Randolph sat up straighter. "I took Gray Eagle to help me inspect the area where the incident happened. There were some marks in the sandy earth, but nothing distinctive. I guess I was hoping for a piece of cloth or a personal item to tell us who it was. Anyway, it was a vain hope."

"So... what next?" asked Turner. "Where do we go from here?"

"The most important thing is this man is brought to justice," said Randolph. "And he is never able to do this again. Mrs. Sinclair said to me early this morning, a man like this *will* try, given half the chance. I agree with her. However, we are all aware of the difficulty of smoking him out, when we have so few facts to go on. And there is the overall success of the train to think of."

"What do you mean by that?" Lillian asked.

"I mean the hardest part of the journey is still ahead. After the South Pass, we go into disputed Indian territory. The major at Fort Laramie gave me some troubling news. A missionary group somewhere on the Columbia River was attacked by Natives this winter. More than a dozen killed."

A small gasp escaped Grace. Zachary had mentioned settling near the Columbia in his letter.

Lillian's hand went to her breast. "What could have caused such a dreadful thing?"

"These tribes are seeing more and more of their ancestral lands disappear. Even peaceful contact leads to destruction, it seems." Randolph leaned forward. "The major told me there was an outbreak of measles. Half a tribe died, but the missionary outpost was untouched, so they're blaming the white men. Who knows? Maybe they're right. Maybe it *was* their fault. No matter, our whole expedition will have to work as one, should the worst happen and a war party attempt to stop our progress. And that means absolute trust between the overlanders and the military."

"Are you suggesting we do not act until Fort Boise?" asked Lillian, frowning.

Randolph rubbed the evening stubble on his chin. "I had thought of that. But then, how do we protect the women in the weeks between here and the Fort?"

"We could form a special team from all those who can be ruled out," said Turner. "You know, the officers, anyone of slight build—"

"One moment, sir," said Grace. "We have no way of knowing it *wasn't* an officer. It could have been *anyone* of average to strong build. Even yourself and the captain come into that reckoning."

There was a silence as Turner raised his eyebrows at Randolph, and Lillian shuffled in her seat.

Grace's cheeks were on fire. "I'm sorry," she mumbled. "I didn't mean to imply... Of course neither of you would—"

"No need to apologize," said Randolph, giving her a reassuring nod. "I take your point. It could even be an overlander dressed to *look* like a soldier."

Lillian sighed. "So where does this get us?"

"Well, we could consider a general announcement of what has happened, and then everyone would be on his, or her, guard," Randolph said. "But, as you know, I'm against this because of the possibly disastrous effect on morale and discipline."

"Miss Eliot would find it very painful," said Grace.

"Would people need to know who the victim was?" asked Turner.

"It would soon seep out, I'm sure," she replied.

"What about her family?" asked Lillian. "When will you tell them, sir?"

Randolph swept some imaginary dust from the table with his hand. "I find this point difficult. It does not feel right, knowing about this, when the girl's mother and father remain ignorant. I know Grace feels bound by a promise she made to the girl—even though it was under duress." He made a slight nod toward her. "At the moment, Jane wants no one to know. I'm sure if the Eliots were informed, it would be all round the camp in no time. The father could rightly seek justice; Mrs. Eliot would be distraught..."

The group fell silent again.

"We seem to be going round in circles," Turner said.

Randolph poured more coffee into Turner's mug, but the rest had hardly been touched.

Lillian looked at Grace meaningfully and nudged her arm. They had discussed a plan during the afternoon, and seeing as no better idea had come up, the time had come to propose it.

"Grace has a suggestion, sir," Lillian began. "I think it may be worth considering."

TWENTY-THREE

They looked at Grace. She took a deep breath. It had seemed like a good plan when sitting in the wagon earlier that day. With the captain's tall and imposing figure sitting so close, now she was not so sure, but there was no going back.

"When I was a girl, I stayed at Grandpa's farm most summers. He kept chickens. One time, he lost a chicken to a fox. The next night, he made sure the chickens were locked up in the coop good an' proper, and sat out in the dark all night with his shotgun. The fox never came.

"So, the following night, he sat out again. Nothing happened. Grandpa thought maybe the fox had gone to worry someone else's chickens, and gotten the message that these were guarded. So the third night, Grandpa went to bed."

Grace took a gulp of coffee.

"That night, he was woken by the rumpus of chickens squawking. He ran out, but the fox had already disappeared, leaving feathers everywhere, and two chickens gone. So, the fourth night, Grandpa decided to try something different. He left one of the chickens out in the run for the night, and then settled down for the evening with his shotgun on his lap.

"Sure 'nough, the fox couldn't resist the smell and noise of the fresh young creature. But when he came close to the run, bang! My grandpa shot him dead."

Grace glanced round at the three people at the table. Randolph was looking at her intently, a line between his dark eyebrows. He was going to take some convincing.

"Now, sir, please listen to the *whole* of my plan. You might not like it, but I hope it's worth consideration. I'm sure you catch the drift of my story."

"The attacker is the fox," said Randolph.

Grace nodded. "He won't strike again unless he thinks it safe, or there is something to lure him. We need something... *someone* to lure him but be ready to take him when he makes his move."

Grace flicked her eyes across to Lillian, who smiled to encourage her.

"I propose I try to repeat the situation Jane Eliot found herself in. We make it look like, well, like I have an understanding with one of the soldiers."

Randolph started to protest.

"Sir, please. I beg you. Hear me out. Once this is general gossip among the men, I arrange to meet the soldier in a secluded place. Something must prevent him from meeting me. Then, just like the fox, the man will think it safe to strike once more. But this time it will be different. I'll be expecting the attack." She looked from Turner to Randolph. "And I will have two protectors watching over me, pistol in hand, ready to arrest him."

Turner whistled a long breath.

Randolph's face was dark. "That plan is *entirely* unacceptable."

"Why, sir?"

"*Why?*" Randolph threw up his hands. "You need to ask why? First, it's too dangerous."

"But it's *not* dangerous," Grace said, "because *we* would be in control. We would know when the attack would happen. I would be expecting it, so I could defend myself—and you would be there to seize the man."

"But what if he attacked *before* we are ready. On a day when we were not expecting it?"

"That, sir, with respect, would be no different to the situation now. When I walk out of this tent tonight, I will be at risk. And so is every other woman."

Randolph opened his mouth to reply but could not find the words. He raked his fingers through his hair. "Think what this would do to your reputation. You are a married woman. You're suggesting setting up... secret assignations with a soldier. You will be the subject of malicious gossip."

Grace sat up, straight as a stalk of corn, knowing that she would have to speak rationally if she was going to persuade him. "Thank you for your concern, sir, but that's something I'm prepared to take. Once this journey is over, I will go to my family in Oregon. I am unlikely to ever meet any of these soldiers again. I'm not terribly concerned about what they may say of me. I will know the truth—that I have not behaved dishonorably." Grace glanced up at Randolph. "Indeed, the dishonor would be in *not* doing *everything* possible to catch this monster. And once we have caught him, the truth will out."

"But, Mrs. Sinclair," Turner said, shaking his head, "it would not just be the soldiers. You can be sure folk would talk. The other overlanders won't be kind to you. And they may be part of your life beyond this journey. Mud sticks, your reputation would be soiled. And what would your husband say?"

Grace dropped her head. Truth was, this action *was* risky. But she *needed* to do it, propelled onwards by some sense of atoning for what had happened in Independence. She couldn't put this into words, didn't even quite understand it herself. She was sure about one thing, though: the immediate threat.

Somehow she had to persuade them. Grace wanted to speak calmly so they would all understand, but struggled to keep the emotion from her voice.

"I found Miss Eliot. I listened to her sobs. I cleaned the blood from her thighs. If I found out that another girl had been put through that ordeal in weeks, months, maybe years to come, because *I* had held back from doing what was needed... if fear of gossip or a bad name or a few moments' danger made me a coward... then I do not think I could live with myself."

Randolph stood and poured a drink of water from the jug on the table behind him. There was the slightest tremor in his hand. "Mrs. Hollingswood, what do you think of this plan?"

Lillian looked at the back that was turned to them. "Sir, I have the advantage of having thought about it all afternoon. At first, I was as shocked as you. Put up all the same objections. But, y'know, we've not come up with a better plan. What choice do we have?"

"Turner, what's your opinion?"

He sighed. "I don't like it. Not one bit. But I can't think of anything better either."

Randolph paused a moment and turned back to them. His face looked grave. "Very well. We will go with Mrs. Sinclair's proposal. But we do *everything* possible to prevent any risk to Mrs. Sinclair's person." He finally glanced at her. "And at the end, when we are successful, I will do all I can to restore your good name."

"Thank you, sir. Thank you for giving me the chance to help put this right." She sank a little in her chair, feeling a weight lifted from her.

Randolph sat back down at the table and took out his pocket watch. "Time is passing. How can we put the plan into action?"

"We need to set up a believable liaison between Mrs. Sinclair and one of the soldiers," Turner said.

"But, as Grace pointed out earlier, we must be careful," said Lillian. "The beast could be almost anyone."

Grace raised her face and found Randolph looking at her, a slight frown on his brow, even though his eyes were kind.

"What if *I* were the man in the liaison?" Randolph suggested. "That would give the advantage of my being able to stay near to keep Mrs. Sinclair safe, while keeping the number of people who know the plan to a minimum."

Turner sucked his teeth and said nothing.

"Well, why not?" Randolph asked the surprised faces in front of him.

"We said the situation must be believable, sir," Grace said, treading carefully. "I don't think our attacker, or anyone else, would believe in a secret assignation between you and me. I mean... your..."—she searched for a word that was not too strong —"*antipathy* toward women in general, and me in particular, is well-known. Everyone knows you'd rather I wasn't here."

Randolph leaned back in his seat and narrowed his eyes, looking as if he was about to challenge what Grace had said, but thought better of it. He held her gaze, and for a moment she felt her face flush at the boldness of what she had said. He wasn't a man used to being contradicted.

She looked down, and fiddled with the tin mug in front of her.

"So, who do you propose?" he asked.

"What about Corporal Moore?" suggested Lillian. "We know he wasn't the attacker. Jane is sure of that."

"No, I don't think so," Grace contended. "Again, it would not be believed. Even the captain knew of his attachment to Jane."

"*Even?*" asked Randolph, raising an eyebrow.

"Corporal Flanagan?" suggested Turner. "We've already agreed he can't have been the assailant. He doesn't drink or smoke."

"But was he not a clergyman?" asked Lillian. "Hardly a man likely to set up a dalliance."

"Trained for the clergy," said Randolph with a wry smile. "And the reason for failing to take up his calling was his... weakness... for the fair sex."

"Is that generally known?" asked Grace.

"Yes, among the soldiers."

"He would seem like a good candidate then."

Lillian nodded in agreement.

"In that case, I will brief him first thing in the morning," said Randolph. "And then, Mrs. Sinclair, I think it best if you manage the next stage of the plan between you. However, we must proceed with extreme caution."

He looked directly at Grace. "I want to make sure you are in company whenever possible. Turner and I will do whatever we can to keep watch. I do not want to put you at *any* unnecessary risk."

They heard the taps being played on the bugle.

"It's getting late. Thank you all for your time. Let us hope there will be a satisfactory end to the situation. And may I remind you—for the moment, not a word, even to close family." The captain looked at Lillian and Turner.

They all stood. Randolph shook hands with Lillian and thanked her once more. He then took Grace's hand. His palm was warm and strong, and a vibration ran through her.

"Good luck. We will be watching over you."

She glanced up and saw a soft expression in his eyes, the same one she'd noticed earlier. Her stomach tightened, but she was unable to find anything to say in reply.

TWENTY-FOUR

By the next morning, Jane was missing her family, so Grace took her back to the Eliot wagon. They walked arm in arm, Jane never raising her eyes from the ground, but wincing as they went over uneven ground.

"She's better than before," Grace said, when they reached the Eliots. "But needs some kindness and care."

"It's usually my Sarah demanding attention," said Mrs. Eliot. "Let's hope Jane's not picking up her fancy ways as she gets older."

Jane did not say a word but climbed onto the bench behind her father, Sarah by her side, chattering aimlessly.

Even with the burden of setting the trap, Grace was excited to see the granite mound of Independence Rock in the distance, bulging out of the ground like an ancient animal with scales slipping off its domed back.

According to trail wisdom, the pioneers needed to reach the Rock by Independence Day to be sure of beating the snows in the last part of the journey through the mountains. As the first train of the season, there had been little doubt they would reach the marker ahead of schedule. Nevertheless, tradition required the travelers stop and celebrate, and carve their names into the gray granite.

At the noon halt, Corporal Flanagan came to her wagon. Grace was tongue-tied. How were they to start their supposed love affair? How obvious should they be?

Flanagan coughed to clear his throat. "The captain briefed me this morning. A shocking business."

Grace looked around to make sure Tom was not close enough to hear. "Yes, indeed; but we must be discreet about it."

"Discreet?"

"About the... incident. Folk must not know that such a dreadful thing has happened. Not yet, anyway."

"I see. But we cannot be too discreet about other things." His warm Irish lilt suggested a smile behind the words. "Otherwise the plan would not take effect."

Grace studied the ground beyond him. "I feel awkward about this, even though it was my idea."

"Mrs. Sinclair, I daresay your previous experience of illicit love is smaller than a grain of sand. Sadly, my past is not as honorable as it should be, so it seems I must take the lead. But I believe Captain Randolph has made my legion failings clear to you. I would have been a disreputable priest."

Corporal Flanagan's twinkling eyes matched his warm smile. His fair complexion had gone red across the cheeks and nose from traveling in the sun, despite his corporal's cap. He was slightly taller than Grace and built on the heavy side. Grace was amused by his self-deprecating comments and could see why Randolph thought he might be the right person to help them.

Flanagan looked at the trail they were to take that afternoon. "We reach Independence Rock today, so tonight there'll be singing an' dancing an' making merry around the fire. May I suggest we meet then?"

"Yes, of course. I look forward to it, Corporal Flanagan."

"In view of the closeness of the relationship we are supposed to be having, we ought to be using first names. Would you call me Patrick? Named after the Irish saint by my good Catholic parents, even though I failed to live up to their hopes."

"And you may call me Grace."

"Never was a lady so befitting her name," he said with a flourish of his cap.

"So you have the Irish blarney about you too. Remember, you don't have to use flattery with me. I proposed this union, did I not?" she said with an arched eyebrow.

Flanagan chuckled and made a slight bow, and they parted.

As evening fell, travelers gathered around the campfire in the lee of the looming gray mound of Independence Rock, to celebrate reaching this milestone. A fiddle, guitar, and a small drum soon appeared and Mr. Gingham began a round of songs.

Grace sat on a small bench and Corporal Flanagan approached.

"Would this seat be free?"

"Indeed it is," she replied as he sat beside her.

They did not speak at first, and as the next song was an Irish melody, Flanagan joined in with gusto.

"So, you enjoy singing, Patrick?" Grace asked, forcing herself to start a conversation, even though she felt uncomfortable.

"Me? I'll sing anything—a good hymn, a rousing song, even the occasional tearful ballad—but that isn't a pretty sight. D'you not sing yourself?"

"I do, but not particularly well. And on this trip I've got used to being as quiet as possible."

"Why should such a lovely young lady be quiet?"

"Y'know, the captain not allowing women to travel alone an' all. I promised him I'd be no trouble. So thought it best if nobody noticed me."

"Well, I say well done for sticking with it. You're good as any man."

"Thank you," she said with half a grimace. "Was that another compliment?"

He grinned. "Anyway, the captain can't send you back now. So you can be as wild and raucous as you like."

Grace laughed. "I still feel that would be breaking my agreement with the captain."

"Ah, but we have a new agreement now. The captain *expects* you to be noticed. Otherwise the plot won't work."

"True."

"In view of which, Mrs. Sinclair—Grace—would you do me the honor of joining me for this dance?"

A country tune had started up and couples were filling the sandy area beyond the fire. Grace took Flanagan's hand and they joined three other couples for a reel.

She felt part of the community, perhaps for the first time since the beginning of the journey. True, some heads turned to watch the attention being paid by Flanagan. Folk were always looking for something new to gossip about, that was the way of the world. As Flanagan had pointed out, it was part of the plan. And pretending to flirt with a soldier was nothing compared to what she had actually done, just three months before. What would people say if they knew she had shot a man, that she had fled rather than facing the consequences?

"I was thinking about when we could next meet," said Flanagan as they danced. "Perhaps tomorrow evening?"

"That would be a fine idea."

"Should I come to your wagon?"

"Would that be too... obvious?"

"I thought obvious was what we wanted." Flanagan grinned and spun her round faster.

Not since that dance at the beginning of their journey, had Grace allowed herself to enjoy the sensation.

Randolph patrolled the edge of the camp. He had not relaxed since he had first learned of the vicious attack. He scrutinized suspects and made a mental list of the most likely culprits. What did he really know about the men who had joined them at Fort Laramie: men who were new to the group, and yet to prove themselves? All day, he had observed and counted. Where was this soldier? Where that? As evening fell, his unease grew.

Randolph stood in the shadows and watched the group around the fire. Many of the soldiers had joined the pioneers. He mentally marked them off, but his attention was drawn time and again to Grace and Flanagan. They sat close together, Grace laughing at some witticism of the corporal's, before he took her hand to join the dancing.

It was the first time Randolph had seen her dance since that fateful night when he discovered Mr. Sinclair was not traveling with them. That felt a lifetime ago. He watched her movements as she danced; she had a lightness of foot, an elegance which shone through, even with this country dance. She laughed as the reel circled and wove in and out. Flanagan placed his hand in the small of her back.

He removed his hat and ran a hand through his hair.

A sudden hot pang of envy took Randolph's breath away. To be there, dancing with her, feel her hand lightly placed on his shoulder, smell her chestnut hair. Pulling her closer as the dance went faster. She would look up at him with those deep brown eyes, her lips slightly parted. For the first time, he allowed himself to admit to himself that she drew him to her, that he thought about her more than was wise. Not just in these past days since the attack, but before. Had he actually felt relief that she had succeeded in getting to Laramie, that she would continue to be part of the train?

He banged his hat against his thigh. She was a married woman, for goodness' sake.

"Sir." A voice pulled him away from his thoughts.

Randolph glowered at the young private who saluted him.

"Quartermaster wants to open a new barrel of beer. The lieutenant said I should ask you, sir."

Randolph had the irrational fear this boy could hear his thoughts. He hadn't felt this overwhelming attraction to a woman for years. Not since Arabella. And what a disaster that had turned out. He paused to compose himself.

"No, that would not be a good idea. It will leave us low for the remainder of the journey." Although Randolph usually allowed a drink or two, he now knew there was someone among them with unspeakable impulses, which he could not risk being released by drunkenness. His duty was to protect the women on this journey—in particular Grace, who had chosen to make herself so vulnerable.

TWENTY-FIVE

The next evening's camp was pitched at the mouth of Devil's Gate, a gorge between two outcrops which stared angrily at each other, ready to lean in and throw rocks. A lone tree stood proud between the cliffs. The Sweetwater splashed through the gap, but it was too narrow for a wagon, so they would need to make a detour, come the morning.

Randolph climbed the northern outcrop. The ground was rocky and dotted with small shrubs. He sat down, took out his field glasses, and watched the comings and goings of the camp below.

Women sat chatting while repairing clothes, darning socks, and scrubbing pans. Men relaxed further from the camp, smoking in the evening sun. Some boys played chase, and were hollered at as the game grew too rough.

Randolph spotted Turner picking his way up the ridge, stopping frequently to draw breath. It had been his turn to check all was safe, and they had arranged to rendezvous at this isolated spot.

"Everything as it should be?" asked Randolph as Turner drew close.

"All present and correct, sir. But, Lord knows, this constant watching is wearing me out."

"Here, take a seat." Randolph indicated the smooth stone beside him.

"Wonderful," said Turner, and let his large body drop heavily.

"If it's any consolation, I'm not happy with the situation either." Randolph raised the field glasses again.

"Anything happening down at camp?" Turner asked.

"It's the usual evening calm."

He handed the glasses to Turner, who traced the figures below.

"Tell me," said Randolph, "do I really have a... a well-known antipathy toward women?" Randolph had been dwelling on these words from two days before.

Turner chuckled. "The truth?" he asked, glancing over.

Randolph nodded.

"Then I guess, if the shoe fits. I mean, you aren't exactly sociable. You don't join the Saturday music-making if you can avoid it. You're not one for small talk with the ladies."

"I'm not good at all that." He grimaced. "The smiling and fawning and talking about... ephemera."

"And then there's your whole thing about women on the trail."

"That's for a darn good reason. No one can deny that women are weaker and they give up easily."

Turner raised his eyebrows. "Mrs. Sinclair...?"

"Look, Alfred, the fact that I was wrong in *one* case," Randolph said, "does not mean the general principle doesn't stand. It's still madness to bring women on this trip alone. Mrs. Sinclair is... the exception that proves the rule."

Turner carefully put down the glasses, but continued to watch the camp. "I think you're wrong about women giving up easily. Seems to me, once a woman makes up her mind 'bout something, she pretty much sticks to it, like a burr on a woolen coat. Now, that something may be ephemeral, as you say, but it may also be a large or noble idea. I bet you half those men in the camp wouldn't be here if it weren't for the women holding fast to an idea of something better in the West."

"You mean nagging them on?"

Turner shook his head. "It doesn't have to be like that. A good marriage is like two halves coming together to make something better, stronger."

"Like your marriage."

"Yes, indeed. Y'know, James, I would heartily recommend a good marriage, even for you. You're looking for perfection. I'm afraid, my dear friend, it doesn't exist."

Randolph grunted. "I know that well enough. I thought, once, that I'd found it. Perfection. Look how badly that turned out!"

Turner took a sideways glance. "Arabella?" he asked cautiously.

Randolph grimaced and shivered at the memory.

Arabella had been the beautiful daughter of a major general at West Point. All the cadets had competed for her hand, Randolph among them. She was sophisticated and witty, and when he was talking to her, she made him feel like the rest of the world had disappeared.

When Randolph had won Arabella's love, he'd felt elated and, yes, proud. He was doing well and was widely expected to move swiftly up the ranks once he graduated. He had proposed marriage and she had eagerly agreed, spending captured moments with him, talking of their future life together—a home in a fashionable part of Washington, which breed of pet dog, whether they would have an open or closed carriage.

Then one of his fellow officers was given a commission ahead of him. Randolph had been frustrated but not particularly surprised. After all, the other man came from a long line of soldiers, and was very well connected. He knew his commission would come, he just had to be patient. But soon after, Arabella broke off the engagement. That blow felled him. Never saw it coming. Soon afterwards, she switched her attention to the newly promoted officer.

Randolph was shattered, though he had no choice but to stand by and, as a fellow West Point man, even attended the wedding. But he admitted to himself he was humiliated. He hated the fickleness of women's affections—that they could switch so quickly! He despised women for setting so much store by outward status in the world. He had felt all his fellow cadets' eyes on him. Pride came before a fall. He had been the lovesick fool who'd given his heart to one who did not really want it.

Randolph had begun to drink, was quick to disagree with his friends, eager to escalate disputes into fights. He had joined Sam Houston's troops in the Texas Revolution, and threw himself into battle with the reckless abandon which gained him the promotion he had previously hoped for, along with a fair few medals.

Turner's friendship had been the one constant through this time. Gradually, Randolph had felt himself return to being the level-headed young man of his early years, before Arabella. Experience made him an excellent leader of men—or at least, that was his hope. But, dear God, he had never lost his disappointment with the frailties of women. His relationships over the past years had been brief, meaningless liaisons with saloon girls and camp followers. His heart had never again been touched.

Never until this journey.

"James," said Turner gently, "have you thought about Flora Williams, by any chance?"

"Flora?" Randolph opened his eyes wide. "Why should I—?"

"We'll be seeing her again when we reach Fort Boise. A

pretty young thing. Knows about military life, what with her father the major there. Eunice thinks she was sweet on you, when we passed through the Fort last year."

Randolph snorted. "Have you and your dear wife been discussing my prospects?"

"We all need pastimes to fill the cold evenings. Seriously, though, she might be a good match."

Randolph stretched out his left leg, which had grown stiff. "I grant you she's a sweet, bonny girl. But I honestly can't remember anything else about her. Shouldn't there have been... *something* between us when we met? Some sort of, I don't know... excitement?"

Turner shook his head and grinned. "James, one day you'll find the right woman for you, and you won't know what's hit you."

Randolph picked up the field glasses again. Corporal Flanagan approached Grace's wagon. He watched her fetch her bonnet and set off with Flanagan for a stroll.

"Yep. I'll find the right woman," he said with a grim smile, "and find she's already married to someone else."

Turner looked at his friend, and followed his gaze down to Grace and Flanagan. He nodded slowly, and Randolph wondered if perhaps his friend had recognized his feelings sooner than himself.

They sat in silence again. A buzzard wheeled overhead.

"Tell you who I'd like to meet," said Randolph, handing the field glasses to Turner. "*Mr.* Sinclair. I hope to see him when we make it to Oregon City."

Turner surveyed the camp.

"I mean," Randolph mused, frowning, "what sort of man marries a woman like that, and then leaves her? Leaves her to fend for herself and their son in the East, for I don't know how long. Yet, she is so determined to be with him again. What sort of man can inspire that devotion? It astounds me." He pulled at a weed and stripped the leaves from the stalk, throwing the pieces back on the earth. "Particularly as he seems such a goddamn fool, letting her make this journey by herself with no one to protect her. I can tell you, if she were *my* wife, I would not want her away from my side for a single day!"

Turner put a hand on Randolph's arm. "But she is *not* your wife."

"No... no. I didn't mean—"

"James, I know what you mean," said Turner with a sigh.

Randolph lay on his back and stared at the first stars of the evening. He had said more than he intended, said things he was not even aware of feeling.

"You can always hope for some good news at Oregon City," said Turner. "Mr. Sinclair may have died of some disgusting disease by the time we get there."

The two men broke into laugher, releasing the tension of the moment.

"Or been gored by one of his cows," Randolph suggested.

"Trampled by buffalo."

Randolph looked at his pocket watch. "Ought to get back down there. Do another check," he said, standing up.

"Yes, and Eunice will be wondering where I am." Turner puffed as he stood up and stretched the stiffness from his legs after sitting on the hard rock.

The friends made their way back down to the camp.

TWENTY-SIX

Grace tied the bow of her bonnet and was glad the brim extended forward to hide her face. Yes, the intention was for people to notice, but she didn't want to catch their eye while doing so.

Corporal Flanagan and Grace set off through the gorge. The Sweetwater gurgled over rocks, and the high cliffs on either side echoed every sound. They emerged to the wide valley beyond, with mountains to the north. Flanagan suggested they sit by some cottonwood trees, the gray bark twisting up the trunk like old cracked skin.

"So your family emigrated from Scotland?" Flanagan asked. He was a good listener and Grace enjoyed his company.

"My grandfather came first, looking for a better life. Grandma came over once he was settled." Grace leaned back against the trunk of the tree. "He loved inventing things. But was not good at working out how those things could become something useful. The trick of changing them into products folk would buy always fell to others. Luckily, as my father grew up, he developed a talent for engineering. The two of them were a great team: Grandpa with ideas, Pa finding ways of making them work."

"What sort of things did they make?" asked Flanagan.

"Well, over the years, they concentrated on firearms. Ways to make them more accurate, less dangerous to the person firing them."

"So that's why you're such a sharpshooter yourself?"

Grace shrugged. "Guess so. Hours spent with Pa, testing new adjustments. Of course, I can't take all the credit. I'm using a better type of gun—a much truer aim."

"I've heard of Sinclair Rifles. Would that be it?"

"Yes. That was some years back. Unfortunately for the family, they were made by another company that got sold on. But..." Grace looked at Flanagan. "You know how to keep a confidence, don't you?"

"That part of being a priest would have been no problem. You can trust me." Flanagan shuffled closer.

"Father had been developing a special pistol before he died. He made a few prototypes—y'know, models to see how they worked. They're wonderful. Shoot as straight as a line, and at more distance than anything you can buy today. But he died before he could arrange for manufacture. That's one of the reasons I'm going out West. My father made me promise to take these prototypes to my brother, in the hope he would develop them properly."

"So that's another reason why you're so eager to make it to Oregon?" Flanagan asked, rubbing his ginger hair with his hand, making it stand stiffer than the dry grass on the plain.

"Well, I guess there's lots of reasons." Grace had relaxed and said far too much. God forbid she start blabbing about her violent landlord in Independence. She inwardly cursed herself for revealing her father's name was Sinclair, not her "husband." Her face felt hot. Would Flanagan notice this slip? A lump came to her throat and she quickly changed the subject. "And you, have you lived in the States all your life?"

"Indeed I have. Father died when I was very young, so I hardly knew him. Mammy had come across from Ireland with the rest of her family. It was a lovely close community. Endless aunts and uncles."

Flanagan told how he had tried to enter the Church, mostly to please his family, how he had failed abysmally and signed up with the army to escape, joining Captain Randolph in Texas. Flanagan maintained a deep love for the Catholic church but knew it was not his calling.

The conversation ranged over many subjects, but settled on their fellow travelers, the foibles and vanities of the officers and overlanders. Grace wanted to know who Flanagan trusted and respected.

"And the captain?" she asked. Deep down, she knew she wanted to know more. "What about him?"

"What d'you want to know?"

"What is there to tell?" she asked with a smile.

"Not very much, I'm afraid."

"Oh, come on! I won't tell anyone. I can keep a secret as well as a former priest." She barged him with her shoulder. She had glimpsed a gentler side of Captain Randolph and was intrigued by the contradictions.

"There's not much to say. I've heard hints of a wilder youth, but the man I've served with for years has always been reserved," said Flanagan. "The men trust him. He can be very stern, and has stricter morals than many a priest. But he makes good decisions."

"The men respect him?"

"Completely. He's fearless in battle, so inspires the men to think they're invincible. I saw that in Texas."

Grace wrinkled her nose. "Surely everyone has something to fear."

"Maybe. The difference is, he doesn't show it."

"Doesn't he *ever* show emotions?"

Flanagan thought for a moment. "Anger. That's his main failing. Gets mad at things too quickly."

Grace acknowledged that she had seen this trait. "No other feelings?"

"Aha, now, my friend! It wouldn't be *love* that you're thinking of?" Flanagan said with a cheeky wink. "I've seen many a woman set her bonnet at him. Doesn't have much effect. Look at poor Sarah Eliot. However, and this is something *you* must keep in confidence"—the two drew closer together—"I have heard it rumored he's got some sort of unofficial engagement with the daughter of the commander of Fort Boise."

"Really?" The muscles round Grace's chest tightened uncomfortably, but she had to know more.

"I once heard Mrs. Turner mention it. Thought to be a good match on both sides."

Yes, a military man's daughter probably would make a good match. "Have you met her?"

"I haven't been formally introduced, if that's what you mean. Remember, I'm only a lowly corporal."

"But you know more, I can tell." Grace bit her lip, wondering why she was asking these questions when the replies were making a knotted feeling right there in her stomach.

Flanagan grinned. "A little. Her name is Flora."

"That's a pretty name."

"She's a pretty girl. All ribbons and curls."

"And he loves her?" Grace asked tentatively.

"Who knows?" Flanagan snorted. "He'd think of the practicalities first. Is she companionable? Does she have childbearing hips, that sort of thing."

Grace gave him a gentle thump. "You're jesting!"

"Yes, I am. I don't think *anyone* knows what's going on in

the captain's heart. And it was just a bit of gossip, there's probably nothing in it."

Grace surprised herself by how fervently she hoped there was nothing in it.

She changed the subject again and they sat under the trees, chatting until disturbed by Kane bounding up to Grace. Tom was close behind. She felt a pang that he would be confused by her uncharacteristic behavior. Tom must have seen them setting off for a walk some time ago, and eventually convinced himself that Kane also needed a walk up the river through the gorge.

The three set off back to camp. Flanagan spoke mostly to Tom, making friends with the boy. Grace would need a long chat with Tom that evening. She could not reveal the real intention of the public dalliance with Flanagan, but she would reassure Tom it was nothing untoward; this was purely a friendship and would never be anything more.

In the late evening quietness, Randolph leaned back in his chair, smoking a cigar. Corporal Flanagan was the only man with him.

"How do you think things are going?" It was Randolph's job to collect intelligence, and he tried to convince himself that this conversation was nothing more.

"I think I'm thoroughly the subject of camp gossip by now," said Flanagan, his eyes twinkling.

"Good." Randolph studied the glow at the end of his cigar. Truth was, he didn't think this was good at all. "Then we should proceed to the second part of the plan very soon. The trap is set. Now it's time to catch the fox. I'll talk to Turner about it."

"You mean within the next few nights then?"

"Yes. But we must consider the terrain. I don't want Mrs. Sinclair put in any danger by being in the wrong setting. Somewhere with too much cover for our criminal, for example. In the meantime, make sure you keep very close to her."

Randolph poured a glass of water for Flanagan and a whiskey for himself.

"How's she taking it?" he asked. "Mrs. Sinclair, I mean. Is she having second thoughts?"

"No, none at all. She's very strong."

He grunted, concerned she might be putting on a brave face.

"What do you talk about?" This was more than simple intelligence gathering, but he could not help himself.

"Many things, sir. She now knows the entire history of the Flanagan family. I know somewhat less of the Sinclairs." Flanagan put his head to one side. "Y'know, there's something missing about her family story. I can't quite put my finger on what it is."

"Have you talked about... well, fellow travelers? Given any thought to who our man might be?"

"We seem to have chatted about many folk, both settler and soldier."

"Ever talked about me?" Randolph leaned forward. He felt like a schoolboy, trying to find out if the girl next door had noticed him.

Flanagan looked sheepish.

"I can take the truth," said Randolph with a slight smile.

"Doesn't *everyone* gossip about the person in charge? Just, not to his face."

"Any mention of my antipathy toward women?"

It was Flanagan's turn to smile. "Not in so many words."

Flanagan could not know that the captain had continued to think about this phrase, turning it over in his mind and examining his life in relation to it.

What had happened to him recently? First, his conversation with Turner, when he had revealed feelings he didn't know he had; now he was questioning Flanagan about what people thought of him.

Randolph had always thought it nobody's business what happened in his private life. Indeed, he quietly congratulated himself on his lack of attachment in affairs of the heart, and secretly thought others would admire him for it.

But were people judging him as ungentlemanly in relation to the fair sex? As someone to be condemned, or pitied, or even sniggered at? Damnation! These were uncomfortable thoughts; if only Turner was here to tell him he was considering things too deeply, taking things too personally.

TWENTY-SEVEN

Captain Randolph led the way, skirting south of the Devil's Gate ridge and west into the wide Sweetwater valley where the river meandered down from the Continental Divide. The air felt cleaner, softer, even in the heat.

Around midmorning, he rode to the Sinclair wagon, and Grace gave a tiny nod of acknowledgment. The sun was strong and her face was partly hidden by the wings of her cotton bonnet. He traveled alongside for a while.

"That's Split Rock in the distance." He pointed at the distinctive cleft cutting into a range of mountains to their right.

"They weren't terribly imaginative when naming places on the journey," Grace said. He caught her smile.

"Oh, I don't know. Devil's Gate?"

"You got me there, sir."

Randolph laughed. "And beyond is South Pass. That's the wide saddle between the Wind Mountains to the north and the rest of the Rockies to the south." His horse swayed rhythmically. "Where's Tom?"

"Traveling with his friend in the Hollingswood wagon for the morning. I'll have the two kids with me this afternoon."

Randolph didn't know whether to be pleased or not: he had resolved to speak to Grace but wasn't sure of the words. Now there was no excuse for putting it off to another time. "If you have second thoughts, you just have to say the word."

Grace glanced at him. "No, I'm all right." Her voice was soft.

"What I mean is," Randolph pushed on, "as the time to... spring the trap... draws close, you may feel afraid. There is nothing to be ashamed of in that. No one would condemn you, if you found you couldn't see this through. We can search for other ways to catch this man."

"Thank you for your consideration," said Grace. "To tell the truth, I already often feel afraid. I then... then think of Jane on that night... I know it will only be a short time for me to be frightened, and then it will be over."

He scrutinized her calm face, her gloved hands firmly holding the leather straps. His jacket suddenly felt too warm and he loosened the collar.

"Very well. But please remember, just one word from you..."

They rode on in silence for a while and he considered riding forward to the next wagon. He often did this, checking on each wagon's progress as he went. But he needed to speak out loud what was laying heavy on his heart.

Randolph cleared his throat. "I've been thinking about what you said. About my antipathy to women—"

"Sir, I didn't mean anything by those stupid words," Grace cut in. She looked across, straight into his eyes. "I didn't mean to..." Grace searched for the words, "to insult you."

"No, I was not insulted. I'm afraid it's true." He shook his head. "Women seem concerned with such silly things: the curl of their hair, the cut of their dress, how expensive the lace on a bonnet is. Some take joy in gossiping about people and spreading the worst."

"Oh, sir, I must defend my sex," said Grace with a laugh. "We cannot be as bad as all that!"

"I daresay I'm being harsh on womenfolk. I know it is a prejudice. And as with all prejudices, it is defined by one's experience of the individual."

Grace frowned and looked at him, shielding her eyes from the sun with her hand.

"What I mean is, early experience with an individual may color one's views for many years. But then, perhaps getting to know a *different* individual will improve my view of the whole sex. You, for example." He now gazed directly at her. "You are as brave as any man I know. And completely selfless. You are prepared to put yourself in danger, to sacrifice your good reputation, for the sake of a woman you didn't know a couple of months back. You're hardworking, taking on the burden of two people to keep up with the wagon train, but I've seen you giving the time to help your fellow travelers."

The color rose up Grace's neck and across her cheeks. She fixed her vision on the mules ahead.

"I'm sorry," Randolph said. "I've embarrassed you. That was not my intention. I only wanted you to know the regard in which you are held."

"Sir, you are very kind." Grace gave a slight slap to the backs of the mules. "Indeed, you are much too kind. This only shows how little you know me. I hide many faults, as I expect we all do. I'm sure if you really knew me, you would be disappointed."

There was an obstruction on the trail ahead and the wagons came to a pause. Randolph circled his horse so it was close to the driving bench.

"I regret I'm unlikely ever to be able to really know you. However, I'm happy that you will remain faultless in my eyes."

Randolph spurred his horse on. Surely he'd said far too much. And yet, amazingly, he didn't care. He had spent too many years being cold and reserved, never expressing his feelings, for good or bad. Maybe, just this once, he could speak the truth.

Grace sat open-mouthed, her heart beating faster than the swiftest antelope running across the plain. To be held in such high regard by a man she thought despised her. And his final words! He regretted not being able to know her more. She wanted to cry out to him that there was no barrier between them, she was unmarried, they could court each other without guilt or shame.

But that brought Grace sharply to her senses. Every day, she lived a lie by pretending to be Mrs. Sinclair. Perhaps not the worst lie ever told. Perhaps the captain would forgive her. But the cause of the lie was the bigger obstacle. The captain's idealized picture of her did not include the possibility she was a murderess.

Randolph was destined to marry the daughter of the major at Fort Boise. That was how it should be. Someone of his own kind, not an ordinary pioneer girl, with no family, no money, no connections. And a dangerous past.

These thoughts wound round Grace's head all morning. At noontime, her eyes searched out Randolph, but he did not look her way. During the afternoon ride, she was sharper than usual with Tom and Benjamin, objecting to their noise and childish observations. By the evening camp, she had resolved to store the words in a secret place in her heart and not examine them for a very long time.

TWENTY-EIGHT

As the day went on, the land got steeper and the jagged outline of the Rockies drew nearer, snow lying on the peaks. When the train stopped for the night, the pioneer wagons extended over most of the flat area near the river. As usual, the soldiers pitched their tents on slightly higher ground.

Corporal Flanagan grabbed a moment to speak to Grace as she prepared dinner. "The captain wants to set the trap as soon as we can, but he doesn't like the lie of the land here. He's asked us to walk together this evening as usual. Establish a pattern. Hopes tomorrow the area will be more level so they can keep watch better. I'll meet you over there in an hour." He indicated a clump of Rocky Mountain juniper trees a little way to the west.

Grace agreed and he returned to the soldier's encampment.

Before the hour was out, there was an accident. Young Private Lewis was making coffee for his squad. Somehow, he got careless and poured boiling water over his hand. He yelled and grasped his wrist, the pot clattering to the ground.

Flanagan leaped up to give advice. "Here, put it in this cold water."

Others crowded round. "Spread grease on it," someone suggested.

Dr. Trinkhoff bustled in and dressed the wound. Lewis groaned with pain.

As the fuss died down, Sergeant Knox took charge. "Come on now," he barked. "Time to go to your posts for the first watch. Flanagan, take Lewis's place."

The corporal had not finished his coffee. "But I'm on night watch."

"I'll get someone else to cover that."

"Can't you find someone else to do *this* shift?" asked Flanagan. His meeting with Grace was on his mind, so something in his tone provoked Knox.

"You questioning an order?"

"No, I just thought—"

"I ain't asking you to *think*, Corporal."

Flanagan got to his feet. "It's just I've made arrangements—"

Knox took a step closer, the men watching. "You should think more 'bout being a soldier and less 'bout your romantic assignations. Picket duty. Now!"

Flanagan would only make the situation worse by protesting, so saluted and left. He thought of Grace waiting for him, vulnerable, alone. He should defy the order and go straight to her. But Knox would be watching, and it would create an almighty commotion that would be difficult to explain.

Flanagan took a few steps toward the captain's tent to tell him the situation. Randolph would make sure the watch duty was switched. But then he stopped. They had invested so much effort in trying to trap a violent man; the whole plan could come tumbling down if Randolph acted out of character by overruling his sergeant's order.

Flanagan rushed to his own tent, grabbed a pencil and a scrap of paper, and scribbled.

Sir,

*Due to circumstances beyond my control, unable to keep my
meeting with Mrs. S. Will explain reasons later. V. concerned she
is <u>alone</u>. Arranged to meet at juniper trees west of camp.*

*With my regrets,
Cpl. Flanagan.*

He folded the letter, and once outside looked for someone
he could trust. Private O'Hara was nearby.

"Private, have you a moment?" O'Hara was young and
keen, a fellow Irishman, and kinsmen should stick together. "It's
very important that you take this note to Captain Randolph,
right now. Put it in his hand," he said. Then a thought struck
him. "Or Lieutenant Turner. He would do."

"So who shall I take it to?"

"Either! Whichever you meet first. But *quickly*, man."

O'Hara scuttled away and Flanagan went to take his watch.

Grace stood waiting, looking out for Flanagan, pulling her
shawl tighter around her shoulders. The sun had set and
twilight slipped into darkness. She shivered. Maybe she'd got
the wrong spot and he was waiting somewhere else. A half-
moon was caught in the branches of the stubby gray-green pines
before being enveloped in clouds. The darkness between the
trees deepened.

She walked a little further on, picking her way carefully on
the soft earth, the smell of juniper filling the evening air. She
wondered whether, if she didn't see him soon, she should go
back to the camp.

She heard a whistling sound, then a whispered, "Grace,
over here."

"Thank goodness," she said, "I was about to give up on you."

She took a few paces toward the voice when her arm was clasped hard, and she was twisted around and grabbed from behind, knocking the air from her chest. One hand went over her mouth, the bitter taste of tobacco on the fingers. The other arm enveloped her waist.

Grace kicked and struggled, but the man just held her tighter.

"Now, don't do that," he said, his mouth close to her ear. "You'll just git more hurt."

He yanked her head back and pain spiked down her neck. She stopped struggling, trying to think what to do. Fear made her mind freeze.

"That's better. Over here."

He tried to drag her to the ground. Grace bit the hand over her mouth and made a sharp jab backwards with her elbow.

"You bitch!"

The man spun her round and hit her, a sharp blow with the back of his hand across the side of her head and she reeled to the ground.

"No point shouting. No one can hear."

He was on top of her, his hand again over her face and his body weight crushing the air from her lungs. His other hand fumbled with his pants, and then pushed at her skirts.

Grace wrestled a hand free and jabbed her fingers into his face above the neckerchief he was wearing. He pulled back in pain and Grace twisted out from under him. As she was pulling free, he grabbed her and flung her back in fury. Her head hit a rock, the throbbing pain making Grace dizzy. She closed her eyes and felt herself slipping away.

She heard the click of a cocked gun at close quarters, and then everything stopped.

TWENTY-NINE

"Get away, you vermin!" The voice was deep, angry, forceful.

The crushing weight lifted as the attacker got up.

Grace opened her eyes and turned on her side, shaking with fear and relief.

The attacker laughed. "Come to join in the fun?"

The captain tossed his pistol to his left hand, and threw a punch on the man's chin. He crashed to the ground and the captain strode over to him. "You're not fit to walk this earth," he hissed, and then discharged the gun close to where the man lay. The sound echoed through the clearing.

A moment later, Grace heard more voices.

"Captain?"

"Over here, Turner."

Turner was out of breath from the run, O'Hara close behind.

Randolph hunkered down where Grace lay. "Are you all right?" he murmured.

"Yes... I think... I think so." She struggled to breathe.

"Did he..." The words hung in the air.

"No... no. He didn't have the chance." Grace closed her eyes, the lids squeezing a tear onto her cheeks.

"Thank God Private O'Hara got Flanagan's note to me," he whispered, and then called to the soldier. "Private, fetch Mrs. Hollingswood. Bring her here fast as you can. Tell her... tell her the trap has shut and the fox is caught. Got that?"

O'Hara sped off through the darkness.

Turner walked over to where the man was still moaning on the ground. He crouched down and pulled the neckerchief from the man's face.

"Private Croup," Turner said in disgust.

The man started laughing again, and as the clouds parted, the moon gave a white sheen to his face.

"One of the men who joined us at Laramie," Turner said to the captain.

Randolph reached for Grace's hands and helped her sit.

She pulled her knees up tight, her head resting forward on her arms, blood still pumping through her veins. The man's laughter was ringing in her ears, making her feel nauseous.

"You're shaking," Randolph said. "Are you cold?"

"A little."

Randolph took off his military jacket and spread it around her shoulders, its weight comforting and warm.

Soldiers and pioneers, drawn by the sound of the gunshot, began arriving at the clearing.

"You two," Randolph spoke to the first soldiers to appear. "Take any weapons this man may have. Then place him under armed guard. Private Croup," he spoke directly now, "I am charging you with the rape of Miss Jane Eliot and the attempted rape of Mrs. Sinclair."

There was a ripple through the crowd as this information registered.

Mrs. Hollingswood pushed her way forward and knelt by Grace.

"Is she all right?"

"She is unhurt. Take her back to her wagon, would you, and watch over her?"

Lillian helped Grace to her feet. She felt sick and dizzy.

"My head," she whispered. "It hurts real bad."

With her next step, all power over her legs disappeared. Lillian tried to hold her. "Captain!"

Grace was aware of Randolph stepping towards her and sweeping up her collapsing body.

Lillian supported her head. "There's blood. Grace must have struck something."

"This is all my fault," he said. "I should never have allowed her to take this risk."

Randolph was already making his way out of the thicket and toward the camp, Turner following closely. The military tents were much closer than the wagons.

"Get Trinkhoff," Randolph called over his shoulder as he carried Grace toward his tent.

Turner held the canvas flap to one side, and Randolph laid Grace gently on his camp bed.

As he was lighting the lamp, the doctor entered. "Did O'Hara explain what happened?"

Trinkhoff nodded and knelt by the bed. He raised the back of Grace's head: there was a cut that had already grown to a large lump and was bleeding freely. Trinkhoff opened his black case and took out a pad of muslin. Dampening it with water, he cleaned dirt from the wound, and pressed a new pad to the cut.

Randolph rubbed the back of his neck.

"Do not worry," Trinkhoff said, "head wounds often bleed profusely."

Grace was coming round again. She squinted at the lamp-light and screwed up her face in pain.

"It is difficult to judge how serious it is," said Trinkhoff. "She certainly should not be moved again tonight. Someone should watch over her for any change."

He wanted to be the one to keep watch, but it was unthinkable that he could remain all night with a married woman. "Of course. I'll sleep elsewhere so you can look after her."

Trinkhoff raised both his hands. "*Nein.* I am a military doctor. I'm not sure I should…"

Lillian had slipped inside the tent. "I'll stay with her."

Randolph cast her a grateful glance and swept up his personal items: some clothing, his shaving gear, and the logbook.

"There's something else you need to look after." Lillian put her hand on his arm, just as the captain was leaving. "Her good name."

Randolph nodded and stepped outside, handing his effects to O'Hara.

Corporal Flanagan was waiting. He had been sent for, as many of the soldiers assumed there was an intimate relationship with Mrs. Sinclair.

Randolph gave the order for all available soldiers to meet outside the mess within five minutes. There, with Turner and Flanagan beside him, he gave a brief account of the situation, of a vicious criminal within their ranks, that this evening's events had been an attempt to smoke him out. Things had not gone precisely to plan, but they had got their man. He made clear Mrs. Sinclair's role and that no suggestion of improper behavior should be attached to her. The men were dismissed and he asked Turner to explain things to Tom.

Randolph took a moment to pause. He looked up at the sky, dark except for the moon lighting up the scudding clouds. They had caught the man. That was a good thing; he ought to be feeling proud. Instead, he could not help thinking of Grace looking so fragile, feeling so delicate in his arms.

He breathed in deeply, feeling a need to steady himself. There was work to do. He walked to the overlanders' wagons to seek out Jane Eliot's family. This was not an encounter he looked forward to, but it was one that must be undertaken urgently.

THIRTY

The whole camp was alive with rumors about what had happened. They had heard a gunshot, and knew a woman had been carried to the captain's tent. Many of the overlanders were soon convinced it was a lovers' quarrel and that the woman was dead. Grace Sinclair's name was whispered, so some thought Corporal Flanagan was the perpetrator. But then others said they had seen him walking free, while a different man was under guard—a private.

The captain paced through the pioneer camp, looking for the Eliots' wagon. Those who tried to ask questions, he dismissed with the shake of a hand. He had only one thing on his mind.

Randolph approached Caleb and Betty Eliot. "I need to speak to you. Can we sit in your wagon?"

Caleb frowned in puzzlement but led the way. They climbed up the steps and sat close together on boxes and benches under the canvas. A single lamp cast shadows.

Randolph took a breath. How to start? "This evening's incident closely affects your family."

Both the Eliots stared at Randolph, too surprised to speak.

"On Monday morning, your daughter Jane appeared unwell. Am I correct?"

They nodded.

"She's been out of sorts for a few days," said Betty. "But I don't see how—"

"She had in fact been attacked by a soldier, and violated in the most dreadful way."

Betty let out a cry and lifted her knuckles to her mouth.

Randolph shook his head. He was used to dealing with soldiers and speaking in a direct way. "I apologize, Mrs. Eliot. I do not mean to appear insensitive."

Caleb's jaw tightened. "Sir, tell us what's happened."

Randolph leaned forward so he could speak more softly. "Mrs. Sinclair informed me she found your daughter in great distress Sunday evening."

"Mrs. Sinclair?" Caleb scratched his wiry hair. "What had she to do with this?"

"She simply happened to be walking with her dog, I believe, and came across your daughter."

"But Jane shouldn't have been out by herself. What was she doing?" Caleb asked.

"She was meeting Corporal Moore."

Caleb's face went dark as he squared his shoulders. "And he attacked her? I'll kill him. I'll damn well kill him!"

"No, that's not what... Mr. Eliot, were you not aware of a bond of affection between them?"

Caleb shook his head.

"I had an inkling," whispered Betty, with a sideways glance at her husband. "Well, more than an inkling. Knew she was sweet on him."

"So... who attacked her?" Caleb asked.

Randolph swallowed hard. "That was our difficulty. She could not identify the man. Hence, I talked it through with my lieutenant and we decided to set a trap. Mrs. Sinclair volunteered to help."

He thought back to the plan that had so nearly gone wrong. No, it *had* gone wrong: Mrs. Sinclair was injured and now under Mrs. Hollingswood's care. Responsibility for it rested upon his own shoulders.

"Tonight the rapist has been caught. It is Private Croup. I don't know much about him, but I assure you he's now in custody."

Randolph watched in alarm as Caleb sprang to his feet and opened a box nearby.

"Mr. Eliot?"

Caleb took out his pistol. "I'm going to finish this, right now."

"Sit!" Randolph stood, needing to bring the authority he used to lead a company of soldiers. "I understand how angry you are. But that's not how this is going to play out."

"*Angry?* You got a daughter?"

Randolph stood his ground until Betty took her husband's arm and coaxed him back onto the seat.

"So, what now?" asked Betty. Her voice shook as she tried to control her breathing.

"He'll be tried when we reach Fort Boise. I'll ask an officer to collect evidence. Your daughter's testimony will be vital, of course."

"You better make sure he damn well swings for it!" Caleb put his head in his hands and started to sob. "I want my girl in here. Now." His voice thick with emotion. "Sarah," he called out. "Fetch your sister."

Sarah had been standing just outside, apparently straining to find out why the captain should be in their wagon.

In a moment, Jane was there. Her mother drew her down to sit next to her, but she kept her eyes on the wooden floor, her mouth a thin line. Randolph wished he could leave, but knew he had to remain until things were resolved.

"Why didn't you tell me?" Betty asked, her eyes wide, still trying to understand everything that had happened.

Jane looked at her, and burst into tears. "I couldn't," she said between sobs. "I was so ashamed... and I thought Papa would be angry 'bout me meeting Daniel..."

"Damn well right," her father growled.

Betty shushed her husband. "But still, you could have come to me."

Jane shook her head from side to side. "Maybe I got what I deserved."

Betty rocked her daughter in her arms and soothed her head. "Now, you must be very brave, my sweet, and in the morning tell the captain's officer everything that happened."

"I can't. It was... I just can't." She looked up at her mother, her eyes full of tears. "I heard someone say Mrs. Sinclair has just been attacked. She can do it. She's stronger than me. She can tell them everything."

"That's not possible for a number of reasons," said Randolph, looking at Betty. "Jane, I need to make sure this man Croup faces justice."

"But I don't want to. Folks will stare at me, like I'm..." Jane wiped her wet face with the corner of her shawl.

Randolph's jaw tightened, thinking of the woman he had just carried to his tent. "You need to understand. Mrs. Sinclair *chose* to put herself in danger, purely to save what had happened to you being repeated by this vile man. She didn't *have* to do it. She showed great courage and fortitude. No doubt people will stare at her, even though she is blameless."

Jane sniffed back her tears.

Randolph stood. "Now, may I suggest you take some time to talk and comfort each other." He picked up his hat. "In the morning, Lieutenant Turner will start the investigation. I trust you will tell him everything you can."

He got down from the wagon, followed by Caleb, who was muttering to himself.

"You know, Mr. Eliot," he said, putting on his hat. "Corporal Moore is a good man. Hardworking, honest. If there is still a bond between them, I think you should encourage it. Jane could do a lot worse."

He walked swiftly to the soldiers' camp, ignoring people as he went.

Randolph crept back into his tent, where Lillian was keeping watch over the patient. He found Tom sitting at the field desk, his face pale, his glazed eyes fixed on Grace. He briefly squeezed the boy's shoulder.

"How is she?" he asked, looking over to where Grace lay.

"Sleeping," replied Lillian.

"Good... good." He turned to go.

"Sir, it would be helpful if I could fetch some things from my wagon, if I am gonna stay here for the rest of the night. And I could take Tom to spend the night with my family. Perhaps you could stay a short time, while I sort myself?"

"Yes, of course," he said. "Anything I can do to help."

Lillian left with Tom, and Randolph sank down in his canvas chair opposite the bed. He glanced at her again, but thought it best to try to keep his attention elsewhere.

His military jacket hung on a nail, a brown-black stain on the back where blood had seeped from Grace's head wound. Lillian must have hung the jacket there. Grace's shoes were by the bed, her outer garments folded on the table. A group of black hairpins were near the logbook.

An oil lamp burned on his table. He reached for the book he

was reading and tried to concentrate on it. But his attention pulled back to the woman sleeping in his camp bed.

Soon he gave up, put down his book, and leaned back in his chair, watching her face. Grace lay on her side, her mouth slightly open as she breathed very lightly. Her long dark eyelashes contrasted with her pale cheeks. Her locks trailed across his white linen pillowcase.

After a few minutes, she stirred, opening her eyes and focusing on the soft lamplight. Her gaze moved across to Randolph, and she gave a slight smile.

A sense of relief like nothing he had felt before flowed through him. He dropped to his knees beside the bed, his face close to hers, fighting the urge to take her hand.

"How are you feeling?" he asked as gently as he could.

Grace raised her fingers to the wound. "Like I've just been hit on the head."

He shook his head. "I am *so* sorry—"

"Don't," Grace interrupted, her voice soft. "We got him, didn't we?"

"We did."

"Who was it?"

"Private Croup." Just saying the man's name filled him with disgust.

A small furrow appeared in Grace's brow. "I don't recall..."

"Joined us at Fort Laramie."

"Oh... I see. But it won't happen again?"

"No, he's under guard. And will remain that way."

Grace closed her eyes a moment, then opened them.

"Are you comfortable?" Randolph asked, wondering what he could do to make her better.

"Perfectly," she said with a smile. "I have never felt a softer pillow, or smoother linen."

Randolph bit his lower lip and tried not to grin. She had

found him out. "My one luxury. I cannot bear anything other than crisp linen."

"Very sensible too," Grace said, drifting away and closing her eyes once more.

Randolph sat back in the chair and watched her fall asleep, praying that it would bring her healing. He was grateful for these few moments with her, and would have stood guard all night if necessary.

Lillian Hollingswood returned with a basket of mending and took over the vigil from Randolph. The camp quietened, and gradually the needle slipped from her fingers as she settled into sleep.

A tremulous whisper from Grace jerked Lilian awake. The lamp was still burning as Lillian bolted upright and realized Grace was asleep but experiencing a vivid dream.

"Leave. Leave me alone," Grace hissed. Her voice was not loud but anguished.

Lillian stepped forward to feel Grace's brow.

"Don't touch me!" said Grace. "I told you to go."

Lillian was uncertain what to do. Her movements seemed to take Grace deeper into the nightmare.

Grace mumbled and became more agitated. "I'll shoot if I have to," she cried clearly. "I will... I will." She pushed herself up and opened her eyes.

Lillian could see the pulse beating in her neck vein. She fetched a cloth and dampened it, then put it to Grace's head to soothe and cool her brow. Lillian longed to stop Grace playing out the evening's events in her head.

Grace's breath quickened, and her eyes were wide with fear. "Boyd!" she cried.

Lillian stopped still; had she heard that name right?

"Mr. Boyd. I'll shoot if I have to. I will." A sheen of perspiration shone on Grace's face.

"Grace, Grace," Lillian murmured.

She settled for a moment and then opened her eyes again. She looked at her hands. "Tom, all this blood." She clutched at the bedcover. "It's on my apron. I'll have to burn it."

Lillian took her hand. "Grace, you're safe."

Grace looked at Lillian this time, rather than through her. Her breathing calmed and she dropped to the pillow, exhausted by her dream, and slipped back to unconsciousness.

Lillian pulled the bedclothes straight and cooled Grace's face with the cloth.

She thought about the nightmare Grace had experienced. Had it been about that evening's events, all jumbled up in her mind? There had been a gunshot from the captain and plenty of blood. It was to be expected after the dreadful experience of being attacked.

But it didn't make sense.

Lillian stroked Grace's hair. Instinctively, she knew it was a different event Grace had dreamed of—but one no less real. She had suspected for some time that Grace had been running from something. Now that thing had a name: Boyd.

THIRTY-ONE

Shortly after reveille, Dr. Trinkhoff checked his patient and reported to the captain.

"To me, she seems good."

"You sure? Her head wound's safe?" asked Randolph.

"*Ja*. The woman may have a headache for a few days, but then, women complain of that all the time!" The doctor let out a snort, pleased with his joke.

Randolph bristled and drew himself up to his full height. "Refer to her as 'Mrs. Sinclair' and not 'the woman.'" His eye fixed on Trinkhoff, who shifted his feet.

"Anyway," Trinkhoff said, "it will not prevent us making progress today."

"Thank you. You are dismissed."

In the past, he had used the doctor's bluntness to his advantage. They had an unspoken understanding: Randolph wanted to make progress and disdained malingerers; the doctor advised that people were less ill than in reality. Thus the train moved onward.

Today was different. Randolph went to his tent and removed his hat as he ducked through the canvas flap.

"The doctor has just reported. Tell me, how do *you* think Mrs. Sinclair is?" he asked Lillian, seeing Grace was asleep.

"I'm hopeful she will get better, so there's no reason to be anxious, sir."

"But what about now? Can she travel?"

"Daresay she could lie in the back of a wagon, if you need to move out today," Lillian said, rubbing an earlobe. "But it would be uncomfortable for her. A day's rest and sleep would be mighty beneficial for Mrs. Sinclair."

"Then that settles it. We stay here today."

Anyone else, and the wagons would have been on their way by now. But this was not anyone else; this was the woman who had sacrificed herself for the safety of others. That was worth something. Worth making an exception.

Deep down, he sensed maybe this was something more, maybe this was about his softer feelings.

He ran a hand back through his hair and let out a breath. She was a married woman, damn it.

Through the day, Lieutenant Turner questioned Croup and talked to the Eliots. When Randolph read Turner's report that afternoon, his blood ran cold. Croup had admitted everything: he was proud of his attacks and expressed the belief that he had behaved as all men want to, saying that most men would secretly respect what he had done.

By the evening, Grace felt well enough to return to her wagon. She dressed, and Lillian walked her back to the overlanders' encampment. All eyes were on her, but no one spoke. The attitude toward Grace was strange. No one was sure whether to admire her or shun her. The truth of what had happened the previous night was still not fully believed, and of those who did believe the "trap" story, very few understood *why* she had done it.

In the silence, Betty Eliot stepped forward and took Grace's hand. "Glad to see you up and about, my dear," she said, loud enough for everyone to hear. "An' if there's anything—*anything* —we can do for you, you only have to ask."

Grace gave her a grateful smile before climbing into her wagon, and the crowd drifted back to their own business.

Lillian brought a bowl of stew and sat with Grace.

"You all right?" Lillian asked, looking at her face for signs of distress.

"Yes, thank you. I'll be fine. I'll turn in early."

"The captain's arranged for one of the soldiers to drive your wagon tomorrow. So you can join me in ours. You still need rest."

"Thank you," said Grace with a slight nod. "I'd like that."

Evening had turned to night, when there was a knock on the backboard of her wagon, followed by a polite cough.

Tom untied the canvas. "Good evening, sir."

"I have something for your mother." The voice was low and gravelly.

Tom turned to Grace and whispered, "It's the captain."

Her mouth went dry as she moved past Tom, and leaned out over the wooden panel.

"I'm sorry to disturb you so late, Mrs. Sinclair." Randolph was unable to look at her face. "I thought you might like these."

He handed over a bundle. Grace unfolded the burlap cover and found a white linen sheet and pillowcase. Her mouth fell open and she looked at him, her eyes wide. "But I couldn't—"

"I'd like you to have them," he said, pushing the linen toward her.

She pulled her hand over the smooth fabric. "You said they are your one luxury."

"Not exactly," he said, now looking at her with a sheepish grin. "I have a spare set. So that's *two* luxuries."

She bit her lip but couldn't stop herself laughing. "But I still cannot accept—"

"Please, Mrs. Sinclair. It would be of great comfort to know you had them." His head was at the same height and he looked at her. The moonlight made his eyes deep blue. "I find it hard to think of a way to thank you... for what you have done."

"I will... treasure them," she whispered.

He made a slight bow and walked away.

Grace caressed the soft material and put it to her cheek. It smelt of the soap he used to shave. The same warm feeling of security flooded her as had the night before—the sensation when she first opened her eyes and saw Randolph watching over her.

Her thumb traced the corner of the pillowcase: the initials JBR were embroidered there. Such a personal and intimate gift. No wonder there was a fluttering deep in her belly and her heart was beating fast.

The next morning, the wagons moved onward. The day soon became hot and dry. Grace lay in a bed made up in the Hollingswoods' wagon, while a soldier drove her own wagon, as promised. Other Hollingswoods and Tom walked alongside, or looked after the cattle. Lillian sat with Grace in the back, making sure she was as comfortable as possible, despite the wagon lurching as if at sea, and the metal tires creaking on the wooden rims as the wheels complained of the ruts. The two women chatted easily, recalling recent events.

"There's a hidden side to you, my dear. I've bitten my tongue with a dozen questions." Lillian nudged Grace's legs to one side and sat on the quilt. "You know, honey, a trouble shared is a trouble halved?"

"That depends on the trouble."

"Can I ask you plain?" said Lillian, and Grace nodded. "Who's Mr. Boyd?"

The hair on the back of Grace's neck prickled.

"I... don't know of a Mr. Boyd," she said, her gaze flitting around the wagon. "What makes you ask?"

"You called out his name in your sleep. The night I watched over you in the captain's tent. You seemed afraid."

"People say lots of odd things in their sleep," Grace said, smoothing down the quilt. "It doesn't mean anything."

'You're troubled by this, Gracie." Lillian took her hand. "Whatever happened, you can trust me, I won't say a word."

Grace turned away and took a deep breath.

"Is he your husband?" Lillian asked.

"What? No!... My...? No, nothing like that."

Lillian put her head to one side and frowned, like she was struggling with something. "Are you... you see, I've been thinking about this recently... are you actually married?"

Grace froze. What had made her friend ask that?

Her eyes flicked up to Lillian's face. Should she continue the lie? She had wanted to unburden herself to Lillian so many times before. She made a decision.

"I have no husband," she said, barely loud enough to hear.

Lillian nodded slowly. "I thought as much. And Tom? Is he your son?"

She shook her head. "No. My brother."

"I thought you were too young to be his mother."

Grace shrugged slightly. "I don't know how others haven't noticed. I guess he's small for his age. People just accept what they're told."

"So..." Lillian tried to look into Grace's face. "Boyd?"

"He was a man... back at Independence."

"Did something happen?"

She looked sharply at Lillian. "What makes you ask that?"

"You talked about blood—when you were sleeping, I mean."

Grace sighed. Any remaining resistance to unburdening herself melted away. No matter the consequences. "I shot him. I think I killed him."

Lillian's hand flew to cover her open mouth. "Dear Lord above! Gracie! How... how awful." Lillian shook her head. "But I can't believe you did it for no reason." She reached out and took Grace's hand once more. "Tell me the whole tale. It'll make you feel better."

"Very well. But you must let me tell you all, from beginning to end. No interruptions."

Lillian put a finger to her lips and Grace sat up in the makeshift bed, and moved the cushion behind her.

"Pa and Ma died in a cholera outbreak last fall, and since then, well, I've been trying to keep things together. For Tom and me. My elder brother, see, he'd already left after years of arguing with Pa. Went out to the territories in '43. Truth is, Pa was not an easy man. Drank something dreadful. As he was dying, he made me promise to go out to Zach. Wanted his forgiveness, wanted him to carry on the family business. I was left, just with Tom. That's why we were in Independence, gathering everything we'd need to join a train.

"Money was running short, and buying everything for the journey was so costly. So I looked for cheaper lodgings. Silas Boyd was a bit of a character round town. You know, a fixer. He offered a small place—just one room, up and down. The rent was real low, so I took it. I was too stupid to see he expected rent to be paid in other ways. I kept managing to put him off, but it was hard to be too blunt—he could've turned us out on the streets. One night he turned up... it was a little after midnight and he'd been drinking all evening..."

Grace absently rubbed the palm of her right hand with her

thumb, her eyes fixed on the middle distance, and she told Lillian the awful events of that night in Independence.

"Y'know, it's strange how your mind works at those times. I can picture every moment. It was almost as if I... stepped outside of myself, could watch myself. I had to stop him, I didn't know any other way... Then I knew we had to get out fast. We had few possessions, it didn't take long to pack.

"We cleaned up the blood, burned my bloodstained clothes. We left in the dead of night, and first thing, got in line at the Court House to sign up for Oregon. You know the rest, how I lied my way onto this overlander train."

Grace put a knuckle to her nose, sniffing back the tears that were gathering. "So, you see, all this stuff about how brave I've been, trapping Jane Eliot's attacker, it sits heavy on my shoulders. I'm a criminal." Her voice dropped to a whisper. "I've killed someone. I've lied about it. I may never stop running."

She paused, her eyes filling with tears, which she pushed sideways from her face.

Lillian fished a handkerchief from her pocket and gave it to Grace, before hugging her warmly. "So what will you do when you reach Oregon?"

"Well, at least that part of my story is true," Grace said with a hopeful smile. "There *is* a Mr. Sinclair. Our elder brother. Zach has started a homestead in the Dalles. We'll make a life there. Or at the least, Tom will be able to stay—even if I have to move on."

Lillian laid her hand over Grace's. "I'm sure it won't come to that. Look how huge this country is. It goes on for ever. We're like tiny ants crawling our way across it. People are too busy with their own little lives to care about what happened to a bad man half a world away."

Grace traced a pattern on the quilt with her finger. "But, deep down, *I* know what I've done."

There was silence for a while. They listened to the wagon rolling ever onwards.

Lillian tucked a lock of hair behind Grace's ear. "Is that why you were determined to take such a risk for Jane Eliot? Because you knew the fear she must have felt?"

Grace pursed her lips before replying. "I think that was partly it. The idea of a man taking all control, because he's stronger. Yes, that was like Silas Boyd in Independence. But there was something more." Grace paused while she put her thoughts into words. "I think... I wanted to do it because, had it all gone wrong, it would have been my punishment."

Lillian looked at her intently.

"You see, I haven't been punished for shooting Boyd yet. Not that I *want* the punishment," Grace said. "But I was, well... I was prepared to risk it. Risk being punished."

"If you feel this way," said Lillian, "then there's something else you must consider. You've been tested in the fire. Prepared to sacrifice, to atone for what you did in Independence. And you have come through, purified like silver. You must put what happened in that shabby frontier town behind you."

"Do you truly think so?" She looked up at Lillian, hoping for forgiveness.

"Indeed I do."

"Because for a moment, when the man was pulled away by the captain, it was like... like some blessed salvation." Grace felt a warmth deep down inside. These words gave her some comfort. Perhaps Lillian was right, she *had* tried to make amends, and might look forward to a life without fear and guilt.

THIRTY-TWO

With Grace's good health and fierce determination, she was soon up and about. A hidden hand made her daily life less arduous than on the journey so far. Meals were often brought to her; Lillian or Mrs. Eliot would spirit away dirty clothes and return them laundered. Sometimes Corporal Flanagan would arrive to feed, water, and brush down the horse.

What cheered her most was feeling part of a community. She had been the oddity; this woman who dared travel alone, who seemed a threat to husbands and single men alike, who was at ease with weapons and shot straighter than some soldiers. Now the women were kinder and warmer.

It took another week to reach the saddle between the Wind River Mountains to the north and the Antelope Hills to the south. The mountains were huge and granite-gray, a smudge of pines across the lower reaches, but above, the land was barren, with white snow pocketed in the jagged summits. Turner told Grace that behind them it fell all the way down to the Atlantic seaboard, and ahead tilted down to the Pacific. But the South Pass was so long and gently sloping, it meant the Rubicon was crossed with Grace barely noticing.

Captain Randolph kept his distance. Grace found herself looking out for him, and was disappointed if he passed without stopping, simply touching his hat and moving on.

Of course, now Croup was captured, there was no reason for him to speak to her. Probably he was regretting his warm exchanges earlier in the journey—even though she remembered every word.

She buried her head in the linen pillowcase at night and imagined where his cheek had lain. She came close to speaking to Lillian about her feelings for the captain, but then chided herself for being such a dolt.

A couple of days after the wagons trundled through the South Pass, Randolph consulted Gray Eagle and decided they were making good enough time not to risk the Sublette Cutoff. The Cutoff could save them three days, but at what cost? Near fifty miles of desolate flat earth in the summer heat, without a drop of water for man nor beast. There was no need to put the over-landers through that misery. Instead, the train swung south and west, over Pacific Creek, Little Sandy, and Green River. Within the week, they stopped at Fort Bridger, where overlanders with deeper pockets stocked up with exorbitantly priced supplies from the old fur-trapper.

They reached the north-flowing Bear River valley—an oasis after so many days of sagebrush and sand. It was a place of rare beauty, and Randolph found a perfect clearing for a Sunday stopover. The valley about six miles wide, with hills wooded with cottonwoods and pines, providing plenty of fire-wood. The freshwater river teemed with salmon and trout; abundant grass meant the animals at last had plenty of fodder. Friendly Shoshone traded wildfowl and fresh fish for items of clothing, taking pleasure in mixing waistcoats and hats with buckskin shirts.

On the Saturday evening, everyone gathered for their usual hoedown of music and dancing. The barriers between military and civilian had long since disappeared for these evenings, and the dark blue uniforms contrasted with the dun of the pioneers' coats and the patterns of the women's dresses.

Randolph stood at the edge of the merriment as usual. He saw Corporal Moore and Jane Eliot sitting together in the shadows. Not dancing, like that time at the beginning of the journey. But perhaps there was hope for the couple.

Lieutenant Turner danced with his wife, and, at the end, they both joined the captain, laughing and breathless.

"The McClagon reel," cried Eunice, "we must dance to this one." She turned to her husband.

Turner puffed and put a hand to his chest. "I'm worn out, my dear. Couldn't dance another step."

"Oh, come on, you old stick-in-the-mud. It's *such* fun."

"James, perhaps you'd be so kind?" Turner asked.

Randolph stepped forward, gave a slight bow, and held out his arm.

On the other side of the circle, Grace counted partners and made calculations. This was a traditional circle dance where, after each section, the woman moved on to the next partner. She had watched from the corner of her eye as Randolph brought Eunice Turner into the circle.

Her mouth was dry. Was it excitement that he might be forced to acknowledge her? Or embarrassment at allowing herself to daydream about something that could never be. She sensed an emptiness below the ribcage: she was falling for someone who would never be interested in her. She had discovered he was kinder than his reputation, maybe even gentle. But it could never be anything more.

With each round of the dance, she came closer to him. In

her head, she ran through things to say, something casual and lighthearted. But not flirtatious—please not that. He would hate it. But he had spent the last few weeks ignoring her. Why would he give a fig what she said anyway?

She tried to get her breathing under control.

Just one partner behind. They danced so close, her skirt brushed his legs as the ladies spun round. And then they were there, together.

And the music ended.

A long chord indicated a bow and curtsy and the briefest of glances between them before they each looked away.

Randolph undid the button at the neck of his uniform and cleared his throat. "Mrs. Sinclair, it's good to see you so completely recovered from your ordeal."

She inclined her head slightly. "Thank you, I barely think of it."

If he could read her mind! She thought of it all the time: the fear, but also the closeness they had experienced.

Neither of them made to leave.

"I'm sorry we were not able to dance." His voice was husky. "Perhaps you could join me for the next one?"

Never had she so longed for something and feared it at the same time. "Yes, of course," she said, looking at his feet so he would not see the blush on her cheeks.

The fiddle and accordion started up as she spoke. A slow waltz.

He put his hand on the small of her back, pulling her close, and held her right hand. Her heart raced as she reached up and laid her other hand on the epaulette on his shoulder and finally looked up at his face. A whole dance.

THIRTY-THREE

He was an excellent dancer and Grace wondered where he had learned. Officer training perhaps. Did they spend time polishing up the social graces? He led firmly but not too tightly; his sense of rhythm was perfect and they swayed in unison. Although there were many other couples dancing in among them, it felt strangely private. His breath was warm on her ear, and she felt the roughness of his of his fingers holding hers.

"I suppose we must say something," she whispered after a couple of minutes.

Randolph smiled. "Is it compulsory?"

"Surely, we cannot go the whole dance in silence. Perhaps you could share your thoughts."

"Very well. I was thinking how clever your parents must have been."

She put her head back to look at him, both eyebrows raised. "My parents?"

"To know how perfectly your name would suit you as you grew up."

He said it so plainly that she took a moment to register the compliment he was paying. Corporal Flanagan had said something similar, but she'd dismissed him as a flatterer. With Randolph, she was unable to find a reply. She dropped her head and felt her earlobes become unbearably hot.

The music came to an end. He bowed, and tucked her hand inside his arm to lead her back to her place near Lillian Hollingswood. He asked to be excused, and left.

Lillian offered her a glass of cider, sucking in her cheeks to stop herself laughing. Grace took the drink and swallowed it quickly.

"I can't help wondering," Lillian whispered, "what he would do if he knew you were unmarried."

Grace swung round on Lillian. "You must never tell him. Promise me."

"Of course I wouldn't, hon."

"Promise me!"

"If that's what it takes. I promise not to breathe a word." Lillian took a step backwards. "Gracie, I would never betray your confidence. I only meant... Oh, I don't know what I meant. Here, calm your nerves." Lillian topped up Grace's glass with bourbon from a bottle.

Grace shrank back into the shadows as the darkness gathered. Looking round, she realized Randolph had already slipped away from the gathering.

The dance came to an end, leaving just the stalwart revelers to drink, sing, and tell tales. Grace walked back to her wagon, where Tom had already turned in and was deep asleep. Grace was restless, though. She was not used to liquor, even in small amounts, and needed to clear her head and calm her thoughts. The moon was nearly full and cast a watery light between the shadows. She pulled a shawl round her shoulders, untied Kane from his sleeping place beneath the wagon, and walked toward the wood.

Kane chased back and forth, following scents along the ground. Suddenly, he gave a bark and rushed forward.

Grace picked her way through the silver-lit trees to see a hatted man on his haunches, stroking Kane's ears. A soldier on guard duty? She took another step and broke a twig. The man stood up to look her way: Captain Randolph.

"Oh... It's you... Kane was restless. Well, I was restless, to be truthful." She struggled to find words. "I don't usually take him out so late."

"It's a beautiful night," he said. 'I wanted to be alone for a while."

"Oh, I'm sorry," she replied, signaling for Kane to come to her. "We are going back now—"

"No, no I didn't mean... Please stay." He looked down at her. "You must know how dearly I want you to stay," he breathed.

Grace held his gaze, a heat rising up her neck.

Kane picked up a scent once more, and Randolph nodded slightly toward the way he had taken, inviting her to follow the dog deeper into the woods. The trees were widely spaced so the moon lit their way, the sound of their footsteps deadened by the soft, mulchy earth.

"I'm glad you feel safe enough to walk in the evening," he said. "After everything that happened, I mean. But then, courage is not something you lack."

"Ah, Captain Randolph, I lack courage about all sorts of things."

He paused a moment. "Would you... would you feel able to use my name? Call me James, I mean."

Grace inclined her head. "If you wish. James," she whispered, enjoying the feel of the name on her lips.

They continued walking, their strides in step.

"So, tell me, Grace, what are you afraid of?"

"The usual things, I guess." Grace sighed. "The future. Tom's future. Getting us to safety. I feel..."

"Yes?"

She was surprised how comfortable she felt with him. Once, she had thought him so formal and distant. Now she found she wanted to share her feelings with him. Maybe it was being in a shadowy wood: he could not see her face clearly.

"Since Father died, I feel like I've been in a river. A wide one, like the Platte. There's a bank the other side, with safety, and a roof that doesn't leak, and a larder full of food. And if I can just keep on going. Keep on swimming. Keep my eyes on that bank. I'll get there eventually. I'll drag myself out of this river."

Randolph looked surprised at her words, and she wondered if she had said too much.

"That sounds very... wearying," he said.

"Yes, I guess it is."

"And lonely."

Grace nodded. "That too."

Kane lolloped back and pushed his muzzle in her hand before taking off through the trees again.

"No point getting maudlin, though," she said, walking on, thinking it might be better to get some distance between them.

Some broken branches lay across their path. "Be careful now," said Randolph.

He took her hand and helped her over, but did not let it go. And Grace did not pull her hand away.

They stood for a moment, the roughness of his fingers against her palm. Her heart thumped so hard, she could hear a whooshing sound in her ears.

His gaze searched her face. "Was there a reason you felt restless this evening?"

She raised her fingers to the scar on his jawline. "I think you know the answer to that," she whispered.

He put his other hand behind her neck and, leaning down, gently brushed her lips with his. She tingled and opened her mouth as he kissed a little harder. She let out the slightest sigh of pleasure.

Randolph raised his head to look at her face, stroking the backs of his fingers across the down of her cheek, ending at her mouth, thrilling her senses. She closed her eyes and kissed the ends of his fingers.

Grace stepped back and leaned against the rough bark of a pine tree. He dropped his hat to the ground, his eyes locked on hers, and moved toward her, one arm above her head, leaning on the tree, the other around her waist.

Their lips met again, this time with more urgency. She reached her hands behind his neck, her fingers twined in the soft hair that touched the top of his jacket. Her mouth felt the roughness of his stubble, his masculine scent filling her nostrils. He drew her to him and she allowed her body to fill the contours of his, her breasts pressed close against his chest, his thigh between her legs.

He pulled back, his steely blue eyes taking in every contour of her face. "I came to this wood tonight to free myself of thoughts of you."

He slowly shook his head and took her hands from the back of his neck.

"I'm sorry," he said, closing his eyes and letting out a deep sigh.

When he opened them again, there was something unreadable. A vein pulsed at his brow and he stepped away.

"I'm sorry," he said more firmly. "I'll walk you back to the camp."

He dropped her hands and whistled for Kane, who padded toward them. The puzzled look on the dog's face echoed Grace's feelings.

Randolph picked up his hat and brushed the pine needles from it.

They walked back in silence, each in their own thoughts. At the edge of the wood, they stopped and he took her hand.

"You go on from here," he said in a low voice. "I'll watch to be sure you're safe and then make my way round to the east. I wouldn't want..." The words hung in the air.

She took a step nearer, wondering if he might embrace her, but he turned her palm upward and kissed it. She felt confused; his actions were intimate yet formal.

"Well... goodnight then." Grace pulled her shawl closer around her.

"Goodnight," he said, and she walked back to the camp unnoticed, her senses flooded with the passion of that kiss. She was so disappointed by the abrupt end, felt embarrassed that she had revealed the depth of her desire for him.

Perhaps... perhaps she could tell him she was unmarried.

Her shawl became entangled with a bramble in the dark, so she tugged at it, so hard she made a tear. She suppressed a groan. Of course she couldn't tell Randolph she was unmarried. That would lead to the whole truth of why she was here, and what would happen to Tom then?

THIRTY-FOUR

Randolph turned left and made his way through the edge of the wood to the sentry post. He asked if everything was in order.

"Yes, sir. All quiet, sir."

For once, Randolph was relieved at the inefficiency of his picket guard.

He returned to his tent, poured a drink, and sat staring at it for a long time. The scent of her hair was in his nostrils, and when he closed his eyes, he felt her touch. He swallowed his drink, and poured another.

Corporal Flanagan led Sunday morning prayers as usual, the nearest the camp came to a pastor. The soldiers turned out, smart and tidy as always. Most of the overlanders joined the early-morning service of hymns and prayers.

Randolph stood at the head of his men, not a hair out of place. His face was stony as ever, but it concealed the turmoil within. Grace was absent, but then, she rarely attended. Perhaps she was feeling as guilty as he at their licentious behavior.

At least she wasn't a hypocrite. Standing here, mumbling these pious words, and then ignoring them.

Church was one of the duties of military life. Some greater power could be seen in the majesty of the mountains they traveled through, or a mustang galloping free across the prairie—not in the tedious words of men of the cloth, all form and no content.

Look at his love affair with Arabella. She had come from a God-fearing family but had behaved with no morality at all. And everyone around her approved the breaking of a sacred promise, ending their engagement in the hunt for a more eligible mate.

His firm sense of right and wrong was partly guided by the military virtues of duty and faithfulness to one's comrades. But Randolph had a strict childhood brought up on the Ten Commandments, and there was no escaping these rules. He coveted another man's wife. Adultery was a sin. It was dishonorable, to the husband, to the woman, to himself.

And here he was, the captain, supposedly so strong and self-controlled, behaving like a farm boy in the first flush of love. True, she had not resisted his kisses. But he had taken advantage, and barely found the strength to stop. A few caresses more and God knows where it would have ended. Just like those words of Croup: *Come to join in the fun?* That's what he had said. Randolph's skin prickled with heat. He would be a willing adulterer. Perhaps he was little better than that contemptible savage.

Randolph stood, hat in hand, his head bowed, his jaw clenched, stung by the hypocrisy of standing there while prayers were said. Could he utter a few prayers and be forgiven? Yet more weakness. First, he must seek forgiveness from her, the woman he had wronged.

He pictured himself going to her, and his fist closed. To speak to Grace would be impossible. He would never be able to say the words he wanted. He must write it down. That was the solution. Find the right words and give her a letter.

Grace was untroubled by the remorse torturing Randolph. Her heart too light for anything to weigh it down. She had a fluttery feeling in her stomach every time their embrace came to mind. Which was nearly all the time. She had kissed before—of course she had—but that had been an adolescent clutching with a friend of her elder brother. More of an experiment to see what it felt like. And it had been chaste: two pairs of lips briefly touching and parting with giggles, Grace wiping her mouth with her hand in embarrassment.

But this was—and would always be—her first proper kiss. A feeling that started with the lips, but spread through her body and soul. For the first time, she understood the passion that propelled men and women toward a bond that nothing could break, not land or sea, not war or peace.

She knew enough of the world to realize the captain would not be part of her future. Even if Flanagan had not mentioned Flora—the woman waiting for him at Fort Boise—Grace knew captains didn't marry penniless pioneer girls.

But he had feelings for her, of that, she was sure. She longed to hold him again, to feel the roughness of his lips on hers. If he felt just half the passion she did, just a fraction of her need to be near him, drink in his smell, his taste—it could not end with just one kiss. Was that such a dreadful thing to dream of? To embrace for a second time?

Through the day, Grace looked for Randolph, for a moment of exchange. She saw him at prayers and then striding around the soldiers' camp, but he did not come near the overlanders' wagons all day.

In the early evening, she returned from washing dishes in the river and found a letter just inside the wagon. She snatched it up and ran her fingers over the paper, knowing it was from him. He must have waited until Tom joined the other boys after supper. She eagerly climbed into the privacy of the wagon to read it.

Dear Mrs. Sinclair,

I am sure you have been as tormented as I over last night's occurrence. I have nothing but the deepest regret and apologies and can only offer my assurances that nothing of the sort will ever happen again.

I take complete responsibility for the mistake. I took advantage of your weakness and vulnerability. I have no doubt you were lonely for your husband and that led you to forget the Seventh Commandment. St. Peter tells us women are the weaker vessel, so it is the duty of the man to protect the woman's good name.

A man who looketh on another man's wife with lust hath committed adultery with her already in his heart. I have behaved little better than Private Croup and I humbly ask your forgiveness.

I would understand if you felt unable to forgive. Indeed, I imagine you may now only feel anger toward me. Possibly you wish to denounce me publicly, which, though painful, I would accept as just punishment.

I ask that you write, if you feel able. But if there is no letter, I will not press you.

I remain respectfully yours,

James B Randolph, Cpt.

A heaviness sat in the pit of her stomach.

Grace read the letter again, trying to search for comfort, but there was none. That he could feel so differently about their kiss! He was ashamed, even disgusted, by their encounter.

Grace screwed the letter into a tight ball. To compare the passionate feelings they had exchanged with the violence of Private Croup—the two were completely opposite. And his consideration of her as the "weaker vessel." How dare he? Was that the way he thought of her? As some poor foolish thing who did not know her own mind, who would let her feelings run away on a whim. It was so insulting.

Grace unfolded the paper, read the words again, and groaned. *Of course* he would feel this way! Flanagan had told her that he had stricter morals than many a priest. The strength of her feelings had allowed her to forget she was playing a part every day. She knew what she must do: go at once and tell him their feelings were not sinful. She was not married.

But Grace covered her face with her hands. Why did that thought dismay her so? Did she not, deep down, want him to know that she was single, unattached, that the way was clear? For a moment, her mind crept toward the idea: she might become the captain's wife...

She let out a low moan as she flung the fantasy aside. How could Randolph ever love her if he knew the truth? That she had shot a man and left him for dead. That one day, she might be arrested and dragged back to Missouri to face charges. She could never bring such shame on the man she loved.

Grace had never felt so empty and alone. She doubted her own actions. Was she wanton because she had *not* felt tormented by their embrace?

She tried to smooth out the creases before folding the letter and pushing it into the deep pocket of her apron. She would reply, but not yet. Not until she knew what to say. He would not have his quick forgiveness. He would have to wait.

THIRTY-FIVE

Grace hardly slept all night. In the morning, she was rushed and disorganized.

"Why didn't you get the halters untangled last night?" she snapped at Tom.

"You never asked me to." His face was puzzled.

"Tom, do I have to ask every time something needs doing? Now we're going to be late!"

He separated the leather straps wrapped around the harness, muttering loud enough for Grace to hear, "That's not fair. I did all my chores. I always do."

Grace balled her fists and groaned at the sky, angry with herself for taking things out on Tom.

They moved out, taking a place near the rear of the train. The sun beat down, and the wagon jolted this way and that, as it followed the difficult track beside Bear River. Even the lush beauty of the valley did nothing to soothe Grace's spirits.

Over and over, her mind went through what had happened. Grace had read the letter many times and knew it almost by heart. All the pleasurable memories of their embrace had gone; now tears of humiliation prickled in her eyes.

Midmorning, the captain rode back through the train to check the stragglers, as was his habit. He glanced toward Grace and then rode on, his mouth a thin line. Her stomach lurched; if only she could crawl into the darkest part of the wagon, draw a blanket over her head, and hide. But she didn't; she just kept driving the mules onwards, slapping reins and yelling warnings.

At the noon break, Lillian checked how Grace was faring.

"I'm driving your wagon the rest of the day," Lillian announced.

"No, really, there's no need."

"There's every need. Look at you. Dark shadows under those pretty eyes. A puff of wind would blow you over. You haven't eaten a mouthful of that johnnycake."

Grace looked at the corn-yellow pancake in her hand. "I'm just not hungry at the moment. But I'll be all right."

"I'm sure you will be—when you have rested. Now, hush up and stop arguing, for I won't be gainsaid."

Lillian and Grace sat next to each other as the wagons moved on, the leather straps in Lillian's gloved hands. Tom happily skipped off to the Hollingswood wagon for the afternoon.

"I would ask the doctor to see you," said Lillian with a nudge of her elbow, "but he's such a drunken quack, he doesn't know an injury from an insult."

"I'm feeling fine, really," said Grace, her voice faint.

"You don't look fine. You seem very low."

Grace made no reply but kept her eyes fixed on the horizon, the mountains folding into one another, each becoming a paler shade of blue into the distance.

"Something playing on your mind?" Lillian asked.

Grace could not trust herself to speak, there were so many emotions battling inside her.

"You know what I say: a trouble shared is a trouble halved."

A tear escaped down Grace's cheek. Lillian put a

comforting arm around her and the floodgates opened. Grace sobbed, her breathing short and shallow, her head throbbing.

Lillian made comforting noises and waited for the wave of emotion to subside. "Now, Gracie," she said, stroking her hair, "d'you want to tell me what's happened?"

"What happened... what happened was that I fell in love, and he didn't," said Grace bitterly. She took a long breath. "It was Saturday night. After the dance. I was restless, so I took the dog for a walk in the woods. We met by accident, but it felt like... like fate. It was *meant* to happen."

"*What* was meant to happen?" Lilian asked, her eyes fixed on Grace.

"We kissed. I mean... really kissed. Like it..." Grace was unable to find the words.

Lillian's mouth fell open. "The captain!"

Grace nodded, and studied a piece of dirt in the middle of her palm.

Lillian blinked several times. "And then what?"

"And then nothing. He stopped. Just... stopped." Grace looked out at the mountains again. "We seemed to be in another place, deep in that wood. That's how I remember it. A place of... freedom and tenderness. Then, with every step nearer the camp, we left that world behind and returned to his world of duty and order. I was confused, but I didn't think..."

Grace pulled the letter from her pocket. It was folded many times and one of the edges was ragged. She took the reins while Lillian unfolded the letter.

"Captain Randolph's written to you?" Lillian stared at Grace, her eyes wide.

Grace nodded.

Lillian read as quickly as she could.

"Seems mighty formal for one kiss." Lilian pursed her lips. "When did you receive this letter?"

"Yesterday evening."

"Have you replied?"

"No, not yet. I don't know what to say."

Lillian sat quiet for a moment, her back straight as a washboard.

Grace felt more wretched as the silence grew. "You think badly of me, don't you. You think I'm a wanton creature."

"Oh, no, hon! I don't think badly of you." Lillian put a hand lightly on Grace's forearm. "I could see there was something between the two of you. If it weren't for being the captain, I wouldn't be surprised at all. He does seem so buttoned up. Stiff. Straight as the barrel of a rifle." Lillian shook the paper. "As shown by this letter."

"I wanted him. I wanted him so bad," Grace whispered.

Lillian let go a breath. "Honey, you got it real hard. Love is a powerful force, and you've not experienced love like this before, have you?"

Grace shook her head. "I think of him, well, *all* the time. I think I'm going crazy."

A small line appeared between Lillian's brows. "I can understand why he needs to make sure things don't go any further. But this letter, it's so, well, discourteous." She sighed. "But that's what it can be like with feelings. If you crush them down, they just come bursting out somewhere else. Take my Mr. Hollingswood. He gets mad about things but doesn't say, tries to put up with it. Then bang! Suddenly all his anger comes bursting out."

Grace glanced at Lillian. "So you think it was just animal lust for the captain when we kissed? Something he had pushed down but broke out? Is that what you're saying?"

"No... no, I'm not saying that at all. Truth is, the reason he's so agitated is because he cares deeply for you too."

Grace rolled in her lips and sniffed, trying to keep the tears at bay.

Lillian pushed on. "When you think about it, the signs were

all there. His admiration of you for catching Jane's attacker. He was almost beside himself when you were injured."

"I guess that was just guilt that things had nearly gone wrong. He blamed himself for letting me go on with the plan."

Lillian put her head to one side. "Yes, he did reproach himself. But there was more. Oh, my, the tenderness with which he looked at you..."

"So why send such a reserved letter?" Grace held the reins while Lillian read it through again.

"Y'know," Lillian said, "this letter is not so much about what happened. It's that he thinks you're married, that's what's distressing him. Things are either right or wrong with him. Nothing in between. No excuses or explanations. Adultery is a sin."

They traveled on for a while, both with thoughts racing.

"I think," said Lillian after a pause, "if you were to tell him the truth, he would feel very differently."

"The truth?"

"That there is no Mr. Sinclair waiting for you. He might still berate himself for letting his emotions run, but he would not feel the weight of adultery. Ain't no law against kissing. I think it possible that feelings would grow. Feelings that would lead to something."

Grace's pulse quickened as she felt a moment of hope. A future together, that warm feeling of safety when she was with him, protection from the demons chasing after her.

But then cold reality flooded in, just as it had the night before.

"I've thought about that and can't do it. I can't tell him there's no Mr. Sinclair." She sniffed. "He hates lies and deceit. At the very moment I lift the burden of adultery, he will know I've been lying to him from the first day we met. All his early feelings would come back—his conviction that I should not be here traveling alone in the first place. I'd be proving him right. Women are not to be trusted."

Grace closed her eyes and felt her hands tighten into fists. "And Lillian, you know that would not even be the worst of it. That would be nothing to telling him *why* I was desperate to leave Independence. Here's a man troubled that one passionate kiss is adultery. How would he feel about a woman who'd killed someone? Can you imagine? It would stop any tender feelings in their tracks."

Lillian sighed and thought about everything Grace had said. She shook her head. "I guess you're right."

They rode in silence again.

"Look, why don't you get some rest?" Lillian said. "Go sleep in the back of the wagon. I can manage here."

Gratefully, Grace climbed over the wooden panel behind the driver's bench, and curled up on a counterpane thrown over some boxes. She slept fitfully, always dreaming of Randolph and waking with a start to find things no better.

By the evening, Grace had decided how to reply to the captain. She had no paper, so she carefully tore part of a blank page from the back of the family Bible, and unpacked her precious pen and ink from the bottom of a case.

Sir,

Thank you for your letter. I apologize for not answering sooner.

I want to put your mind at rest. As far as I'm concerned, no one need know what occurred. I will never speak of it again. You need not fear my public denunciation, nor my private admonishments.

*I am saddened that you still think me weak and vulnerable. I
thought I had demonstrated over recent months that I take
responsibility for my actions. While you may feel regret, shame,
and guilt for your part in what happened, please do not be so
arrogant as to think it necessary to take on the burden of my feelings also.*

Grace Sinclair

She read through it several times. Was it too angry? Too
formal? He must be assured that whatever attachment there
had been was now over.

She considered how to get the letter to the captain. She did
not want to meet him face to face, but could not risk it falling
into the wrong hands. Finally, she begged Lillian to wait until
Randolph's tent was empty with no one around, and leave the
note on his field desk.

When Randolph returned to his tent for the night, he
immediately noticed the letter. His heart beat faster; no one else
could be writing to him privately. He sat down and unfolded
the paper.

Randolph let out a long breath and dropped his head. She
was furious with him. As he had feared. That stubborn streak
that had so infuriated him came through loud and clear.

He stood by his letter to her: she knew how important duty
was to him. Doing things properly—even after having made a
mistake. She said nothing about forgiveness.

Perhaps the truth was she didn't care for him at all. How
could he have misread the signals so completely? Their warm
embrace was a brief diversion for her: that would explain why
her words were so cold.

He couldn't work out why he was so heartsick at the vehemence of her response. He was the one to make it clear they could never meet again. He should be glad she was in agreement.

Gradually he realized, deep down, he had hoped that somewhere, somehow, she would be part of his future. He leaned back in his canvas chair as images of Grace came to mind. Nothing in her behavior had suggested her caresses were carelessly given. His mind was flooded by memories of her: the softness of her mouth as she stood against that tree in the moonlight, his hand on her back when waltzing, her frown of determination when crossing the river in flood, her joyful kiss on his hand when told she could continue West.

This memory jerked him forward, as he recalled the unknown Mr. Sinclair waiting for her. She was married, for God's sake, even though she never spoke of him.

What was he like? He must have been exceptional for Grace to have given up her independence for him. She would have been very young when they wed. Tom was about, what, eight? They can't have seen each other for two years. Was Mr. Sinclair even alive? Life was hard for a pioneer, everyone knew that.

Randolph raked both hands through his hair as anger bubbled up inside, anger with himself. What if he had written a completely different letter? One that said he was prepared to wait, prepared to see if there really was a life for her in Oregon. Sure, he found words difficult, but he hadn't made any attempt to tell her how he truly felt. Truth was, she filled each waking moment, and most of his dreams. Perhaps he should have spoken on Saturday night, as they walked back in the moonlight. Yes, that would have been the moment.

Now he had sent that damn formal letter and Grace was angry with him in return. Of course she was. From her point of view, he had behaved like so many of his soldiers: seen an opportunity, given in to baser instincts, then tried to cover up what had happened as quickly as possible. Now it was too late to ever tell her the truth of how he felt.

THIRTY-SIX

The trail reached Snake River valley, where they swung west again. The sun beat down on the canvas, making the wagons as hot as ovens. Most people walked alongside the animal teams, but this was no better with the dust kicked up by the hooves, sometimes so thick they could barely see the wagon ahead. Dense sagebrush scratched the animals' legs and pulled at skirts and pants.

What made it worse was the sound of the Snake River roaring through the deep gorge to their right. It was impossible to drive the wagons close. Each evening, Gray Eagle led overlanders and soldiers as they rolled barrels down the steep banks, filled them with fresh water, and hauled them back up with ropes.

Tension was almost visible in the air; they were approaching land lived on by the Cayuse people. Relations had been strained to the limit over recent years as their hunting grounds had been taken by the new settlers. The major in charge of Fort Laramie had told Randolph about the skirmishes. The train would be safe once it reached Fort Boise, but as the darkest hour was just before the dawn, the most dangerous part of the journey would be just before they reached the protection of a frontier garrison.

Added to this, the overlanders were weakening; it was August, they had traveled for months, sometimes straight up and over the hills. Men dragged their feet as they walked beside their wagons, oxen's hooves bled from treading on sharp obsidian. Equipment needed repairs, cattle were bony from lack of grazing.

Perhaps only Turner knew Randolph well enough to notice a change in his behavior. The soldiers respected him, knew him to be stern but fair. He never said more than was necessary, so his silence was nothing new. Turner, however, saw a man distracted. Randolph was doing his job by rote, without his usual diligence and attention to detail. This could be fatal, given the dangerous land they were approaching, so he resolved to speak to his captain and friend.

Randolph lay on his camp bed, his jacket off but boots still on. A single oil lamp burned, and beside it a glass half filled with whiskey. There was a knock on the wooden pole and Turner entered.

"Alfred? Anything wrong?" Randolph asked, swinging his boots to the ground.

"Well, actually, yes. I think there is. May I sit down?"

"Of course. Pour yourself a drink. There's a glass over there, and maybe you could fill mine."

Turner put his hat on the table, topped Randolph's glass, and sat down, facing the camp bed. He leaned back, his tunic stretching over his stomach.

"So, what's troubling you?"

"You are, James," said Turner, smoothing his mustache with one hand. "You're troubling me. I've not seen you like this for a long time. In fact, not since the awful business with that silly Arabella girl."

Randolph took a sharp breath. "I don't know what you're damn well talking about."

"Something has happened. Something to change you. You're drinking more than usual." Turner nodded to the glass.

"You sound like my mother haranguing my father," Randolph muttered.

"And you've not been... engaging with the soldiers. They give you the regular reports, but you don't seem to hear them. You ask no questions."

The hairs prickled on Randolph's neck. This wasn't the usual diplomatic Alfred. "Are you doubting my leadership?"

"No, James, I'm sure you're able as ever. I wouldn't normally interfere. The men should be reliable by now. But we're entering Cayuse territory, we can't afford for you to be anything other than at your best."

"So, I'm not at my best?" he snapped.

Turner scratched at his whiskers, undoing all the smoothing of a moment ago. "To be honest, no, I don't think so."

How dare he speak to him like this, even as his closest friend. Didn't Alfred know how much was resting on his shoulders? "And what do you propose to do about it?"

"I... I don't know if I can do anything about it. Perhaps if I knew what was troubling you, I could help."

Randolph huffed. "No, Alfred, I don't think this is something you can help me with."

Turner leaned forward. "So, there is something amiss. Why not try me?"

Randolph grimaced. What was there to say? It was one of the oldest stories in the world: he had fallen for a woman, and it was hopeless.

He took a gulp of bourbon. "You know that speech I give the men before we start out? The one where I tell them what's expected of them. How honorable and disciplined our life in the army is."

"Yes."

Randolph held the glass but pointed a finger at Turner. "And then I go on about how these raw young privates should be careful of these pioneer girls. How they're looking for a good catch, how they'll reel them in, like a fish on a line, given half the chance. Well, my dear friend, I won't be giving that puffed-up speech again."

He swallowed another mouthful.

"You see, I'd never considered the possibility that it might be *good* for those privates to be caught by a pioneer girl. Maybe a loving wife and a houseful of children would be a fine thing. I mean, look at you and Eunice, look how happy you are."

"We don't have a houseful of children," Turner said, almost too quietly to hear.

Randolph gave him a chastened look. "No, Alfred, I'm sorry. That was stupid of me. But Eunice loves you, and she cares about you. What do I have? I'm gonna grow old and hard and angry." He looked at the empty glass in his hand. "Become one of those generals in those clubs back East, who sit up drinking all night, because they can't bear to go to an empty home, who talk endlessly about their battalion, because they have no real family."

"James, not all women are like Arabella. What about Flora at Fort Boise? And if she's not right for you, I'm sure if you looked, you would find many ladies who might make a fine wife."

"Many?" Randolph looked up. "It's not many. Just the one. And I *have* found her."

Turner sighed and looked like this was what he was afraid of. "But, James, we've talked of this at Devil's Gate. She's married already."

"Yes. She is married." Randolph got up and refilled both the glasses.

Turner took the glass and leaned forward, nearer to Randolph, an arm resting on each leg, holding the whiskey between them. "Has something happened?"

There was a silence as Randolph considered what to say. He wanted to share his burden because his feelings were eating him up, and this was the one man he could talk to.

"I don't know what to do, Alfred," Randolph whispered. He sat down on the camp bed. "You're right about my soldiering these last weeks. I hardly hear a word anyone says to me. I can't eat, because there's a sick feeling at the pit of my stomach."

He put the glass on the ground. It felt good to finally admit these things. Maybe it would be good to tell Alfred more.

"We met one night, by accident."

"Met?"

Randolph nodded. "It wasn't planned. I kissed her and, well, she kissed me back. She's not seen her husband for several years. It's not surprising she takes comfort elsewhere, it's human nature. But for me it was... it was like everything had been leading to that embrace."

Randolph swallowed hard. "I touched her hand and felt her wedding ring. Like a Bowie knife running through me. Reason came flooding back. I stopped. Think I may have even pushed her away. We walked back to the camp—we'd met in a wood, you see—and instead of telling her how sorry I was, how perfect she was, but that... I said nothing. Tongue-tied. By the next morning, my stupid, overblown sense of moral superiority rushed in. And guilt." He passed a hand over his face. "So I sent her a damned stupid, rude, pompous note, telling her it should never have happened."

He looked into Turner's face. "Now she's angry and hurt. Daresay she thinks I'm just like every other soldier who sees a chance to take advantage of a woman."

Turner leaned close enough to put a hand on Randolph's

shoulder. "I'm certain she does not see you like that. If you're so sure about her, then wait for her. James, this is a dreadful thing to say, but it's crossed your mind too: she may already be a widow. Why don't you tell her how you feel, and how serious your intentions are, should she become free? We've only got one life, my friend. We have to seize it."

Randolph's jaw tightened and his teeth pushed together. "I have considered doing that, even began to go find her once. But it's a crazy idea. I can't put that burden on her. It's just as likely the husband has set up a farm somewhere in the Dalles. She'll have to build a marriage again. At the moment, she can forget our embrace as a brief..."—he searched for the word— "aberration. It will have little meaning in the length of life. Me telling her how I feel, won't help when she picks up her life with this Mr. Sinclair."

"I swear I'm not tempting fate," Turner said, "but what if something happens in the next few years? Life can be dangerous for those frontier men."

Randolph leaned back on his bed and looked at the canvas above him. "Then fate will make sure I find out somehow, and I will ride up on a white horse, and put her on the saddle in front of me, and never let her go," he said with a wry smile.

Turner chuckled. "You're just the man to ride in on a charger and steal away your bride. You pretend all this discipline and order, but I know underneath there's a wild romantic." He stood up, arched his stiff back, and picked up his hat. "But in the meantime, James, I urge you to find that old steely soldier. The one who makes absurd speeches about the weaknesses of mankind. Because that's the soldier who will lead us through Cayuse territory if the going gets tough."

"Agreed," said Randolph. "I will do what I can."

He poured the remaining whiskey onto the dirt at his feet. "From tomorrow, you will see the old self. Just as rigid, despotic, and tyrannical as I used to be."

THIRTY-SEVEN

The Snake River escaped its high canyon walls and the valley opened, craggy mountains beyond. The river was wide, and Grace could see the islands in the middle which would ease their crossing. The overlanders and soldiers had crossed many rivers, big and small, but the Snake was dangerous.

Grace carefully stowed her belongings, making sure everything was secure. Tom had become a skilled horse rider over the months, and would be safest riding their mare. The goat would swim with the cattle when time came to drive them across.

She joined the line of wagons and carts. As she reached the front, Grace set her shoulders and whipped her mules into the fast-running water. They shied at first but then pulled forward to the first island, looking for safety. From there, it was a shorter distance to the next island, the mules following the wagon in front.

Once on the island, she could see Tom urging their horse onwards. He had been swept slightly downstream, but the horse was swimming to the far side. He reached shallow water and rested, before Tom urged the horse onto the bank. He turned and waved to Grace, who waved back, a metallic taste in her mouth from the relief flooding across her.

The last branch of the river was fast-flowing, so the wagons were roped in a chain, three at a time. Grace took her place behind the Hollingswoods and Eliots. The wagons plunged into the cold water, men on horseback guiding them onwards, oxen lowing in distress.

Halfway across, Grace could tell that the wheels were losing contact with the riverbed and the wagon was drifting downstream. How could she ever get control? What if she dragged the other wagons with her?

There was a sudden movement as the rope broke away from the wooden wagon tongue extended between her team. Dear God, she was going to get swept away! She cried out as loud as she could, desperate for help. Her arms were shaking as she grasped the reins. Someone shouted at her, but she could hear nothing over the sound of the water.

Gray Eagle splashed to her on horseback, and grabbed the harness, pulling the mules onward, calling to them in words that were strange to her ear. She thought of using the whip to help drive the team but did not dare leave hold of the leather straps connected to their backs.

She could have wept with relief as the wheels made contact with the bed once more, and gradually they reached the shallow water by the northern shore. Sergeant Knox pulled the mules onto the bank.

Grace climbed down from the driving bench, her legs still shaking and her skirt sopping. She put her hand up to Gray Eagle as he sat on his horse.

"Thank you, sir. From the bottom of my heart, thank you."

He looked straight at her, his face unreadable. He briefly touched her hand and wheeled his Paint horse away.

.   .   .

Grace and Tom were exhausted after the long day, and argued as they hauled their wagon into place for the night, having found a level patch of ground not far from the riverbank.

"No, you can't go play with Benjamin 'til we're done here," Grace said. "There are chores to be finished."

"But I'll do them later," the boy whined. "What's wrong with that?"

"It'll be too late, later."

"I'll be back way before nightfall."

Grace put her hands on her hips. "And what if you forget? Then I'll be left to do all your jobs. I thought we were a team. These things need drying out, the water fetching for tomorrow's journey. That canvas needs repairing and our mare needs a good rub down."

Tom dropped his shoulders, and spied up through the scruffy hair on his forehead. He looked just like Kane when the dog knew he'd done something bad. "What's wrong with leaving things undone, just for one day?"

"This is no time to get slapdash, Tom. We might need to move on at a moment's notice. You know it could turn dangerous here."

Tom kicked a wheel. "But it's not fair. None of the other boys my age do all these jobs."

She sighed. "It's tough for just the two of us. But we're going to make it to Oregon. I promised Pa we'd make it to Zachary."

Tom scowled up at Grace. "I didn't make no stupid promises. I can't even remember Zachary. I wish we'd stayed in Missouri, even though you killed that man."

"Tom! For God's sake, be quiet," cried Grace.

Tom's eyes were blazing, his hands held in fists. "Why should I? You can't tell me what to do!" And he turned and ran.

Grace went after him a few steps but was terrified of creating more of a scene.

She whirled round, her eyes scanning the area. Had anyone

heard? Please let no one be nearby. Thankfully, everyone seemed to be going about the business of setting up a new camp. She prayed to God no one had been listening.

Tom ran up the river. He was out of sight of the camp and his instincts told him it would be dangerous to go further. He'd stepped over the line but could see no way back. Tom collapsed on the bank and watched the Snake flowing in front of him. The water eddied around a rock in the middle and he flung a stone at it. The satisfying crack of stone on rock made him want to throw more. He threw another, angry and frustrated.

"Hey!"

Tom spun round to Sergeant Knox.

"You're not supposed to be out here," said the sergeant, his voice gruff. "What you doing?"

"What does it look like?" Tom hurled another stone with all his might.

"Don't get clever with me, boy. It's dangerous out here."

Tom dropped his head. "I'm sorry, sir."

"Now go on, back to the camp."

"I don't wanna go back, sir." Tom clenched his fists. "I'm sick of it."

The sergeant put his head to one side, and Tom felt himself being studied.

"Some of you kids have a tough time. I remember from when I was a boy." Knox dropped down next to him on the bank, looking out at the river. He picked up a couple of stones. "What is it, son?"

"This journey goes on for ever," Tom said.

"I don't know. We're nearly at Fort Boise. Less than a week, I'd say. Then one more push to Oregon."

"But it's nothing but work. Do this, do that." Tom threw another stone. "And Grace has been *horrible* for weeks. She never used to be moody. Just takes it out on me, telling me to do stuff. I mean, why should I take it? It's not as if she's my mother!"

Knox stopped mid-throw, then tossed the stone up and down in his palm.

"No, it's not right, is it?" Knox agreed, picking up more pebbles and weighing them in his hand to see which one would be best. "Boys should have time to themselves. She's no right to say all that. I mean she's... what? Your stepmother?"

Tom shook his head and frowned. He shouldn't be telling a soldier all this, but Grace made him *so* mad. "She's my sister," he said, stealing a look at Knox, who nodded slowly. "It's just us. Cholera took Pa and Ma last fall."

A long breath escaped Knox. "And... there's no Mr. Sinclair waiting at some pretty-looking smallholding in the Dalles?"

Tom looked up and wiped his nose with the back of his hand. "Oh, yep, that bit's true. Our elder brother. He's Mr. Sinclair. He moved out there some years back. You know, when folks first started going further West. We're going to settle with him."

Knox nodded slowly. "Well, that's... that's good. Good you've got somewhere to settle when you get there." He pushed himself up. "Come on, young Tom. Better make our way back."

Tom scrambled to his feet, and stood with his arms hanging slack at his side and endured the sergeant ruffling his hair.

"It's not for much longer. The journey. Life, well, it can be hard, but it'll make you strong."

"You won't say anything, will you?"

"I won't say a word to Mrs. Sinclair," Knox replied.

Tom wanted a wider promise but was too afraid of the sergeant to press him. He'd said far too much. What a blatherskite. He didn't know if the sergeant could be trusted. Thank goodness he hadn't mentioned what had happened in Independence. Then the game really would be up.

THIRTY-EIGHT

Captain Randolph gathered the six senior staff and Gray Eagle in the officers' mess tent. They sat around two trestle tables, most with a drink in hand. Knox slipped in last, nodded to Randolph, and took his seat.

"Gentlemen, we have made good progress on this expedition," Randolph began. "In normal circumstances, that would be cause for congratulations. However, it means we have reached this stage of the journey earlier than expected. As you know, things aren't as peaceable with the Natives as they once were. Major Williams will send a company out from Fort Boise to meet us, and escort our passage through this dangerous territory. But he won't be doing that for at least another week.

"So we have some choices. First, should we sit tight here, where it seems safer, for a while, then move forward?" Randolph looked round at his officers.

"Problem with that is supplies getting low," said Quartermaster Hooper. "Some overlanders are running low on food. The animals are getting scrawnier every day."

"I agree," said Randolph. "We could stop and let the

animals rest, but that would mean fewer rations to take us through the last part of the journey to Oregon City."

"So we head on, fast as we can?" suggested Corporal Flanagan.

"But then we don't have reinforcements through the Cayuse territory," said Turner.

The men were silent as they considered this conundrum.

Randolph cleared his throat. "What I propose, gentlemen, is that two experienced men go on ahead, travel day and night to reach the Fort, and alert them to our imminent arrival. It will be perilous. But two men on horseback will have a good chance of getting through. The rest of the train continues at its usual pace but on high alert."

There were muttered responses of agreement to this plan.

"However, we should take one day's rest," continued Randolph. "Allow the oxen and mules to recover, stock up on fish and wildlife, make repairs. Then we'll be ready for the push to Fort Boise."

Gray Eagle leaned forward. "I will go ahead."

Randolph nodded. "Good. I hoped you would volunteer. You know this land better than any of us. I want you to take Private Willard. He was a fur-trapper before signing up, and has experience of the Rockies."

The officers discussed details of the plan.

"Well, gentlemen," said Randolph, tapping the table, "anything else, or are we done?"

"I got some interesting information," said Knox, putting one elbow on the wooden table and fiddling with the mustache that framed his mouth. He smiled and Randolph thought he looked like the cat who'd got the cream.

"Well?"

"Our Mrs. Sinclair turns out to be nothing of the kind. We should be addressing her as *Miss* Sinclair." Knox took a sip of his whiskey and looked round at his audience, his smug grin revealing a missing lower tooth.

Randolph stared unblinking at Knox. *Miss* Sinclair? Impossible. She would have said something to him, surely.

Lieutenant Turner was the first to speak. "What the devil do you mean?"

"Turns out she's unmarried. And Tom? Well, he's her brother, not her son."

"I always thought she was young to have that boy," said Trinkhoff, hooking his thumbs under his braces. "Indeed, I think I remarked on it,"

"But... Mr. Sinclair?" Randolph was finally able to ask. His throat was dry and his voice not much more than a growl.

"Oh, yes, there's a Mr. Sinclair. And in Oregon. But not her husband, that's her older brother." He tapped the table with his forefinger to emphasize his point.

"How do you know all this?" asked Turner.

Knox leaned back and stretched his arms. "It was the boy. I came across him at the river, all tired and angry. After sitting with him, it came tumbling out."

"Did he tell you *why* they've been masquerading?" Turner continued to probe as Randolph failed to take the lead.

Knox laughed. "Sure, that's simple. They wanted to get the family together again. If they told the truth, the captain would never have let them travel."

The men looked at Randolph. A prickly heat rose up his body and his heart was thumping. There was silence for a while. Knox moved uncomfortably in his seat.

"So what happens now?" asked Moore.

Turner glanced at Randolph and quickly cut in, "No one does anything. Isn't that right, Captain? The information goes no further than the eight of us. This is just the sort of thing that would unsettle the camp."

Randolph nodded and the officers acknowledged this order.

"Nevertheless, I will speak to her," said Randolph, his words hard as a gun barrel.

Turner shifted so only Randolph could hear. "Do you think that is wise?"

"I need to know what in God's name is going on." Randolph turned his attention to the officers again. "But the lieutenant is right. We concentrate on getting through the Cayuse territory. We can't afford to be distracted by gossip. If any of you show by a word—even by a look—that you know the Sinclair woman is unwed, you will have to answer to me."

Randolph dismissed the officers, but Turner stayed on. Randolph pulled on his jacket.

"You're going now? Wouldn't it be better to sleep on it?" Turner asked.

"She put me through hell, Alfred," Randolph hissed as he buckled his holster. "I want to know why. Why didn't she tell me the truth, dammit, even after what happened between us? I need to understand."

He seized his hat and furiously marched out.

The sun had set behind the mountains and dusk was falling across the valley. Folk went about their business of preparing for the night.

Grace's wagon was on the edge of the camp. She always opted for as much privacy as possible and today had drawn up close to the Snake. After their earlier argument, she hadn't the heart to insist Tom did his chores and had sent him off to play with Benjamin at the Hollingswood wagon. She was brushing down her buckskin-colored mare, looking out over the river to the horizon, when she heard steps behind her.

"*Miss* Sinclair?"

Grace stopped mid-stroke. She paused, taking in the implication of those simple words, and recognizing a note of anger in the familiar deep voice.

Slowly turning round, she swallowed, as the captain's flinty eyes fixed on her from the shadow of the brim on his hat. "How did you find out?" she asked, softly.

"I had the unpleasant experience of being told of your true status by a junior officer. I understand your... *brother* confided in him. I've given strict orders the news goes no further. Assuming it's true."

Grace studied the horse brush in her hand. This was the result of their argument. She should've known this would happen. Tom had kept their secret for so long, but he was little more than a child and it was an unfair burden on him, and she couldn't blame him.

She looked back up at Randolph. His hands rested in his belt and his legs were apart, his boots firmly planted on the ground. He hadn't taken his eyes off her and she could think of nothing to say, nothing that would make this anything other than a dreadful revelation.

Thankfully, they were shielded from most of the camp by the wagon, but Randolph kept his voice low. "What I wonder," he began, his voice hard, "is whether I meant anything at all to you. You see, I feel quite a fool now. I thought I was, well, *something* to you. Turns out you were no better than other women I've known. I was just a passing whim. Who knows? Perhaps one of many."

Grace was stung by the insult. How could he suggest she had had attachments to other men? "Surely you don't think that of me?"

"Then why didn't you tell me you are unmarried?" A vein pulsed at his temple. "When I think of the pain I went through. All that guilt. Thinking I'd been dishonorable."

"I just... couldn't." She knew she was making things worse.

He folded his arms. "Not a good enough answer, Grace.

Not by a long shot. I need to understand. You owe me that much."

He was right, she did owe him an explanation. She closed her eyes and remembered what it had felt like back in April, being so desperate to leave. "It seemed the only way to get on the train. If I could bluff my way on, I would escape Independence. But I wanted to tell you, way back by the Sweetwater. Truly I did. And then when everything happened with Private Croup. You were so caring and gentle."

She turned away from him, reached up and absently disentangled a knot in the mare's mane. "But I couldn't risk it. And, to be honest, I didn't want to lose your regard. As I clearly have done now."

She remembered that night in the wood. Did he think she had followed him there? She needed him to understand.

"I never intended for us to meet that night. But when we did, it seemed as if it was *meant* to happen. Then your letter came and it was so cold and formal. And I realized I had been right not to tell you the truth." She turned back to him. "I thought you regretted everything."

Randolph removed his hat and tapped it on his thigh. He stared at her intently. "My regret was because I thought you weren't free. Surely you knew how I felt? Even before our kiss." He impatiently ran his hand through his hair. "Couldn't you tell that I... I thought about you, night and day?"

Grace found the courage to look up at him. "That's not what your letter said. And afterwards... these last weeks, you have been at pains to avoid me. To be fair, sir, I don't really know you."

"But did you *want* to know me?"

"Yes. Dearly. I would never have kissed you like that, had I not..." Why was she even talking like this, when she knew the barrier was not how she felt, or even how *he* felt? The barrier was what she had done in Independence. "But the bigger problem is, you don't know the first thing about me either."

The mare seemed to sense the tension and became restless. Randolph took the bridle to steady her but did not take his eyes off Grace. She felt the heat of his gaze, so she returned to the animal, pushing the sleeves of her dress back up her arms. She stole a glance at his face. The lines at the side of his eyes had softened, like that night in his tent.

He spoke more gently, his anger having subsided. "I know you are a brave, compassionate woman. The sort of woman I would feel proud to have at my side." He fiddled with the bridle and then looked back at her. "The sort of woman I would want as mother to my children."

Grace's heart beat so hard, it hurt. She shook her head, and swept the brush across the curves of the glossy flank. A moment ago, he had been furious with her. Surely he was not suggesting marriage. She must be mistaken.

The *sort* of woman, he'd said. Not the actual woman.

Before Grace could speak, she heard footsteps and a private approached, saluting smartly. "Sir, Corporal Moore requests your assistance with a matter."

Randolph turned sharply on him. "Can't you see I'm busy?"

"Yes, sir. No, sir. I'm sorry. But it seemed rather urgent."

The Adam's apple bobbed in Randolph's throat. "I'll be there in a minute. Dismissed."

The soldier retreated.

Randolph turned back and looked directly into Grace's eyes. Rising heat made her cheeks feel they were on fire.

He cleared his throat. "I have told you how I feel. And I am hoping, hidden inside, you have feelings for me too. Would you do me the honor of accepting my proposal?"

Grace felt the breath knocked out of her. So it *was* a marriage proposal. "Sir, you can't be serious!"

"Indeed I am. It's not a thing I would joke about, you know

that much about me." He stroked the mare's velvety soft muzzle, now avoiding looking at her. "But if I have mistaken the depth of your feelings toward me, then please say so, and accept my apologies for intruding on your time. As I said earlier..."—he shrugged—"perhaps I was a passing dalliance for you."

Grace brushed harder than necessary at a patch of mud. How could he propose to her and insult her in the same breath? Angry words escaped before she could catch them. "And I say again, you are mistaken. There is no one else. I am not the sort who would... I have never even kissed a man before. Not like we did."

Randolph looked out over the river, taking a moment to absorb her words. He turned back and hidden from the rest of the camp, put his hand over hers. "Grace, I know a proposal of marriage should be more romantically phrased. Unfortunately, I have become used to speaking in a direct way in the army, and expecting a response."

Grace pulled back her hand. She must stop this now. It was too painful to have the possibility of happiness before her, when she knew they could never be together. "Sir, I am able to give a response. I must say no."

Randolph frowned. "May I ask you to take more time to consider?"

She shook her head. "Time will not change things. I must refuse your offer."

Randolph breathed out heavily. "Would you at least do me the kindness of telling me your reason?"

The mare stamped the ground, and Grace put out a hand to soothe its neck. How could she tell him the truth? It was extraordinary that his love was strong enough to forgive the lies she had been telling him from the very first day. But if she told him the reason for those lies, no doubt his feelings would change.

She tried to speak firmly. "As I say, you do not know me. I

have done something that makes it impossible for us to be together."

He moved a step closer. "Dear Grace, tell me."

His closeness made her want to melt. "I can't... I am too ashamed to speak of it," she whispered.

"Surely it cannot be so great, that love can't overcome?"

She glanced up and saw pleading in his blue eyes. He was everything she could ever wish for and she knew she loved him deeply. More deeply than she had ever imagined loving a man. Perhaps she could say nothing, could keep it hidden. After all, only she, Tom, and Lillian knew the truth, and she was sure she could persuade Lillian to keep her secret.

But he deserved to know everything, even if a confession came with the danger that he would insist on taking her back to Independence. His sense of duty would make him feel obliged to force her to answer for her crime. But that would leave Tom defenseless, a ten-year-old unable to reach the only family he had left, the thing she had fought to avoid every day of this journey.

The sun glinted on his buckle as he moved slightly. She looked at the hair on the back of his strong hands and remembered him fixing the axle of their wagon. Then up to his face, the lines made by the sun and dirt, the kindness in his eyes. He was a good man, a caring man. He would never leave Tom vulnerable, she was sure of it. Her heart was heavy as she realized what she must do. "I will explain to you in a letter. Then you will know everything, and see why marriage is impossible."

"Very well. I hope to receive your letter as soon as you are able."

Randolph put on his hat and marched away. Grace returned to the mare and buried her face in its mane.

THIRTY-NINE

Grace wanted to write the letter immediately but decided she should not rush such an important step.

She slept fitfully through the night, pondering Randolph's words. Even though she knew she must refuse his proposal, it was astonishing that he wanted to marry her, this man who was so full of contradictions. He appeared to live only for the army, yet had spoken of marriage and children. He professed a low opinion of women, yet he had repeatedly shown her kindness and consideration.

In the small hours, she indulged herself thinking back through the long journey, to discover when her feelings for him were born, how they had grown. She had always admired his person, felt a carnal attraction to the man who strode out in the early-morning light, tall and determined. Then the rainy night when they had repaired the axle, and he had lain so close, she had watched his muscles flex. She had needed to lie closer to him, drawn like those magnets in her father's toolbox. His playful grin when he had rolled over her, their bodies touching. Yes, the captain knew the effect of his masculinity. But that was desire she had been feeling, a feminine response to a man's body at the peak of his powers. When he had agreed to let her continue the journey beyond Fort Laramie—was that the moment her heart had cracked open?

And his feelings? Perhaps they had begun during the plan to find Jane's attacker. The very idea of their posing as lovers had been dismissed by all as unbelievable. Yet here they were, a couple of months later, expressing the deepest feelings for each other. And, oh, his tenderness, how gently he had cared for her in his tent, the intimacy of his gift of the pillowcase.

She adored him, she loved him, she longed to say yes to him, to be Randolph's wife. But that could only happen if she kept the truth concealed.

Over and over, her thoughts came back to her final night in Independence and the bloody body of her attacker. Her heartbeat raced. One day, somewhere, someone would point her out in a crowd and cry, "There's the woman who shot Silas Boyd and left him for dead!" She was sure of it. The captain would have married a felon. If she really loved Randolph, she would never risk infecting him with such shame.

It was early dawn, and in the soft gray light, Grace quietly tore another page from the Bible and wrote in small script.

Dear Captain Randolph,

You have paid me the greatest honor and compliment possible with your proposal. However, as I said, we do not really know each other. There is something I have done which, had you known it, would have prevented the offer being made. Once you allow me to place before you a particular incident, you will understand that we could never be wed.

You asked last night why I had not told you the truth of being unmarried. I replied I was desperate to leave Independence, but you did not ask more.

My elder brother traveled to Oregon in '43, after some years of conflict with my father. Pa passed away in the fall. Before he died, he made me promise to tell Zachary that he regretted the rift, and to ask his forgiveness. More than that, Father made firearms and he wanted me to put his final invention—a pair of pistols—in the hands of my brother, in the hope he would continue the family business. One of those pistols proved to be my downfall.

I was left to protect Tom on my own. I saved what money I could and made preparations for the journey overland to Oregon. We would have waited in Independence until later in the season, and a wagon train that would take us—I mean with a leader with less stringent rules than yourself.

We had been staying in cheap lodgings to save money. The land-lord talked of payment in kind where necessary, and I understood this as cleaning and laundry work, which I undertook. On a couple of occasions, Silas Boyd, for that was his name, tried to take liberties, but I was able to avoid him, and simply endured his surly nature. But I kept a pistol loaded, in case I needed to warn him off.

The night before your train left, Boyd entered our lodgings with a spare key he had in his possession. He was very drunk and said my rent was late. I protested I had paid an advance, with the balance not due until the end of the month, but he demanded immediate payment. I offered what little coinage I could spare from our savings, but he insisted payment would be made through my person.

I defended myself, which made him more angry and determined. The pistols were lying on the table. I took one and pointed it at him. Still he would not leave. Instead, he approached, telling me I would not have the courage to shoot. I lowered the gun slightly and fired. The bullet lodged in his leg, but as he fell, I believe his head struck the stone hearth.

The sound of the shot must have roused Tom, because the next moment he was there beside me. I was scared and all I could think of was how to flee. I tried to tie the leg wound, and then packed, on the double. Boyd was still breathing when I left, but I have no idea whether he survived until morning.

I don't know how clearly you remember us on the day of depar-ture. I needed to get out of Independence quick as I could, so I let you believe there were two of us—Mr. Thomas Sinclair and myself—and I pretended to be married. Having left a man prob-ably for dead, just hours previously, it seemed a small step to lie about this.

I lay this before you to act as you see fit. I understand you may feel obliged to send me back to Independence to answer for my crime. But I beg you think of Tom, find some way to take him to his elder brother.

Now you know the truth about me, I am sure you will welcome the fact that I release you from your offer.

Faithfully yours,
Grace Sinclair.

It was bright morning by the time Grace finished her letter. She folded it over itself, which was difficult as some of the script was on both sides of the page. It was a rest day, so Grace looked for a chance to deliver her letter. She walked close to the soldiers' quarters during the morning but lost her nerve with the thought of meeting Randolph, and turned back.

. . .

At midday, Lieutenant Turner visited her. He clapped his hands. "So. How are you?"

"Well, thank you." Turner was looking at her intently. Then Grace realized: he was a close friend of the captain, he must know about the whole "Mrs. Sinclair" deceit. She dropped her eyes to the mending on her lap.

"I thought I would just pop by and see how things were going."

"Thank you." Grace could hardly speak, her throat was so tight.

Turner lowered himself onto a stool close by.

"I wanted to say that the captain sometimes gets things... well, out of proportion. He's sometimes angrier than he means to be."

Grace said nothing in reply.

"You shouldn't take everything he says to heart."

"What do you mean?' Grace asked. Was there a coded message? Perhaps he knew of the proposal, but was warning her it was an impulse to be ignored.

"Well, you know... he doesn't always say what he means."

"That has not been my experience of Captain Randolph." Grace measured her words carefully, although her pulse was running. "He strikes me as a man of few words, and those he says are considered."

Turner shuffled on his stool. "But what I mean, my dear, is, if he was angry with you, you shouldn't take it to heart. What you did—I mean, pretending to be married—wasn't so bad. It was even understandable, looked at from one way. I'm sure James will come round to see it in time."

So, Turner knew nothing of what had actually happened the night before. He assumed Randolph had spoken harshly to her, and was now giving her support in his big, kindhearted way. He spoke of "James," not the captain.

Grace looked up into Turner's face and he smiled at her.

"Well, I just thought I'd... well." He got up. "If there's anything I can do to help..."

Grace put her mending on the box and stood. "There is, if you would be so kind." She reached into her pocket. "I have a letter for him. I can trust you to..."

"Yes, of course." Turner took the letter and tucked it inside his jacket. "I'll give it to him directly."

The officers were about to sit for their lunch in the mess tent when Turner entered.

"James, could I have a quick word?"

"Yes, of course. In private?" Randolph sensed an awkward-ness in Turner's manner.

He nodded.

"Gentlemen, I will be detained for a moment. Please begin the meal without me."

Once inside Randolph's tent, Turner handed over the letter.

Randolph recognized the handwriting, and his chest tight-ened. "Do you know what it is about?"

"No, she just asked me to deliver it," Turner replied, and left.

Randolph sat at his field desk and unfolded the single sheet of thick paper covered with close handwriting. He read care-fully, trying to stop himself rushing ahead. Grace had raised a pistol, shot a man, and fled from the lodgings. He used a hand to knead the back of his neck. He didn't know what he was expecting in this letter, but, dear Lord, it wasn't that.

He went back over the letter a second time. She had lost her father and been alone looking after young Tom. He could see flashes of the determined woman he knew, making preparations for the journey so she could reunite what family was left. His beloved Grace had been so vulnerable. He knew the dross of the world that ended up in these frontier towns and how they would prey on a single woman. No wonder she kept a pistol loaded.

He had faced belligerent drunks himself, but they had always backed down in the knowledge they wouldn't get the better of him. He pictured Grace facing this man Boyd, how afraid she must have felt, when even the threat of a pistol did not make him stop.

Randolph sat back in his chair and a surge of compassion welled through him. If only he had been there to protect her. But he hadn't been there—she had to protect herself in the only way she could. And if she had stayed to face the authorities? Who would have believed her? The way of the world was always to believe the man's story over the woman. He uncomfortably acknowledged his own attitudes towards women at the beginning of this journey—until one woman had changed everything.

Grace believed he would welcome the release from his offer of marriage. Running his fingers over the characters she had penned, he found nothing to make him change his mind. But did Grace *wish* to release him from the proposal? At no time had she written she did *not* want to marry him. This long letter —it was more a confessional.

She had shifted her piece on the chessboard and now it was up to him to decide the next move. He took out a sheet of paper and wrote his response.

Just as he finished, there was a noise outside the tent. "James?" It was Turner's voice.

"Enter," said Randolph, folding his letter.

"I thought I might bring your meal to you." Turner held a plate with a wide bowl over the top.

"Thank you, yes, you can put it here."

Turner placed it on the table. "Is everything all right?"

"I... I'm really not sure." Randolph looked at Turner.

"Would you do something for me? Would you take a letter back?"

"If you wish. Do I wait for a reply?"

"No. There might not be one."

"I'll go now then."

Randolph sat alone, wondering what his fate would be.

FORTY

Grace was scrubbing clothes by the river when Turner approached.

"The captain asked me to deliver this," he said and immediately left.

Grace turned the paper over in her hand, not wanting to open it. Not only must it draw their relationship to an end, but her fate was in Randolph's hands.

She tucked the paper in her pocket and finished her task with even more vigor. She hefted the basket of wet clothes onto her hip, walked back to the wagon, and asked Tom to spread them out on the bushes to dry. She could put it off no longer, and climbed into the wagon for privacy.

His letter was longer than expected.

My dear Grace,

I have read your letter carefully, but I cannot agree that the dreadful actions in Independence prevent us becoming man and wife. Please allow me to explain.

I have been a soldier for some years and have tried to defend our young country as best I can. In the course of that service, I have sometimes—too many times—taken the life of another man.

As I see it, you have been faced with the same situation, albeit in a personal way. This man, Boyd, attacked you. Of course you defended yourself. What else could you have done? You had no choice. He decided to behave unlawfully, the consequences are his fault, not yours.

Far from making me want to give you up, your experience only increases my desire for us to be together. Had I been there to defend you, I would have taken exactly the same action you did. Please allow me to do my best to ensure nothing like this ever happens to you again. I want to protect you and keep you safe, to the best of my abilities, for the rest of my days.

I cannot tell from your letter if you have any further reason for not accepting my proposal. You say we do not really know each other. I think—I hope—you love me. If this is true, then please allow us to be together.

However, perhaps your reluctance is toward me personally. I know I have rough edges and may not be what a woman seeks in a husband. I am ashamed that even yesterday I insulted you with my careless words. If I do not receive a response to this letter by sundown, I shall assume these are the reasons for your refusal, and I assure you, I shall not trouble you further.

I remain your sincere and faithful servant,
James Randolph, Cpt.

Grace read the letter again more slowly, making sure she understood everything Randolph wrote. She found she was shaking, and for the first time, she allowed herself to see what had happened a different way, a soldier's way. Maybe Randolph was right and there was nothing else she could have done.

With the burden of her confession lifted, her spirit soared. By the good Lord above, he still wanted to marry her! He knew all, and believed they could be together.

She closed her eyes and pushed the letter to her chest, feeling her heart beat so strong, she thought she might burst. This was her moment to grasp happiness. In the middle of this wide continent, with danger all around—incredibly—she had fallen in love.

She longed to be with Randolph, to find out every detail of his life. She craved his touch, wanted to be held by him again, to feel his thick hair run through her fingers, breathe in his masculine scent, feel his lips on hers.

Grace grabbed her bonnet and climbed down from the wagon, feeling so light, she might float away. She would give her acceptance in person, and have the pleasure of seeing the effect on Randolph.

"I'll be back in a little while," she called to Tom, drawing her shawl around her.

At the soldiers' camp, she told the duty officer she wished to speak to the captain.

"I'm sorry, that will not be possible, ma'am," he said.

Grace's face fell. "Even for a moment?"

"The captain is not here. He's leading a scouting party for tomorrow's route. He'll be a few hours."

Grace's shoulders dropped and she pulled her bonnet forward to hide her face. Now she would have to screw up her courage all over again.

She returned to the wagon and picked at different chores, all the time trying to keep an eye on the officers' camp to look for his return.

. . .

It was late afternoon when the small scouting party rode back into camp. Once more, Grace walked over to the army tents.

"May I speak with the captain?" she asked.

Once more, she was rebuffed. "He's in a conference with the officers and cannot be disturbed."

A somber atmosphere had fallen over the army camp. Soldiers kept coming back and forth to the officer's mess, some carrying rolled-up maps.

"May I sit and wait awhile?" Grace asked.

"Might be a long wait, ma'am."

Grace sat on a log, wondering what to do for the best. She did not want to draw attention to herself by sitting outside for too long.

"I'll try a bit later," she said, and returned to her wagon with a heavier heart.

Lillian called by to return the tinderbox she had borrowed when George had mislaid theirs. "All sorted," she said.

"Where was yours?" Grace tucked the box inside the canvas bonnet.

"He'd shoved it into a boot last night to stay dry," Lillian said with a roll of the eyes. The women stood next to each other, leaning their backs on the wagon bed. "All a bit worrying, don't you think?"

"What is?"

"Mr. Hollingswood says the scouting party found signs that hostile Natives are nearby."

Grace was hardly listening; she kept her eyes on the mess tent. Then the captain appeared at the door, he stretched and looked around. Grace gathered her shawl once more.

"You must excuse me," she apologized to Lillian. But no sooner was Grace out of her wagon than Randolph was gone.

She must do something. What if he had been looking for her? He had wanted a response by sundown. She walked back to the army camp and went to Private O'Hara who was standing guard.

"Please could you pass a message to Captain Randolph?"

"He's very busy at the moment. Important things to consider."

"Yes, I know, but this is important too." She put her hand on his arm.

"Very well," he relented. "What is the message?"

Grace realized she had not written anything down. She must seize the moment.

"Tell him..." She thought for a moment. She needed something innocuous for general hearing but meaningful for Randolph. "Tell him the proposed changes to the domestic arrangements are acceptable."

She got O'Hara to repeat it back before allowing him to enter the mess tent. Her future happiness lay with this soldier giving the message correctly.

She returned to her wagon to wait.

FORTY-ONE

Inside the mess tent, the air was a fug of tobacco smoke, and the oil lamps spread a yellow haze. The scouting party had found a recently abandoned Cayuse camp nearby, and Randolph needed to decide whether to push on, or wait and hope for an escort from Fort Boise.

"Thieves and rogues," said Sergeant Knox. "Only thing they're good at is stealing horses."

"The impudence of these Indians," agreed the quartermaster, "asking folks to pay, just for crossing their land."

Randolph tapped his fingers on the map. "It bodes ill that the agreements aren't being honored. On either side."

"I am thinking it is safe to stay here," said Dr. Trinkhoff. "We can build up defenses in case of attack and wait until the escort reaches us."

"The problem is we have no guarantee the escort will arrive," said Turner. "Gray Eagle and Willard are good men, but how do we know they will reach the fort?"

Trinkhoff stuck to his guns. "Fort Boise is expecting us soon. Won't they be sending an escort anyway?"

"We're a week or more ahead of time," said Randolph. "The Fort might decide to wait it out longer. Maybe even a month."

"Do we have supplies for a month?" asked Sergeant Knox.

They looked at Hooper.

"Doubt it," the quartermaster shrugged. "The overlanders would need to slaughter stock for food."

"What's the point of traveling West, if you arrive with nothing," said Randolph.

"So we move on and take what may come?" asked Flanagan.

Randolph swept some cigar ash from the map. "I think so. It's better than being a sitting duck here. On balance, we should travel as fast as we can to Fort Boise. If there is a relief, they'll reach us sooner. And we can pray that the threat has been exaggerated. The tribes rarely want to provoke a battle, in my experience."

As they discussed the actions needed for swift progress, O'Hara entered the tent and skirted round behind Randolph.

"I have a message from Mrs. Sinclair," he said in a matter-of-fact tone.

Randolph turned round from the table to face the young man. "Yes?" He raised an eyebrow; he had been hoping for a response, but surely his most private business was not going to be played out in public.

"She says she can change the domestic arrangements."

"I'm sorry?" Randolph cocked his head.

O'Hara frowned and pursed his lips. "I guess she means the food or something? She can change it."

There was a message somewhere in there, he was sure of it, and he must not make the wrong interpretation. "Can you remember *exactly* what she said?"

"Yeah... the changes... No, the proposed changes to the domestic arrangements are possible... No, are acceptable. That's exactly her words." The boy smiled sheepishly. "She made me remember them."

Randolph bit his lip. "Thank you. Dismissed."

O'Hara saluted and returned to his post outside the door.

He caught the look of interest on Turner's face, and put a hand to his mouth to hide the smile creeping to his lips. Turner let out a slight noise, and Randolph could see the pieces falling into place.

Turner rose and poured two whiskeys. Taking one to Randolph, he whispered in his ear, "A celebratory drink may be in order, I think."

Randolph turned away from the officers to hide the wave of happiness that flowed over him. He had made the most momentous change to his life. Nothing would be the same again.

Composing himself, he pushed back his chair and stood up. "Right, gentlemen, time to return to your posts. We have an early start ahead of us. I'll do a quick round of the camp now to settle any nerves."

He took his hat and left the men behind.

The temperature had dropped sharply. The night sky was the dark blue of a military coat and the semicircle of the moon shone brightly. Most overlanders had gone to bed; a dog barked and oxen shuffled in their corral. Randolph went to a group round a fire, greeted them, and urged them to get some sleep before an early start. He checked one or two more tents.

Then he reached Grace's wagon on the edge of the camp, the one place he truly wanted to be. The canvas covers were tied down. Standing close to the back, he whispered her name.

In a moment, Grace pulled back one of the awnings. Wisps of her burnished hair escaped her braid, and she pulled her shawl over her cotton nightdress.

He stepped nearer and took her hand. Leaning upwards, he kissed her gently and then rested his forehead against hers.

"So you got my message," she whispered with a smile. "What do we do next?" She pulled back to look at him.

He held her chin and looked into her eyes. The dark brown irises were almost black in the moonlight, and his voice was husky as he said, "We marry at Fort Boise."

Her eyes widened. "So soon?"

"What is there to wait for?"

"Nothing, I guess. If you're sure."

He kissed her again, a long, lingering kiss. She smelt of lavender soap and woodsmoke. Her skin was as soft as the white boll on a cotton plant.

"It can't be too soon for me," he breathed. "But I'm afraid we need to keep this secret until then. The coming days will be difficult so I can't have soldiers or overlanders distracted by gossip. I don't know if I'll be able to speak to you privately, but be sure you are always in my thoughts. Promise you'll keep yourself safe."

"I will try my best."

He kissed her hands and reluctantly left. Never had reaching Fort Boise been so important to him.

FORTY-TWO

"Need a break from my own clan," Lillian said, climbing up beside Grace on her wagon bench. "I hope you don't mind."

The wagons moved out early, mist still hugging the ponderosa pine trees. Grace felt a warm ball of happiness inside her, and wondered if her face had given her away. Her friend must know some great event had taken place, just by looking at her. She longed to share her news but knew the engagement had to remain a secret, even from her closest friend. She had to wait until they were settled at Fort Boise.

"I'm guessing you didn't come here for an idle chat," Grace said, giving Lillian a friendly nudge.

"Well, no. That's true." Lillian looked serious for a moment, searching for words. "Some of the women were listening to the men talking. During the rest day. And they asked me to speak to you."

Grace's mouth felt dry, fearful the women knew of her relationship with the captain. How on earth had that happened? Perhaps they had been overheard. Now all hell would break loose.

"We all know we're going through dangerous territory,"

Lillian continued. "The men try to hide it from us, but we know what's what and there's no point treating us like kids."

Grace was relieved Lillian was not talking about the captain but bewildered by what she was saying.

Lillian shifted her seat. "Some of the women feel... vulnerable. I mean, we're all afraid, but it's made worse by not feeling able to defend ourselves. I'm here to ask for your help."

"But what help could I give?" Grace asked in amazement.

"You're the only woman on this train who *really* knows firearms. You know how to shoot them, handle them, load them. My George says you're a better shot than most men here."

"But I don't understand. The soldiers will protect us, our menfolk will do everything possible."

Lillian shrugged. "We want you to help us... well, to help ourselves."

Grace's eyes opened wide. "You mean to use the guns?"

"Yes, that's what we thought."

"But that takes time. It's not something I can show someone in a moment. And guns are dangerous if you get them wrong."

"Grace, think what it's like for us other women. We could be attacked at any moment. The soldiers, they're all trained, they'll each have their role. And our men, they're ready to defend us. But us women, what will we do, other than cower in a corner?"

"You'll keep the children safe," said Grace, giving the reins a slap to move the mule team onward.

"Yes, we will. And we will do that with the last breath in our bodies." Lilian turned to Grace. "But some of us would like to do more than prayers and wishes. We'd like to be able to defend the children. And ourselves."

Lillian spoke with such strength and passion, Grace was completely wrong-footed. "I'll need some time to think about this," she said, her eyes fixed on the mules' backs in front of her.

"Well, hon, time is something we ain't got," Lillian said. "We don't know when danger might strike."

Grace had hardly given the Cayuse a thought. She had been so wrapped up in her own story, she had not noticed anything else. The tense atmosphere of the camp had seemed nothing compared with her own anxiety. She had watched the soldiers return from scouting but looked only to see Randolph; she had given no heed to the significance of their task. And then her own elation had blotted out all fear of attack.

But surely Lillian was exaggerating the threat. While Randolph was their protector, no one would dare attack.

How foolish this notion was. Randolph's own last words had been about keeping safe should the worst happen. With a shock, Grace saw the desperate seriousness with which he viewed the threat.

Which meant Lillian was right: the women were horribly unprepared. The men would each have a job to do. The women would sit and wait and hope, fear cutting into them like a knife.

"How many women?" Grace asked. "How many are you speaking for?"

"There's four of us."

"And what of the other women? Would they wish to learn?"

"I'm not sure," Lillian said. "One or two might be handy already. Particularly the ones who grew up on farms. And others would be too afraid. As you said: guns, they're dangerous things."

"If you're right, and those women are the most timid, then they would suffer even more deeply under attack."

"You wanna try teach *all* the women?"

"No. But..." Grace chewed her lip. "Take the reins. I need to get something."

She climbed into the bed of the wagon and found her pen and ink, and her Bible.

Scrambling back to Lillian, she asked, "How many women are there? Counting everyone, I mean."

"Why, 'bout thirty, I would guess."

"I want you to name each one of them."

Lillian did as asked and Grace wrote down the initials on the edge of the Bible frontispiece. She counted the list. "Now, that's twenty-nine women. And how many children?"

"I included some of the older girls already. I'd say 'bout thirty-five children."

"And who are the women who have spoken to you?"

Lillian gave the names of the three other women, and Grace put a mark by their initials. She was surprised that Betty Eliot was among them. Perhaps the journey had changed her mouse-like timidity, and the attack on Jane had made her more determined to be able to defend her two daughters.

Grace looked at her list again, and quietly put marks by the names of other women, thinking of each one and their character. Some she hardly knew and had to ask Lillian.

"And Mary Corn? What's she like?"

"Sensible enough woman," Lillian replied.

"Good with children?"

"I don't know. She doesn't have her own."

Grace made a mark and moved on.

By the time she finished, the wagons were slowing down for their midmorning break. "Now, Lillian, we haven't much time. The captain will move on as soon as the animals are fed and watered. Please ask your friends to come to my wagon at the noontime rest, soon as they're free. We need to talk about this."

Lillian climbed down. "Wouldn't it be better if we met at my wagon? We don't want to draw attention to ourselves."

"Yes, that's a fine idea."

.   .   .

That lunchtime, Tom helped Grace to quickly water her team, the mare, and goat. She tucked a johnnycake and some dried beef into her apron pocket, and went to the Hollingswood wagon.

Inside, two women were already there with Lilian: Betty Eliot and Harriet Long. They were joined by Hanna Gingham, whose husband had accompanied Grace hunting all those months ago.

"Ladies, time is against us," said Grace. "So I will talk plainly. Lillian has told me of your wish to learn about firearms and I will show you the basics. But I think there is much more we can do.

"All of us are afraid of what might befall the train, but no one has thought what we can do to help. I propose we divide the women into three tasks. The first group is yourselves, who wish to help the men fight." Glancing round, Grace saw all eyes fixed on her. "Then we need a group of women who are willing and able to help the injured. If there is an attack, you can be sure there'll be casualties."

"Sounds sensible," said Lillian, patting a finger against her lips. "And the third group?"

"They'll look after the children; keep them together, calm, and cheerful." Grace picked up the scrap of paper torn from her Bible. "I've made a list of each woman and what group she would be best in. I propose we ask Mrs. Turner to be in charge of the medical group. She's traveled with the army before, she must've seen wounds at some time. Mrs. Perriman should look after the children. She was a teacher and will know what to do."

"But what if they don't want to help?" Betty asked, nervously picking at her apron.

"Of course, they're under no obligation," Grace said. "But I think any of us would be better with a clear task, should the worst come. It is up to each of you to convince them." She turned to Harriet. "You know Mrs. Perriman well, do you not?"

Harriet nodded in response.

"Talk to her this afternoon. Explain what is needed. Should the attack happen, her group of women must gather the children in the safest place. Comfort them with songs, little games. She must plan now, because if faced with hostiles, we will all be too far out of our wits to think clearly."

Harriet shuddered for a moment but agreed to take on this task.

"And, Lillian, you're best to speak to Eunice Turner. She may be anxious about stepping over the mark, having lived with the army so long. Be persuasive."

Lilian smiled and gave a brief mock-salute. "I'll do my best."

"We can all help right now. Look." Grace brought out a cotton petticoat wrapped in a bundle. "We will need bandages and we will not have time to make them should we come under attack. So..." She got out her sewing scissors and made a small cut, ripping the petticoat in two.

"But that was such a pretty petticoat!" gasped Betty. She blinked her mouselike eyes.

"And I shall manage with one less. Each of us must."

"But what if we don't get attacked? Then we'll have ripped our underwear for nothing." Betty smoothed her skirt as if trying to protect her petticoat from those scissors.

"If we don't get attacked, then I will praise the Fates and be grateful," said Grace. "But if we are, then I will be glad to have done what I could."

She made another small cut near the edge. Harriet picked up the fabric and, with one swift arm movement, tore it into a bandage.

"What about the four of us?" Harriet asked.

"I'll teach you to reload a musket with bullets. That's what slows things down. You can leave the men to take aim. Betty and Hanna, you two travel with me in my wagon for the beginning of the afternoon, and then Lillian and Harriet."

The women looked at each other. There was a frisson of excitement; at last, they would be able to *do* something.

A bugle sounded to signal that the train would be moving on soon.

"One more thing," said Grace, putting out her hand to stop them leaving. "We need to be quiet and calm about this. If we go flurrying about like chickens, we will simply cause more anxiety. In fact, we should avoid letting the men know of our preparations. They would be sure to try to prevent us. And the army would be angry as a pack of coyotes if they knew you were learning about firearms."

She wasn't thinking so much of the army, as of Randolph. He would be furious if he knew what they were doing. This was a dreadful start to their engagement; already she was going against him. But she could not deny her friends when they had asked for her help, and everyone—including Tom—would have a little more protection.

"And might they try to prevent us, even if an attack happens?" asked Betty.

Grace gently put her hand on Betty's arm. "Let's still hope and pray it doesn't come to that."

"But if it does?" Betty's voice was almost a squeak.

"It's my guess that everyone will be so hard-pressed, they will be glad to have any help possible."

In the general activity of moving on, no one noticed five women climbing from the Hollingswood wagon. Lillian went off to travel with Mrs. Turner, Harriet to find Mrs. Perriman. Betty and Hanna went to their families to make their excuses before returning to Grace's wagon.

Tom sat on the front bench, his chin up and back straight, holding the reins as the wagon swayed back and forth. Grace had told Tom over breakfast that she knew he had confided in

Sergeant Knox but that she hoped their news would not fly around the whole camp. For now, their pretense was to continue. Tom had apologized and they had hugged each other. "Things will get better," Grace had whispered. After lunch she had then explained her plans with the women. Now Tom wanted to do all he could to make amends and help.

Under the canvas, Grace uncovered her father's rifle and placed it before Betty and Hanna, alongside the neat wooden case.

"This was my pa's best rifle. He designed and made it, and you won't find better."

"And in the case?"

"That's a pair of pistols. Again, handmade."

"But you mentioned muskets."

Grace nodded. "The soldiers use the Springfield musket with round balls, but I'll have to use the rifle for us to practice the moves. Now, listen as I name the parts."

She talked them through the lock, barrel, trigger, and stock.

"Now, you stand the musket upwards and take the barrel in your left hand like this. Then take the cartridge and tear it open. My pa would do this with his teeth. We haven't got anything to practice with, I'm afraid. And as we're new to this, it might be best for one lady to tear open the cartridge while the other sets up the musket. Now imagine pouring the contents of the cartridge into the barrel, and then the lead ball." Grace mimed the actions. "Draw out the rammer and ram the cartridge and ball firmly into the base of the barrel. Like this. Then give the musket to the soldier. He'll prime the cap to ignite the gunpowder. So, ladies, let's practice as far as we can without cartridges."

She took Betty and Hanna through the actions of loading the gun, time after time.

"Remember," she said, "if you ever need to do this, it will be under fire, with noise and chaos. You'll feel scared, so really concentrate."

"What about firing it, Grace?" Hanna asked.

"You'll be more use making sure the men have guns to fire quickly."

Hanna had a stubborn look on her face. "I want to be able to protect myself from those savages."

Grace thought about the Sioux women and children they'd seen living around Fort Laramie. They didn't look like savages. Nor had the family groups they had sometimes encountered on the journey; they had traded fish and buffalo, treated them kindly when the overlanders were in desperate need. She thought of Randolph's admiration for Gray Eagle, a Lakota who had guided them.

This journey had brought her closer to their land, to understanding the challenge of surviving all its hostile contrasts. They seemed to have mastered it while the white folks struggled against it. She didn't understand why there was so much fear of the Cayuse, and why now. But savages? She didn't think so.

"Ladies, I'm sorry, aiming at a man and actually pulling the trigger: that's not something you want to do. It's something that stays with you." Even now she felt a little sick at the memory.

The wagon slowed up and stopped. It was the afternoon break.

"We shouldn't think on such things," Grace said, feeling the oppressive heat under the canvas. She patted Betty's arm. "We're gonna be fine. We'll be riding into Fort Boise before you know it."

Betty and Hanna stepped down from the wagon.

Lillian and Harriet took their places under the canvas bonnet as the train moved on and Grace began her explanations once more.

"What did Mrs. Turner say?" she asked Lillian as they began to practice.

"She was rather taken aback to begin. Said the military would sort all that stuff. But I said Dr. Trinkhoff might not be able to manage with just a couple of orderlies—a few women could do a lot of good. I think it was the mention of Dr. Trinkhoff that changed her mind. He's half-drunk much of the time—who knows what he'd be like under fire."

"So she agreed?"

"It took a bit more persuasion, but, yes, she'll do it."

"And Mrs. Perriman?"

"That was much easier," said Harriet. "She loves to be needed—even more to be in charge. She could picture herself as some saintly woman protecting these children, singing in the face of danger."

"Well, good. That's exactly what we'll need. She'll organize the other ladies. And they'll both keep this quiet? I mean, some of the men might be alarmed, and we don't want to set prairie rabbits running."

"They'll be discreet."

The two women continued practicing loading the guns until the wagons slowed up for the evening camp.

FORTY-THREE

As the army tents were being set up, Randolph slipped away to grab a quiet word with Grace as she took her mules for water. "I need to see you. I'll come to your wagon during my evening check."

Her pulse quickened, but she shook her head. "No."

Randolph frowned.

"I want more than a few stolen words, afraid that Tom might hear," Grace said. "I beg you, can we meet properly?"

Randolph scratched the back of his neck. "I don't see how—"

"Meet me in those pines beyond the camp. It will be like the night after the dance. I have something I need to give to you."

Randolph nodded. "Very well. See that larger tree? I'll wait for you there, after my rounds."

Grace put a burlap bag over her shoulder and wrapped her shawl tight. It was a cold night, scattered with stars. She picked her way through the pines, aware of every animal cry, every breath of air through the trees. Her stomach turned over: there was Randolph, waiting for her, tall and still, his familiar stance, his hat hiding his face. She slipped her bag to the ground.

He took her hands and gently kissed them. "I need to make things clear with you." His voice was husky near her ear. "Tomorrow, we cross the river plain between the low ridge of mountains to the southwest and the Rockies to the northeast. This is Cayuse land and they know how to make the most of it. If they attack, it will be there."

Grace looked up into Randolph's face and could see the strain in the tiny lines around his eyes. "Then why not wait for the men from Fort Boise?"

"Troops may be here tomorrow. Or they may take weeks. I have no way of knowing. Gray Eagle told me the Gathering is soon, when the Native people move south through this area from their northern lands. The longer we wait, the more we may have to face. I want to get through without bloodshed."

She shook her head. "Don't speak this way."

He hugged her to his chest, his body warming hers. "I do not mean to upset you. Because if we live, I plan to wed you as soon as we reach Fort Boise."

They stood in silence for a moment and then Grace pulled away.

"I have something for you," she said. "Shall we sit?"

He dropped his hat beside the bag, and shook off his blue jacket, laying it across the smooth carpet of pine needles. The moonlight made his white shirt shimmer in contrast with his dark hair. Grace swung her shawl from her shoulders and Randolph spread it across the ground.

She sat and opened her bag, pulling out a flat box. "These were my father's and I want you to have one."

He sat beside her, one leg extended, and unclipped the box. Inside was the pair of exquisitely fashioned pistols. He weighed one in his hand. "It's heavier than I'm used to."

"You will not find a truer aim," Grace said. "My father and

grandfather were both gunsmiths. They labored long hours to make new rifles and pistols. It has a revolving cylinder so you will be able to make six shots without reloading. You'll find this more powerful than any other pistol you have used."

She ran her hand over the remaining gun. The name Sinclair was engraved on the barrel. "It was my father's dream to make our name and fortune with these pistols. He wanted my brother to follow him in the business. Before Pa died, I made a solemn promise to get these pistols to my brother, somehow."

She closed the box.

"Thank you. I shall keep it with me tomorrow."

Putting the gun on top of the case, he leaned over and kissed her lips, his arm on the ground behind her.

She put her hands behind his neck to draw him closer. Her lips parted as his tongue explored her mouth. The heat inside grew stronger, a tingling through her body. She stopped kissing and put her brow to his.

"I want you to know," he whispered, "tonight and forever, how special you are to me. When I began this journey, I was alone and full of anger. Now I see how pompous and stupid I was. You have changed me. So if tomorrow it is my time to... if it is my time... you have made my life complete."

She paused, knowing there was something she dearly wanted to ask of him, but being unsure of the words, and fearful of his response. "You say I have made your life complete," she said. "But there is something I want you to do to make *my* life complete."

He placed delicate kisses down the side of her neck. "Anything," he breathed.

"I want you to take me. I mean... now. As a woman. As a wife." She knew what she wanted but struggled to put it into words.

He stopped and swallowed as he looked at her.

"James, I don't want to wait until Fort Boise."

"You mean—?"

She pulled away and crossed her arms in front of her, rubbing her upper arms. "Please do not think less of me. The world is a dangerous place. I want to live to the full. Today. Not waiting until tomorrow."

"I don't think less of you. But are you sure?"

She nodded. "I know what I'm asking of you."

He smiled. "It's more what you are giving me."

"And it is something you want?"

As an answer, he spread her shawl further. She felt a flutter in her belly, part fear and part longing. Lying back, she smelt the mulch that made the earth soft. Randolph lay beside her, leaning on one elbow so he could study her face.

He took a tendril of hair in his fingers. "I'm never quite sure what color your hair is. Sometimes, like now, it looks rich and dark as coffee. Then sometimes, on the trail, the sun will strike it and it seems there is honey running through it."

He put his face in her hair to breathe in the aroma, then inched his lips along the line of her chin.

Her heart beating faster, Grace undid the small buttons of her dress, one by one, and unclipped the split-busk at the front of her corset.

Randolph pushed her cotton chemise to reveal her shoulders and traced a finger over her pale skin, leaning down to kiss the dip between her collarbones. Even with the cold night air, her skin was on fire, a deep need burning inside her.

He sat back to tug off his boots, tossing them in a pile, then swept his shirt over his head in a single movement. Grace gazed on the muscles, honed taut by the daily physical work. She tentatively touched the dark curly hair that spread across his chest, and let her fingers trace the darkness down to where the hair disappeared below his belt. She unthreaded the leather strap but struggled to undo the clasp. Randolph grinned and helped undo the belt, then unbuttoned and slowly slid off his pants.

He lay down close once more, the full length of her body, looking into her eyes. "And you are sure?" he whispered.

Grace bit her lip and nodded. Her desire for him was unlike anything she had ever felt before.

His mouth grazed over her shoulders once more and toward her breasts, planting kisses as light as feathers. His hands moved downwards, pushing back the dress and then the petticoats, her underwear, caressing the curve of her rear, the inside of her thigh. Their legs entwined, each responding to the needs of the other, his arousal hard against her leg. Her breathing tightened as his hands explored further, encouraged by the slight moans of pleasure that escaped her.

He moved above her, gently parting her legs. She tensed her fists, uncertain of what would happen next, apprehensive, yet yearning to be one with him. He gently entered her, but a sharp intense pain made her gasp.

Randolph paused and looked at her questioningly, seeking reassurance whether to continue. But she pulled him to her, fingers reaching into his dark hair. His lips were on her mouth, his tongue exploring, and she closed her eyes, taking in his taste, his smell.

The initial pain forgotten, she responded to his rhythm, arching her back, pleasure flooding her body, feeling his warm breath on her face. Her muted cries mixed with his animal growls as the whole of her body tensed and then unwound. Randolph held her closer, his chest taut and hard as he climaxed and rested his forehead on hers, gasping for breath.

Both of them spent, he rolled to lie beside her, one arm across her waist, the other beneath her head. She felt complete, even joyful. She was unified with this man for the rest of time. Looking up through the trees, she watched the blue-gray clouds rushing across the moonlit sky. All the colors seemed so bright.

She felt strangely detached from the world, as if she were floating close to the stars.

Grace closed her eyes, and breathed in the scent of the man beside her. She stroked the cluster of muscles on his forearms.

A coyote howl reminded them that time was passing. Randolph raised himself on one elbow again and kissed her forehead, her nose, her lips.

"We'd better get back," he said.

They were the first words for some time.

He tugged on his pants, his boots, and drew his shirt over his head.

Suddenly feeling cold, Grace pulled her skirts straight and sat to hook up her corset and button her dress.

Randolph stood and buckled his belt. The movement was familiar—then she remembered: the dawn when she had disturbed his shaving. She realized each one of his movements—his dressing and undressing, the way he brushed his hair, whether he slept on his back or his front—would become familiar to her once they were married. And hers to him; he would come to know her better than anyone on earth. A warmth spread from within until it filled her chest. So this was love: a willingness to trust, to be open to whatever he brought her. In a life full of striving, she finally felt safe and secure.

He reached down a hand to help her stand and then swept up the shawl, shaking it free of pine needles, before tenderly spreading it round her shoulders. He retrieved his jacket and brushed the leaves from it before shrugging it back on.

Grace handed him the pistol and he tucked it into the back of his belt. He took her hand and they made their way back in silence, reaching her wagon at the edge of camp.

"Tomorrow evening," whispered Grace, "we will meet again, I promise you."

FORTY-FOUR

The captain ordered everyone to rise before dawn. Dew drenched his boots as he walked through the camp, tapping the sides of wagons. People spoke in low voices, the still air pierced by tin cutlery clattering on breakfast mess bowls. Men fetched the cattle that had wandered off in the night.

Randolph led the departure, mist still hanging over the wide pass between the mountains before them. He rode at the head of the train, the Snake River to his left. Next came the wagons, but today they were flanked, not by overlanders, but by soldiers, each with a gun at the ready. Children who were used to running alongside were safely under canvas. Pioneer men sat bolt upright, reins in hand, making sure the oxen kept a steady pace. At the back of the train, the cattle were hurried along by soldiers riding in formation.

Randolph set off at a brisk rate to make progress early in the day. Beyond was Fort Boise, perhaps just one day's travel away. To the northeast, a single line of smoke floated into the pale blue sky: the Cayuse encampment. He kept his eyes on the horizon. He didn't want to create fear by appearing constantly watchful, but he scanned to his right, looking for signs of the

Cayuse in the north, then to the northwest in front of him, where their destination lay. For the hundredth time, he wondered if Gray Eagle and Willard had reached the fort. Then there'd be a company of cavalry riding out to join them. But there was no way of knowing.

At midmorning, they stopped by the river, long enough for the animals to drink, before pushing on quickly. At noon, with the sun high above, Randolph spotted movement in the hills to his right. He raised his field glasses: a group of Cayuse riding toward them. Not the vast crowd he had seen in earlier army days, but there could be more behind.

He gauged the distance in front: they had several more hours' riding ahead of them. No way they could cross the valley before the Cayuse caught up. He made a hard decision: they must stand and defend themselves.

Ahead lay a flatter area by the river, a position that would give them protection, a loop in the river where they could corral the cattle and horses. Randolph called the bugler to sound a rapid advance, praying they would get there in time.

The overlanders looked to the horizon to see the danger. Mules brayed as they bolted forward, leather straps striking their backs. The oxen lumbered onwards. They reached the river and Randolph ordered the wagons and carts to form a barrier.

Each soldier knew his place. They pushed crates which had held supplies between the wheels to provide cover. Three wagons were hauled into the center, where women and children gathered, as the men built up the defense.

Still mounted, Randolph directed his men. Horses and cattle were driven to the riverside. If more Cayuse braves joined their brothers and they were overwhelmed, then the women and children might escape on horseback over the river.

Randolph assessed the advantage of their position. The Cayuse could not spread their attack around the whole camp, so the soldiers could concentrate their defense. Nevertheless, Randolph gave orders to the small group of men crouched behind the wagons by the riverside to stand firm, and be ready for any hostiles who might try their luck at this weaker point.

He quickly scanned the group of women for Grace but could not see her. He shook himself; he had to trust that she was safe and his duty now was elsewhere.

Grace's pulse raced as she grasped her rifle, and tucked her father's remaining pistol into her belt, the twin of the one she had given to Randolph. The best thing was to keep low: it would be hard for a man to fight, knowing a loved one was nearby. Randolph's mind must be completely on the battle ahead; he must not be distracted by seeing her in danger.

Keeping Tom by her side, she drew together the four women of her troop. "Remember, do not rush to assist quite yet," she said. "Wait until the battle starts and watch carefully. When a man falls or falters, that is the moment to move forward and assist with the ammunition. In the heat of gunfire, they will be relieved to be handed a loaded musket."

The women embraced, Lillian with tears in her eyes.

"Courage, my ladies," Grace cried, hoping she was hiding her fear inside.

She could not help but admire Mrs. Perriman as she gathered the children and started an action song to absorb the little ones' attention.

Giving her shotgun to Tom, Grace rolled a water butt to Eunice Turner, who had cleared two supply wagons to make space to lay down the injured. Other women found whatever fluid they could: water to clean wounds, strong spirits to ease pain. Sarah Eliot gathered bandages and extra linen in readiness. Dr. Trinkhoff glanced at Grace in bafflement at all this activity around him, as he set out his two black leather cases of instruments and remedies. He turned to remonstrate with Mrs. Turner, and she nodded her head, patted his arm, and quietly continued preparing the space.

Grace could see the cloud of dust beyond the wagons, raised by the hooves of the horses. She crouched out of sight and her heart contracted as she heard Randolph shout to his troop.

"Keep your nerve, men. Make each bullet count. We will come through this. God be with you."

Dear Lord, she silently prayed, *you can do as you want with me, but please, please keep him safe.*

The ground shook as horses thundered closer to the wall of wagons. The braves raised a yelping and screaming that made Grace shiver in terror.

Randolph's voice rang out as he gave the order to fire.

Grace crawled forward to peep through the spokes of a wheel. Horses in the vanguard reared up, screeching at a high pitch when struck; others instinctively turned away from the danger. As the first attackers fell, those behind pulled up and veered to the left. There was a brief lull before the horses bore down once more. The previous line of braves had fallen some distance from the wagons, but this time the attackers got closer before being repelled.

Grace watched, appalled. She knew she should move to safety, should be doing something useful, but she was paralyzed, hidden behind the wheel. The Cayuse were brave and deter-mined; another wave came, this time reaching closer to the line of defense. Those thrown from their horses crept toward the wagons, and Grace prayed the soldiers would pick them off. Mostly, the Cayuse brandished their traditional weapons. Some had guns, however—more guns than Grace had expected. Fear-less Cayuse fought right up to the wagons, where Grace could see them clearly, see the damage the soldiers' bullets did to human flesh.

A woman screamed behind her, and Grace finally

wrenched her body away. She turned to find Tom had remained by her side, and was ashamed she had allowed him to witness the carnage. The Perriman wagon was rocking side to side, until suddenly it fell with a crash, as wood splintered and the metal wheel tire broke.

Three warriors broke through the gap they had made, so some soldiers who had been watching the riverside rushed toward them. The Cayuse were quickly cut down, their blood turning the dust into scarlet mud. A boy and girl stared, wide-eyed and clutching at each other. Grace grabbed their hands and dragged them to where Mrs. Perriman had gathered the children.

She stood in the center of the corral, the noise throbbing in her ears as she looked around in bewilderment. The battle was like a river in flood, the water rising higher, swirling, the bank beginning to fall. As a farmer will hurriedly repair the bank with more sand and soil, so the soldiers rushed to dam up the breach of any gaps in their defense. The line was once more complete, and fading sounds suggested the Cayuse had withdrawn.

In the pause, a soldier cried out close by. Calling to Tom, he and Grace each hooked under the man's arms and found an unexpected strength to drag the soldier to Dr. Trinkhoff's wagon. Grace looked at her hands, covered in the man's blood, her nostrils filled with the smell of wet iron. She shivered with the memory of that night in Independence.

The juddering beneath her feet warned her that the Cayuse were bearing down on them again. Grace looked around, close to despair, terrified for James, somewhere in the middle of this. She saw Lillian gathering weapons from where they had fallen and standing them ready for reuse. Lillian had not panicked, she had not been overwhelmed by a fear so strong it made her nauseous. Grace needed to live up to the faith put in her by her friends.

Soldiers and overlanders crouched behind the wagons and on top of carts. Fewer men defended the riverside: those who had moved to fend off the Cayuse who had broken through the wagons had not returned to their posts. Perhaps the desire to be in the thick of things had gotten the better of them: only a cowardly soldier would move back to the quieter place.

But didn't those soldiers know a chain is only as strong as its weakest link? It wouldn't take long for the Cayuse to notice this weakness. Thank heavens, Sergeant Knox spotted the gap and ran to join them, shouting orders that men and soldiers must not abandon their positions by the river.

Grace could hear the new attack begin, and sensed the soldiers flex to defend their line once more. Over Knox's shoulder, her eye was caught by a movement upriver: a narrow canoe came around the bend with six braves paddling fast. Then a second canoe appeared behind it. A breach in the defenses would be a disaster.

"Come with me," Grace called to Tom. She picked up her skirts, and darted to take a place beside the few men. Tom laid ready their powerful family rifle, alongside the one he had been clutching. Grace checked the pistol in her belt.

Sergeant Knox narrowed his eyes but nodded to her; despite his hostility, they both knew her true aim was needed.

Although protected by lying low in the dirt, Grace's view of the river was poor. "It's no good here. I can't see them well enough," she shouted to Tom. "Follow me."

She climbed onto the nearest wagon and pulled a crate into place to stand on. Her hand shook as she sliced a vertical tear in the canvas with her pocket knife, giving her a perfect view of the river. She straightened her back, raised her rifle and rested her cheek on the stock. With both eyes open, she aimed at the brave at the front of the first canoe. Sweat ran down her spine.

She couldn't do it. She couldn't deliberately fire on a man. Not again. She lowered the rifle.

"It's them or us," Tom yelled, seeing her hesitate.

Them or us. Those words summed up everything. There would never be a place for both overlanders and the people who had lived here for generations. Tears came to her eyes as she looked at Tom. Us. Her duty was to protect him.

Grace raised her rifle again, fired, and felt the recoil thump into her shoulder. The man in the canoe jerked backwards and slumped onto the brave behind. The powder left a smell of rotten egg hanging in the air of the enclosed wagon.

She handed the rifle to Tom, who exchanged it for a loaded one. She wiped the sweat from her palms. Once more: aim and fire. Her eardrums throbbed from the noise.

With two brothers now dead or injured, the remaining fighters in the canoe fell to confusion. Grace had no choice but to keep firing. She struck a man in the second canoe but injured, rather than killed him. Despite his wounds, the warrior continued to shout his orders, and the three remaining Cayuse in the first canoe started to paddle once more.

Grace aimed, but this time she missed. She hurriedly pushed back the hair that was falling into her face, and took the reloaded rifle from Tom.

The Cayuse were now within firing range of the soldiers on the earthen bank, and a barrage of shots rang out. Some jumped from the canoes and swam to shore, but the soldiers were prepared and waiting.

A third canoe appeared.

"Please, God, not more," she whispered, terrified this would be the wave that broke over their defenses.

A fierce warrior at the front urged them onwards and this canoe traveled faster.

Them or us. Grace took her pistol from her belt. "Remove the man in command," she murmured to herself, and steadied her nerve to take aim. She fired, and the warrior fell backward into the water. Cayuse leaped into the Snake, some powerfully swimming to the bank, but none reached the wagons.

The noise of battle was diminishing.

"What's happening? Can you see?" Grace called.

Tom cautiously raised the canvas bonnet. "I think they're retreating. They're riding back."

"You're sure?"

Tom climbed onto the wheel to get higher. "I can see dust between the mountains over there. Fort Boise must have sent a troop to help us."

"Get down, Tom. Now! It's still dangerous out there." Grace stayed at her post, a bilious taste in her mouth. She kept a rifle trained through the gap in the fabric bonnet, her eyes not leaving the river for fear of another canoe.

Across the river, a brave waded to safety, his gun held aloft. The lethal shots had come from one of the covered wagons. Looking closely, he could see the muzzle emerging from the canvas. He lifted his precious gun, took aim, and fired.

PART THREE

FORTY-FIVE

Randolph watched the retreat but could not see the cause. The air around the wagons was thick with dust, but he guessed at what had happened. He called four men together and ordered them to mount their horses. Putting Turner in charge of the encampment, the soldiers rode forth with him.

Looking to the northwest, he saw horses in the distance, mounted by men in dark blue uniforms. The Cayuse were retreating into the hills to the northeast. He turned back to the small, vulnerable collection of wagons and carts. Danger was still all around in the form of the warriors fallen before the camp; some might still be alive and armed.

Randolph dismounted and began his bloody business with the four other men. They overturned the leaden weight of bodies, and gathered weapons from the dead. He found a wounded man near death, a gaping wound in his chest, vivid red blood bubbling from his mouth with each remaining breath. He dispatched him with a *coup de grâce*.

From the corner of his eye, he saw the flash of a knife as a soldier dragged a dead man up by his hair, ready to scalp him. "No!" Randolph roared. "Halt, soldier."

The man stood, arm crooked above him, gripping the knife.

Randolph marched toward him. "Private Lewis, there'll be no mutilations here."

Lewis let the body drop. "I was only taking a trophy."

"I know *exactly* what you were doing."

Lewis looked at the dead bodies around him. "I don't understand, sir. They're just savages."

Randolph grabbed the front of Lewis's uniform with his fist and pulled him to within inches of his face. "Savages? Yet you're the one with a knife in his hand." He pushed him away. "Return to the wagons. See if you can find something useful to do there."

The cavalry troop from Fort Boise rode up and the officers exchanged a salute.

"Your man reached us last night," said the leading officer.

Randolph nodded. "Good to see you. Just the one man?"

"Yes, a private. He said a second man perished trying to reach us."

Randolph felt he'd been punched in the stomach. Gray Eagle. A man he respected and admired. Gray Eagle had known the dangers of traveling ahead but went anyway. And now he was another dead Indian. Randolph looked around at the twisted bodies lying in the dust. Manifest Destiny. This was the reality of the destiny for Europeans: bloodshed and destruction.

"Sir?" The officer was waiting.

Randolph shook his head. "Let's get out of here. I need three of your men to help search the prisoners. The remainder report to my lieutenant and prepare the wagons to move out."

The soldiers carefully searched the injured Cayuse, bound their hands, and dragged them to a tree outside the camp; dead bodies were left where they fell. Randolph needed the wagon train to move on as fast as possible, and he knew the Cayuse would return during the night to collect the bodies of their fallen comrades.

Corporal Flanagan rode to his captain. "Lieutenant Turner has drawn up a list of our dead and wounded, sir." He handed over a sheet of paper. The list was mercifully short.

"And the civilians?" Randolph asked.

"One dead: Mr. Long. God rest his soul. Another six injured, one badly, might not pull through. And... and I'm afraid there's Mrs. Sinclair."

"Grace?"

"Yes, sir. She took a bullet during the attack."

Randolph's mouth went dry. He could not even form the question he needed to ask.

Flanagan seemed to sense what he wanted to know. "She's alive, but unconscious, sir."

He turned on his heel and mounted his horse. Why had she not been safe among the women?

"Sir?" Flanagan asked.

"Continue here," he said, his voice cracking. "And I expressly forbid all trophy-taking."

He kicked his heel into the horse's flank and galloped back to the wagons, passing the relief troop without acknowledgment. A bitter taste rose at the back of his throat.

He already had a sense of what had happened. The woman he had fallen in love with was not the sort to huddle under canvas. He remembered that day on the Plains when he first discovered how well she could handle a gun. But he was angry that she had not kept herself safe: he'd only just found her and was not prepared to lose her.

The camp was full of movement and activity. Men rocked and hauled the wagons back onto their wheels, women and children gathered belongings. A horse had broken free and two young men were trying to catch it.

"Get the wagons loaded fast as you can," shouted

Randolph. "It doesn't matter if it's your own. We can sort belongings at Fort Boise."

The injured lay on three flatbed supply wagons, those with superficial wounds sat on the earth, waiting to be seen. More seriously injured men were in wagons out of the sun—and away from eyes if Dr. Trinkhoff had to operate.

Randolph leaped down from his horse. "Where's Mrs. Sinclair?" he asked a soldier giving water to one of the injured men. He was met with a blank look.

Eunice overheard him. "This wagon here, James."

He climbed into the back where they were shielded from the chaos outside. Grace lay on one side of the wagon, her eyes closed. Her left arm was bare and her shoulder bandaged.

Dr. Trinkhoff tended to the civilian lying on the other side of the wagon. The man roared in pain as Trinkhoff removed a bullet from his leg.

Randolph knelt by Grace's side and took her hand. It was warm. "Grace, Grace," he whispered.

As Mrs. Turner bandaged the man's leg, Dr. Trinkhoff turned to his captain.

"Not too bad, sir." He waved a hand in a wide semicircle. "Not too bad at all! All things considered. I have certainly seen worse on the battlefields of Europe."

"Will she be all right?" Randolph asked, caring nothing for a whole field of soldiers, if this one woman was lost.

"Mrs. Sinclair?" Dr. Trinkhoff raised his eyebrows. "Well, sir, I cannot tell exactly."

"Will she live?"

The doctor polished his glasses with the hem of his shirt. "I'm not sure of her injuries."

He balled his fists. "But—"

"She's unconscious, James," Eunice said gently. "She's breathing, but it's like a deep sleep we can't raise her from. She was in a wagon at the river side of the camp. Young Tom was with her. He ran for help, just as the battle was ending. I don't know quite what happened, but she took a bullet in her shoulder."

"How bad is the wound?"

"It's clean. She's lucky, the bullet has gone straight through."

Randolph's brows lowered. "But that would not have made her lose consciousness."

"She must have struck her head. See, here, there is already a large lump."

"Head injury, you see, sir," interrupted Trinkhoff, making his presence felt. "Maybe it's the same as the one earlier in the journey. You can never tell. The patient may wake in an hour. Or maybe, suddenly they die." He clicked his fingers for effect.

Randolph turned away, his teeth clenched, and heard a dog barking and a voice outside the covered wagon.

"But I want to see my sister!"

"The captain's there, son," said a man.

Tom slipped in, evading the arms trying to stop him.

"Your sister?" asked Eunice, but Tom didn't hear. He was distraught.

"Is she okay? She shot loads of them. One after the next." He sat beside Randolph. "Then something happened, she just flung back. Like she'd been punched. And hit the metal thing on the wagon bed. She'll live, though? Won't she?" Tears welled up in his eyes. "Please, sir, she can't die. Not Grace as well. I don't wait to be left alone."

Tom crumpled into Randolph's side and he put his arm around the boy's shoulders. "You won't be, Tom. Come on, let's get this wagon off to the Fort."

Randolph was grateful to have someone to look after to distract him from his own fears, and he led the boy into the busy camp. Kane started barking again.

"Tom, can you find some rope and make sure Kane is settled into a wagon with you?"

The boy nodded and left to go on his mission.

The light seemed unnaturally bright and all the colors were washed out of the sky, the earth, the wagons. Men surrounded Randolph, trying to report information or request orders. He felt sick, and dizzy, as if on a boat.

"Turner, status?" he asked.

"Should be ready to move out within half an hour. One of the wagons is damaged beyond repair, but that one over there should be moving soon. As you can see, it's all pretty much in order."

Randolph's training as a professional soldier reasserted itself. "Private O'Hara, go to Corporal Flanagan and report back on the body check. Sergeant Knox, take two men and do a thorough perimeter check. I don't want any sudden surprises. Examine the riverside carefully—including those canoes." He turned to the Fort Boise lieutenant. "Forgive me, I forget your name."

"Meade. Lieutenant Charles Meade."

"Set up guards around the camp until we are ready to leave. The Cayuse could yet decide to mount an attack."

"What do you want to do with the prisoners who can't walk?" Meade asked. "They'll slow us down. Shall I send a soldier to dispatch them?"

"No. We leave them all here. Walking wounded as well."

"All, sir? Is that wise? Major Williams would value some prisoners for exchange."

Randolph looked at the small group of Cayuse sat by the tree. "Leave them. It's more important that we reach Fort Boise quickly."

Each person had their role until the wagons were ready to move on. The relief cavalry rode in a column down either side of the wagon train, as Randolph and Meade trotted at the head.

"We'll be there by nightfall, Captain."

His jaw remained fixed, as he rode onwards.

Once on the trail, there seemed to be an outward sigh from the pioneers. Women were covered in dirt, some comforting children who began to cry, remembering what they had seen. Men cleaned out clay pipes and pulled hard on tobacco, frowning at the women who had not behaved as they had expected.

"You seemed mighty organized back there," said Caleb Eliot to his wife Betty.

"What did you expect? That me and the two girls would sit quivering? Those days are over. Jane, Sarah, and me, we're made of stronger stuff."

The women who had helped with the firearms caused the most puzzlement.

"Don't you ever go putting yourself in harm's way again," said Mr. Hollingswood to his wife.

"Don't recall you complaining, when I was handing you your next loaded rifle," Lillian replied, raising an eyebrow.

"And where d'you learn all that any way?"

"Grace Sinclair," Lillian replied. "She showed a few of us women what to do. We've been practicing."

"God in Heaven," cried Mr. Hollingswood. "There'll be ladies in the army next."

FORTY-SIX

Randolph remembered the adobe walls of Fort Boise as they loomed up out of the gathering dark, and the heavy gates opened to the company. Now they had reached a place of safety, tension melted from his limbs, but his mind was aware of every wagon movement to and fro as he thought of Grace unconscious within one.

His behavior had been indiscreet earlier that day, with the shock of hearing that Grace was a casualty, and he hoped it had not been noticed in the melee at the end of the battle. He was relieved that only Eunice and the doctor had witnessed his reaction to seeing her. He hated the idea of Grace—or himself—being the subject of gossip, and hoped to keep their relationship confidential until she had recovered.

They entered the earthen square in the center of the fort. A flag flapped on its pole, but the breeze was too light to lift the fabric.

Most of the buildings were made from wood, but a few were stone covered with plaster. Wooden pathways joined the structures. When he had been here the previous year, a storm had turned the dirt beside the pathways to deep mud.

The occupants of the fort watched the arrival of the wagon train. Randolph and Turner drew up their horses in front of the main building on the square, just as Major Williams came out to greet them. They exchanged salutes.

"Very good to see you, Captain," said the major.

"Likewise, sir."

"You all look on your last legs. Let's get you settled in. Sergeant, take the injured to the infirmary."

The soldier to the major's left sprang to action. "This way," he said, indicating the wooden building on the east side of the central square. The garrison took charge and the fort filled with activity.

"I'd like to see my private first," said Randolph, "the one who made it through to you."

A soldier took him to the infirmary. In the lamplight, Willard looked even bonier than usual but was overjoyed to see his captain.

Randolph clasped his hand and drew a chair up close to the side of the bed. "We've gotten a lot to thank you for. I don't know how much longer we would've held back the Cayuse, if the relief had not come from the fort."

"I'm sorry it took so long to get here," said Willard.

"What happened to Gray Eagle?"

Willard's eyes narrowed. "We ran into a hunting party. Sudden and unexpected. Luckily, they were just as surprised to see us. There were about six of them. Gray Eagle started to parley, but they got real angry. I don't know. Seeing an Indian in a blue uniform might've just made them worse. You know, raised voices, took out their weapons. Gray Eagle, sir, he told me to ride on while he held them back."

Willard shook his head at the memory. "I saw him go down, and I whipped my horse hard as I could. I thought I'd gotten away, but one of them infernal arrows caught my horse in the leg. He went lame pretty fast, and all my provisions were lost in the attack. So I was a sorry sight, trying to pick my way across the hills to the Fort. Worse than when I was a fur-trapper. Lord, I thought you all would reach here before me," he said with a grim smile.

"You did a good job, Willard, and I'm proud of you." Randolph rose. He tried to keep his voice steady but was deeply moved by what had happened to his friend Gray Eagle. "And now I must go see how the other casualties are faring."

Garrison soldiers carried the injured into the room. Those with minor wounds lay on blankets on the floor, but the ones with the worst injuries groaned as they were helped onto camp beds.

"Corporal Moore, you fought bravely," said Randolph as soon as the man was settled.

"Thank you, sir."

"What's the injury?"

Moore held up his arm and grimaced. "Bullet smashed the bone. The surgeon says he's taken it out." The bandage was brown with dry blood.

"Good. Make sure to get some bromine on it."

A skirt rustled behind Randolph. He turned to Jane, her weather-beaten hands twisting a handkerchief.

"Miss Jane Eliot." He gave a slight bow and left the young people together.

Randolph worked his way round the men, checking how they were, exchanging words of comfort and encouragement. He then stood in the corridor at the end of the ward wondering where they had taken Grace, the person he most wanted to see.

A woman walked past, carrying a bowl of bloody water.

"Madam," he said, and she stopped. "Is the young woman overlander here? The one injured in the attack."

"Aye, sir. In that room down there. We wouldn't want her in here with all these wounded men."

"And how is she?"

"That's not for me to say. The wee lass is still not back with us, so to speak."

They walked toward the wooden door of Grace's room. "May I see her?"

The nurse looked up in surprise. "I hardly think that would be proper, sir," she said, straightening her back, her Scots accent more pronounced.

He nodded and left, since there was nothing more he could do without raising unwelcome questions from this severe woman. He must take care not to set off malicious gossip.

Randolph reluctantly put on his hat and made his way to the major's residence across the square, even though he would much prefer to go and find his own quarters and get himself bedded down for the night.

Many of the men drank heavily that night, with relief at still being alive. They talked about the battle, and alcohol loosened their tongues as they lounged round the stoves in their quarters.

Already the garrison of Fort Boise, who had seen many a train come and go, sensed things had been different on this expedition. Some of them remembered Randolph from his previous trips: they knew his reputation for discipline and order, so the stories of how women had behaved during the assault baffled them. Although only a handful had assisted the men with ordnance at the front line, the number grew with retelling. Nevertheless, some of the soldiers spoke in praise of the women who had quietly, calmly, helped with the injured men.

Although the stories of military heroism also grew with the telling, Sergeant Knox was angry he had been left to hold the line by the river.

"You abandoned your posts," he admonished the men who had moved during battle.

Private Lewis tried to justify himself. "The Indians nearly broke through the other side of the barricade."

"You left us vulnerable to attack from the river," said Knox. "And what's more, we very nearly cracked. You saw those canoes on the riverbank? Every one of them full of Indian braves. And just me and Private O'Hara to defend it."

"Oh, come now!"

"'Tis true," O'Hara spoke up. "Sticks in my craw to say it, but if it'd not been for Mrs. Sinclair, we might have been overrun."

"The woman lying in the infirmary?" asked one of the garrison men.

"Indeed. She was shot by one of the natives, but not before she dispatched a fair few of them."

A Fort Boise man roared with laughter. "What? That slip of a thing?"

"You may well scoff," retorted Knox. "But I'll tell you something. Months ago, near the beginning of the trail, she taunted me in front of the captain. She'd shot a whole clutch of rabbits. I missed one sitting close by. She smiled and asked not to be behind me if ever we was attacked. I hated her for that. Couldn't wait for the captain to kick her off the train."

Knox pulled on his pipe, and he looked up at his companions who had been caught by the intensity of his words. "I tell you now, I'd rather have Mrs. Sinclair beside me under fire than many a man I've served with."

Some of the men laughed, and a couple whistled. Knox leaned back in his chair and surveyed the fire.

"I heard she's the captain's mistress," said a Fort Boise man, with a mischievous grin.

"No!"

"Yes. That Mrs. Sinclair and your Captain Randolph."

"I heard she's not a missus anyway," said another man. Rumors had been whispered that evening.

"Dr. Trinkhoff said it's true. And someone heard the boy, Tom, calling for his sister."

"He could just be confused, in the battle an' all."

"That's crazy. You don't confuse that sort of thing."

"It's true." A voice came from the back of the room. Turner had quietly entered and had been listening to the conversation. Now so many had heard the rumors, he thought it best the truth be out in the open. "She's unwed and Tom's her brother."

"You sure?"

"Quite sure. It only came to our attention recently. And we've had more important things on our minds since."

"And what about the captain?" asked the soldier who had set this hare running.

"The captain is an honorable man and soldier. The best you could hope to serve with," said Turner. "I suggest, if you know what's good for you, you spread no more gossip. It would be an idea for you to call it a night now anyway."

The men could take a hint. It was the early hours and many could feel exhaustion in their bones. They creaked to their beds and most fell into deep slumber.

FORTY-SEVEN

If any of the men had been early risers, they would have seen a clear blue sky. As it was, the soldiers slept on, given furlough in recognition of the danger they had come through. Some of the overlanders were livelier, looking at their wagons to see what damage had been done, what personal items had been left behind in the rush.

The Perrimans' wagon was entirely lost in the skirmish: as it had been turned over, the long wooden tongue had split from the reach running under the bed, and there had been no time to repair it in the field. Mrs. Perriman wept and was close to despair, wishing she had never set out on the journey. Then, one by one, out came pieces of furniture saved from the accident months before. The Hollingswood boys brought a chair they had stowed away. Mrs. Perriman sat in it once more, and cried even harder, partly for joy at finding an old friend, but more with grief for what had been lost.

Tom fetched Mr. Perriman to see the heavy crib they'd salvaged, and the two of them carried it back to Mrs. Perriman. She ran her fingers across the carved wood.

"Thank you, Tom. You've a kind heart. Shows you've been brought up properly."

It turned out Captain Randolph was billeted in the major's own house. Although he would have preferred to be nearer his men, it had a few advantages: he took a long bath in the morning, shaved, and had his hair trimmed. He wore his dress uniform while his day uniform was cleaned. His thoughts rarely left the infirmary, as he wondered if Grace had regained consciousness but knew it would raise eyebrows if he were constantly at her door.

The major invited him, Lieutenant Turner, and Eunice to lunch. As Randolph walked into the room, Major Williams introduced his daughter.

"You remember Flora, I'm sure," said the proud father.

"Yes, of course," replied Randolph, taking her hand and making a quick bow.

In front of him stood a young woman in a floral dress with a profusion of lace, nipped in at the waist by a ribbon with a bow. Her blond hair was parted in the center, and curls fell like barley sugar twists over her ears. Her cheeks blushed pink for a moment, as she dropped her eyes and then lifted them to his.

"And I remember you, sir," she said, looking up at him through thick lashes.

He recalled Eunice describing her as a beauty and he supposed it was true, but his thoughts drifted back to the Grace's simple elegance, the way she would push back her hair from her large brown eyes.

They took their seats at the table. The major sat at the head, Randolph on his left and his daughter on his right. The food was good and there was plenty of it. The major told them all what a long but excellent winter they had had, how the men had endured much hardship but had come through it the stronger, how the impudent local Natives were now making trouble. They were the most notorious rascals west of the Rocky Mountains.

Flora was eager to hear whatever news came from the East —what the fashions were, the latest music and dances. She addressed all of her questions to Randolph.

"And James—may I call you James?—are skirts fuller in New York now?"

Randolph was carving a piece of meat on his plate. "I cannot say. I have not been to New York for some years."

"I have a magazine and it looked that way," she continued. "It came all the way through Fort Vancouver, so is somewhat out of date."

As Randolph had never looked at a woman's magazine, he was at a loss for an answer.

Eunice broke in. "I believe skirts are going a little fuller, for evening wear. The gentlemen may not have noticed yet."

Flora's laughter was light and sweet; she continued with her questions. But all the time Randolph wished he could be sitting with Grace, rather than in this dining room.

At the end of the meal, the gentlemen rose and thanked their hosts for the hospitality. "Duty calls," said Randolph, "I must check on my men."

"We'll see you at seven for dinner then," said the major.

Randolph was caught off guard. "With regret, sir, I have a task I must undertake this evening. A private matter which must be resolved. And then I had planned to eat with my officers tonight."

"I'm sure they'll all understand the attractions of my table," the major replied, with a chuckle and a slap on the back.

"I am afraid I must abide by my plans."

"Mrs. Turner," said Flora, her color rising once more. "Why don't you stay a while longer for a cup of tea?"

Eunice could see what was needed of her, and agreed to stay. Randolph and Turner bowed and left.

Turner had a wry smile on his face as they strode across the drill square. "If you don't mind me saying, James—may I call you James?—you have a pickle of a situation developing there."

Randolph tapped his hat on his thigh. "Do you think it's serious?"

"Indeed I do. I told you some weeks back that Eunice thought Flora was sweet on you the last time we reached Fort Boise. That young woman has probably been waiting for you the whole year."

"I think you are very much overestimating my charms. If there were some slight attraction, it will be easy for her to get over it."

"But will her father? And will your career? Looks to me like the major has settled on marrying off his pretty daughter to a promising captain."

Randolph stopped still and ran his hand through his hair.

"If I may venture some advice?" Turner said. "You need to get out of this as quickly and plainly as possible. I'm sure my Eunice would agree." They stopped outside the infirmary.

"The problem is," Randolph lowered his voice and stood closer, "to my shame, I don't know quite what I let them assume last year when I was here. I know no promises or declarations were made." He shook his head. "You know, until a few months ago, I might have gone along with this. I had such low expectations of marital happiness. Flora seems no worse than many." He looked at the infirmary door. "No, that's unkind of me. She is pretty and charming and lively. And deserves a life away from a frontier fort. What I mean is, things are different for me now." He lifted the latch and they went in.

. . .

The injured men were all improving. Those with minor wounds had moved out that morning and were back in their barracks.

Again, at the end of his visit, Randolph went down the corridor and stood at the door of Grace's room. He took a deep breath and knocked. The same woman emerged as last night.

"Afternoon, sir," she said, looking him straight in the eye.

"I was wondering if there was any news."

"Well, sir, I think so, although you should speak to the doctor."

"She's conscious?" His voice was hopeful.

"Not exactly. But I've seen movement under the eyelids, and her lips have moved as if to speak."

A muscle contracted in Randolph's jaw. "Has she said anything?"

"No. No words as such."

Randolph drew himself taller, frustrated that the woman was so taciturn. "I have a responsibility for all those who have traveled on this train. That means the overlanders as well as my soldiers. So, Mrs...."

"Mrs. McKinney."

"Mrs. McKinney, it is not unreasonable for me to ask if you think she'll recover."

The nurse adjusted her apron over her ample bosom. "I would be a foolish woman to say that! I've seen worse pull through. And I've seen healthier slip away. It comes down to grit, I always say. How much the person fights to stay with us. Good day, sir."

She turned and went back inside, closing the door.

Randolph had no option but to return to his men.

Surely Grace would fight. Fate could not be so cruel that at the moment of finding the woman who gave his life meaning, she would be taken away.

FORTY-EIGHT

Grace was coming to the upper reaches of consciousness. She struggled with bad dreams, her lips forming words, then names —many different names. Sometimes she was vaguely aware of someone else in the room. A good person or bad? She wasn't even sure where she was.

In the early evening, Grace's eyelids fluttered. She felt like she had been drowning deep in a river but was thrashing her way to the surface. She came to the surface more often, as if gulping air, before being dragged back down by the water. As the evening fell to darkness, she opened her eyes wide.

A large woman wiped a cold cloth across her face. "How are you feeling, my wee one?"

Grace could not answer. There was a throbbing pain in her head, a pain so strong she felt sick.

"Can I get you some water?" the woman asked.

"I... maybe. Yes. I'm thirsty."

The woman had a mole close to the side of her mouth with several large hairs sprouting. She brought an earthenware mug of water. It was cool and refreshing.

"May I ask who you are?"

"I'm Mrs. McKinney and I've been nursing you, my dear. You may call me Nellie if you choose."

Grace looked at the rough wooden walls. "Where is this?"

"Fort Boise."

"We made it then. Why is my head hurting so?"

"You had a nasty knock. We weren't sure you would come through."

The throbbing got worse and Grace closed her eyes again.

"Try to sleep if you can," said Nellie, pulling the blanket straight. "I'll go find the Fort doctor."

Sleep was impossible. Tom. She didn't even know if he was alive. She didn't know any of it. Oh, God, why didn't the nurse mention him?

Grace tried to get up, but a throbbing pain filled her skull.

"Doctor," she called. Her voice trembled and barely left her mouth. "Mrs...." What was the nurse's name?

Grace tried to order her thoughts. She went through the journey of the previous months, but there were gaps. The beginning was clear, the early days across the Great Plains. Then, a dark night, a metallic taste of fear in her mouth. There had been an attack. The rank smell of a man's breath filled her nostrils.

"Doctor!" she called out louder this time, pushing through the pain to get herself sitting up.

Presently, the door opened, and an older man in uniform appeared.

"Good to see you back with us," he said, his eyes crinkling in weather-beaten folds of skin.

"Are you the doctor?"

"Indeed. Doctor of Fort Boise. Fredricks at your service." He made a kindly smile.

"I need to know everything."

"Now, there's a challenge. Everything?"

Grace shook her head. "I can't remember what happened. We were attacked. But I don't remember it. Is Tom alive?"

"Tom?"

"My…" Grace's breath caught as she wondered what to say. Brother? Had the truth slipped out? "The boy I was traveling with."

"Yes, he's fine."

"Thank God!"

"I'll send your brother to you."

Ah, brother. That told her something.

The doctor pulled a wooden stool next to the bed and held Grace's head still so he could look at her pupils. "It's quite normal not to remember things when you've had a nasty blow to the head."

"But will I get better?"

"Probably. Possibly. Sometimes the memory never comes back."

Grace's mouth fell open.

"But it usually does." He patted her forearm. "The mind can play many strange tricks. But don't you worry about that. It usually gets sorted out in the end."

Fredricks began to stand, but Grace pulled him back. What about the captain? "And what happened during the Cayuse attack?"

"Surely you don't want to think about that, my dear."

"How many of us survived?" Grace persisted.

"Nearly everyone. You were very fortunate."

The doctor hadn't mentioned Randolph and surely he'd think it strange if she asked outright.

"And what happened to me?" Grace's hand involuntarily made its way up to her head, where there was a bump and a knot of hair and dried blood.

"You have a bullet wound in your shoulder. And you have a lump here at the back of your cranium. Your brother says you fell backwards and struck your head. I'm told you also had a nasty knock earlier during the journey. So that may have made it worse. All in all, you should be far more careful, young lady."

"Were any of the womenfolk wounded?"

"No. Just you. The unlucky one."

Tears filled her eyes and ran down her cheeks. She did not know quite what she was crying for, but something was lost to her. Something she could see in the corner of her eye but vanished when she looked at it.

The doctor rubbed the back of his neck. "Come now. No tears." He left with advice that she should sleep.

That evening, Randolph walked through the fort gates to the shamble of cabins around the boundary wall. In one, an enterprising mountain man had set up a bar. As Randolph ducked through the low entrance, the smell of liquor and pipe smoke hit him in a wave.

The owner's attention was on high alert in the presence of a military man. "What can I get you?"

Randolph removed his hat and gestured that he was not interested in liquor. "I'm looking for Jedediah Meek. The fur-trapper. I heard he was here."

The owner nodded to the table in the half-light at the back.

Randolph bought a whiskey and placed it in front of the bear-like man. "You Jedediah Meek?"

"Who's asking?"

Randolph scraped out a chair and sat opposite him, placing his hat on the table. "Captain Randolph. Just brought in a wagon train."

"Yep, I saw it. So, what does a well-dressed captain want with the likes of me?"

"You been north trapping pelts through the summer?"

The man nodded. "Not that there's much of a living to be made these days."

"I heard you were at Independence earlier this season."

"Maybe."

"Were you, or no?"

The man leaned back in his rickety chair, his eyes gleaming below his bushy brows. "Seems to me like I got something you want, and you're expecting me to give it to you for nothing."

Randolph sighed but he had come prepared. He placed a dollar on the table. "That should loosen your tongue."

"Indeed it will." The man pocketed the coin. "Yes, I visit Independence regular. Trading my pelts, and as agent for other fur-trappers who prefer to stay in the mountains. They trust me."

"When were you there last?"

The man scratched his head. "It was spring. I'm usually there late spring."

"Which month?"

"April."

Randolph drummed the table. "Early or late?"

"I'd say later that month."

Randolph leaned forward. Now for the important question. "You know a man called Silas Boyd?"

Meek frowned at Randolph, who held his eye.

"A dollar pays for more information than your travel itinerary," said Randolph.

The man swallowed his whiskey. "Sure. I know Silas Boyd. Done business with him. He's got fingers in most pies in Independence. Have to look sharp with him. Liable to cheat his own grandmother."

"Did you trade with him this year?"

"Believe I did."

Randolph let out a long breath. "So he was in robust health in late April?"

Meek laughed, showing how few teeth remained in his mouth. "Don't know 'bout robust. He was like a black bear that's had its kill stolen from under his nose. Blundering round in fury."

"Why?"

"Busted his leg. It was slowing him down."

Randolph narrowed his eyes. "Did he say how it happened?"

"My guess was he'd tried cheating the wrong man. Someone took a bullet to him. But no, Boyd wasn't easy on the details."

Randolph nodded. He stood up and put out his hand. "Much obliged to you."

Meek raised his eyebrows. "That's about the easiest dollar I ever earned." He grinned.

"And I assure you"—Randolph's smile was just as wide—"it's the best dollar I've spent in many a year."

FORTY-NINE

Grace had a restless night, moving in and out of dreams. Moments from the past few months merged with her childhood; imaginings mingled with real events until she could not tell which was which. Her father sitting with her mother on the wagon's driving bench, teasing her and laughing. A man raising his rifle against Chimney Rock. *Look, I bet I could knock that chimney down with one good shot.* He turns. It's her brother Zachary.

Nellie came into her room with breakfast of eggs and grits. Grace's skin was clammy and she did not feel up to speaking. The window just above her bed overlooked the drill square, but the view was hidden by a gauze, dirty with years of dust. Boots brushed the earth in unison, a bugle rang out.

"They're raising the color," said Nellie, "and, look, morning inspection."

Nellie helped her sit up in bed.

Pain shot through her shoulder as Grace reached up to pull the gauze to one side and wipe a hole in the grime. The men fell into their ranks, and her breath grew quick and shallow as none of the soldiers were familiar.

"Where are our men?" she asked anxiously.

Nellie sat by her at the head of the bed and peered out. "There's your company. Look. On the right."

"Of course." Grace's shoulders relaxed.

Two soldiers marched smartly to the white flagpole and raised the color, each movement like a mechanical doll. After the flag was raised and saluted, an inspection began. Captain Randolph walked along in front of the men.

"The captain's safe, thank God," she whispered. Her stomach clenched. A memory of an early morning, the dew still on the ground, the captain striding purposefully, his boots leaving footprints on the grass. He seemed like that now, so familiar yet so distant.

Nellie watched him. "Fine figure of a man," she said in her lilting Scottish tone. "He'll make a grand husband for Flora."

"Oh?" Grace glanced at the nurse.

"He's promised to young Flora, the major's daughter. He's been staying in the major's quarters. Not a courtesy offered to other captains coming through this place. I'm expecting an announcement any day now."

Grace felt sick. Some of this sounded familiar. Flora. The major's daughter. She heard an Irish accent in her head: Corporal Flanagan. That was it. He had told her, way back at Devil's Gate.

"What's she like? The major's daughter?"

"Flora? The prettiest wee thing you can imagine. And charming. That's the word for it. Always knows the right thing to say. Always been a kind young lady." Nellie looked back out of the window and sighed. "And a perfect match they'll make— her so pretty and fair, him so dark and handsome."

Was this possible?

Turning back to the inspection, Grace's pulse had quickened. "Has... has anyone been to visit me?"

"Aye, there was the lady with the large brood."

"Mrs. Hollingswood?"

"That was her. But the doctor said absolutely no visitors until you are stronger. So I sent her away."

Grace looked out through the dirty window, her heart sinking. "And the captain?"

"No, not yet."

So, he hadn't been to see her. She clutched at the covers.

Nellie smoothed the blanket again.. "But he's visited all the injured. I daresay he'll visit you too, now you're more yourself. Seems to see it as his duty."

Grace pushed the food around her plate. "I'm not really hungry yet."

"You must get that down you. It's good for you."

Grace felt she was crushing ashes into her mouth. "I really can't," and she moved the plate away.

"Maybe you should rest now." Nellie took the tin plate and closed the door behind her.

Grace's mind was racing. How could he have changed his mind so quickly? Was that the man she thought she knew? But her mind was so mixed up, she wasn't sure what was real and what was false. She had a rush of images of the captain, but she doubted them. Other things she had dreamed of so vividly were not real. Her ma and pa had never been on the trail, after all. But that heat when she saw the captain out on the parade ground was true enough. But desire on her side didn't mean it was reciprocated.

Maybe he had reached Fort Boise and realized the folly of their liaison. How could she compare with the beautiful Flora? A major's daughter—that was the right thing for him. Perhaps things between her and Randolph were not as she had imagined.

Grace lay down and rested on the rough cotton of the pillowcase. Feeling the fabric, she remembered a soft linen pillowcase touching her cheek. A dark evening, a gift. Perhaps that was all that was left of their liaison. Perhaps everything had changed. Her tears were absorbed into the rough cotton.

Grace did not know what time it was when Nurse McKinney gently shook her awake. "I said the captain would visit once he knew you were conscious."

Grace's head shot up, eyes wide. She was not ready for this. She still wasn't sure if her memories of him were true. And if they *were* true, he might be coming to tell her it was over. "Do I have to see him?"

"It's just a courtesy call. He's visited all the men each day."

"But I don't want him to see me like this."

Nellie gave a light laugh. "Like what, dear?"

"With my hair all awry. Not decently dressed."

"This is hardly a military inspection. But give me a moment."

Nellie returned with a brush and a checkered shawl.

"Let's untangle what I can of your hair," she said. "Now you're awake, I'll wash the blood out properly."

Grace spread the shawl around her shoulders as Nellie pulled at the tangles and pushed the chestnut hair back from her face, tying it with a piece of twine. "There, now your hair's straight."

Nellie stood up to fetch the captain. Maybe it was for the best to get this over with, no matter how much it hurt.

"Mrs. McKinney," Grace called out, "you won't leave us alone, will you?"

"Of course not. The very idea. That would not be at all proper now, would it?"

A few moments later, Randolph followed the nurse back into the room. Grace took the briefest of glances when he wasn't looking. In this small room, he seemed so tall, his shoulders broader than she remembered. She tightened her hands and that slight feeling of nausea returned.

He took his hat off while Nellie pulled out the chair and placed it near the bottom of the bed. He sat formally, almost stiffly, as Nellie took her post by the door. He stared at Nellie, but she faced him down and refused to leave.

"It was good of you to come, sir." Grace spoke the words she had just prepared in her head.

"Of course I've come," Randolph said. She heard no warmth in his words. "How are you feeling?"

"Better than I was. Or so they tell me. My head still hurts."

"You must rest."

"So everyone keeps telling me," she snapped.

This was unbearable, to have him so close. A stream of memories came to her mind. But were they memories? The doctor said the mind can play tricks. She looked at his familiar hands and thought she remembered them touching her. Embarrassed, she turned her head away to the wall.

"Are you in pain?" Randolph asked, his voice had softened.

Grace nodded.

"Let me get you some water." He passed the cup to her, but she avoided his gaze.

She could not endure this a moment longer. "I'm feeling a little tired, sir," she mumbled.

Nellie coughed. "Perhaps it would be best if you were to leave now."

He spoke in a low voice to Nellie. "But we've barely spoken. I had some news to give her, in private."

"You can see you're upsetting her," Nellie hissed, opening the door.

Randolph had no option but to stand and take his leave, giving a short bow. "Until you're a little better, then," he said, glancing back.

Grace dropped her gaze to her blanket and he left. A tremor

ran through her, inside and out. "Mrs. McKinney, I don't really feel like people visiting just yet."

"Right you are, my wee one," said Nellie, settling her back down again.

"And if Captain Randolph asks to visit again, can you prevent it?"

"If you wish."

"I do. I really don't want to see him. But Tom—" Grace looked up. "Please could Tom come soon? He would cheer my heart."

Outside, Randolph paced the corridor. Dr. Fredricks waited calmly.

"But she doesn't seem to be herself."

"You must not expect too much," replied the doctor.

"It felt like she barely recognized me."

"Well, that can happen, I'm afraid, particularly with a blow to the head."

Randolph absently ripped a splinter from the wooden lath wall. "Are there other things that she's forgotten?"

"She has been asking questions. I think her memory of recent things is hazy."

Randolph stood still and studied the doctor. "But will it come back?"

"She asked the same thing. Probably. But it doesn't always."

Randolph left the infirmary to return to his room in Major Williams's house, struggling to hide his frustration and fear.

FIFTY

Captain Randolph sat down at Major Williams's table for the evening meal. He felt a queasiness in his stomach when the major showed him to the seat opposite Flora once more, and the only other guest was Lieutenant Sandsten, the major's right-hand man. Randolph recalled him from the previous year: close to the major and cognizant of where preferment lay for his career.

Deal with this quickly and plainly, that's what Turner had said. But raising this matter with the major present was just darn impossible.

"The overlanders seem in pretty good shape, all things considered," observed the major.

"I consider myself fortunate," Randolph replied, "not only have I had the privilege of an excellent company of soldiers, but many of the ordinary men proved themselves brave and resourceful on the journey."

"You have that man in irons, of course," said Sandsten.

"Yes. Croup. There always seems to be one bad apple at the bottom of the barrel."

"My, what did he do?" asked Flora, her eyes widening.

Randolph ran a finger round his collar to loosen it. "That's difficult to say just now, Miss Williams, but I trust the court-martial will find the appropriate punishment."

"Call me Flora, do."

The major's eyes twinkled as he looked at his daughter. "Not like you to praise your civilians, though, James. I remember you a year ago, condemning many for their foolishness in traveling West so unprepared."

"Perhaps the pioneers have improved their preparations. Or maybe I have grown more generous in my judgments," replied Randolph.

The major laughed. "Good, you needed to soften up a little!"

"I acknowledge I was too harsh on people in the past. I would look for the bad before seeing the good. However, I maintain that if there is anything in this world that will bring to the surface a man's bad traits, it is a trip across the continent with an ox team."

Flora handed Randolph a tureen of potatoes, smiling prettily. The neckline of her dress was low, and she wore a jeweled necklace.

"But tell us about this... this *situation* with the women settlers," said Sandsten.

"Situation?" asked Randolph, shooting him a look.

"That you are happy for them to fight beside the men."

Randolph snorted. "Pardon me, Lieutenant, but I don't know to what you are referring."

Sandsten was a tall, thin man, with the blond hair and pale complexion of his forefathers. His alert mind made up for any limitations of physical strength. He took his time to cut a slice from the steak on his plate. "A year ago, in this very room, you said it wasn't yet safe for women settlers to be brought out West."

"Yes, I think I said that." Randolph put down his glass.

"My men tell me that when you came under attack, the women were in what you might call, the front line, shooting along with menfolk and soldiers."

A vein pulsed at Randolph's temple. "I assure you, I never once saw a woman fire a gun during that attack." Randolph spoke clearly and slowly, trying to halt the questions. He knew from his soldiers' reports that Grace had joined the defense. But he had not actually *seen* it.

"I'm quite sure James is right," Flora said, putting her small hand to her breast. "The very idea of shooting at those Indians, it makes my heart stop. I'm sure I would have been huddled at the back, with all the other women."

Flora spun a blond ringlet around her finger. Randolph thought how different Grace was from all other women he had met.

The major cleared his throat. "Yes. Those Indians. My Lieutenant Meade said you left prisoners at the pass. Refused to bring some back to the fort. You know how important intelligence is to get the better of those savages."

Randolph looked directly at the major. "My priority was getting the wagons to the safety of your fort. I didn't want to slow us down."

"So why didn't you dispatch them? Now they're out there to prey on the next train. I must say I was shocked."

"It seems to me, the rules of war are the same out here or fighting down in Mexico," said Randolph, his jaw tightening. "At some point, we're going to have to make a treaty with these people. Massacring them isn't going to solve anything."

Sandsten poured water into his glass and scoffed. "The major said you needed to soften up a little. Looks to me as if you've taken that too far. Going yellow."

Randolph and Sandsten locked eyes.

Major Williams put up both palms. "Now, now, gentlemen.

Let's keep things amiable. What with a lady present." He gave an indulgent nod toward his daughter.

Flora took her cue. "As we've finished eating, perhaps you gentlemen would care to move into the parlor."

The three men followed her through.

Flora sat at the upright piano and entertained them with songs. After a while, the major rose.

"Sandsten, there's some business I need to go through with you," he said, and very obviously left Randolph and his daughter together.

This was the chance to act quickly and plainly. Randolph took a breath. "Flora."

"Yes, James." Flora ceased her piano playing, and turned to him expectantly.

Randolph silently let out a long breath and rubbed at his scar, all the time thinking how to get to the point quickly but gently. "Last year, it was suggested that a man in my position should consider the advantages of marriage. It was even suggested to me that you yourself might condescend to grace my hand."

His mind snagged on the word. *Grace.* He thought of her, lying injured, and felt a surging feeling in his chest, telling him she *must* get well. The alternative was unthinkable.

He pushed on, having rehearsed these words during the afternoon. "But over the past year, I see the presumption on my part to even entertain this idea. I see that it would be quite impossible to ask such a... cultured and delicate young woman to take on as rough a soldier as myself."

Flora let a momentary "oh!" leave her lips.

"It was a foolish idea, an overreach on my behalf. A woman with your sensibilities needs to be looked after properly. For example, I'm sure you would wish to live back East. There, with your beauty and elegance, you would be a leader of fashion. I see now that I would hold you back from your rightful place at the heart of society."

"But I thought you would want to live back on the coast," Flora blurted out.

"I'm not sure who gave you that idea. No. I know myself to be a soldier, a man of the frontier. It was foolish of me to raise my thoughts to you."

Flora picked up the fan lying on top of the table, and cooled her neck. "So you mean never to be married?"

Oh, it would be far easier to say that, indeed, he meant to remain a bachelor. But that would be a lie, and Flora may know the truth of his feelings one day, and be even more hurt. God, what a mess!

"The wife for me is someone more... more like... like Mrs. Turner. A woman who is able to travel with her husband if need be."

Flora wrinkled her nose. "But she's so... homely."

Randolph could not help a smile cross his lips. "A plain woman who could be happy with me would be better than a pretty one who was miserable."

"And I would make you miserable?" Flora had borne it well so far, but now tears sat on the lower rims of her eyes.

"No, you misunderstand me." Randolph moved closer to the piano. "I'm quite sure that *I* would make *you* miserable. Not deliberately. But... but I would be unable to give you the things you need, deserve. Things befitting your position as a major's daughter."

A tear escaped down her cheek. "People have already said what a fine couple we would make. I was kinda expecting... I shall be so humiliated."

"Indeed, you shall not," said Randolph. He must make the best job he could to lessen Flora's hurt feelings. He took her hand. "It is *I* who bear the humiliation. I think others will comment on my utter stupidity in thinking I might be fit for you. They will say it's clear I could never be good enough to give you the position in society you deserve."

Flora seemed a little cheered by this thought. "Do you think that's what people will say? Truly? After all, Daddy is an important person. And I *am* his only daughter."

"I have no doubt of it," he said gently.

Flora pushed away her tears with the back of her hand. "If you will excuse me, I think I will retire early this evening."

Flora left Randolph in the parlor wondering what to do. He wanted to leave as soon as possible but knew there was the father to be faced.

Soon enough, the ample bulk of the major appeared at the door. He frowned. "Where's Flora?"

"She felt a little weary and has retired to her room."

"She seemed in good spirits earlier." Williams poked the fire, making sparks dance in the air. The heat was unbearable. "Have you something to ask of me?"

Impossibly, the evening was getting worse.

"Your daughter and I had a very helpful conversation," Randolph said. Wouldn't it be better for Flora if it seemed that she was the one who had rebuffed him? "She kindly made it clear that I could never hope to keep her in... the manner to which she is accustomed. A young lady such as Flora needs to be in elegant society. This is not something I could offer her."

The major's face turned red. "An honorable man does not break his promises."

"I believe myself an honorable man, and no promise has been made, in the past or present."

"We both know what was expected of you."

"Expectations are not promises. I'm sorry if, in your sight, I have fallen short."

The major strode around the small parlor. "I thought you a promising young man with a good career in front of you." He wagged a finger at Randolph. "Do not make an enemy of me, sir. You may find that career faltering."

Randolph's tone changed in response to this veiled threat. "I hope I may be promoted on my own merits, sir, rather than the merits of a father-in-law."

"You are dismissed." Major Williams spat the words.

Randolph swept up his hat and walked into the cool night air. He steadied his breathing, aware of blood pumping at his temples.

What a shambles. Flora deserved better. But he couldn't pretend to be something he was not. And it was now all very delicate. His personal effects were in the major's house, but he could not stay there.

He went to the officers' mess and asked for Turner to be found. Soon, the whole sorry imbroglio was explained. It seemed that few of his secrets stayed hidden from his close friend.

"We have the anteroom in our quarters. Use that tonight," said Turner. "I'll fetch your belongings once the major has quietened down."

Randolph was grateful Turner managed everything with discretion, and that night he slept a little more soundly, relieved that at least things with Flora were resolved.

FIFTY-ONE

Randolph and Turner were the first to enter the building where Croup's court-martial would take place. Randolph wanted to get a feel for the space. It was the largest room in the fort. Light flooded onto the wooden floor from the two windows which overlooked the drill square. A single chair for the accused was set against the wall opposite the windows. At one end, a large table with an imposing seat was ready for the major as the adjudicating officer. Facing the table were several rows of benches for the witnesses and observers.

The two men took places on the front row as the room filled up.

Randolph pulled out his watch. Five past nine.

The major was late when he marched into the packed room. Silence fell as he took his place at the table.

Major Williams had ruled that both the prosecution and the defense should be made by officers from Fort Boise, reasoning that it would be fairer that way. Having consulted with Turner, Randolph chose Lieutenant Meade to present the prosecution. Meade had acted with calm authority in the aftermath of the Cayuse attack. He had observed in Meade a good mind and clear intellect, a man who did not seem easily intimidated or angered.

A soldier brought in the prisoner, his wrists in iron. Croup's hair was combed back from his face, emphasizing his overlong sideburns, and someone had given him a razor to shave his stubble. He stared around the room intently, moving from face to face, and settled on Randolph. There was a strange blend of fear and contempt in his eyes.

The soldier unlocked Croup's irons and he placed a hand on the Bible to swear to tell the truth. He took the seat on the left of the hall, staring out at the sky through the windows opposite.

The major boomed a few fine words about the sanctity of truth within the court, and then matters proceeded. Meade outlined the case for the charges of rape and attempted rape. Then Croup's defense stood up. He had been allocated Lieutenant Sandsten. The defense was simple: both women had willingly accepted Croup's advances.

Meade had told Randolph he expected this approach. He had spent time with Jane Eliot: she was reluctant to say much, and was still deeply affected by the incident. Although Corporal Moore had stood by her, Jane refused to be called as a witness. She had not even come to court that morning.

Meade decided to concentrate on proving the attack on Grace Sinclair was clearly against her wishes, and thus undermine Croup's position on the first attack.

He called Lillian Hollingswood. She gave the briefest of nods at Randolph as she took a seat at the front of the hall, facing the major but with her back to the people. Meade asked her how things had started, and she told the major that Grace discovered the original attack, and what the two of them discussed as possible actions to stop it happening again. She described the long and difficult meeting with Randolph and Turner.

"Unless this man was caught," Lillian said, "he would be very likely to do it again. The problem was how to catch him."

She told of the decision for Grace to act as a lure in a trap, and of the precautions taken. Finally, Lillian spoke of the night of Croup's attack and how he had been arrested.

Lillian articulated clearly and plainly, and returned to her seat.

Randolph's chest ached from the tension as he listened to the evidence. He lowered his shoulders and let out a breath, as Lieutenant Turner took the oath and stood to give his evidence. Croup had joined the expedition at Fort Laramie. Early behavior showed a sloppy soldier but no worse than many he had seen in his time, some of whom he had turned into reliable men. Croup was inclined to drink and he seemed very full of himself. There had not been evidence of criminal tendencies, however. When he first heard about the rape, he had been deeply shocked.

"*Allegation* of rape." Sandsten jumped to his feet to remind the court.

Turner nodded and continued: he briefly described the evening's discussion with Mrs. Sinclair and Mrs. Hollingswood.

The major intervened. "So, let me be clear, the idea of snaring the unknown rapist—of setting a trap like a"—Williams hooked his wire classes over his ears so they sat at the end of his nose, and consulted his notes—"'fox in a chicken coup,' as Mrs. Hollingswood described it, this idea was not Captain Randolph's?"

"No, it was Mrs. Sinclair's. *Miss* Sinclair, I should say," Turner corrected himself.

"Yes. Confusing, isn't it," the major said drily.

Randolph shot him a glance, but the major moved on.

"And what was the captain's view of this plan?" Major Williams asked.

"He wasn't very happy about it."

"Went against his better judgment, you might say?"

"Well... that's one way of saying it."

Williams was in full flow. "Not very good to have the company's captain being led by a young woman."

Randolph felt a wave of anger flow through him. The major was letting his personal animosity affect the trial. This could prevent Jane Eliot getting justice.

Meade could see where things were heading and tried to pull it back. "So, Lieutenant," he jumped in, "tell us why you took a decision which could endanger one of the overlanders."

Turner adjusted his weight on his feet. "We discussed the predicament at great length. It was essential the overlanders and their army escort worked together with the long journey still ahead of us. If the pioneers thought they were at risk from their protectors, then the security of the whole train could have unraveled. Some might have tried to take matters into their own hands. Therefore, we thought an open announcement of the crisis—that a soldier had made a vile attack—would have put the expedition in jeopardy."

"Why did you not tell just the soldiers, so they could be on their guard?" Meade asked.

"Because the rapist would have gone to ground, only to reappear at some later time. So the idea of treating him like a fox seemed best—to lure him into a trap."

"And this trap," the major interrupted once more, "involved Mrs.... *Miss* Sinclair having secret assignations with one of your soldiers?"

Turner stroked down his beard with the palm of his hand, pulling the hairs to a point. "That was how the previous attack had taken place. I guess we thought we needed to recreate the story."

"Did this woman have no pride in her reputation?" the major asked, looking at Turner over his glasses.

Randolph flexed his hands and gripped them into fists. If it could be established that Grace's behavior was unbecoming, the case could collapse.

Turner had also seen the danger. "Miss Sinclair did not allow *pride* to come before the safety of her fellow travelers. She is a woman of great courage and integrity. *That* reputation is secure."

There was a ripple of comment on the benches behind Randolph. The gossips were enjoying every minute.

Major Williams silenced them with a rap of the gavel. "It seems an enormous risk. To be prepared to entice a rapist to attack. I just wonder what sort of woman would do such a thing." His superior tone grated on Randolph's ear.

"I fully agree with you, sir," said Turner. "It is extraordinary behavior. As I say, Miss Sinclair is a woman of unusual strength and courage."

Randolph smiled at Turner's ability to change the harsh words about Grace to an advantage.

Meade swiftly moved on to the attack and Croup's comments afterwards—comments which showed his self-knowledge of wrongdoing.

Meade finished his case for the prosecution by midday, so the major broke for lunch. Everyone filed out of the courtroom.

Randolph ate with Turner and Meade in the officers' mess.

"The major's behavior is strangely partial," Meade said. "I didn't expect so many interventions."

"Is he allowed to speak so often?" asked Turner.

Meade shrugged. "It's his court. Truth is, he can do what he likes. But it doesn't feel like due process for the defense to sit in silence, while the judge attacks."

"It might have something to do with me," said Randolph. "I think he has developed a grudge against me. Personally, I mean. He may use any stick to beat me."

"Even if it leads to a rapist walking free?" asked Meade.

"Let's pray he doesn't take it that far," said Randolph. "But if he can pin some blame on me, he will."

After they had eaten, Randolph excused himself and walked over to the infirmary. He was still eager to share his knowledge that Silas Boyd was alive in Independence. Grace had no need to fear the law. Having checked on other soldiers as a cover, he found Nellie McKinney.

"I hoped Miss Sinclair might be well enough for another visit."

"I'm sorry, sir, that would not be a good idea."

"Has she got worse?" he asked, his eyes narrowing.

"No, sir. She's getting better, in fact. But she's not happy having visitors other than her young brother at the moment."

"Could I not go in for a brief word?" He was not used to asking permission for his actions, and was getting increasingly frustrated by this nurse being so obstructive.

"To tell ye the truth," she said, straightening her back, "she particularly asked for *you* not to visit her again."

Randolph stepped back in surprise. "Very well." He turned on his heel and left.

Not want to see him? Something must have happened, but he couldn't for the life of him think what.

Crossing the parade ground, he followed everyone back into the courtroom, anxious that, with the decision lying in the hands of just one man, Croup might yet escape punishment, despite all Grace's courage.

FIFTY-TWO

Randolph took his place on the front bench once more, ramrod straight, his broad shoulders filling his blue uniform. Croup stood, and Randolph's eyes did not leave the scrawny face.

The defense began, Lieutenant Sandsten painting a picture of a model soldier. He asked Croup about the first attack. It had never happened. Indeed, Jane had been sweet on him, and when he rejected her advances, she had spun the whole story. For the second accusation, that Miss Sinclair had led him on. Everyone knew what sort of woman she was.

Randolph's nostrils flared and he had difficulty stopping himself speaking out.

"What sort of woman do you mean?" asked Sandsten.

"The sort of woman who would travel West by herself, for a start," Croup said. "The sort of woman who would lie about who and what she was. You can't trust a word she says. This story about setting a trap for me? It's all lies. She *wanted* me. That's the truth of it."

Croup continued in this vein for some time. Randolph's jaw tightened as he listened to Croup continuing his testimony.

"Right from the start, she found ways to be in the company

of men. Anyone will tell you she would take her rifle and go off rabbit shooting with them."

Meade intervened with questions wherever possible, but he could see cracks appearing in his case. Of his two most important witnesses—the two women directly affected—one could not give evidence, and the other would not.

The defense brought in a couple of witnesses: friends of Croup who told the major what a fine, upstanding soldier he was. Their other function was to undermine Randolph's reputation for leadership.

Private Lewis was called to the stand.

"Tell us about the unbecoming behavior of the women at the end of the trail," Sandsten urged.

"During the Indian ambush, they didn't behave like women at all. They were more like men. I don't mean the ones who were a mighty comfort to the sick. That's what you'd expect of a woman." Lewis rubbed at the sore, red skin on his hand where it hadn't healed after scalding himself. "No, it was the ones loading the muskets as fast as they could. It was unnatural. They were schooled by Miss Sinclair, every one of them. Like that Mrs. Hollingswood: I wouldn't trust what *she* says neither."

"And during this battle," Meade intervened, "were you not grateful to have the guns loaded and ready for action? Did it not mean you were more able to fend off the near-fatal attack?"

"Suppose you could see it like that. Don't make it right, though, does it?"

By four in the afternoon, Major Williams was weary. When the defense finished with its witnesses, Williams announced that the court was adjourned for the day and he would give his verdict the following morning.

Randolph met with Turner and Meade to debrief: the court-martial had not gone well.

"If only I could get Miss Sinclair to give evidence," said Meade.

"Would it be allowed at this late stage?" asked Turner.

"Yes, I'm sure I could make a case. The conduct of a court-martial lies very much with the presiding officer."

"It's out of the question," said Randolph. "She's not well enough. I visited the infirmary today and was not able to see her. I won't let Miss Sinclair be paraded in front of those people."

Turner stroked his beard. "What about Miss Eliot then?"

Meade shook his head. "I spoke to her only yesterday. She kept bursting into tears. I don't think she could do it."

"But if she does not give witness," said Turner, "all our work will be undone. Croup's lies about her will stand."

"And everything Grace did to catch him will be for nothing," said Randolph, drumming his fingers on the table.

"Why don't I talk to Miss Eliot?" suggested Turner. "I may have more luck than an officer of the court."

"You're very welcome to try," said Meade. "And no time like the present."

Turner made his way to the small quarters where the Eliot family was billeted. The welcome was cool, but not frosty.

"I hear that good-for-nothing Croup is spinning a pretty tale," said Caleb. Sarah Eliot had attended the trial, enjoying the attention of being sister to the main victim. But the rest of the family had stayed away.

"I want to talk to Jane, if I may."

"I don't think she'd like that," said her mother.

"It's not about what she'd *like*," said Turner with an edge to his voice. "It's about what's *right*."

Jane entered. Her face betrayed that she had being listening at the door. "I know what you're gonna ask. My Daniel says I don't have to go if I don't want to. He knows 'cause he's a corporal. It's a military court. Not for folk like me."

"And he's right in a way," said Turner. "But this is about justice. Doesn't matter whether you're a soldier or a young girl. It's all the same. Sit down with me... please."

She slid onto a wooden chair at the table.

Turner spoke in a low voice. "Jane, there's a chance Croup will walk free tomorrow. Lieutenant Meade has done everything he can, but without you or Miss Sinclair saying what happened, it's Croup's word against nothing."

Jane kept her eyes fixed on the table. "But I don't want to talk about what happened. I want to forget it all."

"And if Croup goes free? How will you forget it then? Knowing he's around?"

She looked up at him, her eyes round and frightened like a deer. "Daniel will stand by me. He promised."

"And what about other young women? Just like you. Croup will do it again, if he is not locked up and punished this time."

Jane traced her finger through some coffee that had slopped onto the wooden table. She spun it into a shape. "But that's not my fault."

"True, it would be Croup's fault. But how would you feel if you hadn't done everything you could to help?" Turner put his hand over Jane's to get her full attention. "Y'know, I remember asking Miss Sinclair why she was prepared to put herself in danger. And she said she would never forgive herself if another girl ended up like you and she hadn't tried to stop it. This will affect her as well, you know. That sacrifice will be for nothing. The sacrifice she made for *you*."

"But I'm not strong like Grace. I didn't *ask* her to do it." Jane pulled her hand away. "I know that sounds selfish. But I'm scared. And people will stare at me. Forever I'll be that girl who was... who was violated."

She broke into sobs and her mother put her arms around her. "I think you should go now, Lieutenant."

Turner stood and went to the door. "Please, we can't ask Miss Sinclair to do it. She's still all of a muddle and can't be a witness. Will you at least think about what I've said?"

"I'll think about it." Jane's voice was muffled. "But I won't do it. I won't speak in front of all those people."

Turner left the Eliots' room with a heavy heart, fearful for the outcome of the trial.

FIFTY-THREE

Jane kept her promise to think about Turner's words. She thought about them all night. She tried to picture herself in the courtroom, but sweat prickled on her skin at the idea of sitting in the same room as Croup. Sarah had described with great relish how Croup had sat there with a crooked smile, his black eyes fixed on each of the witnesses.

When daybreak came, Jane thought she might as well get up, as sleep had eluded her most of the night. She dressed in a beige skirt, cotton blouse and a jacket buttoned high to the neck. She crossed to the infirmary and asked a soldier the way to Miss Sinclair's room.

There was no one around, so she tapped on the door and went in. Grace was already awake, her face pale, with shadows beneath her eyes. She clumsily tried to sit up without leaning on her injured shoulder.

Jane gently lifted her upright and rearranged the pillow behind. "Can I get you anything?"

"No, I'm fine for the moment. I suppose Mrs. McKinney will bring some breakfast soon. It's Jane, isn't it?"

"Yes. Would you like me to open the shutters?"

"Jane Eliot. You have a sister, Sarah. Flaxen-haired. I remember her dancing with..." Grace paused. "You see, I remember some things so clearly. She danced a lot on those evenings on the trail."

"Yes. Sarah always loved dancing."

"She wanted to catch the captain's attention. Without success."

Jane laughed. "Not even my coquettish sister could melt that iron heart."

"I remember watching her. So bright and lively." Grace straightened the threads at the edge of her blanket. "You think he has an iron heart? The nurse says he's to wed the major's daughter here. Is that... is that right?"

Jane shrugged. "I don't much hear the gossip. I'm not one for company. Not since..."

There was a moment's quiet as Jane pulled the stool out next to the bed and sat. This was not the strong Grace she had known on the journey. The woman in front of her seemed to have had all the stuffing punched out.

"Lieutenant Turner said you're having difficulty remembering stuff. It means you can't be a witness, of course."

"A witness?"

"At Croup's court-martial."

"Oh." A dark look flitted across Grace's face. "Croup. When's the trial?"

"It was yesterday. Major Williams will give a verdict today. That's what I've come to talk to you about. Ask your advice."

"*My* advice? Not much point in that. Half my mind seems jumbled." Grace tried to raise a smile.

Jane leaned in closer. "If you were better, would you be a witness?"

"Would they want me to?"

Jane nodded. "So, would you?"

"If they asked, then I think I'd have to. But I'm not much

use to the prosecution now." Grace's pale hand drifted up to her temple. "My thoughts are all mixed up. I'm never quite sure what was real and what's not."

"Do you remember the night Croup attacked you?"

"Yes, I think so." A line appeared between her brows.

"I remember every moment of what he did to me," Jane said quietly, the taste of bile rising at the back of her mouth. "You see, that's why I don't want to be a witness. It was so horrible. What he did. I remember the smell of him, the sound of him. His breathing all over me. I remember the pain too." Jane looked into Grace's face. Did she understand? "I know it's not fair to be telling you all this. But there's no one else... no one who might understand. Because I remember the fear most of all. An' I'm scared if I let that fear creep inside again, it might never leave."

"Oh, Jane." Grace put out her hand, Jane took it and moved onto the bed. "It's hard, isn't it? I know."

"And that's why I don't want to testify. But they say if I don't, he'll go free. Croup's saying I made it all up. What if they don't believe me?"

"You can't force them to believe you. But you know it was real. It happened. At least you will have told them the truth."

They sat quietly for a while, Jane thinking about the challenge ahead. She noticed a tear on Grace's cheek.

Grace sniffed. "I can't seem to stop crying these days."

"What's the matter?" Jane asked, gently wiping it away with a finger.

"I remember all that too," Grace whispered. "I remember the stench, the hot breath. And the fear. But then I can't sort out everything else. You see, Jane, after that, I picture waking up with my head on Captain Randolph's pillow. And him sitting there, those clear, blue eyes watching over me. But he visited yesterday and was so distant. Even if it did happen, he seems to be regretting it."

Jane pulled a handkerchief from her pocket and gave it to

Grace. She dried her eyes and ran the fine fabric between her fingers.

"And then there was the pillowcase. I remember him giving me one. Finest Irish linen, the softest thing you ever felt on your cheek." Grace looked up at Jane.

"I always thought he kinda hated you. He was so rough on you for joining the train at all." Jane put her head to one side. "What else comes to mind, Grace?"

"That night. Looking up at the stars. The tops of the trees swaying against the dark blue sky. It was so dark. And I remember the captain there with me."

"But he *was* there. He was the person who stopped Croup."

"No, Jane, what I remember is different. I have this strangest feeling, right inside. I love him, Jane. I know that's crazy. But my memories: they are intimate. Just the two of us, in a wood, lying together. Man and wife. It was dark and the sky was full of stars."

Jane was caught by the wistful sadness in Grace's voice. She seemed cut adrift from the world.

"There, now I've shocked you." Grace gave back the handkerchief. "So, if you *are* going to be a witness, you'll have to do it for both of us. Because I'm not much use."

The door opened and the nurse came in with breakfast. She raised both eyebrows at the sight of Jane.

"I'm just going," Jane said. "I've a busy morning ahead." She kissed Grace on the brow and hurried out.

Jane walked straight to Lieutenant Meade's quarters, and asked the private on duty to fetch him. If she was going to have to be strong enough for Grace *and* herself, she'd better capture the feeling quickly.

Jane stepped through the crowd to the front of the courtroom, taking the seat reserved for the witness. Croup was near. The bilious sensation in her stomach threatened again and she held her handkerchief to her mouth. She searched the room until she saw Corporal Moore sitting at the back, his arm in a sling. It was the first time he had left the infirmary. He gave her a smile of encouragement. Her father sat beside him, any expression hidden behind his beard. But at least they were together, a unified front.

Major Williams stood. "I have received a... deputation this morning saying there is one more witness. As this witness is so important to the case before us, I will allow her to testify."

He nodded to Jane, who stood and took the oath.

Jane apologized to Major Williams for being so late in coming forward. Meade guided her through the events which led up to the attack by Croup. Her lower lip trembled and the words stuck in her throat. Williams barked at her to speak up. She described what happened to her with plain simplicity.

Lieutenant Sandsten for defense took the line that Jane was actually a spurned lover. Her cheeks flamed with embarrassment as she listened to his twisted version of events. When the questions were over, she left her chair and almost ran to the back of the room to sit between her father and Moore.

Major Williams took a break to look at his notes. Jane felt the walls of the room pushing in on her and her body began to tremble. Moore slipped his hand into hers, and she looked up into his face. He gave a half smile of encouragement.

Williams returned and stood behind his desk to summarize his deliberations. An accusation against a soldier was a serious matter, and up until that morning there had simply not been enough evidence to convict. However, he had given much thought to Miss Eliot's testimony and, on balance, had decided Croup was guilty. But what to do with him? As they were sitting in disputed territory, it was not clear which country's laws took precedence: British or the United States.

"But this is a court-martial and therefore I sentence Croup

to five years to be spent in a military jail," said Williams. "Take him back to the cell, and he will be transferred East as soon as possible."

A murmur of disapproval rippled around the room at the lenient sentence.

Mr. Eliot squeezed Jane's arm. "At least it's over," he whispered.

The major put up his hand for silence, and told Captain Randolph to stand.

"I have more to say. I am disturbed by what I have heard about the military accompaniment of the overlanders on this journey. There seem to have been unconventional procedures. Had there been stronger leadership, perhaps some of these troubling events would not have happened."

Major Williams turned and scowled at Randolph. "You used to be a promising officer. Discipline on your expeditions was second to none. Had this young civilian girl and one of your soldiers not been... fraternizing, then the whole sorry mess would not have happened. I had hoped to recommend you for promotion. I find I am unable to do that, not until you return to the Captain Randolph you used to be."

All Jane could see of the captain was his straight back as he stood to attention. He could have been made of stone. Jane felt a rush of regret. This public dressing-down was humiliating, and somehow she was responsible.

"Major, I thank you for your frank comments." Randolph's voice filled the room. "You may have a long wait because I am unlikely to return to my previous ways. Discipline is still important to me, but on this journey I have learned that people can surprise you. Leaving some room for that to happen may not be such a bad thing." He saluted the major and left.

. . .

Her father tucked Jane's hand into the crook of his arm and walked her back to their lodgings. Randolph caught up with them. Jane's heart thumped for fear he would be angry with her.

"I want to thank you for what you did this morning," he said, warmly shaking her hand. "I was most surprised. From Turner's report last night, it sounded as if you had decided against being a witness."

"At the time, that was my decision," Jane said. "But I visited Miss Sinclair this morning. I thought her views were important."

Randolph's eyes shone, making his face softer. He stepped close. "You visited her? How was she?"

"To be honest, I hoped maybe she would be better than the reports."

"So she is still very ill?" he asked quietly.

"Not ill so much. But confused. And that is distressing her."

He looked like he wanted to ask for details, but Corporal Moore came up to the group and saluted his captain.

"And when do you two intend to be wed?" asked Randolph.

"Very soon, we hope," replied Moore, smiling down at Jane. "I have come to take my fiancée to meet the fort chaplain right now."

"Good for you," Randolph said with a grin. "You keep Miss Eliot safe. If there is anything I can do, let me know. I'd like to see you two get a good start in life."

Jane was surprised by his generosity and it struck her that she barely knew the tall man walking away. She was afraid of the captain, with his stern reputation and strict rules, but he had asked after Grace with such tenderness. Her hand flew to her mouth as she realized that the strange thoughts Grace talked of really were memories. As real and true as her bad memories of Croup's attack.

She saw she had the chance to return the good that Grace had done for her.

FIFTY-FOUR

Tom Sinclair was bunking up with the Hollingswood family. As soon as the meeting with the chaplain was over, Jane knocked on their door and Lillian replied.

"Jane, how good to see you. Do come in. You must be very relieved today."

"Yes, I am." Jane stepped inside to the small room that served as kitchen, parlor, and bedroom to the whole family. "I've gone into battle and won. It's such a good feeling. I've never really stood up for myself before."

"Sit down and take some tea with me."

"In truth, Lillian, it's Tom I need to speak to. Is he here?"

"Think he's outside the back with Kane and my boys."

"I need his help with something."

Lillian went to the backdoor and hollered. "Benjamin, is young Thomas with you?"

"Yep," a voice came back, "shall I fetch him?"

"I'll go find him," Jane said, jumping up and going outside.

She called Tom over.

"I visited your sister this morning. I thought she could do with some clean things."

"That's all right. Mrs. Hollingswood took clothes to the nurse when we first arrived."

"I think Grace might like a change of bedding."

"I'll ask Mrs. Hollingswood then."

Jane put her hand on the boy's arm. "But, Tom, wouldn't it be more comforting for Grace if she had her own linen?"

"Would it?" He looked skeptical.

"Everyone likes familiar things round them."

Tom scratched his unkempt hair. "I guess. But our stuff is in the wagon."

"Let's go and look now then."

Tom cast a regretful glance at his friends, but he shrugged and walked with Jane to the area of the fort where all the wagons were lined up. He climbed into the familiar space which had been home for so long.

"I'm not sure where she keeps the bedding. I think it was in there." He pointed to a large wooden box.

"Tell you what," said Jane, "if you'd like, I can stay here and look by myself?"

Tom grinned. "You don't mind?"

"I don't, if you don't."

Tom jumped down over the backboard and ran back to his friends.

Jane opened the box. Tom was right: inside were blankets and sheets. A beautiful old quilt looked like a family heirloom. But as Jane worked through to the bottom of the box, there was no pillowcase as Grace had described.

Jane sat back on her heels. Maybe she was on the wrong track after all, and Grace *was* experiencing strange dreams. But that tender look on Captain Randolph's face when he'd asked about Grace's health. That was more than a polite enquiry.

Jane thought where she might put a lover's gift. She would hide it somewhere safe and private. Jane looked through other baskets and drawers until she came across a painted box. Inside were Grace's personal things: a necklace, a hairbrush, some letters.

And there at the bottom was a piece of white cloth.

She took it out and unfolded it. A pillowcase made of the finest linen, just as Grace had described. In the corner was a small embroidered monogram: JBR. Jane tucked it into her pocket, packed away everything else as carefully as she could and climbed out of the wagon. She pulled the rope fastenings of the canvas bonnet tight behind her.

Jane's courage was still high after her morning's experience in court. She went in search of the captain immediately; she was not sure what she would say, but something would come to mind.

She stepped into the officers' quarters.

"May I help you?" asked a soldier she did not recognize.

"Could you tell Captain Randolph that Jane Eliot would like to speak to him in private, please."

"One moment, miss." The soldier disappeared, but returned promptly and showed her into a side room, where Randolph entered a few moments later.

"Good afternoon, Miss Eliot. No problem with the wedding, I hope?" Randolph asked.

"No, nothing like that. I'm just running an errand." Jane took a deep breath. "As you know, I visited Miss Sinclair this morning. Before I left, she asked me to find this pillowcase in a box of keepsakes in her wagon. And she asked whether you might bring it to her."

Randolph stood very still, his mouth slightly open. "I... see."

That was all he said. For an awful moment, Jane wondered if she had everything wrong.

"It seemed a strange request," she said, with what she hoped was a casual shrug. "Perhaps you know why she asked you to bring it?"

Randolph took the pillowcase. "I think I might know. Don't

worry, Jane, I'll make sure Miss Sinclair receives it."

It was of such fine cloth, it folded small. He tucked it into the breast of his military jacket.

Jane gave a slight bob. "Then I'll take my leave. I have much to do today."

She left, biting her lips to stop herself breaking into laughter. Jane had been brought up on a strict path and told never to lie. Yet, she felt not the slightest guilt about the story she had just spun for the captain.

Randolph went straight to the infirmary, and encountered Nellie McKinney as he approached Grace's room. This time, he was determined not to be prevented.

"I looked in on her recently, sir. She's asleep," said Nellie.

"I'll wait in her room until she wakes, then. Thank you so much." He stepped past her and toward the door.

Nellie followed. "I really don't think this will be good for her."

"I won't be longer than necessary. Surely you're very busy and needed elsewhere?" Randolph glanced down at the large metal jug of warm water the nurse was holding.

"Aye, I am..."

"So I'll call you if you're needed."

Nellie glared at him and beat a retreat.

Randolph entered; Grace was sleeping as Nellie had said. He crept over to the wooden chair and watched the gentle rise and fall of her breathing, the fluttering of her eyelids. A warm tingling feeling started in his chest and spread out to his whole body.

In time, she began to stir, as if sensing someone was there. She stretched and struggled to sit up. Grace looked across the room and, seeing Randolph, gasped sharply, putting up her hand to cover her mouth.

"I've brought you this," he said, laying the pillowcase in front of Grace.

She ran her trembling fingers over the soft fabric and lifted it to her face, breathing in the scent. "Where was it?" she murmured.

"Safe in your wagon. Such a beautiful cheek deserves the finest material to lie on," he said, and he leaned down to kiss her cheek. His lips brushed the downy softness of her skin. He then sat on the bed and took her hands. "I've been so worried. You didn't want to see me, seemed not to even remember what we were to each other. But you remember this gift I gave to you."

"The doctor tells me the mind can play tricks after an injury," she whispered. "I have all sorts of memories of things which I'm not quite sure about."

"Why don't you tell me what you remember, and I'll tell you if it's true?"

Grace looked down at her hand in his, the pulse visible in her wrist, her heart was beating so. "No, I really couldn't do that."

"Very well," he smiled. "I'll tell you what I remember. I remember dancing with you, and everyone else melting away. I remember carrying you to my tent after that dreadful night, and watching over you while you slept. And I remember a night together under the stars when we became lovers."

Grace's cheeks flushed pink, and she withdrew her hand.

"And I remember things you do not know of." He ran his forefinger down from the bridge of her nose, over her philtrum and to her upper lip. "Such as watching over you each day and wondering what sort of husband would let you struggle on alone. My fury when I found you were unmarried, and wondering why you had not trusted me enough to tell me. And I remember the most ungracious offer of marriage ever made. In case you have forgotten, you said yes. Eventually."

"I wanted to say yes immediately," Grace broke in.

Randolph laughed, a warmth radiating through his body. "I'm glad to hear it."

"But what about Flora?"

Randolph sat back. "Flora?"

"Mrs. McKinney said you are to be married. I thought you'd changed your mind."

Randolph shook his head, and frowned. "No, my love, of course not. Whatever made you think that?"

"Maybe you'd thought better of it. I mean, when all is said and done, I still did what I did, back in Independence."

Randolph took her in his arms and smelt her hair. His mouth was close to her ear. "That was what I came to tell you about the first time I visited. Silas Boyd is alive. A fur-trapper confirmed it. You have nothing to fear."

He felt her body shake and heard her sobs, stroking her hair until the tears subsided. He sat back and wiped her face with his handkerchief.

"Now," he said. "It's your turn. Tell me what you remember. Tell me some happy thoughts."

Grace stroked the fabric in her hand and looked up into his face. She traced a finger over the scar on his jaw, the lines around his eyes made deeper by the months in the sun. She pushed back the lock of hair forever falling over his brow.

"I remember you striding round the camp early in the morning with the dew still wet, most people slumbering. I thought you the most handsome man I'd ever seen. I remember lying in the mud under my wagon, and you came and lay next to me to repair the axle. My heart beat so fast, I thought you would hear it. And as I watched you working, I feared you would notice my hands shaking as I held the tools."

James leaned forward to kiss her, this time on the lips. She responded to his passion, putting her hand to his neck. Pulling back, he looked at her. "And now we can spend a lifetime making new memories."

EPILOGUE

Grace drove her covered wagon, her heart beating in anticipation of seeing her elder brother again after so many years. Tom walked beside the mules, Kane bounding back and forth. The mare and goat were tethered behind, and the chickens were settled in their baskets hooked over the wagon bed. James rode his black horse beside the wagon where the path was wide enough, going in front when the trees narrowed overhead. Grace smiled to herself as James assiduously pointed out rocks or warned her to take care of branches. She had told him many times that she had recovered, but inside she liked having someone care so deeply about her.

A rocky track led down a hillside to a clutch of wooden homesteads in the valley below. The hills were thick with trees, but in the valley floor, the land was clear and there were green meadows beside a winding river. Some of the land around the buildings had crops grown in neat lines. Larger fields with wooden fences held cattle. It was a parcel of Eden.

A figure working in a field noticed their arrival and stood, his hand shielding his eyes. A shout, and then other people joined him. A couple of children ran forward. As the wagon reached the edge of the fields, a tall, fair-haired man strode toward them.

Grace stood, reins in hand.

"Zachary?" she cried.

He ran, a broad smile across his face. When he neared the wagon, Grace pulled up the mules as Tom dashed ahead, springing himself into his brother's arms. Close behind, Grace abandoned the wagon so she could greet her brother. He hugged her hard and lifted her off her feet, Grace laughing into his shoulder. Kane barked in excitement.

"Let's get this wagon to the farm so you can meet everyone," he said, all three walking back to where the mules were eating grass. At the wagon, Zachary reached up an arm and shook the hand of the soldier escorting his sister. "Thank you, officer, for bringing my brother and sister so far."

"It was my pleasure," said James, a smile playing around the corners of his mouth.

Zachary climbed up next to Grace and Tom, all crushed together on the driving bench. He slapped the leads on the mules' backs to drive the short distance to the homestead.

"We have four families here, living together," Zachary told her. "We find it important to group together. There's so much work to be done, to make a life in this virgin land. It would be a whole lot harder to try to pitch out on your own."

As they passed the fields, he pointed out the different crops and made sure they noticed how healthy the cattle were. He barely stopped for breath, such was his excitement at being reunited with his brother and sister.

"The best is yet to come." He grinned as they reached the homesteads. The sturdy wooden structures were built around a central area, but each had been placed at random, perhaps on the whim of finding the fairest view of the hills.

All the other families came forward to greet them, some leaving the fields where they had been working, others emerging from the barns. They crowded around the wagon as the three siblings climbed down.

Zachary introduced them, each shaking hands. "I don't know why I'm telling you all the names." He laughed. "You won't remember them, I'm sure."

A woman about the same age as Grace shyly stepped forward, one hand resting gently on her rounded belly.

"But I hope you'll make a note of this one. This is my wife, Margaret," announced Zachary, his eyes shining as he looked at her.

Grace whooped in delight. "Zachary? Really?" cried Grace. "Delighted to meet you."

"He's spoken of you often," Margaret replied softly, and they shook hands.

Zachary called to one of the men: "I'd be grateful if you would take the wagon to the barn and see to the mules, my sister's mare, and the dog."

The man nodded his assent.

"You must come in for something to eat and I expect you need some rest." Margaret led the way up a few steps into the small building nearest to them.

Randolph, so used to being in charge of situations, was amused to find himself the observer of this family drama. *His* family now, although clearly Zachary had not paused long enough to be told of the new relationship. He swung down from his horse and unbuckled his saddlebags.

Zachary strode over. He was rangy and lithe, and Randolph could see the similarity with Tom.

"What did you say your name was?" Zachary asked.

"I don't think I did. It's Randolph. I would be happy for you to call me James, though."

"Let us take that magnificent horse. We'll get him fed and

brushed down." Zachary nodded to one of the other men, then turned back. "D'you want to bring your things into the house?"

"Thank you."

Zachary stood a moment as he admired the insignia on the uniform. "A captain?"

"That's right."

Zachary raised an eyebrow and leaped the three steps up to his homestead porch, and stood to one side of the door. "Welcome to my humble abode," he said, bowing dramatically, and followed Randolph in.

Margaret was already preparing coffee and bringing out bread and cheese. "Here, this is the most comfortable chair," she said, pulling out an armchair for Grace. "And, sir, please sit here." She indicated the head of the table, a place which befitted a man of status.

Randolph smiled but took the seat next to Grace. "I will be fine here," he said, catching her eye.

As the table filled with cups, plates and bowls of food, Zachary finally sat down. "So, tell us about the journey. Was it eventful?"

Tom giggled in response, his mouth full of food.

"Yes, it was," replied Grace, winking at her little brother. "Now, Zachary, please hush for a moment, while I introduce my husband. I'm now Mrs. Randolph. This is my husband, James."

Zachary's mouth fell open. He then grinned wider than ever, got up and shook hands across the table, his arm pumping enthusiastically. "Well, I'll be damned! Welcome. I am *so* pleased."

"And I am delighted to meet Grace's family at last," responded Randolph.

"That explains it," said Zachary. "Was wondering what on God's earth a captain was doing, escorting a single wagon so far. Thought maybe the army had run out of troopers."

Zachary leaped up and fetched some wine from a cupboard in the corner. "Deserves a toast. Made this last year. Not bad, though I say it myself. Now, tell us, how did all this come about?"

However, Zachary had not listened long before the subject turned to his own crossing of the continent, of the three years spent setting up the homestead, of his courting Margaret, the daughter of another overlander family.

"We plan to move on soon, though." Zachary took his wife's hand. "Of course, we'll wait for the baby to be safely delivered."

"Why move elsewhere?" asked Randolph. "You seem to have made a good start here."

"We're going to the Willamette Valley," said Margaret.

"You wouldn't believe it," said Zachary. "This summer, I joined men cutting a new road through the mountains so it can be reached without shooting the rapids. I tell you, it is the land of milk and honey. A wide valley, tall trees for building and fuel. And the earth. Rich and dark. You could grow anything in it." He tore off a piece of bread and carried on talking between the chews. "We're going in the spring with the MacKenzies. You'll love it, Grace. Tom will grow up there, strong and healthy."

Tom's face lit up as he copied his brother in taking more bread.

Grace glanced at Randolph. "Things change so unexpectedly. I am an army wife now. Wherever James is, that's where I want to be."

Zachary's face fell, the wind taken from his sails. "An army wife doesn't seem a safe thing to be at the moment. I wouldn't want my sister put in harm's way."

Randolph took Grace's hand. "I will do everything in my power to keep her protected. But our long journey all the way from Independence shows that little in life is sure. We must live it to the full." He glanced at Grace and she nodded.

"Zach, you know I would not want to live a quiet life on the East coast," she said.

"And I'm not cut out for farming. We had an encounter with the Cayuse that showed the West is far from settled."

Margaret handed round a bowl of salmonberries. "We have a peaceful relationship with the Tensino people here, though. They're our friends. Truth be told, we wouldn't have survived without their generosity and help."

"But you heard of the deaths at the mission, not far from here?" asked Randolph.

"That missionary was a damn fool," said Zachary. "Always trying to convert people to his way of believing. He should have shown more respect, and stuck to the agreements made when he was given the land for his mission."

"I did hear something of the unrest when we were at Laramie," said Randolph. "It's worrying where all this is going to lead."

The table fell silent.

"I'm sure there is much to learn," said Grace quietly. "If you think the Willamette will be a fine place for Tom to grow up, then nothing could be more important."

Margaret cleared the plates and mugs.

Grace rose to her feet. "Let me help. You shouldn't be doing so much, in your condition."

"Let us tidy up together," Margaret said. "Perhaps the men would like to go outside for a smoke?"

The two women stood in the kitchen area, sisters who had only just met. Grace poured water from a pitcher into a wooden tub.

"So, you're not long married?" Margaret asked.

"Little more than a fortnight."

"My goodness! But how exciting." Margaret slipped the

plates into the water and picked up a brush. "Was it a grand military wedding?"

"Oh, I wouldn't say grand, but, of course, it was in the military style."

Margaret handed her the first clean plate to dry and a cloth "Tell me. I want to know every detail."

Grace wiped the plate dry, as her breast warmed with the memories. "We married at Fort Boise, in the little chapel there. It was full to bursting with all James's men, and as many of the overlanders as could fit in. Tom gave me away. He was so proud."

"Did you have any maids of honor?"

"No. But I had some good friends around me, friends I made on the journey. My husband's lieutenant was best man."

"What did you wear?"

"My Sunday-best frock, and friends put pink wild roses in my hair and made a lovely posey for me to carry." Grace paused, cloth in hand. "James was the handsomest groom you ever saw, in his dress uniform, every button gleaming, his boots polished like mahogany. He held my hands so tenderly to say the vows."

"And how did you celebrate afterwards?"

Grace bit her lip, not sure how to put things into words. The washing came to a halt as Grace leant against the drainer. "James was not in the commanding officer's good books at that time. The major in charge of Fort Boise, I mean. There had been a misunderstanding. Some of the men—and women—at the fort had reason to resent our marriage. So the wedding breakfast was a quiet affair. Most of the train moved on first thing the next morning for our final stage into Oregon. This last week has been one of painful farewells, as settlers went their separate ways. But you'll know how that feels, having done the journey yourself."

"Indeed I do," said Margaret wistfully.

"James has left his company in the command of his lieutenant so that he could come and meet Zachary, and make sure Tom is content to stay."

Margaret put the plates on a shelf. "And you're sure you won't settle here yourself?"

Grace shook her head. "Quite sure. I will miss Tom dreadfully, but I know he will be happy and safe here, and as long as I'm with James, I'm in the right place."

"But you will stay here some days now?"

"Alas, we cannot. We must leave in the morning. We rejoin the company and set out straight away for the return journey East. We need to reach Fort Laramie before winter draws in."

Grace sought Zachary out as he sat on the steps of the porch, watching the evening sun making the mountains glow pink.

"I need to give you something." She placed the wooden case between them.

Zachary looked at it ruefully. "God knows I remember that case."

"Open it."

Zachary opened the locks as if they might burn his fingers, and looked at the pistols. "Pa always knew how to make a fine firearm."

He took one and admired the curve of the wood handle, the intricate engraving on the stock. He lifted it to test the sight.

"These are what he was working on when he died," Grace said. "He wanted you to have them."

Zachary grunted. "I don't see why. He'd said he'd disowned me."

She put a hand on his arm. "He regretted all that had happened. Was so sorry about all the arguments, knew he was at fault. He was stubborn and short-tempered, but he still loved you, Zach. Every day, he looked to the horizon in the hope that you would walk back over it. He never gave up hope that you'd carry on the family business."

Zachary shook his head wistfully.

"That's why he made me promise to get these to you," said Grace. "And to make sure you knew how much he loved you."

He sighed. "There are lots of things I'd do different, given my time again."

"Things haven't turned out so bad, Zach. Look what you've built here. You have a lovely wife and will be a father soon."

"That's one thing I will do right: boy or girl, I'm going to make sure they know I love them."

Zachary and Margaret gave their bedroom to the newlyweds to make their first, proper honeymoon bed. Margaret had spread velvety petals across the coverlet and sprinkled rosewater on the pillows, filling the room with sweet smells. Grace made sure they used the precious monogrammed pillowcase.

Grace sat at the dressing table in her cotton chemise, brushing her hair by candlelight. She felt shy now they were in the quiet of their own room. James's uniform jacket was draped around the back of the chair he had sat in to pull off his boots. Barefoot, he padded over behind her and lifted her hair so he could caress her neck. Her stomach turned over at his touch. He pushed the fabric of the chemise to one side so his lips could stroke her shoulders.

She turned round, leaning her head back so he could kiss her face. She closed her eyes as his tongue explored her mouth, arousing a desire deep inside her. Pulling his shirt from his pants, Grace struggled with the unfamiliar buttons, and James pulled it over his head, dropping it to the ground. Her fingers traced the defined muscles of his torso, stroking the dark hair. He untied the ribbons of the chemise and pushed it downwards, running his palm over her breasts, pausing over her heart to feel its urgent beating, his rough hand contrasting with her smooth skin.

Grace stood, and he slid the chemise down over her hips and to the floor. With one arm around her shoulders, the other hooked below her knees, he carried her to the bed.

He removed his pants and they lay full-length, facing each other. His hand stroked down her spine, his thumb exploring the two dimples low on her back before his fingers skimmed over the curves of her rear. A tremor shivered through her body. Moving her onto her back, he returned to her breasts, circling each nipple with his tongue, his hand sweeping down between her thighs.

Grace moaned as she writhed against the effect of his fingers. She slipped her hands into his hair, twisting the dark locks. She surrendered to him as he moved on top of her, no longer able to hold back from possessing her completely. Thrilled at the rhythmical thrust and fall of his body, she gasped as they climaxed.

James rolled back, his body damp with a light sheen, one arm still beneath her head. A floorboard creaked somewhere in the house, and both giggled, realizing their exertions may have been heard.

"We're newlyweds," James whispered. "What else would they expect?"

The following morning had a chill in the clear air. The whole community came out to wish them farewell. The tenderest goodbyes were between Tom and Grace.

"You've grown from a boy to a man, on this journey," said Grace, kissing the top of his head. "You know, this trip across the continent is a sort of magic mirror. It exposes everyone's qualities of heart connected with it. It's shown that you are steadfast and brave and honest. You're gonna thrive here. I just know it."

He suddenly hugged her round the waist, hiding his face so no one would see his tears. "I'm going to miss you."

"And I'll miss you too. Every day. I've never been so proud of anyone in my life."

"Except perhaps Captain Randolph?" Tom tried to joke, standing back and quickly wiping his sleeve across his face.

She looked across to where James was patiently waiting on his horse, a mule behind loaded with gear. Her breath hitched as she took in his steel-blue eyes and firm jaw. How strange that this man should be her husband. "Yes, except my James. But you..." she sniffed. "You come a very close second."

She patted Kane, who sat by Tom's side. "Now, you look after my brother."

The dog wagged its tail, seeming to understand.

She walked over to Margaret and kissed her on both cheeks. "I'll be praying for you. For an easy birth and a healthy child."

Zachary stepped forward with the case with the pistols. "You should take these. There isn't a place for them here."

"Pa wanted you to have them."

"We're trying something new. Like when Penn first arrived in New England, and tried to set up a peaceable state. I know it might sound crazy, but we've got to try."

"But surely these would help somehow."

Zachary shook his head. "We need good rifles to get food and protect us from bears and the like. But these pistols? They're about killing men. We have no place for that here."

Grace secured the box in a sidebag on her mule, and Zachary helped lift her onto her horse. She was sad to leave behind the wagon that had been her home for so many months but knew it would be more use with Zachary.

. . .

As the horses and mules picked their way up the hillside out of the valley, Grace looked back to that little patch of paradise to fix it in her mind one final time, but her brothers and their community had already returned to their fields.

James looked across and, sensing her sadness, drew his horse closer and reached out an arm. She took his hand and clutched it for a moment.

"It won't be the last time you see them, I promise you, my love," he said.

She smiled, knowing deep in her bones that she could trust him to make it be true.

"There's so much of this land I want to see," she said, pressing her heels into her horse to move faster.

James laughed, and matched her pace. "And so you shall. The oceans, the mountains, the forests. We'll see them, side by side."

A LETTER FROM THE AUTHOR

Dear Reader,

Thank you so much for reading *To the Wild Horizon* and I hope you enjoyed Grace and Randolph's story. If you would like to join other readers in keeping in touch, here are two options. Hear about my new releases and bonus content by clicking this link:

www.stormpublishing.co/imogen-martin

Or you can pop over to my website and sign up to my monthly newsletter. You'll get giveaways, sneak peeks, and historical snippets:

imogenmartinauthor.com

Or do both! I look forward to meeting you.

If you enjoyed this book and could spare a few moments to leave a review, that would be hugely appreciated. Even a short review can make all the difference in helping other readers discover my book for the first time and every single review helps. Thank you so much.

The origins of this book go back a long way. When I was a teenager, I took a Greyhound bus from San Francisco to New York. Over those three days of staring out of the window at the majestic mountains and endless flat plains, stories wound themselves into my head: tales of brooding, charismatic men captivated by independent women. My first novel, *Under A Gilded Sky*, is set in 1874, the dawn of the Gilded Age. You'll find out more if you sign up to the newsletter.

I have, of course, done years of research, and this book draws on some events that really happened. But it's fiction: an imagined story. If you want to make contact to find out more, the best place is my Facebook page or the feedback page on my website.

I can also be found on other social media platforms. Come and say hello.

Thank you again for being part of this amazing journey with me, and I hope you'll stay in touch—I have so many more stories and ideas with which to entertain you.

Imogen

facebook.com/ImogenMartin.Author

x.com/ImogenMartin9

instagram.com/imogenmartinauthor

bookbub.com/profile/imogen-martin

ACKNOWLEDGMENTS

Just as it takes a village to raise a child, it takes a whole publishing house to produce a book. I am so proud to be part of Storm Publishing.

My biggest thanks go to Vicky Blunden, the best editor a writer could hope to have. She has an instinct for making a story stronger. Vicky has helped me think deeply about my characters and how to make sure you, the reader, are with them every step of the way. Self-doubt lurks around the corner for most writers, and I am so lucky to have Vicky giving me confidence and encouragement.

Thank you to all the Storm team. To the visionary Oliver Rhodes, to Elke Desanghere for marketing and Anna McKerrow for publicity. I am hugely grateful to Jade Craddock, my insightful copyeditor, and to Maddy Newquist, my eagle-eyed proofreader.

Thank you to Katrina Kirkwood, the first person (after my husband) to read this book, when it was—frankly—in a pretty ropey state. Her tactfully worded feedback spurred me on. This is an American story, and I'm grateful to Trish Richards for reading an early draft and identifying many of my British phrases.

Any new writer needs to find her crowd. I am grateful for the ongoing support of RNA Cariad—who will meet for coffee and cake at the drop of a hat—and to the Bookcamp Mentees, whose hilarious WhatsApp messages have brightened many a drafting day.

Every writer should have a husband like mine. Peter is my first, and most enthusiastic, reader. He makes sure there's food on the table and shoos me back to my desk when I'm flagging. Thank you, Peter, I really couldn't do it without you.

This is my second book and I dedicate it to my second daughter Naomi. Witty, clever, and wise, I wish she lived nearer, but her long phone calls always have me laughing. The fact that she can still see the funny side of life is a testament to her resilient spirit.

Naomi has gone through more than someone her age should have. One of those things was growing up with an older sister whose medical condition meant Naomi often had to take the back seat. But she never once complained as they grew up. Naomi gave up everything to be with her sister, Becky, during her last five months of life: reading to her, putting cream on her hands, making her laugh—sleeping on a chair in the hospital on those really bad nights when we feared what the next day would bring. Thank you for helping me and Becky through that final day, and the weeks that followed. I will love you forever.

Made in the USA
Monee, IL
19 May 2024